Praise for Babs Horton's first novel, *A Jarful of Angels*:

'I loved this book. The story is earthy, harsh, grievous even – and yet so funny, so cunningly and powerfully told, so lit up by the sense of what it was like to be a child then, full of terror and delight, caught in the snare of adult mysteries. Above all, Babs Horton captures the physical intensity of being a child – the smells, the tastes, the ghoulishness and sudden ecstasies.' Helen Dunmore

'Convincingly fuses a nostalgic glance back to the long, hot summers of childhood with a detective story and a dollop of old-fashioned romance . . . Small-town secrets provide plenty of darkness to dapple this atmospheric tale, but its happy ending is all the more pleasing for being so unexpected' *Daily Mail*

'The ever-surprising developments of the story are written with original and lyrical prose' *Good Book Guide*

'A mystery shot through with elements of the magic of folk tales . . . Unusual and cumulatively moving' *Big Issue*

By the same author

A Jarful of Angels

Brought up in London and Wales, Babs Horton now lives in Plymouth where she teaches at a school for children with special needs. Her debut, *A Jarful of Angels*, won the Pendleton May Award for the Best First Novel of 2003.

Dandelion Soup

Babs Horton

POCKET
BOOKS

LONDON • SYDNEY • NEW YORK • TORONTO

First published in Great Britain by Simon & Schuster, 2004
This edition first published by Pocket Books, 2004
An imprint of Simon & Schuster UK
A Viacom company

1 3 5 7 9 10 8 6 4 2

Simon & Schuster UK Ltd
Africa House
64–78 Kingsway
London WC2B 6AH

www.simonsays.co.uk

Simon & Schuster Australia
Sydney

A CIP catalogue record for this book is available
from the British Library

ISBN 0 7434 4972 X

Typeset in Palatino Medium by SX Composing DTP, Rayleigh, Essex
Printed and bound in Great Britain by
Cox & Wyman Ltd, Reading, Berkshire

To John, Laura and Jack, with all my love.

Acknowledgements

I would like to thank my family and friends in Plymouth and South Wales for their support and unstinting hospitality. The students of Senghennydd Court House B at Cardiff University for my late night lessons in philosophy. The Cowan family for sharing many happy and hair-raising adventures in Spain. To Clare Alexander and Kate Shaw of Gillon Aitken Associates for help and support and the best Italian lunch ever. Kate Lyall Grant and Nigel Stoneman for their unwavering enthusiasm and some memorable nights out. To Melissa Weatherill for sure advice. Nadina Gray and David Mann at Simon & Schuster who have done me proud with front covers.

Helen Dunmore for words of praise that I treasure. To the people of Guildford Arts and Pendleton May for honouring me with the first novel prize.

I have Nina Epton to thank for information on Spain in her fascinating book, *Grapes and Granite*. Ruth Bill, a boss in a million who I will miss. As always my deepest thanks to all my colleagues and students at the Hospital School and the Young People's Centre. My friends at Tavistock Hockey Club who make me laugh. The fabulous Book Shop, 'In Other Words' in Mutley.

To Mrs Edna Fuge of Brighton for my first fan letter.

Especially to my husband, John, for always being there, Laura for making me a real writer's den and Jack for imaginative financial advice. Sister Campion and the sisters of St Mary's Abbey School, Mill Hill for teaching me to fly all those years ago.

Absence diminishes commonplace passions and increases great ones, as the wind extinguishes candles and kindles fire. Maximes (1678) No. 276, Duc de la Rochefoucauld

Prologue

Recipe for Dandelion Soup

Take a fistful of garbanzos
A clutch of white beans
A handful of dandelions
Two wide-brimmed hatfuls of spring water
A slosh of olive oil
Some slivers of monastery beef
Two cloves of silvery garlic
One enormous wrinkled tomato
An old potato, and one stout stick for stirring

Pick only the leaves of the most succulent dandelions. Be sure to select only those that bend westwards in the breeze. A breeze not too cool, neither too hot. If the dandelions are in flower check the petals carefully, the petals of the dandelion are the most beautiful of all the flowers, petals that are sparks of fire thrown straight from the sun.

Soak the beans overnight. Toss the beef in a pan with the olive oil and stir until cooked. Add the rest of the ingredients and simmer for three hours over a fire of pine cones and olive branches until the beans are tender. Sprinkle with dandelion petals.

Eat in the best company under a sky full of stars.

Part One

Spain 1946

THE OLD PILGRIM

It was almost dark when the Old Pilgrim found her, a small wide-eyed child abandoned in the long waving grass. As the sun dropped behind the mountains and the smoky mist drifted up from the river far below, he had sat cross-legged on the soft grass beside the weeping child.

Away in the distance the narrow arched windows of the monastery of Santa Eulalia reflected the dying embers of sunset. A soft wind carried the sound of the monks at prayer and brought with it the smell of wild rosemary and thyme, candle wax and incense. Overhead a hawk screamed and plummeted to the earth and a large moon drifted above the far off mountain peaks.

The Old Pilgrim had taken a silver flask from the folds of his black cloak, poured the golden liquid into a battered tin cup and handed it to her.

'Dandelion soup. Favoured dish of saints and martyrs. Provider of sustenance to weary pilgrims. Succour to the dispossessed, nectar of the vagabond and the outcast.'

She had never forgotten those words.

'Food of the gods, fare of erstwhile virgins,' he'd said.

And she had smiled, dried her tears and drunk deeply. Then, she had taken his proffered hand and he had wrapped his filthy cloak about her small shoulders. Together, as the moon rose higher and the first stars lit the sky, they had walked into the darkness of the night.

They made a strange couple; a tall man in a dark cloak and a wide-brimmed hat and a small skinny-legged girl in clumsy boots and a shrunken blue dress carrying the few things she owned in a battered suitcase.

For almost a year they tramped the roads of the Camino de Santiago in search of her mother.

Eventually they had followed the road out of Spain and into France, but to no avail. There was no sign of her mother.

Then he too had abandoned her, given her money and directions and carefully written a name and address on a label, hung it round her neck on a piece of string, as though he were bestowing jewels upon her.

They had stood together for one last time. He stooped to kiss her and then his face had crumpled and her own eyes were blinded by icy tears. Then she heard only the sound of his broken boots on the ground as he hurried away and the whispering swirl of his cloak in the cold Parisian wind as he, too, was gone from her.

Ireland 1947

BALLYGURRY

Ballygurry was a small village of dank, dimly lit houses, crouched low in a mossy hollow and blasted on all sides by the wild winds and inclement weather that came down from the mountains and in from the restless ocean.

Twice a week the clackety steam train wheezed through the station but rarely stopped unless it had a new batch of orphans to unload for St Joseph's, or parcels done up with string and sealing wax sent from those now fled to America or London England.

There was a musty, fusty shop-cum-pub called Donahue's, a dim den reeking of whiskey and yellowing sprouts, old newspapers, dying cabbages and fresh gossip.

There was a sweet shop run by a sour-faced old crone, and a butcher's shop with a carpet of sawdust and sad-faced pigs hanging on hooks. There was the polished, flower-filled church of Saint Bridget and a graveyard where the yew tree bent double in an easterly, groaning and moaning and throwing its black twisted shadows across the cough-lozenge gravestones.

There was a spotless presbytery that housed a succession of lonely but well-fed priests. On the roof of the presbytery a weather vane whirled and spun until the dizzy cockerel begged for mercy.

In the centre of the village there was a horse trough with magic powers where you could make a wish when the time was right: when the moon was full to bursting and the presbytery cockerel blowing anti-clockwise. On the stroke of midnight you'd to kneel down and stare into the horse trough and make a wish without blinking, only if the water was completely still mind, and then you would see the face of whomever you wanted to see or wanted to see you whether they were dead or alive.

Out past the village along the shore there was a crooked chimneyed schoolhouse with a bell on the top and a schoolmaster's house next door.

And at the end of Mankey's Alley there was a big, dilapidated old house with a foreign-sounding name where the Black Jew lurked behind misty net curtains and was said to count up his ill-gotten money over and over.

*

The orphans were sent to St Joseph's from all over the country. There were newborn babies whipped from the freckled arms of bold, brassy girls who opened their legs for love or a pickled gherkin and a glass of port and lemon. Beautiful little pink and blue babies, take your pick. Bonneted and mittened babies who were swiftly snapped up by wealthy families from Cork and even as far away as Dublin. Sweet little Cinderella babies who fitted the Silver Cross prams a treat. Prams with rattles on elastic and banana-shaped glass feeding bottles with rubbery teats. Delrosa and rosehip. Virol and gripe water. Babies who were reborn and renamed on the ride back to the cities. Babies who would grow up in the leafy avenues and staid villas of distant towns and cities.

Then there were the ones who came and stayed. The snot-faced boys of St Joseph's. Hard, pinchy-faced things with styes on their eyes and warts on their fingers. Boys who kicked sullenly at tin cans and piddled over the top of privet hedges. Bleary-eyed boys who yawned through mass and scratched through benediction. You could tell just by looking at them that they would have liked to shoot cats if only they could get their hands on a gun. Dirty-minded snickering things; bad boys in the making.

And there were whey-faced little girls with eczema behind their knees who cried nightly into their pillows, chewed their nails to the quick and peed the beds. Stick-legged girls who metamorphosed at fourteen into po-faced little madams with contraband lipstick and bottles of cheap scent. Brazen-faced girls clutching battered suitcases, mouths painted as red as wild poppies, chins set firm on a life in the big city. Giving two-fingered salutes to the charitable nuns of Saint Joseph's. The sound of their high heels clattering down the lanes of Ballygurry on the way to the station and freedom.

*

It was dark in the Guardian Angels dormitory except for a weak glimmer of moonlight that had wormed its way in through the high narrow windows. Padraig O'Mally stirred in his sleep and was woken moments later by the whistle of the train and the low warning call of the white owl that lived in the Dark Wood.

Padraig lay still and listened to all the usual night-time dormitory sounds, the soft snoring, the wheezy breath of the weak chested, the creak of rusty bed springs and the occasional whimper from the sleeping boys.

A cat wailed outside in the grounds and the wind blew through the leafy boughs of the conker tree like the echo of a restless sea. Stray leaves rustled on the gravel drive and somewhere a loose drainpipe clattered.

Padraig wanted to get up, slip on his clothes and sneak out into the blustery night. He longed to stand out there in the dark beneath the stars and feel the cold wind on his face, but there was no way out of St Joseph's after dark. The heavy doors were locked and bolted and the keys were probably under Sister Veronica's hair vest next to where her heart should have been.

The wind was gathering in strength and Padraig smiled. The only good things about living in Ballygurry were the great rough winds and the wild weather that came roaring in off the sea or sweeping down from the mountains. He loved the winds and the fiercer the better. When other people pulled up their mufflers and hurried away indoors all he wanted was to be out there in the middle of the raging winds.

There was nothing as grand as the feel of an icy wind on your face whipping up your blood and making your heart beat like a drum. Sometimes out in the schoolyard when the gusts came rampaging in from the Atlantic he ran with his arms stretched wide, the wind puffing up inside his orphanage jacket. Round and round he went, like an out of control airplane, nose diving, gliding, weaving and curling, in and out of the clouds of shivering kids, lost and happy in a world of his own. He imagined that if he shut his eyes he could be up and flying, off out of Ballygurry for ever, stealing a ride on the mad wind's back.

Above his head he could hear the creak of floorboards as mad Sister Immaculata paced backwards and forwards in the attic where she was locked up at night for her own good.

Padraig knew the names of some of the winds now. Mr Leary, his new teacher, had taught him. The Chocolatera from Mexico. The Cat's Paw from the USA. Matanuska, Mistral, Moncao. Sirocco, Suestado, Zephyr.

There were soft warm winds and sultry wet winds. There were scorching, dry desert winds that could whip the hair off a camel's arse no sweat. Arctic winds bringing icy sleet and blizzards of snow enough to freeze the knackers off a polar bear. There were typhoons, tornadoes, cyclones and hurricanes.

The winds were free; there weren't any rules that they had to obey. They could blow on any bugger they fancied. They could whip the hats off the poor and lift the skirts of the rich. They could batter the castles of lords and ladies; hammer the farms and barns of paupers and peasants. They could ring the church bells and blow out the altar candles of Catholics and Protestants. All the people of the world were at the mercy of the winds: Aborigines, Eskimos and Bedouins. Snot-faced tinkers and sniffy-nosed bishops.

He lay still for a long time, hands clasped behind his head, thinking of some of the places in the world that Mr Leary had told them about in school.

England. Capital London. River Thames. Red buses. Orl

right mate. Shuttya mouf. Uppyabum. Jellied eels and boiled beef and carrots.

France. Capital Paris. River Seine. Bonjour. Au revoir. Zut Alors. Frogs' legs and snails and bread with chocolate in the middle. In Paris there was a dance hall full of forgetful women without knickers.

Spain. Capital Madrid. Rio Manzanares. Rio meant river in Spanish. Hola. Adiós. Hasta la vista. Paella and tortilla. Bloody bullfights and dizzy guitar music. Toreador. Matador. Picador. Madrid was freezing in winter and scalding hot in the summer. The people there had a sleep in the middle of the day; lazy sods.

Siesta. Fiesta. Flamenco.

Mr Leary had been to Spain to fight against a madman called Frank O. He never told them that in class but Jimmy Hoolistan's da said it was true, Mr Leary told him once when they got slaughtered together in Donahue's Bar. Hoolistan's da said Mr Leary got shot and he had bullet holes in his legs that missed his mickey and his knackers by inches. Jimmy Hoolistan's da said you could see daylight through the holes. Padraig wondered when Mr Leary went swimming would he sink or would bubbles come out of the holes when he jumped into the water.

He listened. Someone was sobbing. It was one of the smaller kids, over in the bed by the window, probably the new boy Donny Keegan.

Padraig sat up in bed.

'Donny, what's up?' he called out quietly so as not to wake the rest of the kids.

No answer from Donny Keegan's bed, just the sound of stifled sobs.

'Donny, for Christ's sake what's up with you?'

'Nothing.'

'Have you had a bad dream?'

Bad dreams came free at St Joseph's.

Silence.

'Have you shit the bed?'

'I have not, so.' The voice was small, tearfully indignant.

Padraig grinned.

'Have you pissed it then? Have you, Donny? Tell the truth and shame the devil.'

A stifled yes and a huge sob.

Padraig slipped out of his bed and hopped and skittered across the cold cracked linoleum.

'Jesus, it's feckin' freezing.'

He pulled back the rough grey blanket from Donny's bed. The boy tried to hold on to it but gave up without much of a fight. He was curled up in a ball, his hands covering his head, his small body quivering inside the regulation striped St Joseph's pyjamas.

'Ah, don't cry, Donny. It's not the end of the world.'

He put his hand gently on the little boy's head. His fair hair had been cut short; the regulation crew cut of Saint Joseph's, rough and scratchy as a badger's arse.

'The worst thing about pissing the bed isn't the first bit, Donny. It feels nice and warm, comfy like.'

Donny took his hands off his head, lay still, listening but trembling violently like a man waiting to be shot.

'It's half an hour in when you start to feckin' freeze.'

Padraig felt sorry for the boy, he knew how he was feeling. He'd pissed the bloody bed himself when he'd first arrived in this shite hole.

That first night he was only six and he'd dreamed that his mammy had come to his bed in the night and lifted him out to use the piss pot. She'd done that every night when he was small just in case of an accident. In the dream it was just as if everything had been a mistake and she'd come back to life again. He'd felt her arms scooping him up out of the warm bed, smelled the lovely smell of her scent, the touch of her tickly hair against his face, his sleepy head tucked up against her soft breasts. He'd even felt the cold of the china piss pot against his small arse, his mother's finger gently poking his mickey down between his thighs so he didn't squirt a fountain of pee all over the bedroom floor.

It was the last dream he'd ever had of his mammy. He rarely dreamed while he slept, just daydreams now that went on for hours but these were getting fewer since he'd been in Mr Leary's class.

'That's a good boy,' his mammy had said in the dream and he'd peed for Ireland.

Then he'd woken up, the sweet soft smell of her still lingering in the air. Jesus, he even had a smile on his face and then he'd realized with a shock where he was. He remembered the tearful train journey to Ballygurry, the long lonely walk up the gravel drive of St Joseph's holding hands with the old priest. Father Behenna had stopped three times on the way from the station to piss and four times to drink from a silver bottle that he kept in a little brown suitcase. Padraig remembered with a shudder the first sight of the unsmiling holy nuns; the stink of disinfectant and boiled greens.

He'd lain awake, petrified and freezing in the stinking wet bed, biting his fist until he'd drawn blood. Then as the first grey light had illuminated the dormitory he'd heard the far-off sound of the bell. Sister Arseface had come crashing into the dormitory and pulled him from the bed, yanked off his pyjamas and made him stand on the freezing linoleum, naked and quaking in front of the other boys. Then the belting he'd had from Sister Veronica. For pissing the bed! Ah, Jesus! That was ages ago.

'Donny, get out the bed quick in case Sister Arseface comes round on patrol.'

'I can't.'

'Come on, if she catches you she'll warm you up with the feel of the strap round your bare arse. Get out the feckin' bed, Donny!'

The small boy, afraid of the tone in Padraig's voice, scrambled quickly out of the bed.

'Get your jamas off.'

The boy wavered.

'Now!'

Donny loosened the cord on his green and grey striped pyjama trousers; the green was the colour of over-boiled cabbage. He struggled to pull the sopping trousers down over his skinny legs, stepped out of them and then shuffled them into a heap on the floor at his feet. The smell of cooling piss was strong in the icy air, with the reek of ammonia the way small kids pissed. It didn't bother Padraig, he'd smelled it too many times. It was as much a part of the St Joseph's night as the moon and the stars.

Padraig hurried back across the dormitory and quietly, cautiously moved his bed, kneeled down, prised a floorboard loose and carefully lifted it up.

Donny Keegan, naked now and shivering violently, had his hands cupped over his mickey as he watched Padraig with wide watery green eyes, as if he was watching a magic show. Padraig pulled a white sheet from beneath the floorboards the way a magician pulled silk scarves from a top hat. He bundled the sheet up in his arms and hurried back to where Donny stood.

'Help me get that wet sheet off of the bed.'

Donny didn't argue and between them they wrenched the wet sheet from the bed and Padraig rolled it swiftly into a ball.

'Quick, now the mattress, help me turn it over!'

Padraig took most of the weight. Together they hauled

the mattress over and lowered it down on to the bed springs.

'Sunny side up!' whispered Padraig and grinned.

Donny smiled weakly, his chin wobbled like Sunday blancmange.

Padraig flicked out the clean sheet across the bed.

Padraig was a dab hand at making beds. He could have won prizes. He folded and tucked and smoothed and patted.

'Get in the washroom and wash yourself off, get rid of the smell. The old cow has a nose like a demented bloodhound. Use the middle tap; the others make too much noise. And be quick!'

Donny scarpered, his bare feet squeaking on the cold brown linoleum.

Away down in the village the church clock chimed the witching hour.

When Donny came back a few minutes later, he smelled faintly of carbolic soap and diluted tears. Padraig chucked him a pair of clean pyjamas and then hurriedly stuffed the wet sheet and pyjamas back beneath the floorboards, pulling the floorboard and bed back into place.

'You just goin' to leave them there?' stammered Donny.

Padraig tapped the side of his nose with his finger.

'Secret,' he said. 'Abracadabra and all that! I'll get you a piece of oilcloth for tonight. In case you do it again.'

'I won't!' the little voice was full of shame and outrage.

'Nearly everyone here pisses the bed the first few weeks including meself. Now get back into bed and try and sleep a bit. It's a good few hours before the old cow comes round ringing the wake-up bell.'

Donny Keegan smiled an embarrassed wobbly lipped smile. 'You won't tell anyone, will ye, Padraig?' he said.

'Nah.'

Donny climbed back into his bed. Padraig winked at him, pulled the blankets up and tucked him in tight.

'Thanks, Padraig.'

'Not at all. All part of the service.'

Poor little bugger.

Padraig climbed back into his own cold bed and lay staring up at the flaky ceiling, listening to the winds. No one in St Joseph's would get the strap for pissing the bed if he could help it. So stuff them! Feck the hard-faced old bags with their talk of charity and the boundless love of God. They wouldn't know what love was if it slapped them between their tits. Anyway, one day he'd escape and he wouldn't come back. They could shove their lumpy porridge and semolina pudding where the squirrel stuffed his nuts. No way was he staying in St Joseph's until he was fourteen and then being packed off to some farm at the arse end of nowhere. He wasn't going to spend his life digging up turnips and swedes until his head turned the same shape and his skin darkened to the colour of a boiled beetroot. Oh no! He was lucky, he might not have stuff all else but he had brains, like his mammy, and that was the one thing they couldn't take away from him however hard they tried.

Mr Leary had told him that he could try for a scholarship to a school near Cork. If he passed the scholarship he'd have a proper school uniform, new shoes and a leather satchel. The best bit of all was that he'd sleep at the school and only have to be in St Joseph's for the holidays.

He couldn't wait. He wasn't going to be thankful for what the good nuns did for him was he hell as like. They could eat monkey sick and die. One day soon he'd be off and away from Ballygurry and he'd be glad to see the back of the sisters. Except for old Sister Immaculata, she poor old thing wanted to escape as badly as he did.

*

Midnight. The sky above Ballygurry is peppered with stars. The rusty echoes of the presbytery clock hang in the air and an owl calls out from the Dark Wood that borders the orphanage of St Joseph. A pigeon hiccups nervously beneath the eaves of Dr Hanlon's house. The wind is steadily rising, whipping across the ocean, wobbling the great white moon and scattering the stars across the firmament. Ballygurry shivers and creaks and the bells above the shopkeepers' doors tinkle and tin bathtubs and buckets play percussion in the backyards. False teeth clack in jam jars and the penny candles are snuffed out one by one in the Lady Chapel.

The waves, white tipped and frothy with spume, pound on to the beach and rattle the empty shells of crabs and mussels, winkle and cockle, shunting the barnacled boats up the beach towards the dunes.

The long, rough grass by the tadpole pond rustles and sighs. A newborn lamb bleats with fright and is answered by a dog fox loping round the famine wall where generations of orphans and villagers have scratched their names. Wild cats grind out their mating wail and field mice and voles, moles and shrews are on the move, stirring the moonlit grass.

Along the coast away past the schoolhouse where a light still burns, the wind screams now like a banshee through the cave they call the Giant's Cakehole. In the horse trough the moonlit water ripples and clouds.

The whistle of the mail train cuts through the night. Clouds of steam balloon into the sky and drift above the roof of St Joseph's. The train pulls into the deserted station and draws to a slow squealing halt. The black and white station clock clanks and whirs but the hands have long since seized at ten to two. A carriage door opens and closes. Small footsteps cross the platform, pause and then echo along the lonely lane that leads to Ballygurry.

In the attic room of St Joseph's, by candlelight, Sister Immaculata trod the boards. Five paces across the room and then turn. Five paces back. Turn. Most nights she walked for miles and miles and sometimes she was still walking when the cockerel crowed and the first bell called the nuns to prayer.

Tonight she was more restless than usual. There was something afoot in Ballygurry, she could feel the brittle tension in the night air, as though a spring was poised, the bait set ready for the unsuspecting mouse.

She could feel the constriction in bone and sinew, a tight squeezing of skin around her skull, a dull, steady ache in her eyeteeth. She could see the tension in the curve of the candle flame and in the shape of the nervous shadows hiding in the wings, the slant of filtered moonlight across the crucifix.

She could hear it in the cool lick of the new wind, the feverish whispering of the trees and the distant pounding of the waves.

Sister Immaculata shuddered and caught her breath. Time was peeling back its calloused old skin and revealing hidden wounds.

Suddenly a gust of wind caught at the window and rattled the glass. She stopped her pacing and listened. She could hear the train coming towards Ballygurry station. Usually it gathered speed but tonight it was slowing down. She crossed to the attic window and looked out. Above the trees in the Dark Wood the stars were bright, stars making a grand highway across the night sky. She listened. Ears pricked for any sound. The dog over on Kenny's farm barked a warning and his chains rattled and clanked. Sister Immaculata stood with her nose pressed against the cold window.

Footsteps! She could hear the sound of someone walking along the lonely lane. The click of hobnailed boots echoing faintly, growing closer.

The footsteps paused.

Sister Immaculata held her breath.

Moonlight dusted the lane and a silver leaf drifted down from a tree.

The old nun stared incredulously at the sight before her. She made the sign of the cross. Dear God, it couldn't be true, could it? After all these years they'd sent someone to rescue her and bring her back home.

A cloud crossed the moon.

The vision was eaten up by the blackness. The sound of the footsteps grew fainter. Sister Immaculata wiped a tear from her face and continued her pacing. Five steps across the room. Turn. Five steps back.

In Nirvana House the grandfather clock in the hallway chimed the hour and in his four-poster bed the Black Jew tossed and turned in his sleep but did not wake. He was dreaming a dream where smiling dwarves riding piebald ponies were chasing him up a steep hill towards a crumbling monastery. Behind the dwarves a grinning nun turned cartwheels on the dusty road and a clown banged fiercely on a drum.

Moments later he was woken with a start and he sat up in bed, disoriented and sweating profusely. He shook his head to clear the noise of the drum and then realized that someone was banging loudly on his front door.

He turned on the bedside lamp and checked the clock. Ten minutes past midnight. He wondered who would possibly come calling on him at this time of the night. No one ever called on him except the postman and the occasional tramp on the cadge for a few Woodbines or the loan of a bob or two. And why for heaven's sake were they banging on the door like a lunatic when there was a perfectly good bell to ring? He climbed unwillingly out of bed, crossed the room, pulled back the heavy curtains and looked out of the window into the darkness of the wind-swept night.

Away through the trees in the orphanage he could see the silhouette of a bent-backed nun pacing across the arched attic window and he shivered.

The banging continued but he could not see anyone down in the garden. He switched off the lamp and looked again.

Moonlight flickered softly through the branches of the restless trees and lit up the path.

Suddenly he gasped. He stared in astonishment then growing alarm at the vision below. He tried to recall how many whiskies he'd drunk after his evening meal. He was sure it was just the two as was his habit but perhaps he'd poured larger measures than usual? He put on his spectacles and looked again. It had to be a trick of the moonlight. He closed his eyes, opened them and blinked rapidly. Whatever it was, it was still down there banging away madly on his front door.

He breathed deeply. He was a logical man most of the time and he pondered now on the likelihood of a dwarf turning up on his doorstep at this unearthly hour. For standing down there in his garden was what looked like one of the dwarves from his dream.

The banging stopped. The dwarf stepped back from the door and stood quite still, patiently staring solemnly up at him with enormous eyes that sparkled in the moonlight.

His heart was beating wildly. He struggled to steady his erratic breathing. Be rational, he told himself; if he went down and opened the door he was hardly likely to be overpowered by a dwarf and bludgeoned to death in his own porch, was he?

The night air was cold and he shivered. The wind whined mournfully around the old house. He snatched up his dressing gown, hurried down the wide staircase and unbolted the front door. As he opened the door a strong gust of icy wind blew into the hallway bringing with it a swirling whirlwind of leaves.

Solly Benjamin blinked rapidly and shook his head like a man emerging from cold water. He wasn't dreaming at all. He stared in amazement at the small person standing before him. It wasn't a dwarf, but a small white-faced child who was shivering uncontrollably. A little girl with a cloud of dark hair that framed her ghostly face, a face etched deeply with hunger and tiredness. She was dressed in a dark cloak with a hood and from beneath the cloak two thin legs dropped down into enormous scarecrow boots. Beside her on the path was a small battered suitcase. She looked like a dirty-faced wide-eyed fairy escaped from the mists of time. They stared at each other but neither of them spoke. Solly leaned forward and peered more closely at the child.

She looked like a wartime evacuee, for round her neck was hung a length of cord bearing a name-tag.

It must be some mistake. She must be one of the orphans on her way to St Joseph's and had somehow got lost.

At last he opened his mouth to speak but as he did so the girl stumbled forward; her eyes closed, her legs buckled and she slumped to the floor. Solly rushed forward, gathered her up in his arms and picked up the battered suitcase. He marvelled at the lightness of her as he carried her into the house. He shut the door with his foot and wondered what on earth he was to do with her.

He looked down at the child. Her eyelids fluttered, she opened her eyes for a moment and smiled weakly up at him. She had the most beautiful blue eyes he'd ever seen, and long dark eyelashes that cast sweeping shadows across her pale cheeks.

Outside the wind was howling now. There was nothing for it, it was too late to do anything. He'd have to keep her for the night. None of the beds in the spare rooms was aired so he'd have to put her in his own bed. When she woke in the morning, perhaps he'd get Dr Hanlon to take a look at her and then deliver her to the nuns at St Joseph's.

He carried her slowly up the stairs and laid her down on his own bed. He undid the ties of the cloak round her neck, slipped the name-tag over her head and put it on the bedside table. He removed the worn-down boots from her feet. She did not stir but he was relieved to hear that her breathing was regular. He pulled the bedclothes up around her, left on the light in case she woke and was afraid of the dark. Then he tiptoed down the stairs and into the sitting room where he poured himself a very stiff whiskey.

Sister Agatha burst through the door of the Guardian Angels dormitory like a medieval soldier breaking down a drawbridge. She stood beside Padraig O'Mally's bed, raised her arm and rang the handbell with a vengeance. The noise of the bell reverberated around the sparsely furnished room. Ten pairs of hands were flattened over ears and a terrified mouse skittered across the icy linoleum and fled behind the broken skirting board.

'In the name of the Father and of the Son . . .'

Blankets were thrown back hastily and twenty bony knees hit the linoleum with a communal thud. The boys, their fingers numbed by the cold, made the sign of the cross and a mumbling of prayers hissed through chattering teeth.

Aremen.

'O'Mally!'

'Yes, Sister.'

'Sister Veronica wishes to speak with you now.'

The other boys in the dormitory looked across at O'Mally and wondered what he'd done now. He was always in trouble. Sister Veronica couldn't stand the sight of him. O'Mally was the oldest boy in the room, ten going on eleven but small for his age like most of them were. He was a dark-haired boy and if nature had been left alone he would have had a mop of shiny dark curls, but Sister Veronica took the scissors to him regularly and savagely as though his hair were an affront to decency. Padraig had deep-blue lively eyes that glistened in the half-light of the bleak dormitory.

'Shift yourself, O'Mally!'

Sister Agatha turned her back on O'Mally and began her morning inspection round of the dormitory, sniffing and pulling back sheets. O'Mally flicked her a two-fingered salute, winked at Donny Keegan who smiled shyly back. Then he pulled on his grey shorts and woollen jersey, pulled on his darned socks, thrust his feet into his boots and left the room.

Sister Veronica was waiting for him down in the hallway. She was a cold grey figure of a woman, her enormous feet splayed on the green linoleum at ten to two like the hands of the station clock.

Mr Leary had told them a story about King Midas and said that everything he touched turned to gold. With Sister Veronica and her band of nuns it was the opposite, everything they touched turned grey or brown or bogey-coloured green. The uniforms, the paint, the lino, and they even managed to wash the colour out of the food. The porridge was grey and lumpy as sick, cabbage the colour of old men's phlegm, the mutton brown and gristly.

Padraig looked up at Sister Veronica. It was a long way to look for a small boy. She was almost as tall as the top of the door. Sister Veronica had eyes like pools of stagnant bog water and her eyebrows were birds frozen in flight above her arctic face.

'I have some messages to be run and seeing as you are supposedly the quickest runner in St Joseph's I have chosen you, O'Mally. Hopefully the exercise will tire you out and keep you out of trouble for a few welcome hours.'

Padraig sighed. He'd miss his breakfast, not that it was ever worth eating, but at least it kept the hunger pains away.

'There are two letters to be delivered. The first one is for Miss Carmichael at number nine Clancy Street and the second for Miss Drew at the sweet shop. And keep your hands to yourself if you have reason to step inside there.'

Padraig didn't like Miss Drew one little bit. She was horrible and he wondered why a crabby old thing like her would want to keep a sweet shop. She hated kids. You could tell just by the way her lips thinned up and her nose twitched at the sight of them.

Padraig took the letters from Sister Veronica. He winced at the touch of her skin, like the feel of a well-chilled corpse.

'And lastly, you've to run down to the schoolhouse and tell Mr Leary that I wish to see him at the end of school today.'

Padraig's spirits lifted at the sound of Mr Leary's name but he bit the inside of his cheeks to keep the smile off his face. Sister Veronica didn't like Mr Leary; her nostrils widened like a spooked horse when she said his name.

Mr Leary was brilliant. Better than Mr Gobshite Flynn the last schoolmaster, who had only ever told them what they couldn't do. Mr Leary was dead clever and he never used the stick on them, not even the once.

Once he'd shown them pictures of a chameleon. Chameleons could change the colour of their skin to match their surroundings, so their enemies couldn't see them to catch them. It was called camouflage. He'd like to be a chameleon. In St Joseph's he'd have to change his colour to dull colours, grey, green and brown.

At school though he'd have to work hard to be a chameleon. He'd have to be all kinds of colours there. Mr Leary's classroom was full of colours. Chameleons were dead good but not as good as the invisible man. Now, he was something else. He wrapped himself round and round in white bandages and when he took them off no one could see him. God, if only he could be the invisible boy just for a day he'd have some fun all right. He'd fill Sister Veronica's shoes with steaming donkey shite. He'd put live crabs in Sister Arseface's bed, no, dead ones; it wouldn't be fair on the crabs. He'd stick out his foot and trip her up. Arse over tit. He'd ram a piece of the sloppy grey fish that they were served up on Fridays right up her snotty nose.

Sister Veronica opened the front door with an enormous key that she kept on a chain hidden beneath the folds of her stiff grey habit. He'd read somewhere that you could make a wax impression of a key and make a copy, only he didn't know quite how to do it. He'd have to puzzle his brains over that one.

Padraig stepped outside the door and breathed deeply. He loved the smells of the early morning, the dew and the nettles, cuckoo spit and steaming cow shit, the breath of foxes on the run.

He ran away down the gravel drive, kicking up his heels like a colt, pumping his arms, and listening to the lively beat of his heart.

High above him in the lightening sky a bird soared upwards and a squirrel chattered at him from a hole in a twisted old tree. Over in Kenny's broken-down farm a scabby dog barked excitedly.

Clancy Street was quiet. The curtains were still drawn on the windows of the cottages but fires had been lit and smoke coiled up lazily from the chimneys.

As he passed Dr Hanlon's house, the only big house on Clancy Street, he heard someone tapping at an upstairs window. He looked up to see Siobhan Hanlon standing at the window in her nightclothes, waving at him. God, Siobhan gave him the irrits, she was always smiling at him in class and making mad cow eyes at him. No harm in her though. He gave her a lazy half smile. She blew him a kiss and he blushed, then suddenly a hand pulled Siobhan roughly away from the window. Dr Hanlon's maid Nora filled the window frame, waggled her finger at Padraig and pulled the curtains fiercely shut.

Miss Nancy Carmichael was on the orphanage committee and came to meetings at St Joseph's. She was always in St Bridget's church polishing the pews and tidying up the flowers. He posted the letter carefully through the letterbox and headed on down towards Miss Drew's shop, which was on the other side of Clancy Street.

The brown paper blinds were pulled down over the window hiding the display of sweets from his view. He bent down and pushed the letterbox open and peeped into the shop. It was dark inside but he could make out the outline of the huge jars of sweets on the shelves, the bran tub in the corner . . .

He pushed the note quickly through the letterbox and ran off down the street.

Ballygurry School was a hop skip and a jump from the beach. It was a grey stone building divided into two. On one side was the school with its one big classroom and cloakroom. On the roof there was a rusty bell that was rung for the start and end of school. In the other half of the building was the schoolmaster's house.

Padraig stood in front of Mr Leary's door. He was nervous about knocking. What if Mr Leary came out in his nightshirt? What if he disturbed him when he was out the back on the lav?

He rapped the door knocker timidly, shuffled his feet and waited. There was no answer. He knocked again, louder this time. He felt shy about seeing Mr Leary out of school hours.

'Will you mind out of the way you blithering eejit!'

Padraig jumped back in alarm as the door was flung open and Mr Leary stood before him, his eyes screwed up against the light. He was only half dressed in a cream vest and corduroy trousers and his braces dangling down to his knees.

'S-sorry, sir, but Sister Veronica told me to . . .'

Mr Leary smiled.

'Oh, it's you, Padraig, my eyes are not the best in the morning. And the eejit I was referring to was the dog and not yourself. Come in, do, and tell me what message the warm-hearted Sister Veronica has for me today?'

Padraig hadn't expected to be asked inside the schoolmaster's house.

'She wants to see you after school, sir.'

'Well now, Padraig, the anticipation of such a meeting fills the heart of a poor man with hope.'

Padraig gawped at Mr Leary.

Mr Leary smiled again.

'Come in, Padraig, I'm only teasing. It's cold out there. Get inside and warm yourself up for a while. Mind the dog, the lazy beast wouldn't move if his ar— his behind was on fire.'

Padraig stepped inside the house and carefully skirted the black and white collie that lay sprawled across the hallway.

'Nice dog, sir.'

'It's not mine, Padraig, he knows I'm a soft touch and comes down from one of the farms to warm his behind and cadge a bit of food.'

Padraig looked around him in wonder. He'd only ever had a peep inside the house when the last schoolmaster was here. Then it was drab and dingy with withered palm crosses stuck to the yellowing walls and flypapers curling in the breeze. Now it was like no house he had been in before. The walls were whitewashed as most of the little houses were in Ballygurry, but hung upon Mr Leary's walls were enormous paintings. They weren't the usual sort of paintings of suffering saints and pale-faced sinners writhing in agony, but big colourful pictures in wonderful bright colours that made his eyes ache. Paintings that made your mouth water, paintings as tantalizing as sweets.

Sometimes, as a treat, if they did well in class, Mr Leary let the kids use his own private paint box. Jeez, it was wonderful.

Crimson, Cobalt, Carmine, Cadmium. Magenta, Burnt Sienna, Raw Sienna. Lovely names to wrap around your tongue. All the colours of nature in the one box.

Mr Leary watched Padraig's face with fascination as the boy gazed at the paintings and after a while he said, 'Do you like paintings, Padraig?'

'No, sir. Well, I like these ones. Did you paint them yourself, sir?'

Mr Leary laughed loudly and said, 'I wish I had, Padraig. If I had I would be sunning myself in the Mediterranean and eating grapes handed to me by sun-bronzed maidens.

I have not the talent for creation, Padraig, merely the willingness to admire and encourage it.'

Padraig stood before the most beautiful painting that he had ever seen. It was a picture of a lopsided house, and above the roof of the house was a fantastic night sky where the stars were like fireworks exploding and the moon like molten syrup. It was just bloody wonderful.

'That one, Padraig, is my pension.'

'How do you mean?' Padraig asked.

'This was painted by a true master, Federico Rafael Luciano. I bought it before he became well known, when I was living in Spain.'

'How will it be your pension?'

'Well, one of Luciano's was sold in America for a fortune recently. The trouble is I don't think I would be able to part with it!'

'I know what you mean, it's wonderful.'

'Tell me, Padraig, what are the first thoughts that come into your head when you look at that painting?' Mr Leary asked.

Padraig blushed; he wasn't used to being asked to give an opinion on things. He studied the painting and said truthfully, 'I'd like to be able to think the way the person who painted this thinks. I'd like to live somewhere like that, with a lot of colour.'

'How do you mean about the thinking?'

'I don't know, sir; just looking at it makes me feel . . .'

'Yes?'

'Bold. Unafraid. Like it's okay to enjoy things.'

Padraig knew that the person who had painted this had a different sort of mind to the people he lived amongst. It was a happy painting, a mad, bad, glad to be alive painting and not meant to frighten the life out of you like all the wounded and mutilated figures in the St Joseph's paintings.

Mr Leary noticed that the boy struggled to take his eyes from them.

'Come into the kitchen when you've had your fill of those.'

He could have stood there for ages looking at the paintings but he dragged his eyes away and followed Mr Leary.

The kitchen was a plainly furnished room. There was an old dresser with a scattering of odd cups and tin mugs, a pile of postcards and letters with foreign stamps. There was a large scrubbed wooden table and chairs and in the middle of the table there was a huge jar full of dandelions.

Padraig stared curiously at the dandelions. He had never seen a bunch of weeds in a house before. Grown-ups didn't usually like dandelions. They thought they were a pest and were always digging them up and yet Mr Leary had them on show as though they were prize roses.

'I am an eccentric fellow, Padraig, and I have an enormous inexplicable love of dandelions.'

Padraig beamed. That was funny. So did he.

In one corner of the room an ancient stove belched out heat and a red kettle hummed contentedly upon it.

'Take a seat, Padraig. I was just going to put on some bacon, cook up some eggs. Do you fancy a bite?'

Padraig blushed and could barely answer for the spit rising in his mouth. His belly rumbled loudly.

'I'll take that as a yes then,' Mr Leary said, nodding at Padraig's stomach.

Padraig sat up at the table and watched curiously as Mr Leary prepared the breakfast; he had never seen a grown man cooking before.

Mr Leary lifted an enormous black frying pan down from a hook on the wall and set it on the stove beside the kettle. He went off into the larder humming as he went and came back out holding four thick rashers of bacon. He placed them in the pan and slowly the kitchen filled with the gorgeous, salty, mouth-watering smell of bacon cooking.

'Nothing like a fry-up in my estimation. In fact, the one thing I missed when I was on my travels in Spain was bacon. Some days I could have died for the smell of bacon sizzling. The Spanish are a dab hand at producing wonderful ham but they have not a clue about bacon.'

Padraig stared at Mr Leary's back and wondered whereabouts exactly the bullet holes were in his legs.

'Were you a long time in Spain, sir?'

'Two years since I was there last. I've been there a few times.'

'Did you have a job when you were there, sir?'

He was hoping Mr Leary would tell him about the war and the bullet wounds.

Mr Leary was silent for a moment as he cracked two speckled brown eggs into the pan along with the bacon.

'I didn't have a job exactly. I was there to travel, I got jobs here and there just to pay my way. In fact, Padraig, the truth is I was on a mission to find a lost Irish virgin, but that's a long story. I'll tell you about it some time.'

'Thanks. Were you in the Spanish civil war, sir?'

Padraig jumped as Mr Leary laughed loudly.

'Me? No. I was there just after the war had finished.'

Padraig looked disappointed. Mr Leary grinned.

'The legend has it in Ballygurry that I have bullet holes in my legs from fighting in the war, is that right?'

Padraig could feel the hot flush that spread across his face. He nodded. Bugger. He wished he'd never listened to Jimmy Hoolistan.

'Truth is I do have bullet holes in my legs, but they were caused by a drunken monk let loose to shoot wild boar and he, I'm afraid, mistook me for a porcine marauder.'

Padraig tried unsuccessfully to close his mouth.

'Was it nice, sir?'

'Being shot in the legs?'

'No, sir, I meant living in Spain, sir.'

'Padraig, to a man brought up in a small wet Irish village not dissimilar to Ballygurry, Spain was a glorious distraction, an education in enjoying both the body and spirit, a Utopia for a narrow-minded lazy soul such as myself.'

Padraig loved the way Mr Leary spoke. All the big words that rolled off his tongue no effort like.

'Listen; while I finish cooking the breakfast, go into the dresser drawer over there, there's a scrapbook of Spain in there. Take a look.'

Padraig got up from the table, walked across to the dresser and opened the drawer. God, he was having the time of his life. A cooked breakfast! And a two-sided conversation where he got to ask questions!

He carefully lifted out a leather-bound book and carried it back to the table.

'Fried bread?'

Padraig didn't answer. Mr Leary smiled and put two slices of bread into the frying pan. The boy had his head bent over the scrapbook and was completely immersed in its contents.

Padraig looked with interest at the photographs. One that took his eye was of an enormous higgledy-piggledy building that looked as though it had been dropped from the sky and had fallen to rest on the top of a mountain. Underneath in Mr Leary's spidery writing were the words SANTA EULALIA.

'Is this place a prison, sir?'

Mr Leary leaned over Padraig's shoulder. Padraig thought he smelled nice, of soap and old books and turpentine.

'Oh, if only it was, Padraig, I would commit a felony and stay there for life. No, it was a monastery where I lived for a while, not the last time I was there but just after I'd left university. It was where, in fact, I was wounded by the bullets.'

'Were you a monk then, sir?'

Padraig tried to imagine Mr Leary with a bald head, brown robes and sandals like the pictures of smiling red-cheeked monks he'd seen in books.

'No, God forbid, I wasn't a monk. Santa Eulalia had rooms for pilgrims to occupy. I did all sorts of odd jobs while I was there, helped out with the harvest and did a bit of cooking and polishing. It was a grand place to stay. The food was tip-top and the company second to none. There you go, Padraig, eat and enjoy.'

Padraig closed the scrapbook unwillingly but the sight of the heaped plate before him claimed his full attention.

Mr Leary was a great cook. Padraig hadn't tasted eggs and bacon since, well, since a long time ago.

They ate together for a while in silence and Mr Leary thought it was a pleasure to watch the hungry boy eat. He was all skin and bone. A few good meals inside the little fellow and he'd double in size.

Mr Leary poured two cups of tea, gave one to Padraig and pushed the sugar bowl towards him.

Padraig put a spoonful of sugar into his tea and stirred it slowly.

'Have as much sugar as you like.'

He helped himself to three more spoonfuls and lifted the cup to his lips. He could smell the syrupy sugar as it melted. He sipped the tea and then licked his lips. God, it was lovely.

'Tell you what, Padraig, why don't I telephone Sister Veronica and say I have a few errands to send you on myself. Then you can have another cup of tea, take a good look at the book, save you running back all the way to St Joseph's.'

Padraig could barely keep the smile off his face, and when Mr Leary spoke to Sister Veronica on the telephone Padraig marvelled at how good he was at telling lies. Not even the Pope would have guessed.

Padraig turned back to the scrapbook. Underneath the photograph of the monastery was a picture of an alleyway. It was a narrow place with houses squashed up tight on either side. You could have leaned across and held hands with someone living on the other side. The houses had wobbly looking balconies with pots of flowers all over them. There were beaded curtains strung across all the front doors. Underneath the photograph Mr Leary had written PIG LANE, CAMIGA.

Padraig screwed up his eyes and peered intently at the photograph. He couldn't see any pigs anywhere. There were no people in the photograph, except . . . Going into one of the houses was a shadowy figure, a strange-looking man wearing what looked like a swirling black cloak and a wide-brimmed hat.

'Who's the funny-looking man, sir?' Padraig asked.

Mr Leary peered at the photograph through his thick-lensed spectacles.

'What man, Padraig?'

'There, sir, see, going into that house.'

Mr Leary leaned closer to the photograph and looked again.

'Look, sir, there.' He pointed the figure out with his finger.

'Are you tricking me, Padraig?'

'No, sir.'

'Wait while I fetch my magnifying glass. I'm as blind as a bat most of the time.'

Mr Leary lifted the lid off a pot on the dresser, pulled out a magnifying glass and held it over the photograph.

'My God, Padraig! I don't believe it. It just goes to show that one needs to see the world through the eyes of a child. I've looked at this photograph a hundred times and never noticed him before.'

Mr Leary sat down heavily on a chair, took off his glasses and rubbed his eyes.

'When I was in Spain, Padraig, I was hoping against hope that I'd bump into this fellow, but he was as elusive as a rare moth. And now I discover that while taking this snapshot I was standing not fifteen feet away from him.'

'Why did you want to see him, sir?'

'He, Padraig, is an enigma. They call him Peregrino Viejo, which in Spanish means the Old Pilgrim. There were all sorts of tales about him. That he was an English axe murderer or a defrocked Italian cardinal. One thing is for sure, that he knew more about that part of Spain than any man alive. I wanted to pick his brains.'

'Why, sir?'

'I'll tell you the story when there's more time.'

'Promise?'

'Cross my heart and hope to die.'

The next photograph was of two women who looked like sisters, an old woman with her eyes shut and Mr Leary, who looked different with a moustache and a beard. They were standing outside a café.

'That,' said Mr Leary, 'was taken in a little fishing port called Camiga. I worked in the fish cannery there, the worst job ever. Those three were friends of mine. See that's the Café Cristobal where they sold the most delicious tortilla and fresh sardines that you've ever tasted.'

'I've never tasted any, sir.'

'You will one day.'

'Is the monk one of the ones from the monastery where you got shot?'

Mr Leary studied the photograph with the help of the magnifying glass and then stared at Padraig. Sure enough, sitting at a table outside the café was an old monk talking to a young woman who was big in the way with child; beside her chair was a package wrapped in paper and tied up with string.

'Why yes, Padraig, that is old Brother Anselm. A very erudite but rather peculiar old man who spent many years studying in Paris before he became a monk. Well, I must have a lend of your eyes again one day soon. Now I wonder what on earth he was doing down in Camiga. Good Lord, look at the time and I'm not even properly dressed.

'You must come again, Padraig.'

Padraig smiled.

'Thank you, sir.'

He closed the door to Mr Leary's house and leaped over the wall into the schoolyard. The sound of voices drifted across as the children of Ballygurry wound their way from the village towards the school.

In all his life Padraig had never felt better. His belly was full for once and his mind was racing. He stood alone in the playground. A fierce gust of wind came in off the Atlantic. Padraig shivered with pleasure at the touch of the wind on his face. He stared out to sea for a long time. One day, one day he was going to escape and go and see all the things in Mr Leary's scrapbook.

After the boy had gone Michael Leary stood quite still and deep in thought. Then he picked up his magnifying glass, sat down at the table and looked again at the photograph taken in Pig Lane. Sure enough the shadowy figure was without a doubt the Old Pilgrim. He screwed up his eyes and tried to see which house the man was going into. He was amazed to see that it was the lodging house run by Señora Hipola, where he'd been staying himself. Surely to God he couldn't have been under the same roof as this fellow and failed to come across him.

He took a good look at the second photograph. It had been taken about ten years ago. He remembered it vividly. It was a few days after the robbery at the monastery of Santa Eulalia. There'd been all hell up in Santa Eulalia, the police involved and all. They'd arrested a funny little fellow who'd been hanging around the place. Muli! That was his name, an odd little nubeiro chap, but nothing was ever proved and they'd had to let him go.

The monk in the other photograph was definitely Brother Anselm, he could tell by the large hooked nose and the determined set of the chin. Michael Leary had never really liked Brother Anselm, there was something not quite right about him, he was a veritable chameleon of a man, a different face for every occasion.

Then his eyes settled on the face of the girl, a beautiful dark-haired girl who reminded him of the girl he'd left behind in Spain. He smiled to himself and his heart skipped a beat. He couldn't wait to see her again, though God only knew when he'd next be able to get out there.

The chiming of the grandfather clock at seven o'clock woke Solly Benjamin from a restless sleep. He realized that he must have slept the night in the high-backed chair in his sitting room. He stood up stiffly and tiptoed out into the hallway to listen for any sound from upstairs. He wondered now had he dreamed the whole thing, but then he saw the small brown suitcase beside the front door.

He picked it up, carried it into the kitchen and put it on the table. He wondered if the contents of the case would give any clues as to where on earth this child had come from or where she was meant to be going. There were small triangular stickers stuck to both sides of the case, the sort of stickers that tourists bought to show off where they'd been. He fetched his spectacles, put them on and read the names of the places on the stickers. Some of them looked quite recent and others were faded and peeling. Vigo. Leon. Camiga. Burgos. Pamplona. Logrono. Bordeaux. Paris.

Carefully, quietly, he undid the clasps and lifted the lid. The inside of the case smelled faintly of rosemary and thyme, of wild flowers and something else besides. What was it? He sniffed. The unsettling whiff of incense and candle wax.

There was an assortment of grubby clothes in the case: a threadbare dress, a pair of unsightly drawers with string where there should have been elastic. He lifted the clothes out gingerly and put them on the table. The nuns of St Joseph's would soon sort the child out with a good bath and some ugly but respectable orphanage clothes.

There was a red rag at the bottom of the case and he picked it up. Something was wrapped up inside it and he carefully unwrapped it. He looked at the scallop shell inside and turned it over in his hands. He thought at first it was a cheap tourist souvenir but as he studied it closely he could see that painted upon the smooth inside of the shell was a picture of the Virgin Mary. A tiny figure hardly as big as a child's finger and yet he could see the soft, tired smile on the Virgin's face, the lift of her eyebrow as though she wanted to ask a question but didn't know quite how to. Beneath her soft dark eyes there was the shadow of a teardrop. A tremble forming on her parted lips. Whoever had painted this was a very fine artist indeed. Along with the scallop shell was a clumsily made silver rosary with strange heavy milky coloured beads. Whoever this child was, she was obviously a Catholic and no doubt her destination was the orphanage. On closer inspection the red rag was in fact a shrunken, moth-eaten old cardigan. He was about to wrap the small treasures back up when he noticed the label sewn into the back of the cardigan. It was a French label and as he read it his heart missed a beat. *Madame Mireille!* It was, or used to be, a small exclusive shop in the Rue Bernard in Paris. His mother used to shop there when he was a child and he'd spent many a dreary morning staring in boredom at his feet while Madame Mireille had served his mother. She'd probably been dead for years, although perhaps she hadn't been that old really; children had a strange perspective on the age of adults. The cardigan was made of cashmere and it must have cost a pretty packet in its day. Slowly, thoughtfully, he replaced the things in the case and closed the clasps.

He crept quietly up the stairs and nervously approached the bedroom. The child still slept soundly, her dark hair spread out across the white pillow. One small hand cupped beneath her cheek, a thumb firmly wedged between her lips. He guessed that it would be a long time before the exhausted girl awoke, so he thought he might take a walk down into the village, speak to Dr Hanlon, ask him to visit and check the child over and then arrange for the nuns of St Joseph's to collect her later.

Siobhan Hanlon rubbed her right ear, which was still smarting from when Nora had yanked her away from the window. She sat on the stool and stared into the dressing-table mirror. She stuffed her tongue behind her bottom lip so that her face ballooned out and she squeezed her eyes to a constipated squint. She giggled. Dear God, she looked ugly when she did that.

'Just watch out, Madam Muck, that the wind doesn't change and you'll be stuck like that,' Nora said over her shoulder as she left the room. 'Sometimes, Siobhan Hanlon, you can be as bold as the bath! Making eyes at a rough-necked boy like that and you from a good family!'

Siobhan didn't care. She hoped the wind did change. Anything would be better than being Siobhan Hanlon. Ten going on forty her mammy said. But she wasn't, she was ten going on eleven and soon she would be sent off to school in England. Following in her mammy's footsteps. Going to her mammy's old school so that she could learn to be more English than Irish. She didn't want to go, she wanted to stay in Ballygurry and go to school local, and then maybe the university in Dublin to learn to be a doctor. When she grew up she'd pull out poor people's appendix whether they wanted her to or not, but she'd do it for free. Or else maybe she'd be a fisherman. Anything rather than go to the soppy school in London where she'd learn shorthand and typing and how to walk properly with a book on her head and cook feckin' fairy cakes.

She let go of the awful face, stood up and pulled back the curtains. Perhaps, if she was lucky, she'd get another look at Padraig. She liked Padraig O'Mally. Not a little bit but a lot. He was mad, bad and funny; he could make a bloody cat laugh if he put his mind to it.

Siobhan stared out of the window and down into Clancy Street. There was no sign of Padraig. She wondered where he'd been off to at this time of the morning. Up to some mischief no doubt. Then her heart jumped against her ribs. A man was walking down Clancy Street. It was the Black Jew. He lived all alone in the spooky old house at the end of Mankey's Alley. She'd hardly ever seen him in the flesh. They said he only came out in the dark when decent Christian folk were in bed.

Dear God, now he'd stopped beneath her window. He looked up and down the street as though he was afraid of being followed and then he disappeared from sight. Siobhan moved across to the other side of the bay window to watch where he went, but then she realized that he'd walked through the door that led to Daddy's surgery.

Fancy that! She knew from listening at keyholes that the Black Jew had hardly ever visited the doctor, or any of the shops in the village. He was like a hermit. Sometimes he went off on the train and didn't come back for weeks. Perhaps he was seriously ill; maybe he'd been struck down with a terrible disease. The Black Death. You could catch that from rats. She wondered if her mammy got the Black Death would they still make her go to school in London? Maybe she'd get kept at home to lance the boils and stick leeches over Mammy's belly. Someone would draw a cross on the front door. Atishoo atishoo we all fall down. Anything would be better than being sent away.

Siobhan crept down the back stairs that led to the corridor at the side of the house where the waiting room was situated. Mammy was always telling her to keep out of the waiting room because of all the germs that the poor people from the farms brought in. Daddy didn't mind her going in there; he said it was an education in itself meeting the world and its wife. There were arguments between Mammy and Daddy over that and Mammy usually won.

She pushed the door open a crack and peeped inside. She liked spying on people. It sent a delicious shiver up her backbone. In London there were loads of spies. There were even shops where they could buy disguises: black moustaches and beards, false noses, spectacles and big hats. Today she was the Mata Hari of Ballygurry.

The Black Jew sat quite still on the old high-backed settle, his head tilted to one side like a bird with an ear out for cats on the prowl. He didn't look at all scary close up but everyone in Ballygurry said he wasn't safe to be around. He had wandering hands and filthy habits. They said he made his tea from the water in the toilet.

Siobhan jumped as the Black Jew looked up suddenly. She held her breath.

The Black Jew spoke to the door.

'Good morning.'

Siobhan realized with a jolt that he was speaking to her and blushed. She was about to scamper back up the stairs but she could hear Mammy and Nora deep in conversation away over in the kitchen. Curiosity overcame her and she slipped quietly into the waiting room.

'Good morning, Miss Hanlon, I hope that you're well.'

'Oh, I've not come to see Daddy, I mean yes, I am well. And yourself?'

'Tip-top.'

Siobhan tried to keep the disappointment off her face. If the Black Jew was well then why had he come to see her daddy?

The Black Jew smiled. He had a nice smile that made his dark eyes crinkle. You had to be wary though, people practised their smiles to fool children, they bought sweets and chocolate and said would you like to come and see a secret. And then, God help you, you could be murdered and found on a lonely road with your legs round your neck and your gizzards cut out.

'I've merely come to consult your father about the health of an orphan.'

Siobhan swallowed hard and wondered if he could read her thoughts.

'An orphan?' she stammered. 'It's not Padraig O'Mally is it? I mean he's not ill or anything? I wouldn't be surprised if he was ill mind you, the nuns are real cruel to them at St Joseph's.'

'They are?' Solly asked.

Siobhan sat down on the other end of the settle, keeping a careful eye on the door. It would be one thing to be caught in the waiting room hobnobbing with the poor, but talking to the Black Jew, that would have Mammy donning a black cap and pronouncing the death sentence. 'Siobhan Hanlon, you have been found guilty of smiling at orphans, shaking hands with the poor without wearing gloves and worst of all . . .'

'How cruel are they, Miss Hanlon?'

'You can call me Siobhan,' she said. 'Terrible cruel. They beat them with a stick for the smallest thing and sometimes they lock them in a dark cupboard with spiders. Padraig says that one day he's going to run away and join the circus.'

Solly Benjamin smiled as he remembered his strange dream of the night before.

'What would he do in the circus then, this Padraig?'

Siobhan smiled.

'Ride elephants, put his head in the lion's mouth. He says he'd rather look at a lion's tonsils than stay in St Joseph's.'

'Does he now?'

'They have grubs in the cabbage and they're not allowed to leave them on the plate. They have to swallow them without making a fuss for the greater glory of God. And there's a mad foreign nun that they keep locked in the attic and away from sharp knives.'

Solly smiled kindly. He'd been such a long time away from the company of children that he'd forgotten how funny they were.

Siobhan smiled back. She thought he was a nice man; he was easy to talk to and he didn't make her feel afraid the way people had warned her.

In the distance the Ballygurry school bell began to toll, and from the kitchen Nora the maid called out impatiently for Siobhan.

'Hell's teeth, I have to go. Goodbye. If Mammy comes in you'll not say I've been speaking with you?'

'My word, Miss Hanlon, is my bond.'

He sat for a few moments listening to the sound of Siobhan Hanlon galloping up the stairs and then he got up and quietly left the waiting room. He'd call on Dr Hanlon another time. He wasn't quite ready yet to deliver his blue-eyed sprite into the hands of the nuns of St Joseph's.

In number nine Clancy Street Miss Nancy Carmichael was getting ready for a busy day. First she was having breakfast with Miss Drew, who ran the village sweet shop, and later that afternoon they were both going to the monthly meeting of the St Joseph's Orphanage Committee. Nancy always liked to look smart for these occasions, so she took a little more trouble about herself than usual.

She stood in her bedroom in the cool grey light of early morning in front of the oval mirror that had supposedly been a wedding present to her mother. Thinking of her mother she automatically crossed herself and felt tears of anger spring too readily to her eyes. She blinked furiously and made an effort to pull herself together.

It had been such a shock finding the box of letters after her mother's death, letters that made a mockery of everything she'd ever believed to be true. No wonder her mother had had so many airs and graces, acting like she was better than she was. God, she'd had a dog's life when her mother was alive. She could never do anything right, nothing was ever good enough! Thankfully, though, no one in Ballygurry would ever know the truth about the Carmichael family. If they did, the shame would kill her.

She contemplated her reflection carefully in the mirror. She wasn't, she supposed, a bad-looking woman considering she was almost forty-five. Although she had noticed of late that the powder she had used since she was a young girl no longer floated across her skin, but filled the wrinkles that were deepening round her mouth. Laughter lines some people called them but Nancy Carmichael had never indulged in a great deal of laughter. She looked more closely; yes, she was definitely getting that dried-up matronly look. She winced; another few years and she would be an old maid. She took a step back from the mirror, stretched out her thin pale lips over her good strong teeth. Then she bared her teeth and scrutinized them. She was very proud of her teeth. Most of the women of her age in the town had lost their teeth and wore false ones, great clacking things that sometimes slipped out when they spoke too fast. Some of them had no teeth at all, real or false, and their faces had sunk into an awful shrunken ugliness. She'd taken good care of her teeth even in the days when money was tight. She had cleaned them night and morning using a little salt and soot from the chimney, rubbing them furiously with a rag twisted round her finger.

Since her mother's death five years ago, things had looked up financially. She still couldn't get over how much her mother had left in her will, considering how mean she'd been when she was alive. Now Nancy bought Eucryl tooth powder from the chemist's in the town and visited the dentist once a year in Cork. Oh yes, she'd been able to push the boat out a little these past few years. Not that she was extravagant or foolish with her money, but she did treat herself a little; she had butter on her bread instead of margarine, she put two scoops of tea in the pot and bought pink iced fancies on Fridays and lamb chops instead of mutton. And of course the medicinal bottle of brandy that she bought each week and kept under the bed inside a pillowcase inside a suitcase in case of burglars.

She applied a little shocking-pink lipstick to her top lip. Then she pulled her bottom lip against the top to even out the colour. It wouldn't do at her delicate age to slap on too much war paint, as her mother had called it. She certainly didn't want to give the wrong impression to the new priest, not like some of the brazen trollops she knew. It was mortifying the way Nora O'Brien and Bridie Gallivan flaunted themselves in front of him, pushing out their floppy bosoms and batting their eyelashes like demented hussies. Quite disgusting, it was, carrying on that way in front of a man of the cloth. She smiled at the thought of young Father Daley. He was a nice-looking young man for a priest and from a good family, you could tell by the way he held his teacup.

She replaced the top on the lipstick, popped it into her handbag and snapped together the clasps. She brushed a speck of imaginary fluff from the fur collar of her coat, took her black felt hat off the peg near the front door, put it carefully on her head, turned off the light and pulled the front door closed behind her.

As she stepped out on to Clancy Street a keen gust of wind caught at her hat and almost carried it off, she had to wedge it firmly down on her head and keep a hold of it. There had been no mention of strong winds on the early weather forecast on the wireless. Another stronger gust that seemed to come from nowhere lifted her best grey woollen coat and her sensible plaid skirt above her white dimpled knees, revealing a glimpse of goose-pimpled flesh and the voluminous legs of her salmon pink winter drawers. Frantically, with one hand she held on to her hat and with the other she fought with her clothes in an effort to restore a level of decency to herself. Then, as she looked up, she was mortified to see a man on the other side of the street, walking in her direction. Of all the men in Ballygurry it had to be the Black Jew. For a second she thought she detected a lascivious smile pass across his thick red lips and she bristled with indignation.

Nancy Carmichael, baker of cakes for priests, cleaner of the church, flower arranger, pillar of the Orphans Society detested the Black Jew and everything he stood for, even if she didn't know quite what it was he did stand for; it was bound to be something unpleasant. The very thought of the filthy old devil ogling her thighs filled her with a mixture of emotions: disgust and something else, something she couldn't quite fathom.

The Black Jew slowed his step, lifted his hat in her direction and tilted his head in a gesture of friendliness.

'Good morning, Miss Carmichael.'

Nancy Carmichael glared at him, the pupils of her pale-blue eyes dilating, and then she dipped her head into the wind as though she were a human battering ram. She wouldn't have any truck with the likes of him. He wasn't safe to be let out and about amongst god-fearing people.

Father Daley had taken a wrong turn and he cursed himself for his stupidity. How easy was it to get lost in a one street village? He should, he realized too late, have carried along the lane that led out of the village towards the station and taken a right turn, but instead he'd turned into the alley between the houses on Clancy Street.

At the end of the alley he came to two large iron gates. A peeling sign bore the word PRIVATE. Behind the gates there was a view of an imposing old house, run down and in need of a lick of paint but nevertheless still rather splendid. This must be the house where the man the villagers of Ballygurry called the Black Jew lived.

It would take him ages to walk back down the lane and according to his watch he was already ten minutes late for his first meeting of the St Joseph's Orphanage Committee. Over to his right above the trees he could see smoke rising from a large red-brick chimney. If his sense of direction proved right for once that must be the orphanage. It wouldn't do any harm if he went in through the gates and cut across the overgrown lawns; there was bound to be a wall or fence he could climb and if he found his way through he would only have to cross the road and it should bring him to St Joseph's.

He slipped in through the gates and stepped warily across the gravel drive. There was no sign of anyone in the garden so he made his way quickly across the lawn. At least there hadn't been any Beware of the Dog signs.

Sure enough at the far side of the garden was a crumbling wall covered in ivy. He took a leap at the wall, got one leg over and was about to drop down on to the other side when he heard a scream. The blood-curdling eerie scream of a child that made the hairs on his neck bristle and his stomach turn over.

He looked back at the house. Everything was still. There was no sign of anyone. It must have been a hawk or his imagination running away with itself, he'd been very jumpy of late.

He dropped down on to the other side of the wall and began to run through the dark woods like a fearful child.

Michael Leary was furious, and as he faced Sister Veronica across the table his face was white and a rapid pulse beat in his neck. Behind his thick-lensed spectacles his eyes were bright with anger. Sister Veronica stared coolly back at him, the trace of a contemptuous smile on her lips.

'Has the boy no living relatives?'

'None,' said Sister Veronica. 'His mother died in Dublin and, er, I'm afraid he has no father.'

Michael Leary laughed.

'Now that would be a miracle indeed, Sister, if the boy has no father. As adults we'd both agree that apart from the Immaculate Conception we have all been brought into this world as a result of our biological parents being involved in a double act, would we not?'

Sister Veronica glared at Michael Leary. How dare he speak to her like that? Just who did he think he was, not five minutes in the job and wanting to call the shots?

'Mr Leary, I think you know as well as I that Padraig O'Mally has a birth certificate that omits to name his father and as such he is presumed to be an orphan and is under the care of the church.'

'So the boy is illegitimate, so let's beat him about the head with a stick, make him pay for his mother's wanton ways, is that it?'

'I think, Mr Leary, that it is high time you left.'

Michael Leary stood up and leaned on the table, his knuckles were white, his voice quiet, and the anger in the air between the two of them palpable.

'I came here today to ask permission for the brightest boy and the most talented artist I have ever had the good fortune to teach to take an examination for one of the best schools in the country. In your infinite wisdom you intend to deny him this opportunity because the school is not Catholic. Well, Sister, go ahead, let's make sure that the boy knows his place, doesn't get too big for his orphanage boots. I suggest, Sister Veronica, that you examine the dark recesses of your soul, because in my book what you are doing is just plain evil.'

'Mr Leary, I did not ask you here today to discuss Padraig

O'Mally but merely to let me have the name of the child who has excelled in school so far this year.'

Michael Leary angrily tossed a brown envelope on to the desk, turned on his heel and left the room, and almost fell over a thin-faced nun who had her ear glued to the keyhole.

When Father Daley turned into the drive of St Joseph's he was red faced and breathless. He hurried along the drive with a sinking heart. He hated committees and meetings and he was already nearly twenty minutes late.

He looked up at the orphanage building and his heart sank even further. It was like a building from the pages of a Victorian novel, more like a prison than a home for small parentless kids.

The windows were uncurtained arrow slits. The brown paintwork was blistered and peeling. The red-brick walls were cracked and weeds grew within the fissures and the drainpipes were coated with layers of rust.

St Joseph's reminded him of his Catholic prep school in London, where he had spent several interminable, miserable years. It had the same air of melancholy and dismal dilapidation. The institutional smells of cold cabbage and disinfectant pervaded the air and mingled with the whiff of old Wellingtons and the inevitable beeswax polish.

Father Daley stepped nervously up to the front door, took a deep breath and tugged the bell pull. Inside the building a bell clanged dolefully.

The door opened slowly and revealed a small nun, her wiry body swamped by a grey habit that was at least three sizes too big for her. She had a long thin pinched face with the stamp of medieval asceticism etched into her features. She nodded grimly at Father Daley without any trace of welcome or good humour. He felt like a small, frightened schoolboy arriving in class without his homework, his socks slipped down miserably into his shoes and a blanket of gloom settling on his soul.

'Good afternoon, Sister. I must apologize for my lateness. I got rather lost on the way.'

The nun ignored him, turned swiftly on her heel and, with a pale hooked finger that reminded him of the worm in a Tequila bottle, beckoned him to follow her.

He chided himself for his uncharitable thoughts. She was probably not allowed to speak because she was under the rule of silence. He suppressed a smile. Or perhaps she was just a miserable old cow, and he decided from the set of her rigid shoulders that it was the latter. Dear God, fancy one of the poor orphans waking from a nightmare and seeing that ugly mug bending down over them!

He felt the urge to turn round, run back down the gloomy corridor, out of the door, away down the crunching gravel drive. He wasn't brave enough and instead he followed the nun meekly along the green tiled hallway. His footsteps sounded overloud and his breath came out in clouds of huffy steam in the chilly air.

The nun ground to a squeaky halt outside a wood-panelled door that bore a name on a highly polished brass plate. SISTER VERONICA. PRINCIPAL.

The stone-faced nun knocked fiercely on the door with her tiny knuckles and Father Daley winced at the sound of fragile bone against oak. The knock was answered immediately by a sharp, irritated voice.

Father Daley was ushered brusquely into the room. The nun turned on her heel and disappeared back into the shadowy hallway.

Sister Veronica was a thickset woman of indeterminate age, somewhere, he guessed, between forty and sixty. She rose from her seat as he entered. Dear God in heaven! She was a woman of gargantuan proportions. Suffering angels!

She must have been nearly six and a half feet tall. Beneath her habit her arm muscles rippled powerfully and the bosom on her was a grey mantelpiece that could have housed a carriage clock and a set of ornaments. She had a large red bulbous nose that separated two eerily grey-brown eyes, a wide humourless mouth and a strong square jaw. On one of her cheeks there was a mole that sprouted a clutch of fierce black hairs.

Father Daley shivered. It was even colder inside Sister Veronica's study than in the hallway, even though a small coal fire burned lackadaisically in the grate. A low watt bulb burned, giving off a weak light that coated the room in a dismal luminescence. Father Daley could just make out three other figures sitting round a large bare table.

Sister Veronica nodded to him to take a seat. Father Daley sat at the far side of the table next to an enormous bookcase lined with religious tomes. He screwed up his eyes and looked round the table. That was Miss Carmichael opposite him next to Sister Amazon. He'd already met Miss Carmichael at mass. She was a rather intense woman, over pious and pernickety, forever rearranging the flowers and dusting the pews when they didn't need dusting. She smelled faintly of eau de cologne laced with brandy. Was that Donahue who ran the village bar sitting next to her? It was indeed, and the man was looking acutely uncomfortable, his battered face scrubbed and shining, wearing a tight navy double-breasted suit. His enormous red neck was squeezed into a white starched collar a size too small. He smelled of shaving soap, fresh sweat and an overdose of Brylcreem. Next to Donahue was a small dismal-looking woman with a sharp pinched nose and lips that moved without making a noise. He had been introduced to her at mass but couldn't remember her name. Miss Shrew or something like that.

'Now that you're finally here, Father Daley, shall we make a start? Miss Carmichael, I believe, is going to discuss the organization of the Summer Fair.'

Father Daley glanced across at Donahue, who looked as though he was badly in need of a stiff drink.

Miss Carmichael proceeded to give a long-winded breathy talk on who would be running the white elephant stall, who had pledged cake and bun donations, followed by a seemingly interminable list of those ladies willing to assist Father Daley with the coconut shy. The bric-à-brac collection was going well. The sales of raffle tickets were a little slow but the running total on the sale of tickets in aid of black babies was looking encouraging.

Father Daley glanced again at Donahue and tried unsuccessfully to stifle a grin. Donahue was almost asleep, his chin resting on his chest, his breathing heavy.

The next to speak was Miss Thin Nose, who talked in a high-pitched squeak about a letter that had been sent by the Bishop about a wonderful opportunity that would be offered to some of the orphans: a brave new initiative to give them a new life in the colonies. Australia to be precise. It was hoped that all the older children of St Joseph's would soon make the journey.

Father Daley stifled a yawn. His mind began to wander. He remembered a geography textbook at school about Australia. It had pictures of hopping kangaroos with cute little babies in their pouches and wide-eyed koala bears clinging to tree trunks, chewing contentedly on eucalyptus leaves. There were pictures of boomerangs and wide-jawed men wearing dungarees and hats with dangling corks on string. There were hot orange suns and yellow sandy beaches.

He was woken from his pleasant reverie by a loud and pointed cough. He looked up and was caught in the glare of Sister Veronica's icy eyes.

'As I was saying, Father, the annual pilgrimage to Lourdes takes place each year, but I expect Father Behenna explained all about it to you.'

Father Daley nodded and panicked. Father Behenna, his predecessor, God bless him, had barely been able to string a sentence together. He had been sloshed for almost the whole of the time they had spent together.

'I'll refresh your memory, Father. Each year we plan a pilgrimage to Lourdes; the trip is open to any residents of Ballygurry who wish to go, although usually it is a small, select party. Miss Carmichael is, of course, a regular, as is Miss Drew. Mr Donahue is unable to go because of business commitments.'

Donahue nodded and immediately conjured up a sorrowful expression that made Father Daley want to laugh out loud. He'd bet Donahue would rather drink rancid bull's piss than go on a trip to Lourdes with a priest and a few poker-faced spinsters who had taken the pledge.

'We always have the most wonderful time, Father, although the food isn't always quite, well, what we're used to. Miss Drew and I always take a few provisions with us. Some tins of corned beef, Spam and sardines. Just to keep body and soul together you understand.'

Donahue snorted and all eyes were turned towards him.

'I had an aunt once from Dublin. She went to Lourdes and was cured of her ingrowing toenails, but she ate some of the food over there and was taken bad. She's never been right since. In fact, she's dead now. Took the lining off her stomach. The food was disgusting. A pile of muck and the meat half raw, she said. Her guts were never the same again, God bless her soul. And she said there was no butter to go with the bread. Imagine dry bread! And the lavs, beg pardon, Sister, the toilets, well they were just holes in the ground. One pull of the flush and she was up to her knees in, well, you know. Jesus, them foreigners still live in the Dark Ages.'

Miss Carmichael coughed and Miss Thin Nose sniffed and twitched next to her. Sister Veronica glared at Donahue.

'Last year, Father, there were six on the trip including Father Behenna. Father Behenna will have already made and paid for all the bookings for this year and I'm sure Miss Carmichael and Miss Drew will run through with you anything that you need to know.'

Father Daley's heart sank.

'And now, time is pressing on and we need to announce the lucky child who has been selected to accompany you to Lourdes.'

Father Daley watched Sister Veronica with interest as she picked up an envelope from her desk, slit it open with a paper knife and took out a piece of paper.

'Perhaps Father Behenna forgot to explain to you, Father Daley, but every year a child from the school is selected to make the trip. The child chosen is the one who has accumulated the most gold stars for progress at their school work and in sport.'

As she looked down at the piece of paper her face grew rigid with irritation; her mouth set into a thin vexed line while in her neck a pulse beat rapidly.

Sister Veronica cleared her throat with a sound like wet cement being shovelled.

'This year Padraig O'Mally has been chosen.'

Donahue started in surprise and stared at Sister Veronica as if she had uttered a string of filthy words.

Nancy Carmichael sat bolt upright in her chair.

Miss Thin Nose Drew gasped.

'Padraig O'Mally!' they chorused.

'Padraig O'Mally indeed,' said Sister Veronica, and her voice was like an easterly wind off an icy sea.

Donahue snorted.

'O'Mally,' he said. 'Isn't he the little bas— isn't he the one who set fire to Siobhan Hanlon's first Holy Communion dress with a magnifying glass?'

Sister Veronica nodded curtly and visibly stiffened, the enormous muscles of her arms rippled powerfully beneath her habit.

'Is he the same boy who interfered with the harvest supper drinks?' asked Miss Carmichael in a whisper.

'The very same. But it seems that Padraig has come out undisputedly at the top of his class. Indeed Mr Leary was asking me only this afternoon if it would be possible for him to take the examination for the Abbey School.'

'But, Sister, the Abbey School is not a Catholic school,' said Miss Carmichael in a scandalized voice.

'Quite so, Miss Carmichael. It seems that our erudite schoolmaster, Mr Leary, feels that education is more important than the keeping of our faith. Of course permission has most definitely not been granted. I have already told Mr Leary so this very afternoon.'

Father Daley cleared his throat.

'Is he a very bright boy, this Padraig?'

'The brightest boy ever to pass through the school here according to Mr Leary, but as we all know, Father, intelligence isn't everything. Education may buy you a loaf of bread, but religion allows you to enter the Kingdom of Heaven.'

Father Daley lowered his eyes and said nothing.

Suddenly Miss Drew leaped to her feet and began to screech like a madwoman.

'What the hell!' Donahue was roused from his doze.

'A mouse!' wailed Miss Carmichael. 'It was sitting in Miss Drew's lap as bold as brass!'

'Kill it!' shrieked Miss Drew.

Sister Veronica rose from her chair, picked up a fire iron, brandished it menacingly and began to stalk the room.

'It's only a little mouse, for heaven's sake, what harm will it do?' asked Father Daley.

The three women stared at him as though he were a halfwit. He made his decision. He was going to get to the mouse before Sister Veronica did.

While Sister Veronica jabbed about under the table with the poker he caught sight of the little creature. It was halfway up the curtains and clearly in a state of abject terror.

Father Daley leaped to his feet, pushed past Sister Veronica, took hold of the curtain and flicked it. As he did so he offered up a prayer. The terrified mouse flew through the air and landed in the middle of the table. Miss Drew continued to screech like a banshee and Miss Carmichael slumped into her chair in a fit of the vapours.

Father Daley lunged at the mouse but it fled over the top of the table, slithered over the edge and hit the floor running. Father Daley got down on his hands and knees and followed it. The mouse scurried away through a crack into the cupboard beneath a large bookcase. Father Daley, panting now, opened the door and almost screamed out in alarm.

He stared in amazement at the sight before him. At the back of the cupboard an ancient wrinkle-faced nun and a small pale-faced boy sat huddled together. Father Daley gazed in astonishment. The boy looked terrified out of his wits. The nun merely grinned at Father Daley, winked and held a finger to her lips. The boy was holding the quivering mouse in his cupped hands.

'What is it, Father?' said Sister Veronica.

She was close behind him, her shadow a cold cloud across his shoulders.

The boy's eyes widened with fear.

'Please, Father don't kill it,' the boy mouthed.

The boy handed him the mouse.

'No one panic now. I have it,' Father Daley called over his shoulder.

Swiftly he closed the cupboard door on the boy and the nun, edged past Sister Veronica without looking at her, hurried from the room and away down the corridor, the small mouse trembling in his hands. He opened the front door and went out into the gardens. He could feel the frantic heartbeat of the mouse and also his own. Dear God in heaven, what sort of a lunatic place had he come to?

He stooped and put the mouse down on the lawn. It glanced up at him and then escaped into the long grass. He hoped that by now Padraig O'Mally and the queer little nun had made their escape too. He knew without a doubt that the boy was Padraig O'Mally. He liked the look and the sound of the boy. At least he'd liven up the trip to Lourdes a bit.

Solly Benjamin replaced his hat and smiled to himself and thought that Miss Nancy Carmichael would be quite a good-looking woman if she occasionally took the trouble to smile. Mind you, those drawers she was wearing were out of the ark! Another big puff of wind whistling up the legs of those gargantuan things and she might take off! He turned up the Astrakhan collar of his coat against the cold and walked briskly on down Clancy Street towards home.

When Solly arrived back at Nirvana House, for the first time in years he was filled with a feeling of hope. He was surprised to see the front gates ajar. He opened the front door and called out cheerfully. There was no answer. She must be still asleep. He climbed the stairs and peered nervously round the bedroom door.

The bed was empty and the girl was gone. Perhaps it was she who had left the gate open. Maybe when she'd woken she'd realized that she'd arrived at the wrong house, let herself out and was at this very moment on her way to St Joseph's.

He went back down the stairs and into the kitchen. The brown suitcase was gone too. He sat down at the table and closed his eyes. He realized with a shock that he was disappointed that she had gone. On his walk back from the village he had been filled with an irrational happiness at the novelty of going back to a house where someone waited for him. Now he chided himself for his absurdity. What had he been thinking? That she was going to stay a while? That they'd play Happy Families? For God's sake, it was a mystery that she'd arrived in the dead of night on his doorstep. He was a rational man most of the time. There would be a logical explanation. Full stop. Now he needed to get on with things, follow his usual routine. A strong cup of coffee and two pieces of toast while he listened to the wireless and got on with the humdrum pattern of his ordered life.

When Dancey Amati woke in the night she couldn't remember at first where she was. She was lying in a huge soft bed with springy pillows beneath her head.

The last thing that she remembered was staring up at a peculiar man who had large startled eyes and a puckered mouth. He had stared at her as though he had never seen a child before in his life. And all the while as he stared he had hopped from one foot to the other as if the floor beneath him was too hot to stand on.

Then everything had drifted into a warm darkness where she was flying, then falling, falling then flying.

Now she lay quite still, looking out through a large

unshuttered window that framed the night sky like a painting. A moon as delicate as a bauble bobbed above the black branches of shivering trees, a spinning moon throwing out stars into the inky pitch.

A highway of stars stretching out across the top of the world. The same stars that she and Mama had watched that night so long ago . . .

They had lain together in the big bed in Señora Hipola's lodging house watching the huge moon float above the tilting houses of the town, trying to count the stars of the Milky Way.

And Mama had told her that one day soon they were going to escape from Pig Lane. They were going to run away to a place where there wasn't danger round every corner and where they wouldn't have to worry about talking to strangers. They wouldn't have to keep their wits about them or keep their eyes skinned because there were poisoners and lunatics in every town they'd ever been to. Towns and villages where there were cutthroats and pirates lurking in each dark alleyway. Where there were scar-faced bandits and madmen on the loose, who would slice out your tongue and cut out your heart as soon as look at you.

Mama said they were going to escape. They were going to walk beneath the stars of the Milky Way and follow them until they reached the gateway out of Spain.

Dancey remembered now how she had closed her eyes sleepily and listened as Mama said that they were going to cross the mountains on foot. Mountains that were as tall as the moon, and when they reached the top they would reach up and pluck a star from the sky and its light would last until they reached their journey's end.

The mountains were beautiful but dangerous too, and they would have to take great care on their journey because enormous brown bears lived there. They ate up every bit of foolish travellers and spat out only the teeth and the toenails.

In the winter the snows were deep enough to drown in and people had been lost in the drifts and never been found. It had sounded scary and exciting to Dancey. Mama said that it would be a long hard journey but when they got to the other side, oh on the other side there were the most beautiful of places in the whole wide world.

They would live in Paris or New York and they would be rich. Mama would be a famous actress or maybe a dancer and she would buy beautiful gowns of silk and taffeta, velvet and organza, hats with misty veils, shoes with gold and silver buckles, expensive soaps and perfumes. They would drive down the streets in a fine carriage pulled by four pure white horses, and they would live in a grand house with its very own bath, and they would have servants to bring the hot water and kill the cockroaches . . .

After his late breakfast and an hour spent listening to the wireless after which he realized he had not taken in a single word he had heard, Solly had grown restless. By early evening the house was stifling him, the walls crowding in on him until he felt that he could barely breathe.

He went out and walked briskly down towards the village. The wind was keen and restless gulls were swooping and riding the currents above the huddled houses of the town, and he could hear the waves crashing with an almighty force on to the beach.

Solly Benjamin took a deep breath, pushed open the door and stepped into the semi-darkness of Donahue's shop-cum-bar. Above his head a bell jangled lazily. He sniffed the air curiously. The place was a veritable bran tub of smells. Fresh beer and last night's whiskey, potatoes softening in a saucepan out in the back kitchen that was curtained off from the bar. There was no Mrs Donahue to do the cooking. She had hitched up her skirts and taken off on the mail train three winters back, and rumour had it she was living in Dublin with a man who raced pigeons and was on the wanted list for impersonating an English Duke.

Solly sniffed again. Sacks of cabbages, yellowing sprouts and piles of damp newspapers were giving off a musty, fusty air.

Donahue, a huge figure of a man, was leaning across the counter of the bar reading a newspaper and didn't look up at the sound of the bell. Solly shuffled his feet. He coughed. Donahue looked up and squinted through a forelock of sweaty curls.

Donahue stared hard at Solly and Solly stared steadfastly back. Donahue picked up his broken reading glasses from the counter and perched them on the end of his bulbous nose. He carried on staring at Solly.

'Good evening, Mr Donahue,' said Solly.

Donahue gawped oafishly as though the ghost of St Francis of Assisi himself had walked in and asked for a packet of birdseed and a tin of Pal meat for dogs.

In all the time he'd lived in Ballygurry the Black Jew had never set foot in Donahue's. In fact, there were few businesses that he patronized except the newsagent and occasionally the cobbler's.

Donahue blinked and grinned at Solly. There was a joke about that. A Jew and his sons lived in Rome; he was a cobbler who repaired shoes for the Pope. He had written above his shop 'Cohen & Sons, cobblers to the Pope'. And someone had written underneath 'And balls to the rabbi!' Donahue chuckled to himself and then began to cough.

Solly cleared his throat, but Donahue continued to stare at him. Donahue thought that nobody knew where Solly Benjamin did his shopping. Perhaps he didn't. Perhaps the tight old bastard lived on fresh air! Another joke. Why do Jews have big noses? Air is free.

Donahue picked his own nose and giggled.

Air is free, that was a hoot that one. Apparently Sinead Dooley had seen the Black Jew in one of the posh stores in Cork buying some disgusting-looking fish that she herself wouldn't have fed to the feckin' cat even though she hated the mangy-arsed thing.

Donahue took a packet of cigarettes from his waistcoat pocket. He tipped up the packet, took out a cigarette, tapped it against his finger and lifted it to his mouth.

Perhaps he ought to go steadier with the whiskey. Seeing things that weren't there was a sure sign of the delirium tremens.

Pink elephants. Hairy-legged spiders. Naked girls. Young busty ones wearing silky cami-knickers.

He turned round to look for a box of matches on the back of the bar and yelped in fright.

Jesus, Mary and Joseph. Now Solly Benjamin was looking out at him from the mirror behind the bar.

Donahue spun round. He was sweating heavily now, oily beads of sweat running from his hairline over his eyebrows and into his eyes and making them sting.

He blinked rapidly, ran his fingers across the greasy stubble of his chin.

'H-how can I be of of . . .' stammered Donahue.

'Assistance?' said Solly.

'That's right, of assistance, thank you for the lend of the word.'

'That's all right, wash it out and have someone deliver it to me. But, firstly, I'd like a pint of Guinness.'

Donahue stood transfixed, yellow spittle bubbling in the corners of his opened mouth.

Shaking his head like a man surfacing from a cold sea, he

turned and lifted a dusty glass from the shelf, then seeing his mouth agape in the mirror, he hastily closed it.

He pulled the pint with trembling hands and shoved the glass across the sticky counter towards Solly.

Neither man spoke. Solly waited patiently for the dark, deep liquid to settle in the glass. Then, under the mesmerized gaze of Marty Donahue, he lifted the glass up to the light, although the 15-amp bulb barely penetrated its deep, dark depths.

'Let's raise a glass to orphans and sprites everywhere. Especially those who arrive unannounced in the dead of night and like the dew evaporate in the light of day.'

Donahue gawped. The man was mad. A mental case.

Solly raised the glass to his mouth and allowed the creamy head of the beer to seep up over his lips. He drained half of the pint in one go and then set the glass down on the counter.

Donahue watched him warily, nibbling at his dirty nails and unable to think of anything to say for the first time in his garrulous life.

'Secondly,' said Solly smacking his lips together loudly, 'I'd like a bottle of Jameson's whiskey. A tin of ham, a loaf of bread and four flagons of your best ale. For this night I intend to get slaughtered.'

Donahue dipped down behind the counter and crossed himself.

Dear God. Jesus and all the saints of heaven. He wondered was it a mortal or a venial sin to serve a Jew with a tin of ham? The whiskey was okay, he supposed, but a tin of ham?

Solly Benjamin swallowed the rest of his pint and set the glass down on the bar with a satisfied smile. He really was beginning to enjoy himself.

Donahue surfaced from below the counter and with a

shaky hand he placed a bottle of whiskey on it. He dipped down again, took up a tin of ham, wrapped it in newspaper and placed it on the counter next to the whiskey.

Solly took out his wallet and handed Donahue a note, smiled warmly and said, 'A fine pint of Guinness, Mr Donahue. Keep the change.' Then he walked jauntily out of the shop clutching the whiskey, beer, bread and the wrapped tin of ham.

Donahue pulled himself together, ran out through the back of the shop and into the yard and called over the wall to Dermot Flynn, who was holed up in the outside lav smoking a Woodbine and reading the racing paper.

'Dermot! You'll never believe who's just been in here.'

'The Holy Father for an ounce of Old Shag,' muttered Dermot from behind the lav door.

'No, don't be so ridiculous, man!'

'Mother Ignatia for a bottle of gin?'

'No! The Black Jew! He was drinking Guinness and raising his glass to lost orphans. I think the man has lost his senses.'

There was silence from behind the lav door.

'And guess what else he bought.'

The lav door rattled and Dermot Flynn, braces dangling and eyes on stalks, came shuffling out into the backyard. He listened to Donahue without interrupting once.

Within five minutes the whole of the left-hand side of Clancy Street knew that the Black Jew had gone mad. Had drunk a pint of Guinness in two gulps and also had, indeed to God, bought a bottle of whiskey and a tin of ham. Mrs Cullinane who lived in the last house on Clancy Street sent her daughter Sinead barefoot across the street to tell Nelly Kiernan who then passed it on over the wall to the widow O'Shea.

By the time Solly Benjamin had buttoned up his coat and

adjusted his hat the net curtains on both sides of the street were twitching. Fifty sets of startled eyes followed him as he walked with an unaccustomed spring in his step the length of the street then turned left into Mankey's Alley and was lost from their sight.

Padraig ran until he was exhausted, until his ears pounded with the echo of his beating heart and his legs would carry him no further. He wiped his tears away with a small dirty fist and slumped down on to the ground.

It was spooky in the Dark Wood. Weak sunlight filtered through the tangled branches of the trees and dappled on the thick mossy ground. Twigs cracked and leaves rustled beneath the tread of invisible animals. Above his head on a branch a cobweb glistened and a spider dangled on a wispy thread.

The Dark Wood was out of bounds. If he got caught he'd be in big trouble. He didn't care though, what else could they do to him now? They could beat him and shut him in the cellar. He didn't give a tinker's stuff. They wouldn't even let him take the exam for the school Mr Leary had told him about. He'd be stuck in St Joseph's now. Maybe they'd keep him there until he was as old as Sister Immaculata. Until his teeth fell out and his legs went bandy and they'd lock him up in the attic at night.

He lay on his back until his breathing steadied and his heart beat more slowly.

The spider dangled just above his nose. It got closer and closer until he could see its eyes. It landed on his nose and he felt the silky touch of its feet on his skin. Then the spider took off, climbing back up the thread hell for leather.

Padraig closed his eyes. He'd stay here for a while until he'd calmed down and then he'd go back to St Joseph's . . .

When he awoke moonlight was dripping through the

branches of the trees and an owl called out close by. It was then that he realized he wasn't alone in the Dark Wood.

Sister Immaculata was worried. It was only ten minutes until Sister Agatha rang the supper bell and Padraig still hadn't come back. Soon the doors would be locked and bolted and Sister Veronica would call the roll. He'd be discovered missing and then all hell would break out. And it would be all her fault if he got a beating. If she hadn't shown him the secret way that led from the laundry to the cupboard in Sister Veronica's room none of this would have happened.

At least the nice new priest hadn't given them away. She and Padraig had had such a shock when the mouse had scurried into the cupboard followed by the priest. She giggled now as she remembered the look of holy terror on the priest's face when he'd clapped eyes on her and Padraig. The poor man had been shocked out of his wits.

Poor little Padraig. When Sister Veronica said that he wouldn't be allowed to take the exam for the school near Cork he was heartbroken. It was all he could do to stifle his sobs there in that dark cupboard.

When they'd finally escaped from the cupboard they'd stood together in the gloomy light of the laundry. The boy's eyes had filled up with tears.

'I'm not going to stay here, they can't make me! And I'm not going to Australia either. I'm going to run away.'

'Where would you go though, Padraig?'

'Anywhere. Anywhere at all that's not here. I'll catch a ride on the train, join up with a band of tinkers or the circus.'

'Take me with you, Padraig.'

'I would, Sister, if I could.'

He wondered if she'd mind being fired out of a cannon. Probably not, she was a game old bugger.

'I know a grand place where we could eat fresh sardines and drink red wine.'

'Where's that?'

'I don't remember now but it was lovely.'

'How long since you were there?'

Sister Immaculata made a calculation.

'Fifty years and three weeks.'

Padraig had stared at her.

'That was millions of years ago,' he'd said.

Sister Immaculata couldn't remember where she'd left her spectacles half the time and yet she could remember things from ages ago.

'The other night I heard someone coming down the lane. I thought they'd sent someone to take me home.'

Padraig had smiled sadly; she was always going on about someone coming to rescue her. She imagined things most of the time, poor old thing.

'I'll never escape now though,' she had said and felt the tears trickle down her face.

'Don't cry, Sister, something will turn up, you'll see,' Padraig had said, and he'd brushed her tears away with his fingers.

Padraig got down on his hands and knees like he'd seen Indians do in the cowboy films he'd watched with his mammy. He moved slowly through the wood, keeping close to the ground. The hairs on his neck were prickling and a slow shiver of fear slithered up his spine.

The trees were drizzled in silvery moonlight. Above his head through the gaps in the branches he could see a sprinkling of stars in the Ballygurry sky. High in a conker tree the white owl blinked and stared down curiously at Padraig. Padraig wriggled towards the sound that had startled him. He stopped, held his breath, crouched down behind an enormous gnarled old tree and slowly peeped round it.

His heart beat like a tight new tambourine. He swallowed his fear.

Holy Mary!

Shite and double shite.

There, standing before him in the clearing, was the strangest creature that he had ever seen.

A small withered witch with a black pointy hat but no sign of a cat or a broomstick.

Padraig stared, mouth hanging open, his heart turning cartwheels.

It wasn't a witch. It was too small. It was . . . well, it was a raggedy thing wearing a black cloak, the hood pulled up over its head. Its legs were thin as twigs and it wore clumpy clown's boots. It stood quite still in a pool of moonlight.

A ghost?

A leprechaun maybe?

A midget nun?

A sprite or hobgoblin?

Padraig knew if he had any sense in his head at all he should run as fast as he could out of the Dark Wood, but he couldn't drag himself away. He was mesmerized.

A twig cracked beneath him. He held his breath.

Then, slowly, slowly, the thing turned round to face him.

From beneath the black hood two enormous eyes stared out from a pale face. In its arms it held an enormous bunch of dandelions. Probably for making spells or potions.

Suddenly the moonlight grew brighter and caught the heads of the dandelion flowers and they shone with an incredible brilliance. They reminded Padraig of the exploding stars in the painting on Mr Leary's wall.

He looked from the dandelions to the shining eyes of the queer little creature.

He couldn't take his eyes off the thing, though he knew that it was probably already casting its spell upon him and by the morning he would be a frozen statue of a boy or a croaking frog . . .

Then he realized with a shock that the thing was speaking. The mouth was moving slowly. It was chanting. An incantation. Over and over again in a strange language.

Padraig was poised and ready to run. All his muscles getting ready for escape. He didn't think the thing had seen him yet. A sudden breeze ruffled through the woods. He shivered with cold and fear. Then suddenly the hooded goblin threw back its head and howled at the moon like a mad thing.

Father Daley was in a panic. For the past hour he had paced up and down his study and bitten his fingernails down to the quick.

What a hell of a day he'd had! He'd spent the whole interminable afternoon at St Joseph's and then in the early evening Miss Drew and Miss Carmichael had turned up on the presbytery doorstep bearing gifts.

He'd spent the next few hours politely eating every cake and pastry that had been put in front of him and listening to their memories of past trips to Lourdes. They had told him that Father Behenna was very organized and would have already bought the tickets for the trains and the boat. The hotel would be booked and paid for. Father Behenna, they said, would no doubt have stored everything in the safe in the study just as he'd always done.

Later, when he'd finally managed to get rid of the pair of them, he'd opened the safe and had been almost knocked to the floor by the landslide of empty whiskey bottles that came crashing out.

There was no sign of any tickets, any money or hotel

reservations. He'd thought at first that there must have been some kind of mistake. He told himself to stop panicking and do something practical. He'd ransacked the study, pulled out every drawer and cupboard in the presbytery but to no avail.

In the end he'd telephoned the Saint Peter's Retirement Home in Dublin, where Father Behenna had gone when he'd left Ballygurry. A cheerful sounding Sister Patrick told him that Father Behenna had never arrived. Apparently, she said, he had changed his mind and gone to live with his sister in Paddington, London. Yes, she said, she had a telephone number but no address.

Father Daley carefully dialled the number.

The line crackled.

He took a deep breath.

Eventually the telephone was picked up at the other end. No one spoke but he could hear heavy breathing as if the person on the other end was an asthmatic. Loud music was playing in the background.

'Hello, my name is Father Daley.'

'Yes, and I'm the Queen of Sheba.'

'Er, would it be possible to speak with Father Behenna?'

'Now listen here, whoever you are will you kindly fuck off.'

'To whom am I speaking?'

'You are speaking to Madame Mimi from the House of Sin.'

'Dear God in Heaven.'

'Oh God! Oh God!' screamed a distracted voice in the background.

He slammed the telephone back on to the hook and slumped shaking into a chair.

Solly Benjamin sipped his whiskey and watched the enormous moon climb higher into the sky. He smiled to himself then as he recalled the look on Donahue's face when he'd asked for a pint of Guinness. He'd only asked for the tin of ham out of devilment. It had been worth every penny.

Outside an owl called away in the woods. The wind was getting up again, and he got up to pull the shutters across.

As he stepped over to the window he caught sight of a movement in the garden. He stood quite still and watched. There it was again. Someone or something was out there prowling round over near the wall that bordered the Dark Wood. He felt the hairs rise on his neck. He picked up the poker from the fireside, made his way across the hallway and slipped quietly out of the kitchen door into the dark night. He took a deep breath and held the poker aloft.

As he skirted the side of the house and peered round the corner he smiled with relief. Two small figures were crossing the lawn towards the house. They walked together hand in hand. Hansel and Gretel in the moonlight. Hansel carrying a suitcase and Gretel a bunch of flowers. Solly hurried back into the house, replaced the poker and went to open the front door.

He felt as though he had slipped down a rabbit hole and emerged in a different world.

'Curiouser and curiouser,' he said to himself, and then aloud, 'If the pair of you are selling clothes pegs or matches I don't want any. If you've brought an invitation to the Mad Hatter's tea party then I'm busy.'

Padraig O'Mally looked up in fascination at the man they called the Black Jew. He must be off his rocker. Who would come round selling clothes pegs at this time of night? And who the feck was the Mad Hatter when he was out of bed?

Padraig had heard all about the Black Jew. He was a miser with stashes of paper money sewn into the mattress.

He saved up the clippings from his toenails and made pillows out of them. You were supposed to be afraid of him. Padraig wasn't.

'We're not selling anything, sir. I found the little girl all alone in the Dark Wood, I just brought her back for you, sir, I thought you might be worried seeing as it's dark.'

'Why would I be worried?'

'Well, it's getting late and it's scary in there all alone.'

'Are you from St Joseph's?'

'Yes, sir, and I'd best be getting back.'

'Do you know what time it is?'

'No, sir, I haven't a watch.'

'It's nearly eight o'clock.'

'Shite. I'll be skinned alive.'

Solly smiled down at the boy.

He was a beautiful-looking child despite the savage haircut and the filthy face.

The girl held tightly on to the boy's hand as she looked up at Solly.

'Why are you bringing her to me and not taking her back with you to the orphanage?'

The boy scratched his head and looked puzzled.

'Because, sir, she belongs to you.'

'And how do you work that out?'

'She has a label round her neck with your name and address on.'

Solly leaned forward and peered at the label.

Dear God. He hadn't looked at it the previous night when he'd slipped it over her head, but sure enough written upon it was his own name, Mr Solomon Benjamin. Nirvana House, Mankey's Alley, Ballygurry.

This was most bizarre. It must be someone's idea of an unfunny joke.

'I think she must have wandered off into the woods and

got lost. She was awful upset. See, though, she's picked you a grand bunch of dandelions. Anyhow, I'd best be off.'

'What's your name?'

'Padraig O'Mally, sir.'

'Ah, Padraig, the boy who wants to join the circus, is that right?'

Padraig wondered how the Black Jew knew that. Perhaps he could read people's minds.

'Well, I'd rather be anywhere than over there in that dump,' he said, nodding his head in the direction of St Joseph's.

'Why's that?'

'It's a terrible place for a kid. This little one's dead lucky she has you to look after her.'

'Well, Padraig, if that's the case, I'd be very grateful if for the moment you wouldn't tell anyone that she's here.'

Padraig grinned.

'I won't. I'm great at keeping secrets. And if Sister Veronica asks, I'd be grateful to yourself if you'd not tell her I was here. By the way, I think the little girl must be English, I can't understand a word she says, not that she says much.'

Then the boy hurried away. Halfway down the drive he turned back and waved and then he was off and running away out of the gates, disappearing into the blackness of Mankey's Alley.

Solly looked down at the little girl and smiled. She watched the gap in the night where the boy had been for a long time and then turned to face Solly. She stood with one skinny arm outstretched, holding the bunch of dandelions towards him. He reached forward and took the proffered gift, swallowing the inexplicable lump in his throat, and then he led her gently into the warmth of Nirvana House.

*

In the schoolhouse Michael Leary turned off the wireless, lit the lamps and banked up the fire. It was still early evening but already it was overcast and the horizon was an angry weal above which purplish clouds were banking in the darkening sky. By the looks of it the weather forecast was right and a storm was brewing far out at sea; a few hours or so and it would hit Ballygurry.

He sat down at the window, lit a cigarette, then he took out the letter he'd received that morning. He read it slowly and carefully, taking longer than usual because his Spanish was rusty and his eyes always ached at the end of the day.

My dear Michael, I trust that all goes well with you.

Things have not been too good here the past few years. I fear that soon Santa Eulalia will close its doors on over five hundred years of history. We cannot continue for much longer the way things are. There have been no new brothers for many years and only a handful of us tottering old monks remain. Sadly, pilgrims are few and far between these days and the revenue we made when times were good has now dwindled to almost nothing.

Yet, you know for centuries Santa Eulalia was a self-sufficient community. We grew our own food, raised goats, sheep and cattle and were famous for our fine wine. We were a happy refuge for the steady stream of pilgrims who travelled to and from Santiago de Compostela. We were renowned for our gastronomic fare, the warm hospitality we displayed to the pilgrims who stayed here over the years. Why, once we employed over a hundred people to tend to our cattle and work the fields. Now we have only a few sorry beasts, but thankfully a cellar full of fine wine.

Brother Anselm, you will be glad to hear, no longer hunts. I asked him about the girl in the photograph but he got quite agitated and said he couldn't recall her at all. He has good days and bad days and I fear that he, like Santa Eulalia, is breathing his last breaths and is unlikely to live through another winter.

We have had the doctor out to him, and even Violante Burzaco, the pastequeira from Camiga, I think that you met her once when you were here, but nothing has done any good.

The only one of our community who fares well is Quixote, the three-legged dog who was a puppy when you were last here. He seems to have fathered pups in most of the villages around and a good proportion of them also have only three legs! Strange, but no doubt the scientists would have an answer.

Anyhow, Michael, sorry that this is such a gloomy letter, but if you can see your way to visiting us here at some time in the near future you know you would be more than welcome.

I remain, in God, your friend Brother Francisco.

Michael wondered what on earth could be wrong with Brother Anselm. He did remember Violante, the pastequeira. She was a fascinating old woman, an old-fashioned healer. She'd lived alone in a rambling house in Pig Lane. People had great belief in her powers and had come to see her from miles around. Most days from dawn until nightfall there was a steady stream of people queuing outside her door. There were agitated mothers holding the clammy hands of whey-faced toddlers, halfwits or giggling idiots. Old women came too with their infantile husbands in tow, decrepit old men, wide-eyed and dribbling, shambling along obediently.

He felt extraordinarily restless tonight. He wanted to get back to Spain and find out why his girl had stopped writing to him, and visit Santa Eulalia one last time, as it didn't seem likely that it would remain open much longer. Perhaps during the next school holidays he would be able to get out there, God willing.

Michael Leary folded the letter and slipped it back into the envelope. He sat for some time deep in thought. Outside, the first large drops of rain were falling and the rising wind rattled the window-panes.

Sister Agatha closed the door to the attic and turned the key in the lock. She always felt better when she knew that Sister Immaculata was safely installed behind a locked door. There was something unsettling about the old nun. The way she looked at you, the way those eerie glittery eyes bored right inside your head. Sister Agatha was sure that Sister Immaculata wasn't in possession of all her faculties, and yet there was a shrewdness and a sneaky cleverness about her that was unnerving.

Sister Agatha had suggested to Sister Veronica that they should get shot of Sister Immaculata, ship her off to a rest home somewhere, but Sister Veronica wouldn't hear of it. Apparently, when Sister Immaculata passed away St Joseph's would get a large amount of money from the old nun's family.

Behind the attic door Sister Immaculata listened to the soft pad of Sister Agatha's feet as she descended the narrow staircase. She pulled a face at the back of the door. She hated Sister Agatha. She was a devious, wily, cruel old bitch and she wouldn't trust her further than she could throw her.

The weak light of the candle cast fitful shadows across the bare and broken walls of the attic room. Sister

Immaculata kneeled down and pulled a small wooden box out from beneath the bed.

She sat down on the bed with the box in her lap and opened the lid. The inside of the box smelled faintly of camphor and mildew. A name and address had once been written on the inside of the lid but now the writing was faded and the surname had long been obliterated. Perhaps, though, if she sat very quietly and closed her eyes she might be able to remember it. She knew that it was important to remember. Thoughts were difficult for her these days. Sometimes she went into a room but couldn't remember why she'd gone there. There were rooms all over St Joseph's where she'd left her thoughts.

It was no good. Tonight the name would not come to her. She took a faded envelope out of the box, tipped it up and a photograph slid out. It was a wrinkled sepia photograph of a young woman sitting in a high-backed wicker chair with two babies nestling in her lap. They were identical babies, peas-in-the-pod twins. Two pretty little things with wide innocent eyes and tousled curls.

Sister Immaculata traced her finger gently round the outline of the woman's face. If only she could remember who she was and what her name was. The woman looked down at the children with an expression of such intense love that it brought a lump to Sister Immaculata's throat.

She closed her eyes and began to rock backwards and forwards. Slowly, so slowly at first, then faster and faster.

She opened her eyes and looked again at the photograph. She imagined the woman's mouth beginning to twitch, a trembling of the top lip, then the lips curving upwards into a smile that crinkled the skin round the eyes. Warm dark eyes that reflected the swaying fronds of the courtyard palm tree outside the window of the villa. There were small beads of sweat on the downy hairs above the top lip. The woman's skin was smooth and dark and her long hair curved as soft as velvet round her slender neck. Any moment now the mouth would open and call a name . . .

Outside, the evening darkened and the wind moaned around St Joseph's, far away thunder growled. A rook flew past the window and its shadow lingered for a second and then disappeared. The candle flickered and hissed, then died.

In Nirvana House, Dancey Amati was woken by the sound of the rain as it fell through the whispering branches of the trees.

She pulled back the bed covers, got out of bed and crossed to the window. There were no stars in the sky tonight, no Milky Way to wonder at. A storm was on its way and the air smelled strange. A flicker of excitement and fear tickled her spine.

She remembered a storm from ages ago when she'd worked in the fish cannery in Camiga. She'd worked there for a long, long time and the money she'd earned Mama had put into her purse to save for their journey, the one they'd never made . . .

She shivered. She didn't like to think about the past. She'd hated working in the cannery but she'd loved the people. Ottilie and Carmen, who were sisters, and old Dolores who was nearly blind had been really kind to her and she'd never even had a chance to say goodbye.

Inside the cannery it had been cool and dark and the walls oozed a damp fishy syrup; the floor was always wet and slippery as ice. It stank of salt and seaweed, iodine and fish, blood and guts. The heady smells of women's sweat: sweet jasmine and garlic; lilac and raw onion.

Ottilie and Carmen had the worst job of all. They had to

chop off the heads of the fish and toss them into large wooden barrels. Dancey winced at the memory.

Chop and bang.

Bang and chop.

Steel against soft bone and flesh.

Then old Dolores scooped the headless fish from the barrel and stacked them in crates, their tails sticking out of the back.

Slither and slop.

Slop and slither.

She gagged as she remembered the stink of her blood-spattered overall that came down almost to her ugly boots and made her look like a circus clown without the smile.

For a long time after she'd left the cannery she still had the wedding ring marks made by the scissors on the soft skin of her thumb and finger.

She had always had to take a deep breath and close her ears to the sound of the blades meeting.

Flash and snip.

Silver on silver.

Steel on steel.

Snip and flash.

Rip and snip.

She had cut off each little silver fish tail until the floor around her feet was a carpet of small, mercurial wings and the silver sequins of fish skin.

The storm had started just before the end of the shift. The metal fly curtains on the doorway began to jingle and the air grew cold as if a ghost had walked in through the door.

Dancey had gasped as a sudden fierce gust of wind blew the curtains inwards until they were almost horizontal.

A tiny little man stood in the doorway, dressed from head to toe in a mish-mash of ragged clothes. His eyes met

Dancey's and they glittered brightly. And then he was gone.

The wind grew in strength, swirling the fish tails around their feet and sweeping them up into the air until they whirled and swirled high above the rafters. Thunder rolled far out at sea and a flash of lightning lit up the cannery for a split second.

Ottilie and Carmen made the sign of the cross.

As the three of them had left the cannery the sky was dark as octopus ink and the wind blew in squally gusts off the sea and whipped the driving rain across the cobbles. They had run squealing and splashing through the muddy pools of water that had formed in the ruts where there were cobbles missing.

They had sheltered in the doorway of the church, huddled together and dripping. They'd listened to the dreary voice of the priest and breathed in the smell of candle wax and mouldy linen, incense and dying flowers.

When they'd stepped out from the shelter of the church, above their heads the wide-eyed gargoyles spouted waterfalls of frothy water. It was the last time she had seen Ottilie and Carmen. The storm had been a sign, because the following day Mama had disappeared.

She thought that perhaps if the storm had something to do with Mama going then maybe, just maybe, the storm tonight would bring her back. She wanted to see more of the storm so she pushed open the bedroom door and climbed slowly up the narrow winding staircase that led up to the little room at the top of Nirvana House.

The first thunderclap rattled the narrow windows of the Guardian Angels dormitory. Padraig woke with a start and flinched with pain. Hell, Sister Veronica had taken the stick to the back of his legs when he'd missed the roll-call and now they were agony.

The night beyond the window was dark and starless, the dormitory almost pitch black. He could hear Sister Immaculata moving around up in the attic like a wounded moth against a window-pane. He was really worried about her; she had been looking and acting real odd the last few days, as if something was playing on her mind. At nights she was very restless and he could hear the pad of her bare feet on the floorboards.

No one else in the dormitory had woken. They were all worn out because Sister Agatha had sent them on a run round the famine wall. Five times round it and all because someone had stolen two fig rolls from the visitors' biscuit barrel.

Another clap of thunder. A lightning flash. A split second of fierce light that lit up the dormitory. Padraig got out of bed and skittered across the cold linoleum towards the window. It was no good though, he'd wake everyone if he tried to climb up and look out.

And then he had a brainwave.

It was brilliant! If he got caught, though, they'd kill him. So what! He could do it. He knew he could. If only he could get downstairs and into the laundry and through the secret way into Sister Veronica's study.

He knew that her study door was always locked at night but that she left her window open a crack for her cat to come and go as he pleased.

He went back across to his bed, dressed hurriedly then, holding his breath, trying to control his trembling, he opened the door and stepped out into the silent unlit corridor.

Siobhan Hanlon pulled the covers up over her head and tried to stifle her terror. She was afraid of storms. If a thunderbolt were to hit the house they'd all be killed in their beds, or fried alive if it was lightning. She tried to remember all the things that Mammy had told her you shouldn't do in a thunderstorm: stand under a big tree, speak on the telephone, wear big silver earrings or stand by the window.

Another fierce crash of thunder, right overhead now, seemed to shake the house from the bottom up.

Pulling the covers from over her head, she stiffened with fright. She thought she could hear the skeleton rattle on its stand in Daddy's study. The china thimbles in the glass cabinet jingled and a draught of wind startled her rocking horse into a creaking canter.

Across the landing she could hear Nora muttering her tearful prayers and the nervous rattle of her rosary beads.

Lightning speared the darkness. For a split second the eyes of her teddy bear shone with a startling brilliance as though he had come to life like Frankenstien. Then the lattice windows of the dolls' house lit up as if from the inside.

She hated being afraid of things. She was sick of the way Mammy was always putting the fear of God up her.

Don't talk to strangers, Siobhan!

Keep your dress pulled down over your knees.

Proper little girls don't do cartwheels.

Make sure you're wearing a clean vest and pants in case of accidents.

The list of Mammy's don'ts was endless.

Siobhan took a deep breath, pulled back the bedcovers and got out of bed. She tiptoed warily across the room towards the window. The rain was hurtling down outside and a second flash of lightning lit up the room. She froze, then giggled as she realized it was only her own goggle-eyed reflection in the dressing-table mirror.

She stood half hidden by the curtain and looked down into Clancy Street. The rain hammered down on the cobbles and bounced back up again. The sign outside Donahue's was clanking wildly. The horse trough was full to the brim. Then she saw him. Honest to God!

Padraig O'Mally was making his way down the other side of Clancy Street! Where on earth was he off to at this time of night and in this weather, too?

She watched him curiously until he was out of sight. He was as daft as arseholes sometimes, considering he was so clever. It wasn't safe to be wandering around out in the dark like that. He'd be soaked to the skin and catch his death. Anyone could get hold of him and do him in. He was mental. She'd make him tell her what he was up to tomorrow.

Way beyond the trees she could see the outline of the glass dome on the roof of the Black Jew's house. Daddy had told her it was a tiny observatory where you could take a telescope and look at the night sky. Mammy said the dirty old thing probably watched people undressing from up there. Siobhan wouldn't mind climbing up there herself and having a good look at the stars.

The thunder rolled again and she wanted to leap back into bed and pull the covers over her head, but she was determined not to. If only she could be half as brave as Padraig. Just then a flash of lightning lit up the sky and she caught a fleeting glimpse of a very strange sight indeed.

She stood for a long time hoping for more lightning so that she might look again at the strange goings on in the glass observatory in the Black Jew's house.

Padraig was drenched to the skin by the time he got to the beach. He looked across at the schoolhouse where a light was still burning. He wondered if Mr Leary was still up and watching the storm. Padraig would have liked to have gone over there and watched the storm with him.

He sat down on an upturned boat and stared out to sea. The weather was wild and the waves were lashing the beach. He felt the sting of the salt spray on his face and the wind whipped sand around his bare legs until they tingled with pain.

He almost jumped with joy every time the lightning flared across the bay. When it came it was like a gigantic firework. God, it was bloody brilliant. If the wind hadn't been so strong he would have done cartwheels across the beach.

He began to shiver violently. For two pins he would have loved to run up over the dunes and bang on Mr Leary's door, ask if he could have a cup of sugary tea and sleep the night. Instead, he squeezed beneath an upturned boat and huddled in the tarry, salty hidey-hole while the rain hammered above his head.

It was almost cosy under the boat and he yawned sleepily. He must have dozed off then, for he was woken later by a foghorn that sounded far out at sea. It was time he was off. He crept out from under the boat. The storm was moving on; there were just occasional blasts of rain and the squally wind off the sea now.

The night smelled fresh and lovely like the world had been scrubbed and hung out to dry. The moon was a great wobbly egg yolk, and a million stars were sprinkled across the sky.

He scampered across the beach and up over the slipway, keeping close to the shadows of Clancy Street. All the houses were in darkness except for Donahue's. He crept up to the window and edged his nose towards the sill. He peered in through the rain-streaked glass. The clock above the bar said five to midnight. Donahue was asleep on a chair, his head resting on a table surrounded by empty beer bottles. A yellowing newspaper beneath his head riffled with each breath he took. A ginger cat slept contentedly on his huge shoulder.

Donahue was a moody old thing but you couldn't really not like him. Sometimes he looked as if he was going to burst into tears. He was nearly always drunk or dead drunk. He had a shiny black Morris Minor that he kept in his shed at the back of the house. He'd bought it to take his wife out for a spin but after she ran away he'd locked it up and hadn't used it since.

Padraig turned slowly away from the window. The moon shone down on the water of the horse trough. It was as clear and still as glass. Padraig checked that no one was about, then scurried across the road.

Any minute now the Ballygurry clocks would chime the midnight hour. He spat on his finger and lifted it up into the wind. Yes! The wind was coming from the right direction. That meant the presbytery cockerel would be spinning the right way. He kneeled down and stared into the shimmering water of the horse trough. His wide-eyed reflection stared back at him. He began to tremble. The stars and the wobbling moon were reflected round his face in the water. His heart was beating so furiously he thought he might faint.

Somewhere, in one of the little houses of Clancy Street, a clock tinked the hour nervously. Then a louder bolder chime came from the grandfather clock in Dr Hanlon's house.

And then he saw it. A face staring solemnly back at him. He gasped with shock. His startled breath rippled the water and then the face was gone.

Solly Benjamin's life suddenly took on a whole new meaning. He took a trip out to Rossmacconnarty and bought the child a whole new wardrobe of clothes because he couldn't bear to see her dressed in the shabby rags she'd arrived in. He bought new shoes, pretty red sandals with cream crêpe soles. He chose five cotton dresses in different colours with intricate smocking across the bodices, three cardigans with buttons in the shape of ducks and rabbits. He bought a pink fluffy bolero for best and Wellingtons for wet days. He bought pants and socks and nightdresses and a shampoo that wouldn't sting her eyes.

As the days passed she gained slowly in strength. The colour returned to her cheeks and the dark rings beneath her eyes grew smudged and then disappeared.

He knew that her name was Dancey Amati; it had been written along with his own name and address on the name-tag that had hung round her neck on her arrival. Apart from her name, though, he knew nothing else about her.

When Solly spoke her name she smiled shyly at him but she did not speak to him at all, although sometimes when she was alone he thought he heard her whispering quietly to herself.

Early each morning while she slept Solly took a walk down to the village to buy fresh bread and other provisions. It was a pleasure now to buy food for two. The child ate hungrily and politely and wasn't fussy about her food, except for fish. One evening he'd made some toast and opened a tin of sardines and she'd shrunk back from the table and turned quite pale.

On the morning after the storm he walked down the slipway and stepped down stiffly on to the beach. The wind was still wild and as it blew in off the sea it took his breath away. The sea was dark grey tinged with an angry purple and white-capped waves crashed on to the beach, exploding around him and sending up curtains of misty spray.

The beach was empty except for a few wind-blown gulls worrying at empty crab shells, others trying to keep their balance on upturned boats that had been hastily pulled up above the tide line by the local fishermen. Solly walked down towards the water's edge and stood looking out across the restless ocean, an ocean stretching from the simple shores of Ballygurry all the way to America.

Years ago he had made the journey to New York on an ocean-going liner. He'd thought that he might settle in America and make a new life for himself over there. He'd stayed for a while in New York, Boston and San Francisco but in the end he'd decided to come back.

When he'd returned from the States he'd stayed in London with old Uncle Sammy, spent one sweltering summer in Barcelona and a hideously cold winter in Madrid. Then, on a whim, he'd taken the ferry to Ireland and, somehow, he'd landed himself here in Ballygurry, a rain-lashed small town on the west coast of Ireland, and he'd stayed, God knew why, ever since.

He realized that quite unconsciously he had been feeling for the ring on his finger. How odd that he should do that. He hadn't had the ring for years, not since . . .

As he stood there on the beach with the wind buffeting him he was suddenly transported back in time to a day many years ago when he'd stepped off the train in Rossmacconnarty. He had been going to pick up the keys for Nirvana House. It had been a terrible day, the wind was gale force and sheets of rain had whipped across the platform blinding him. He remembered now quite clearly that in the distance he'd heard the tolling of wedding bells. What a day that had been for a wedding! He wondered if the storm had been a good omen for the happy couple. He'd dragged his heavy suitcase the few yards to the station waiting room and in those few seconds he was soaked to the skin. He'd pushed open the door in his rush to find shelter, flung down his suitcase, stood for a few moments stamping his feet and tipping rain from the brim of his hat. Then suddenly he'd become aware that he wasn't alone. A man was sitting huddled on the floor on the far side of the waiting room, his head in his hands, sobbing noisily. Solly had coughed with embarrassment to alert the man to his presence. The fellow had looked up slowly and for the next few seconds Solly had been unable to take his eyes off him.

He was dressed in good quality clothes, smart trousers and an expensive mackintosh with a tartan collar and leather buttons. Yet they were absolutely filthy, spattered with mud as if he'd been chased across rough countryside by a pack of hounds. His eyes were wild, a desperate man by the look of him, and yet Solly had not been afraid.

'Terrible day,' Solly had said quite inadequately.

'Yes, yes, it has been . . .'

He was a well-spoken man, a man fallen on hard times. There had been a lot of fellows like that after the war, men who couldn't settle down in civvy street after war service.

Solly had rambled on, 'Those winds are gale force, there'll be trees down all over the place . . .'

'Trees down, yes, you have to understand . . . I've done the most terrible thing, I've left a child fatherless. Oh God forgive me but it wasn't my fault, my poor mother. Oh Christ, I have to get out of here.'

Then the man had got up unsteadily, drunk with emotion, fear, self-disgust . . .

Solly had given the man all the money he had on him, and as an afterthought he'd slipped the ring from his finger and handed that to him as well. Whatever the man had done he needed the ring more than Solly did. Afterwards he'd worried that the man had committed a terrible crime.

He'd scoured the national and local papers for weeks for news of a murder, an escaped lunatic on the run, but to no avail. He must have just been a demented tramp, a petty thief and a drunk. The ring would have fetched a pretty penny in a jeweller's. Solly only hoped that it had brought the fellow better luck than it had brought him.

He sighed. After the strange events of the previous nights he needed some time to think. He had been a man of careful routine for many years now, a man grown old before his time. Yet suddenly by a quirk of fate he'd been shaken out of his dullness by the arrival of a small mystery girl. Who, though, could possibly have decided to send him a child? And why? And what was he supposed to do with her?

He scoured his mind for a clue. Who did he know who had a child? Apart from Uncle Sammy all his family were dead. Most of his old friends he had long since lost touch with. There was Max in Venice, but he'd never been interested in women and the last Solly had heard he was living with a professor of linguistics called Pietro.

It was quite ridiculous, but somebody somewhere had made a conscious decision to send Dancey to him. They knew his name, where he lived . . . And in the pocket of her dress there had been a piece of paper with directions to his house written in three languages, English, French and Spanish. There was nothing written, though, about where she came from, who she was or what he was meant to do with her. He knew that some time soon he'd have to contact the authorities but he didn't want to hand her over to the nuns at St Joseph's. He felt strangely responsible for her; someone had thought him a fit enough man to put a child into his care and he wasn't willing to hand her over to the ill treatment of the nuns. Not yet, anyway. Maybe he'd phone Uncle Sammy in London. He was a shrewd old bugger. He had contacts in nearly every European city from his work in wartime. Maybe he'd find a key to unlock the mystery, for Solly sure as hell couldn't.

If he'd been a younger man he'd have questioned whether the child was actually his, he'd had a few romantic dalliances in his youth. He knew that was impossible, though, it was well over fifteen years now, he thought sadly, since he'd been involved with a woman.

It was all a total mystery. The only thing that he knew for certain was that he was a different man since she'd arrived. Change had been suddenly thrust upon him, if only temporarily, and it had brought out new emotions in him.

He stood and watched the waves roll on to the beach and thought that he was happier than he had been in many years. He wondered had he ever been truly happy? He smiled ruefully. Yes, for a very short time as a young man he had been blissfully happy. Or at least in the ignorance of his youth and his lack of experience he had convinced himself that he was happy.

He sighed. He didn't like to dwell on the past and what might have been. What was the point? He had his memories, but what were they worth, eh? A head full of useless recollections; snapshots of loved ones now dead, home movies of the mind that he reran and others that he had long since banished.

He wondered how anyone looking at him now would describe him. A lonely slightly hunched middle-aged man taking a bracing walk on a windswept beach. He'd been lonely, of course, over the years but he had learned to live with loneliness the way he supposed one would learn to live with a limp. He'd even got to like it in a perverse kind of way. Until now.

He was comfortably off financially; his investments kept on growing despite his indifference to them. He had his few pleasures, music, books, a glass or three of fine wine or whiskey. He made occasional visits to old Uncle Sammy back in London for old time's sake.

Stooping to pick up a scallop shell from the beach he turned it over in his hands and was about to hurl it into the sea when he was startled by a voice behind him.

'Hello there. Is it cold enough for you this morning?'

Solly, awoken from his reverie, swung round and stared in surprise at the new village priest. The priest was red in the face, his dark hair whipping across his cheeks, his eyes watering.

'Hello.'

'Well, this wind is certainly picking up a bit again. That was a hell of a storm last night. There's another on the way I'll bet, if I was a betting kind of man of course.' The priest said, blushing. 'Sorry, am I interrupting your thoughts?'

'No, no,' said Solly.

'Father John Daley,' the young man said, holding out his hand to Solly. 'I was wondering when I'd bump into you, Mr Benjamin, you're a hard man to track down. I have an apology to make.'

'An apology?'

'Yes, I'm afraid I took a short cut without permission through the grounds of your house the other day.'

'No need to apologize.'

'The funny thing is, I thought I heard a child scream, a terrible ear-piercing scream.'

Solly stiffened. If this man got to know about Dancey he'd no doubt report it to the authorities and she'd be taken away to the nuns.

'They say the Dark Wood is haunted, but in my estimation that's a load of old twaddle. Most likely one of the orphanage kids escaped and was playing in the woods.'

'I expect you're right. Ah, a scallop shell, the emblem of

the pilgrim,' Father Daley said, nodding towards the shell that Solly was still holding.

'Sorry, I'm not with you?'

The priest smiled.

'The scallop shell is the emblem of the pilgrims who walk to Santiago.'

'In America?'

'No. Santiago de Compostela in Northern Spain. They used the shells as makeshift spoons and cups. Anyway, enough of all that, I'm a mine of useless information. I was wondering, if it's not an impertinence, if sometime you would care to come up to the presbytery for a drink and a chat. I think you're the only member of the community I haven't yet got acquainted with.'

Solly smiled.

'I don't think you'd be doing yourself any favours with the folk of Ballygurry by inviting me into your home.'

'But I don't care what the folk of Ballygurry think of me,' the young man said hesitantly.

'Then you're a very brave man,' laughed Solly.

The priest smiled again and blushed sheepishly.

'I only wish that were true. I am, in point of fact, the world's greatest coward.'

'Come now, don't denigrate yourself. How are you settling in to Ballygurry?'

'It's an unusual place,' the priest said with a slow enigmatic smile.

'It is that. I take it you're not used to small Irish towns? More of a city man?'

'I'm not used to Ireland, full stop, Mr Benjamin.'

Solly looked at him in surprise.

'Ah,' said the priest. 'My accent?'

Solly nodded.

'My parents moved to England from Cork when I was

five or six, I never lost the brogue. But me, I'm more used to the dance halls of Cricklewood on a Saturday night than a jig in the village hall. And yourself? I take it you're not a native of Ballygurry.'

'Ah, it's a long, long story. My father was third-generation English; my mother was French. I spent my childhood between Paris and England and other parts of Europe. Then, somehow, I got washed up here.'

'Right.'

'But you're wondering why a wealthy Jew with no visible occupation came to be living in a run-down house on the west coast of Ireland?'

The priest blushed again, more deeply this time.

'Incurable curiosity, I'm afraid. My mother always said that it would be the ruination of me.'

'Mothers can be wrong, you know. Curiosity will no doubt be the making of you!'

'I hope so.'

Solly looked with interest at the priest, an eager young man probably not much older than thirty. An easy man to talk to, thought Solly, a good listener. He'd have plenty of listening to do in Ballygurry. He'd have his handsome ear bent this way and that by every woman under eighty.

'Well,' said Solly, surprising himself, 'I'll decline a drink at the presbytery if that's all right with you, I don't like to be away from home for too long in the evenings, but if you'd care to step up to my house one of these nights you would be more than welcome.'

The priest grinned.

'Thanks, I will. I have a free evening tomorrow, would that be all right?'

'Tomorrow night will be grand. But come under cover of darkness if you know what's good for you.'

The priest laughed an easy good-natured laugh. Then he checked his watch.

'Hell. I'm late. I must fly.'

'See you tomorrow night then.'

And Father Daley was off, sprinting athletically across the beach, clambering over the dunes and on up the main street of Ballygurry.

Solly lingered on the beach for a while longer letting the iciness of the wind seep through his black overcoat, chilling his shoulders and creeping down his arms until the discomfort drove him towards home.

He smiled as he realized that he was actually looking forward to returning to a house that was no longer empty. And he was looking forward to meeting again with the young priest. He hadn't had a decent conversation in years with anyone in Ballygurry, or anywhere else come to that. Of course he made civilized small talk with his accountant in Cork, his Dublin solicitor and the rambling talks about the old days with Uncle Sammy when he visited London, but nothing that ever aroused much interest in him. There was something so eager about the priest, an enormous unbridled energy and innocence about him that was intoxicating. He thought, though, that he had recognized a degree of worry and disquiet in the young man too, and that puzzled him.

Miss Nancy Carmichael woke up with a pounding headache. She'd spent a restless and uncomfortable night sleeping on the floor beneath the kitchen table in case the house was hit by lightning. Now she was so stiff and cold she could hardly move. She filled the kettle and put it on the stove and swallowed two aspirins.

She felt irritable and jittery, and not just because of the storm. There was something decidedly fishy going on in

Ballygurry at the moment. Father Daley, for a start, was looking most out of sorts, and whenever she spoke to him he tried to avoid her. He looked pale and distracted and had stumbled over his words three times in mass on Sunday. Every time she and Miss Drew tried to collar him and talk about the forthcoming pilgrimage he backed away and made some feeble excuse. There were less than two weeks to go before their departure for Lourdes and yet the travel arrangements had still not gone up on the church notice-board.

And then there was the theft of her clothes. Someone had climbed over her back wall in the dead of night and taken her brown paisley dress and two pairs of darned pants off the washing line. And if that wasn't enough they'd taken her old gardening shoes as well. Whatever was the world coming to? And she could hardly report it to Sergeant Kearney in Rossmacconnarty and give a description of her underwear, could she? It would be mortifying.

On top of all that there was the gossip about the Black Jew. After years of keeping himself to himself he'd been into Donahue's for a drink. And bought a tin of ham! God forgive him. There was talk too that he had a loose woman staying with him, though no one had actually seen her. It had been noted, though, that he'd been into Miss Drew's shop and bought half a pound of toffee, a slab of chocolate and four ounces of pear drops. Poor Miss Drew had been half terrified out of her life when the bell above the door had rung and the horrible old thing had walked in as brazen as you like.

And he'd also been seen buying fancy talcum powder and soap in the general store in the next village.

Nancy Carmichael poured a generous measure of brandy into a cup and swallowed it down in one gulp to steady her frazzled nerves. Something wasn't quite right at all in Ballygurry.

Father Daley walked along Mankey's Alley, and as he did he wondered if the rumours he'd heard around the village were true. All the talk in the village was that Solly Benjamin had a fancy woman installed in his house. It had certainly set the tongues wagging in Ballygurry. He'd heard Mrs Cullinane tell Miss Drew that she'd seen lights on in an upstairs window of Nirvana House in the small hours. Honest to God, to get a sight of the windows she'd have had to be perched on top of her chimney, and if not she must have been wandering around Ballygurry in the dead of night. Come to think of it he'd seen Mrs Cullinane skulking down to Kenny's farm once or twice.

He stepped up to the front door of Nirvana House and rang the bell. A few seconds later a flustered Solly Benjamin answered the door.

'Good evening, Father, come in do. I was just having a quick tidy round when you rang the bell.'

Father Daley stepped into the hallway and looked around him. It really was a very beautiful house and, although it looked a bit run down from the outside, the inside was lovely.

He followed Solly along the hallway and into a large wood-panelled sitting room where a fire burned merrily in the hearth. Solly indicated that he take a seat and he sat in a large comfortable leather armchair on one side of the fire.

The only strange thing about the exquisitely furnished room was that on a side table an expensive-looking Chinese vase was filled with freshly cut dandelions. Father Daley wondered was there a Jewish custom regarding dandelions maybe?

'Let me get you a drink. Beer? Whiskey? Gin?'

'A whiskey would be grand.'

Solly poured whiskey from a decanter into two cut-glass tumblers and handed one to Father Daley.

'Your good health, Father.'

'Good health. Please call me John.'

They sat on either side of the hearth for a while in comfortable silence.

'So how are things going for you in Ballygurry, John?'

'Oh, so-so, it takes a bit of getting used to. They don't teach you half the things you need to know in the seminary.'

'What sort of things would they be?'

'Well, I'm inundated every day with broths and cakes, offers of Sunday lunches. I'll be the size of a house by the time I move on.'

'Are you thinking of moving on already?'

The priest blushed and was about to reply when there came a loud bump from overhead and a muffled cry.

Solly Benjamin leaped to his feet in alarm.

'Just excuse me a moment, John.'

He hurried from the room and Father Daley listened intently. He thought he could hear the sound of murmuring voices coming from upstairs. The fancy woman no doubt.

After a few minutes Solly came back into the room and picked up of all things a rosary from a side table and went back upstairs.

Father Daley wondered if perhaps the rumours about Solly Benjamin's fancy woman being a Catholic were true.

Outside an owl hooted and through the windows he saw the huge pale moon rise above the tops of the trees of the Dark Wood.

Father Daley took a long swig of whiskey and sighed. No

smoke without fire, he thought. Still, it was none of his business. There was definitely someone upstairs, though. Maybe Solly Benjamin was like Mr Rochester and lived like a recluse because he had a mad wife hidden in the attic. He thought about the scream he'd heard that day when he'd climbed over the wall into the Dark Wood and he shuddered.

Then he heard the sound of Solly's footsteps as he came back down the stairs.

'Sorry about that. Where were we? Talking about moving on.'

'Oh, take no notice of me. I dare say when it comes to it I'll stick it out. It's just all strange at the moment.'

'And lonely?'

'Yes,' said Father Daley and took another gulp of his whiskey. 'No one warns you about the loneliness,' he added sadly.

The fire was warm and the whiskey had mellowed Father Daley, loosened his tongue, for he spoke again without thinking.

'The thing is, I'm in the most almighty pickle. The last priest, you'll probably remember him, Father Behenna, well it looks as if he's done a runner with the entire amount of money for the pilgrimage to Lourdes.'

Solly Benjamin raised his eyebrows, guessing that the man had been troubled by this for some time and couldn't wait to get it off his chest. Sometimes it was easier to confide in a stranger.

The priest swallowed more whiskey and looked uncomfortable.

'Well, that does put you in something of an awkward position.'

'The thing is, I tried to contact him to sort the whole thing out, but it seems he's vanished to London.'

Solly rubbed his chin and looked thoughtful.

'I'm sorry. I shouldn't have mentioned it.'

'Have the hotel bookings been made?'

'No. I contacted the hotel where we were supposed to be staying but nothing has been booked and, what's worse, all the hotels in the area are already full.'

'There is always a solution to a problem in one way or another,' Solly said softly. 'More whiskey?'

Father Daley held out his glass.

'I'm sorry, I shouldn't unburden my problems on you.'

'Like I said, every problem has a solution. Something will undoubtedly turn up.'

Solly looked at the young priest and his heart went out to him. He was a man of integrity, a good man.

'Perhaps we could exchange our difficulties. I'll have a try at solving your problem and there's a mystery perhaps you could help me with.'

'I don't understand.'

'Let me get us a refill and I'll explain.'

Solly poured two generous measures of whiskey and sat back down.

'It seems to me, John, that you have several options. Firstly you blow the whistle on Father Behenna and the law becomes involved, but I sense that you're reluctant to do that, am I right?'

'Yes, you see the thing is I only spent a few days with the old fellow but I don't think he was, well, quite himself, he was throwing bucketloads of drink down his throat. I mean he must have been eighty-odd if he was a day. I don't really want to set the law on his tail and have him spend his last days in jail.'

'Problem one solved then. Leave the law out of it. So the only other problem is obtaining the money to replace what is missing.'

'You have it in a nutshell.'

'That I can solve for you. I can let you have the money.'

'No, no that wouldn't be right, I mean you're not even a . . .'

'A Catholic, Father? It wouldn't be right for a Jew to pay for a bunch of Catholics to go on a holy pilgrimage?'

Father Daley blushed and smiled weakly.

'Miss Carmichael and Miss Drew would never sleep at night! I'm serious, though. I have more than enough money for my needs. I'll get the cash to you tomorrow.'

'I don't know what to say.'

'A simple yes will do. The third problem is one of accommodation, which is harder to solve, but I have every faith in you, John. Now let's see if you can solve a hypothetical mystery for me . . .'

'Fire away!'

'A man receives an unexpected present.'

Solly paused.

'Through the post?' Father Daley asked.

'No. The, er, present arrives on his doorstep in the dead of night.'

'So someone actually brings the man a present in person.'

'Not exactly. The present arrives but the sender of the present is nowhere to be seen.'

'Ah? So you want to find out the identity of the sender?'

'Yes, but there are no clues except a sort of gift tag on the present itself.'

'And it says?'

'Just the man's name and address.'

'Does the man recognize the handwriting?'

'No.'

Father Daley scratched his head.

'The sender of the present doesn't contact you to make sure the present has arrived?'

'No. No word from the sender.'

'So the mystery sender doesn't want you to know who they are?'

'So it would seem.'

'Is the present a valuable one?'

'Like a good woman, priceless.'

'Does the nature of the present give any clues as to who the sender is, you know, is it maybe a romantic gift?'

'Most definitely not a romantic gift.' Solly smiled bashfully.

'Am I allowed to know what the gift was?'

'Not at the moment, it being a hypothetical mystery.'

'Well, all I can suggest is that you check to see whether anyone was seen arriving at your house in the dead of night. Time may well reveal an answer.'

'Yes indeed. More whiskey?'

With their glasses refilled they sat together in the firelight, talking about all kinds of things until, glancing at his watch, Father Daley said he had to go. He was about to step out of the door when he said, 'Is that yours?' He pointed to the small brown suitcase that was standing against the wall.

'No, it, er, belongs to, er, an old friend of mine.'

'Well, remember when we were on the beach I was telling you about the pilgrimage to Santiago de Compostela?'

'I do.'

'See all those stickers on the side of the case? Most of those are the major towns on the route to Santiago.'

Solly looked down at the suitcase with interest.

'Are you sure?'

'Positive. It's long been a dream of mine to go to Santiago, though I don't suppose I ever shall. Anyway, as I said before, I am a mine of useless information.'

Solly smiled.

'Well, good night, Solly, and thank you for everything. I only hope I can help you out some day.'

'You already have,' said Solly.

Father Daley stepped out into the cold night and set off down the drive. He was filled for the first time in many days with hope. There was a spring in his step and a great deal of whiskey in his belly as he staggered along Mankey's Alley towards home.

Donahue was about to shut up for the night when Michael Leary the schoolmaster came in through the door.

'Am I too late for a drink?' he asked.

'Never let it be said that it's too early or too late to get a drink in Donahue's. What would you like?'

'Whiskey, I think. Something to warm the cockles of my heart, it's nippy out there tonight.'

'The weather's changeable at the moment. Let's hope it calms down a bit before the Ballygurry pilgrims set off. I had Miss Drew and Miss Carmichael in here today. Miss Carmichael bought that many tins of food to take with them they'll need a cure for the backache by the time they carry them all the way to Lourdes.'

Mr Leary grinned, took off his glasses and cleaned them.

'I don't know why they bother. The food is grand abroad.'

'Can't say I fancy it myself, bits of frog and snails, for God's sake. Who in their right mind would want to eat that kind of shite?'

'Ah, Marty, don't listen to all you hear. Travel broadens both the mind and the palate.'

'Anyhow, did you hear the talk about the Black Jew?'

'No.'

'They reckon he has a woman shacked up in the house with him, the dirty lucky old beggar.'

'What's so dirty about that? I wouldn't mind one myself.'

'I thought you had a young woman abroad?' Donahue said.

'Sore point, Marty, she's stopped replying to my letters.'

Donahue leaned across the bar and whispered even though there was no one else there.

'A fancy piece from Cork so they say.'

'Well good for him.'

'Michael, the man is a heathen and the talk is that she's a good Catholic girl.'

'Have you seen her?'

'No, but he buys her chocolate éclairs and coconut macaroons, to keep her strength up I suppose. Oh, and scented soap by all accounts.'

Mr Leary scratched his head. He wasn't quite in tune with Donahue's logic.

'Well, Michael, how is the schoolmastering going? Rather you than me. I couldn't stand being cooped up all day long with all those snotty-nosed little buggers.'

'It's a great job, Marty, and remember you and I were snot-nosed little sods once upon a time.'

'Suppose so. Fancy they're taking that Padraig whatshis name on the pilgrimage.'

'O'Mally. He's a grand little lad.'

'Ah, is he now? Well, they'll all need a rest cure after a fortnight with him.'

'He's just very bright that's all and a bit lively.'

'Ah, brains can be dangerous on that sort.'

'Marty, what sort are you referring to?'

'Well, he could get above himself. People need to know their station in life.'

'That's bollocks and you know it. I'll have another

whiskey and one for yourself.'

'Thanks. Well, from what I've seen of him serve the Australians right. They'll have to cope with his brains and good riddance.'

'What Australians?'

'Haven't you heard?'

'Heard what?'

'They're going to start shipping them out. Make a new life for themselves down under.'

'Who?'

'The orphans.'

'Has anyone asked them if they want to go?'

'You don't ask kids, Michael, you tell them. You should know that, being a schoolmaster.'

'That's disgraceful. You can't ship kids to the other side of the world and then just dump them.'

'The church can, and you take heed, they will. There's talk that St Joseph's will become an old people's home. Less trouble and more money to be made if you ask me. Not that they need the money, there's a lot of money comes into that place.'

'You wouldn't think so from the way they treat those kids. They reckon the food is disgusting.'

'Ah well, you don't want to be feeding them orphans up; they're enough trouble when they're skinny. Big strong ones would be a nightmare.'

'Marty, you're full of shite. How do you mean about the money?'

'Well, years ago there were a couple of rich old biddies living there. Separate from the orphans like, had their own rooms and that. You used to only see them at mass, sitting at the back between a couple of nuns acting like body-guards. A bit simple the pair of old girls were.'

'What were they doing at St Joseph's?'

'The talk was that they were both from wealthy families. A foreigner one of them was, from Italy. They were an embarrassment to the families, a bit on the wild side, like. The one used to lift up her skirts, show her drawers, you know, a bit gone in the head.'

'That's disgraceful.'

'Ah no, Michael, she couldn't help it.'

'No, I don't mean that it was disgraceful that she pulled up her clothes. I mean the families packing the handicapped off, hiding them out of the way.'

'It made good sense, if you ask me. They used to pay a lot of money for them to be looked after, and when the parents died their share of the family inheritance went to the nuns.'

'Dear God, what sort of world do we live in? I wouldn't put a dog in the care of that lot of old bitches.'

'Michael, you shouldn't talk like that about the sisters. They're good women, the brides of Christ and all that.'

'Look, Marty, I have good memories of the nuns that taught me, they were a kind lot, but that Sister Veronica and her snivelly-nosed little sidekick are two nasty bits of work.'

'Sister Veronica is a very educated woman, Michael.'

'She's a bigoted old cow.'

'I've heard she comes from a well-to-do family.'

'They must have been glad to be shot of her.'

'Between ourselves and not a word, mind, I heard there was a man involved before she took the veil,' Donahue whispered.

'What? Never to God.'

'That's what they say. A failed romance. You have to feel sorry for her.'

'I don't. Whoever the fellow was had a lucky escape, if you ask me.'

'You're a hard man, Michael Leary.'

'I am that. Marty, can you hear singing?'

Donahue cocked his head on one side.

'I can.'

Michael Leary crossed to the window and looked out.

'Come and look at this, Marty. This'll set the old spinsters' tongues wagging.'

Donahue lifted the bar flap and walked across to the window.

'Dear God, Father Behenna was bad enough but would you look at the state on him.'

'As pissed as the proverbial pudding.'

And they stood side by side watching Father Daley lurching out of Mankey's Alley and along Clancy Street towards the presbytery.

Padraig was down on the beach looking for signs of life in the rock pools when he heard Mr Leary call out to him. He turned round, waved and smiled as Mr Leary came down through the sand dunes towards him.

'How are you doing, Padraig?'

'Not so bad, sir, and yourself?'

'Grand. Are you looking forward to the pilgrimage? It's not long now.'

'Not really, sir.'

'I thought you'd be pleased to be going.'

'Oh, I mean I'm not ungrateful or anything it's just . . .'

'Just what?'

'Ah, nothing, sir.'

'You can tell me, Padraig, I'm a good man with a secret.'

'Well, the thing is, sir, people go to Lourdes to be cured, right?'

'So they say.'

'Well, there's nothing wrong with me, sir, I'm not a cripple, deaf or dumb and I don't have a terrible disease or anything. I've nothing to be cured of.'

Mr Leary threw back his head and laughed.

'The thing is, though, Padraig, at least you've the chance to travel a bit. You'll see a million things you've never seen before.'

'I know, but look at the company I'll be keeping, Miss Drew and Miss Carmichael!'

'Father Daley seems a nice sort though. Perhaps with a bit of luck the two old biddies will find a cure for the miseries while you're out there.'

Padraig grinned and nodded his head.

'You must take a camera with you and show me the photographs when you come back.'

'I don't have one, sir.'

'Well, I can help you out there. I've a spare one that you can have. Maybe you could even do a bit of painting and drawing while you're there. Do you do much drawing at St Joseph's?'

'No, sir, Sister Agatha says it's a waste of time and I'd be better off learning to paint walls and ceilings for a living.'

Mr Leary spat in disgust.

'Take no notice, Padraig; what does she know? You could maybe do some sketches and keep a scrapbook while you're away.'

'That would be great. Sir, do you remember when I was looking at your scrapbook, you said you'd tell me the story of the lost Irish virgin.'

'Ah, now that is a very complicated story.'

'You did promise though.'

'I did indeed. Well, here goes. Once upon a time, many years ago, there was a great artist who painted a famous picture of the Virgin Mary. You can still see the painting in a museum in France. Anyhow, a few years later he was commissioned to sculpt a statue of the Holy Virgin. It was the most beautiful statue, by all accounts. The statue was based upon the painting and it was crafted in gold with jewels encrusted all over it.'

'Was it worth a lot?'

'Priceless. Anyway, the long and the short of it was that the statue was sent as a gift to the people of Santiago de Compostela in the north of Spain. It was entrusted to the care of a group of Irish monks, who set sail from Ireland. When they arrived in Spain they made their way on foot towards Santiago de Compostela, as the pilgrims did in those days. But the story has it that somewhere along the way one of the monks gave the others the slip and made off with the statue. It was never ever seen again.'

'What about the monk, sir?'

'Disappeared off the face of the earth. Never heard from again.'

'What do you think happened to the statue?'

'Well, that's the mystery, Padraig. Nothing was ever heard of it again until a short while ago.'

'What, they found it?'

'Not the statue, no, but some jewels were discovered.'

'Where, sir?'

'That's the strange thing, Padraig. In Paris.'

'How do you think they got there, sir?'

'God only knows after all this time. But if we were able to find out where the jewels came from, then we could be on our way to unearthing a mystery from the past.'

'Who found the jewels, sir?'

'They were sold to a pawnbroker who didn't immediately realize their worth, but luckily he got in contact with a fellow he knew, a historian.'

'Wow!'

'Now this may be a wild goose chase but one can't help being excited.'

'Things aren't always what they seem though, are they,

sir? Perhaps the poor old monk didn't really steal the statue, sir. Maybe the other monks did and they put the blame on him. Maybe they picked out the jewels and melted down the statue and came back to Ireland.'

'You think he was innocent then, Padraig?'

'Could have been. They might have done him in so he couldn't spill the beans.'

'They could have indeed.'

'Do you want to find the statue so that you'll be rich, sir?'

'No. I expect if the statue was found then it would belong to the church. The reason that I want to find out the truth is that the monk who ran off with it was one of my distant ancestors.'

'Honest to God?'

'Honest injun, Padraig. I found out when I was researching my family tree. So you see I come from a long line of criminals, all of them probably with bad eyesight to boot.'

Padraig laughed.

'Won't it be hard trying to find out about something that happened so long ago?'

'Undoubtedly. Impossible, I expect, but I am not a logical man, Padraig. I am a deluded romantic who also likes to think himself something of a Sherlock Holmes.'

'Perhaps I could be your Dr Watson.'

'Indeed, Padraig, indeed.'

At morning break Siobhan Hanlon cornered Padraig against the wall in the schoolyard.

'If it's a kiss you're after, I've sold out,' Padraig said.

Siobhan grinned a gappy-toothed grin.

'Well now, Mister Big-head O'Mally, it's not a kiss I'm wanting from you, so there.'

'That makes a change. What is it then?'

'I know a secret that you don't know.'

'What secret?'

'It's a secret, daft arse, so I can't tell you.'

'Well, if you're not going to tell me, then push off and play hopscotch or something.'

Siobhan turned her back on him. She walked a few steps across the playground then turned round and said, 'You know everyone says that the Black Jew has a woman in his house, well that's not true.'

'So what?'

'He has a little child hidden there. I know because I've seen her.'

Padraig raced across the playground towards her and slapped his hand across her mouth.

'SHHHH! Siobhan, don't tell the whole bloody school!'

Siobhan sniffed up the smell of his skin. Tree bark and dandelions, powder paint and pencil shavings. She tried to speak through his hand but he kept it clamped fast over her mouth and she was glad, she didn't want him to let her go.

'If I take my hand away, Siobhan, will you promise to shut your big gob?'

Finally, in fear of suffocating, she nodded.

'Siobhan, come over here with me in the corner.'

She went with him willingly.

'Listen, Siobhan, how did you find out about the little girl?'

'It was the night of the terrible storm. I was standing by the window watching. Well, you know that glass thing on the top of his house, well the lightning came and lit it all up and I saw a little girl up there dancing around like a mad thing, like a ballerina with a squib up her arse. Honest to God, Padraig. She was leaping about like a simpleton.'

'I believe you, but she's not simple.'

'Do you think he's keeping her a prisoner, Padraig?'

'Don't be soft.'

'Father Daley told Mammy that when he was in the Dark Wood he heard a child scream. Perhaps the Black Jew steals children the way tinkers do.'

'Why would he do that?'

'I don't know. Perhaps he eats them for breakfast.'

'For God's sake, Siobhan, who's simple now?'

Siobhan blushed.

'Anyway, you're not to tell anyone else.'

'Why not?'

'Because he doesn't want anyone to know.'

'Why?'

'I don't know. He asked me not to tell.'

'When were you talking to the Black Jew?'

'Don't keep calling him that.'

'Everyone calls him that.'

'So it doesn't mean it's right. Just promise me you won't tell.'

'Give us a kiss then and I'll promise.'

Padraig sighed. Siobhan closed her eyes and a slow satisfied smile grew on her lips.

Padraig jabbed his lips against hers and then pulled away.

'And another thing, Padraig O'Mally, what were you doing walking about at nearly midnight the other night in the pouring rain?'

He slapped his hand back over her mouth.

'Shut up, for God's sake, Siobhan, or you'll have me strung up.'

She pulled away his hand.

'I saw you. What were you up to?'

'Looking in the horse trough to see if what they say is true.'

Siobhan's eyes grew wider by the second.

'Honest to God?'

Padraig nodded.

'Did you see anything?'

Padraig nodded seriously.

'What did you see?'

'Can you keep a secret, Siobhan?'

She nodded vigorously, her fair curls leaping around her shoulders.

'Wait while I whisper in your ear.'

Siobhan stepped closer.

Padraig whispered.

Siobhan squealed.

'Padraig O'Mally, you dirty filthy pig! Another kiss or I'm telling.'

He kissed her a second time, a little peck, and then he was gone, off across the schoolyard, arms wide like an airplane, soaring and diving.

Siobhan put her hand up to her mouth. God, he was lovely. Couldn't you just eat him up? When she was grown up she was going to marry him, give him a good wash and tuck him up in bed at night. She just wished that she hadn't already been daft enough to tell big-mouth Sinead Cullinane the secret about the old Jew first.

Father Daley bit the bullet and called a meeting of the Ballygurry pilgrims at the presbytery. All three of them. He told the assembled pilgrims that there had been a slight change of plan due to an overbooking at the hotel in Lourdes. Instead of going to France the Ballygurry pilgrims would be making history. They would be sailing to Spain and there they would tread in the hallowed footsteps of thousands of past pilgrims making their way to the cathedral in Santiago de Compostela.

Padraig grinned from ear to ear.

Spain! Wait until he told Mr Leary.

Miss Drew and Miss Carmichael shook their heads in dismay.

Spain!

A land of lunatics tilting at windmills.

Bullfighters in over-tight trousers and brazen-faced women wearing red dresses and black high heels tap dancing to guitar music.

But so enthusiastic was Father Daley's speech that by the end the two women were nodding and almost smiling. Miss Carmichael thought that perhaps it would make a nice change from the drab hotel in France and maybe the food would be better. Miss Drew had never thought much of the Hotel du Lac; the eiderdowns were positively grubby and the lavatory hadn't seen a brush or the whiff of disinfectant in years. And as for the food, it was a pile of muck.

The sun shone down brightly on Ballygurry and a soft warm breeze rippled across the ocean. Net curtains and tablecloths flapped gaily on washing lines and the smell of fresh whitewash and Reckitt's Blue was strong in the air.

Outside Donahue's shop-cum-pub, strings of brown and red crêpe-soled summer sandals were hung up along with tin spades and buckets for the tourists who never came. White ankle socks replaced the long grey and fawn socks of winter. Flannel underwear was boxed up with mothballs, and aertex and string vests were the order of the day.

Donahue had dusted down the bottles of calamine lotion and plimsoll whitener and put flypapers out on display. Daffodils nodded gaily in the backyards and yellow poppies and bluebells transformed the Dark Wood. Frogs sang down by the tadpole pond. Apple and cherry blossom blew over the walls of Nirvana House and scattered like confetti along Mankey's Alley.

The train puffed slowly into Ballygurry station and came to a grinding halt. Steam billowed above the platform and the enormous black and white clock whirred and clanked but the hands remained steadfastly at ten to two.

Most of the village had come to wave off the small band of pilgrims. A bleary-eyed Michael Leary was there, and Marty Donahue. Mrs Cullinane, Sinead and Dermot Flynn. Dr Hanlon, Mrs Hanlon and Siobhan, who was wearing her best emerald-green dress and white sandals.

Sister Veronica, Sister Agatha and two rows of scrubbed and subdued orphans stood in a line together. Donny Keegan had a lump in his throat the size of a gob-stopper.

Padraig O'Mally clutched a new suitcase containing two new pairs of grey shorts and three T-shirts, two vests and pants and four pairs of ankle socks, which had all been bought out of charity money. On his feet he wore a new pair of brown sandals with squeaky soles; they were a size too big and meant to last. In his pocket he had a twist of sticky barley sugar wrapped in brown paper to stop any travel sickness.

Father Daley and Donahue lifted the suitcases on to the train and struggled with Miss Carmichael's enormous trunk, which weighed a ton.

When Sister Veronica wasn't looking Mr Leary slipped Padraig some money and handed him a camera and a piece of paper.

'There you are, some pocket money for you, all the spare pesetas I could lay my hands on. Listen, I've written instructions on how to use the camera and there are five films.'

'Thanks, sir.' Padraig wanted to fling his arms round Mr Leary and hug him but instead he shook his hand like grown-up men did.

'Have a grand time, Padraig.'

Mr Leary smiled down at the boy and tweaked his ear gently.

'I will, sir. Will I write and tell you if I find the statue or see that fellah with the cloak and the hat?'

Mr Leary nodded.

Sister Veronica stalked across the platform towards them.

Donny Keegan wiped away a tear with the back of his hand.

'Now, Padraig, be sure to say your prayers every night.'

Mr Leary pulled a face behind her back and gave Padraig a surreptitious wink.

'And remember that Cleanliness is next to Godliness. Make sure you wash every night and morning. Living among heathens does not mean you have to sink to their levels.'

'Sister Veronica, Spain is a Catholic country.'

'Yes, well, Mr Leary, as you well know, there are Catholics and there are Catholics.'

The guard blew his whistle and the pilgrims clambered on board the train.

Padraig looked around for Sister Immaculata but she was nowhere to be seen. He'd said goodbye to her last night after supper but she hadn't been her normal self at all. She seemed jumpy, far away, lost in a world of her own.

'Bon voyage,' called out Dr Hanlon.

Siobhan jumped up and down with excitement and blew Padraig a noisy kiss. And then another.

Padraig raised his eyebrows, grinned sheepishly and waved.

Mr Leary put up his thumb.

Donny Keegan blew his nose and looked down at his feet.

'I love you, Padraig O'Mally!' shouted Siobhan Hanlon at the top of her voice.

'The sooner that child goes to school with the nuns the

better,' said Sister Veronica. She thought that if Siobhan Hanlon, the bold-faced little hussy, were an orphan at St Joseph's she'd soon knock some sense into her silly little head.

Mrs Hanlon clipped Siobhan soundly round the ear.

Dr Hanlon sighed and winked at Siobhan.

The train pulled slowly away from the station. Padraig hung out of the window and waved furiously until the people on the platform were just a speck in the distance.

Part Two

Camiga, Spain 1947

Outside the cannery three women sat on wooden crates eating their lunch. Ottilie and Carmen, who were sisters, sat on either side of old Dolores, who was almost blind. They ate sardines straight from the tin with their fingers and when the last of the sardines were finished they soaked up the oil with pieces of bread until the tins were as clean as if they had been washed.

Ottilie poured barley coffee from a battered flask into three tin mugs and handed them round.

'Alberto was telling me just now that the train from the south was held up this morning,' Dolores said.

'By bandits?' asked Ottilie.

'No. That queer little nubeiro they call Muli was asleep on the line. He refused to move until a passenger bribed him to shift himself.'

'There'll be trouble brewing if he's about again. The last time he was in Camiga he conjured up a terrible storm. Remember? It blew the stork right off the church tower,' Ottilie said.

'Look, Ottilie, over there near the customs shed, that's him, isn't it?'

'Who, the nubeiro?'

'No, look! The strange one they call the Old Pilgrim.'

'Oh yes, that's him all right. He hasn't been around these parts for a long time. I thought p'raps they'd locked him up. They say he's wanted for murder.'

Ottilie and Carmen watched the Old Pilgrim with interest. He was standing alone, quite still, looking out to sea as though deep in thought.

No one knew where he came from. Usually he arrived in Spain on foot coming down through the Pyrenees. Occasionally he came by train from the south and once in a while on the boat from England.

Ottilie and Carmen had rarely seen him at such close quarters. News of his arrival in the area usually travelled fast. Someone would report seeing him walking briskly through the dusk in search of a night's lodgings in Los Olivares or bathing naked in the sea at Noja; sharing his supper with horses under a lonely bridge over a dried-up river. Following in the wake of a band of gypsies. Holed up on a snowy night in a shepherd's hut or wining and dining with the monks in the many monasteries of the region.

Once, it was rumoured that he had been seen soundly asleep amongst pigs and goats in the thatched *palloza* dwellings in the mountains. He was an eccentric, a mystery of a man; some said he was on a pilgrimage but that he never ever made it to Santiago de Compostela. For whatever reason he never completed the final steps of his journey. He got within a few hundred yards of the cathedral and always turned back.

Then, suddenly, he would disappear again and nothing would be seen or heard of him, sometimes for several years or more, and then along he would come, like the first cuckoo of spring.

'I don't believe he's a murderer. I think maybe he's a bit

odd in the head but he looks harmless enough.'

'Funny how everyone calls him the Old Pilgrim but he's not that old really if you look at him closely.'

'About forty, maybe even younger.'

'He's a handsome-looking man for a foreigner.'

'The eyes on him would melt any woman's heart.' Ottilie chuckled.

'Even yours, Ottilie?' Dolores laughed.

'Not mine, Dolores. I don't want any man wedging his bollocks under our kitchen table. It's bad enough working all hours to keep body and soul together never mind waiting on a man hand and foot.'

Ottilie and Carmen followed the Old Pilgrim with their eyes as he walked swiftly across the cobbled quay towards the church and then disappeared into an alleyway. He cut a peculiar figure, a tall, slender man wearing a wide black cloak and a broad-brimmed hat.

'Talking of odd people and storms, remember the kid with the funny name, who used to work here before Miguel? The little one who was quaint for her age, she had a mother who was a strange kettle of fish.'

'Yes, of course I remember her. Little Dancey, she was a lovely kid.'

'Well, I was talking to Rosendo the other evening in the Bar Pedro. I haven't seen him for months. He was down for the day picking up supplies for the old folks. He was telling me that last year, the night after the storm, he picked up a woman near the monastery of Santa Eulalia. She was done up to the nines and she paid him handsomely to take her in his cart down to Murteda.'

'So?'

'Well, it was obvious it was the girl's mother by the description he gave, he was quite smitten with her I reckon. Poor Rosendo has been desperate for a wife for years but it's not likely to happen being stuck up there in that god-forsaken hamlet. Anyway, I asked him about the child and he said there was no child with her.'

'That's very odd. It was very strange how the kid was here one minute and then gone without even saying goodbye.'

'She was a very pretty woman although she didn't look old enough to have a kid, if you ask me. She looked more like the kid's sister.'

'I saw her once in Los Olivares buying a fancy pair of high-heeled red shoes, the sort of shoes American film stars wear, and yet it was obvious from the state of the kid that they didn't have a pot to piss in.'

'Poor little thing. Her clothes were threadbare and those boots she used to wear were enough to shame a scarecrow! I don't think she'd had a good meal in her belly in years.'

'I saw the mother going into the whore-house some nights, after she'd put the girl to bed.'

'Dear God! What a way to pay for a pair of fancy shoes. I'd rather go barefoot than lie on my back.'

'Did you ever speak to her?'

'No. She kept to herself. She had stars in her eyes that one. Full of airs and graces, if you ask me. Don't know who she thought she was, teetering about the place in high-heeled shoes and putting the kid to work all hours like that.'

'She was a nice kid though, that Dancey, very bright, and the eyes on her! Beautiful they were, as blue as the Virgin's robes, and eyelashes like feather dusters.'

'Señora Hipola told me that she left owing a month's rent. Did a moonlight flit without a by your leave,' old Dolores said.

'She was a fly one if she could do Señora Hipola out of money,' Carmen grinned.

'Señora Hipola said that once she saw her taking a bath. She said she had a bellyful of nipples like an old sow.'

Dolores shrieked with laughter.

'Señora Hipola said that! I wouldn't believe what she says, she has a wicked tongue on her that one.'

'Fancy, her niece Marta is to marry Ramón,' Ottilie said.

'Ramón! Oh my God, you're joking, the poor girl must be desperate.'

'Poor Ramón, he can't help it,' Dolores said.

'A dog can't help having fleas but I still wouldn't marry one!'

'Hey, look, the British boat is in.'

A large rusty boat had moored alongside the quay and the sailors were yelling and barking out orders and busily lowering the gangplank. Moments later the passengers began to disembark.

'Funny-looking people those British,' Ottilie said nodding towards the boat. 'When they first arrive here in Spain they're as pale as lard and then after a few days of sun they turn as pink as a dog's dick.'

'A very flatulent lot I've heard and fussy with their food.'

They watched with interest as two milky-skinned middle-aged women came staggering down the gangplank. They stood arm in arm on the quayside swaying from side to side, their mouths agape like stunned fish.

Despite the warmth of the sunshine the women were dressed in ankle-length coats with fur collars, woollen gloves and felt hats the shape of piss pots. They wore stout lace-up shoes and thick brown stockings and carried enormous handbags. Both women hurriedly made the sign of the cross and then looked warily around the quayside.

The women were followed down the gangplank by two deck hands sweating profusely as between them they carried an enormous trunk. They set the trunk down with relief on the ground and wiped the sweat from their foreheads.

Next down the gangplank came a tall dark-haired man struggling with heavy suitcases.

'Now there's a man I wouldn't rush to kick out of the sack,' Carmen giggled.

Ottilie laughed loudly.

'I fancy your eyes need looking at, he's a priest.'

'Ah well, a waste of a good man, if you ask me.'

A young boy clutching a small cheap suitcase followed the priest. He was looking around him inquisitively, taking everything in with eager eyes.

He was a skinny little thing with overlarge ears emphasized by a short crew cut. He wore grey shorts, a grey jumper and grey socks. The only colourful things about him were his bright-blue eyes and his pink cheeks. He looked across to where the women were sitting, smiled cheerfully at them and waved excitedly.

Ottilie and Carmen waved back.

'What a cute little fellow.'

'A barrel of mischief, if you ask me.'

'He looks kind of familiar to me. Something about his face. Who does he remind you of, Ottilie?'

'I know what you mean but I can't for the life of me think who it is.'

The women sat in silence for a few moments and then Carmen said, 'Damn! That'll bother me for ages now. He's the spit of someone I know, but I just can't remember.'

Then the cannery siren sounded and the three women rose stiffly from the crates and went reluctantly back through the beaded fly curtains that hung across the doorway of the cannery.

Señora Hipola, on her way back from the market, was so full of the joys of spring that she gave a handful of pesetas to the open-mouthed beggar who was slumped outside the church of San Gregorio.

The beggar gawped in astonishment, stared at the coins in the palm of her hand and bit one to test it. Señora Hipola, who was as cold as a witch's tit, usually gave her a tongue lashing about the evils of begging, being a disgrace to the women of the town. The beggar crossed herself and swiftly pocketed the money in case Señora Hipola had a change of heart. Then she staggered to her feet and limped away across the quay towards the café and breakfast.

Señora Hipola hummed to herself all the way home, and more than a few people who saw her raised their eyebrows and stared after her. Señora Hipola was well known to the townsfolk of Camiga but not for her good humour.

The reason for her uncharacteristic cheerfulness was that she had successfully made a match between her niece Marta and the clock mender's son, Ramón. And in a few days' time the wedding would take place.

Marta was twenty years old and Elvira Hipola had decided that it was quite indecent for a girl of such advanced age to remain a single woman for one day longer. A few more years and she would be an old spinster, dried up and barren and no good to man nor beast. Besides, the clock mender's son Ramón was a good boy, true he must have been standing behind the door when God handed the brains and the looks out but he was a good worker and an obedient son to his father. Perhaps he wasn't over clean about himself and there was the little problem with his bladder, but in the name of Saint Jude, what the hell, no one was perfect.

Marta had been well trained in the arts of laundry and housework and she would make a fine wife for a simple man.

There were other benefits that this wedding would bring too. When Marta moved in to the rooms above the clock mender's shop to start her married life, Elvira would have an excuse to visit almost every day. After all, the clock mender would be a good catch for a widow like herself. Ha! Elvira Hipola wasn't as green as she was cabbage looking. The clock mender had been widowed now for all of fifteen years and had no doubt got a tidy sized pot of pesetas hidden away somewhere for his old age. She could sell up the lodging house, bank the money, marry the clock mender and live the rest of her days in comfort. Marta and Ramón would be on hand to do the heavy work and she would be set up nicely for her old age.

Of course she had expected objections on Marta's part, she was a good-looking girl after all, if a bit too high spirited for Elvira's liking.

Still, luckily there had been the little matter of the man Marta had been seeing on the quiet that she had held over her niece's head. A bit of honest blackmail had done the trick. It usually did. It had been a real stroke of luck that afternoon a few months back when she'd found the box of letters hidden under Marta's bed. Disgusting they'd been! And to think the man was a foreigner too. She'd managed to get the mail intercepted and a tearful Marta had fretted for weeks when no letters arrived. One mention of that liaison to Marta's father and she would be packed off to the nuns at Santa Maria to spend the rest of her days elbow deep in suds in the laundry or making marzipan lambs for feast days.

Marta had tried to delay of course, saying that she would make her own wedding dress, but Elvira had no intention of waiting a year or more while the crafty minx made a dress. Oh no! She'd put paid to that little trick! She had bought the dress herself. It was going to be a worthwhile investment after all!

It was pure luck that she'd walked through the market-place on that particular Friday a week ago and seen the dress hanging above the old gypsy's makeshift stall, blowing gently in the breeze.

It was good quality material the gypsy had told her, made by an expert seamstress in Florence, and she had it on good authority that it had only been worn the once. Señora Hipola had felt the material of the dress, sniffed it, and tugged at the seams to test the strength of the stitching. It was a bit on the big side and there were some dark stains round the hem. Still, with a little careful washing, a stiff scrubbing round the armpits to remove the perspiration stains, it would come up a treat. A good blow out in the spring air, a nip and tuck here and there and it would be as good as new!

She hurried on through the narrow streets. She had a busy day ahead of her. She had a group of foreign pilgrims arriving later and she needed to buy something special to prepare a hearty supper for them.

When Padraig O'Mally stepped down from the boat on to the quayside in Camiga he felt as if he had walked straight into one of the paintings on Mr Leary's walls.

He stood quite still and looked all round him in wide-eyed wonder.

It was a place full of paint-box colours.

It was like an enormous painting that wasn't yet quite dry round the edges. Sky and sea. Cerulean and cobalt.

A spinning sun of cadmium yellow.

The quayside was noisy and busy. Rough-voiced men in sweat-stained overalls pushed trolleys loaded with crates full of weird and wonderful things across the cobbles.

Huddled white birds cooing and shitting.

Hairy coconuts like monkeys' faces.

Purple-skinned onions.

There were market stalls set up around the quay piled high with fruits and vegetables. There were curly-leaved cabbages and whiskery carrots, muddy potatoes and onions as big as babies' heads. There were things he'd never seen before: strange fruits and vegetables in eye-watering colours. Rose madder. Yellow. Olive green. Viridian. Vermillion.

There were wicker baskets full of brown and white shit-smeared eggs nestling on straw.

There were stalls buckling under the weight of silvery sequinned fish, glinting like rainbows in the bright sunlight.

The market traders stood round the stalls talking and shouting, laughing and arguing. Some of them clutched bare-necked chickens as ugly as baby vultures, dangling head first, their mad eyes staring.

The men smoked acrid-smelling cigarettes and spat while the women stamped their feet and waved their arms like drunken windmills. The women wore dark clothes and had arses as black and wide as weathered old ships, their dark hair plaited and thick as tarred rope.

A scabby-arsed donkey hitched to a cart stamped its hooves impatiently and a skinny yellow-eyed dog was digging at its neck for fleas, its shiny balls bouncing fitfully against the cobbles.

There were three women sitting on crates outside a large ugly building. Their skin was as brown and glossy as acorns. Their shiny black hair was streaked with Prussian blue, their eyes as dark as tinned prunes. They wore gold earrings that glinted like crescent moons and their ankles were ringed with bracelets of flies.

Padraig smiled and waved at them as though they were old friends and then jumped with fright as a siren blared out.

Miss Drew and Miss Carmichael stood huddled together like frightened children while Father Daley wandered around trying to find a car or taxi to bring them all from the port to the lodging house where they were going to stay in the place called Pig Lane.

Father Daley returned after a while with an old man following behind him driving a donkey cart. A three-legged dog followed excitedly behind the cart. The dog began to sniff enthusiastically at the ankles of Miss Drew and Miss Carmichael and then feverishly around Miss Carmichael's trunk.

'Shoo,' said Miss Drew timorously and stamped her sensible lace-up shoes.

The dog began to whimper then and paw at the trunk.

'It can smell all that corned beef you've got in there,' said Padraig with a cheeky grin.

'Wishht. Go away!' muttered Miss Carmichael, but the dog ignored them both, cocked one hind leg, balanced precariously for a second, then pissed copiously over the corner of the trunk and then lost its balance and toppled over.

A few of the market traders ambled over inquisitively and helped to lift the trunk and the suitcases into the cart.

The Ballygurry pilgrims clambered aboard the cart and the old man flicked his whip at the sullen donkey, and then they were off.

It was the ride of a lifetime. Once the old donkey got started there was no holding him back. Padraig had to hang on tight to Father Daley to stop himself from being hurled over the side of the cart and into the road. They bounced and lurched through the narrow alleyways and up the steep cobbled lanes of Camiga.

People stopped to stare as the cart clattered through the old town. A withered old woman, leaning heavily on a stick, crossed herself as they passed. Her mouth was a loosely elasticated 'O' and her one tooth a wobbling exclamation mark. Startled chickens and whimpering dogs scattered in panic at their approach. Padraig had to keep his hand slapped over his mouth to stop himself from roaring with laughter.

The old man who drove the cart was more like a goblin than a human being. He was a shrivelled up little fellow without any teeth at all and with eyes as small and hard as rabbit droppings. Every now and then he turned round and winked conspiratorially at Padraig and Father Daley.

All the way through the town he sang at the top of his voice. Every time they hit a bump in the road Miss Carmichael and Miss Drew, who were crammed in between two bales of hay, bounced into the air and screamed hysterically. Every time they shrieked the old donkey pissed with fright and the cart was engulfed in a cloud of heady steam.

Eventually, the cart slowed down, turned into a narrow alleyway and pulled up outside Señora Hipola's lodging house where the Ballygurry pilgrims were to stay for two nights before they moved on to the monastery of Santa Eulalia.

While the grown-ups were shown up to their rooms Padraig went back outside to explore Pig Lane.

Padraig thought that Pig Lane was a strange and exciting place to stay. He had seen a photograph of it before in Mr Leary's scrapbook, but there it had all been shown in black and white. In colour it was wonderful.

The houses were tall and narrow and squashed tightly together as if a giant had stood at each end and concertina'd them up. The doors and window shutters were painted in faded greens and reds. Instead of curtains there were flowerpots on all the window ledges, flowers in every possible hue.

The houses all had tilting balconies that were stacked with even more flowerpots. Faded triangular flags were hung across the lane from the balconies where they fluttered gaily. Hung across all the doorways of the houses were beaded metal fly curtains that jingled in the warm salty breeze that came in off the sea.

Padraig wandered slowly up and down the lane trying to get a peek inside the houses. Every house seemed like an adventure waiting to unfold, every tinkling doorway the entrance to an Aladdin's cave. He longed to pass through the curtains and explore the insides of the houses and meet the people who lived their lives in Pig Lane.

A watchful cat on a window ledge stared malevolently at Padraig. He stared back and the cat twitched its ears with irritation and looked away.

In the gutter a few feet away from where Padraig stood lay a festering eyeless rat, belly up and wearing a vest of flies. Padraig touched it with the toe of his sandal and the flies rose around him in an angry cloud.

He moved on down the lane. The flies resettled contentedly.

Padraig sniffed.

Pig Lane was full of strange exotic smells.

Burnt fat.

Fresh flowers.

Raw onions and onions cooking.

The stench of stale piss that had dried to syrupy blobs on the walls of the houses.

Oranges and lemons.

Ripening tomatoes. Old leather and strange spices.

Garlic, although he didn't know the name of it at the time.

Strong black coffee.

Cigarette smoke that drifted out from the Bar Pedro and scratched the back of his throat.

There was something peculiar besides.

There was a musty, dusty old smell that reminded him of funeral flowers and the inside of crumbling churches.

Guitar music escaped from an attic window high above his head and a kite string of gay musical notes lingered on the air for a few moments and then was sucked greedily away by the breeze. He imagined crotchets and quavers scattering away above the jagged rooftops.

He stepped back through the curtained doorway into the lodging house. It was cool and dark inside the house and a large clock in the lobby clanked and creaked and squeezed out the minutes reluctantly.

Miss Carmichael's trunk was still in the hallway because no one was strong enough to carry it up the stairs. God knows what she had in there but it weighed a ton.

Padraig stared curiously at the trunk. There was something not quite right about it. He scratched his head thoughtfully and then ran up the stairs two at a time to fetch his camera.

Miss Drew, exhausted and mortified by their undignified arrival at the lodging house, lay on her bed, arms folded across her sunken chest, and snored like an old porker.

Miss Carmichael, weak-kneed and still shaky after the horrific cart ride, sat on an orange crate at the makeshift dressing-table and studied her reflection in the mottled glass of the mirror. She'd almost had the life shaken out of her in that damned cart.

Holy Mary, mother of God, what on earth did she look like? The wreck of the Hesperus! She was as pale as death and beads of perspiration had dripped down from beneath her hat and streaked her make-up. Removing her hat, she was horrified to see that her hair was plastered to her head. She looked a very sorry sight indeed.

She felt a little better after a good sniff of smelling salts and a thimbleful of brandy to steady her heart. She poured some water from the jug into the washbowl and washed her face. She carefully reapplied some make-up and pulled a comb through her bedraggled hair.

Miss Drew slept on noisily. Miss Carmichael stepped out into the corridor and closed the bedroom door quietly. She stood and listened for a moment. She could hear someone sobbing loudly in the room opposite. It wasn't exactly a good omen when the other guests were in floods of tears now was it?

She made her way nervously down the well-worn stairs to the dingy lobby. She'd get a few things from her food trunk and then when Miss Drew woke up they could cheer themselves up with a nice little snack and maybe a medicinal brandy to settle their stomachs.

She stood in the silence of the lobby and sniffed. The lodging house had a very peculiar smell about it. It smelled like a cross between a damp library, a church and a stable. Suddenly Nancy Carmichael shivered and the hairs on the nape of her neck bristled alarmingly. She felt for a moment as though someone or something unseen was watching her intently. She looked nervously around her. The lobby was dark and gloomy but there was no one there lurking in the shadows and yet still she couldn't rid herself of the feeling of being watched. She shook herself and tried to pull herself together. She wasn't feeling herself at all and those horrible curtains over the door didn't help; they were a real irritation, jingling and rattling and setting one's nerves on edge.

She sniffed again and pulled a face. There was a most disagreeable smell coming from the kitchen at the back of the house. Heavens above, she'd thought that the smells in France were bad enough but this place! It was full of savages. Why she'd seen people down in the port eating sardines with their fingers, like animals!

What on earth was Father Daley thinking of bringing them to Spain? Old Father Behenna would never have dreamed of visiting such a terrible place. She only hoped that their next stop at the monastery of Santa Eulalia would be better than this god-forsaken hole. She still thought that there was something very fishy about them not going to Lourdes. It was very peculiar that all the hotels had been booked; Father Behenna had always managed to book them in. She wondered where on earth Father Daley had found out about Señora Hipola's lodging house? It was a most peculiar place, ancient and shabby, a bit like a badly arranged museum. Still, she grudgingly admitted that the bedroom was reasonably tidy and the bed sheets were clean and freshly starched.

She kneeled down and as she did she noticed that the hinges on the back of the trunk had been snapped off. Hurriedly she lifted off the lid of the trunk, and stared in horror.

Father Daley lay on his bed looking up at the ceiling. It was cool in the bedroom and the late-afternoon sunlight found its way inside and dappled the room in an underwater light. The sound of far-off guitar music soothed him and lifted his spirits.

He was glad that everything had worked out reasonably well so far. It was only a chance conversation in Donahue's bar that had brought up the subject of the overbooked hotels in Lourdes. He had been so relieved when Michael Leary had suggested they make a pilgrimage to Santiago de Compostela instead and had offered to help him sort out the accommodation.

He liked Michael Leary, he was a very interesting man and a damned good teacher from what he had seen. Dr Hanlon had told him that Siobhan had hated school when Mr Flynn had been the schoolmaster. They'd had to drag her there screaming and kicking, but since Michael Leary had taken over she was up and out in the mornings and raring to go.

Michael Leary was a man with a true vocation, that much was obvious. He really cared about all the kids and not just the clever ones. He'd watched him one day patiently showing little Donny Keegan how to tie his bootlaces. Just a simple thing like that and yet the boy, flushed with his eventual success, had walked away like a prince.

Michael Leary had spoken to him at length about Padraig, said that he was desperate for him to take the examination and get a place at the Abbey School but that Sister Veronica would not hear of it. There was no love lost between Michael Leary and the nun that was for sure.

Father Daley had gently reminded Michael Leary that the Abbey wasn't a Catholic school and that Catholic orphans were normally given a Catholic education.

'Father,' Michael Leary had said, 'do you think that the really great artists of this world divide themselves up into Catholics and Protestants? That they are only influenced by artists of the same religious persuasion?'

'God knows,' he'd replied. He was a complete ignoramus where art was concerned.

'Look, the reason I want Padraig to go to the Abbey School is simple. They have one of the best art masters in the whole of Ireland; an English man. He's the most eccentric, lunatic fellow you've ever met but a wonderful teacher. He was abroad for a long time but had a disastrous love affair and ended up in Cork. He has a tremendous eye for spotting and nurturing talent.'

'And you think, Mr Leary, that this Padraig is talented?' he'd asked.

'Oh yes, undoubtedly. The boy could be a genius in the making. He's drawn things in school that would take your breath away. He has an absolute natural talent. For his age he has a wonderful eye for detail, for colour and movement. And on top of that he has a first class mind to boot. And being shut up in that stuffy orphanage with a bunch of sour-faced old bags could stunt his mind for ever.'

'I don't know about talent but he's a genius for getting into trouble that's for feckin' sure,' Donahue had piped up. 'Like the half-pound of senna pods in the harvest supper cider. There was plenty of movement in Ballygurry that night!'

'It's about time there was some movement in Ballygurry, the place is dying on its feet,' Michael Leary had said. 'The world needs people like Padraig to give it a kick start.'

Father Daley had been perplexed. He felt that he'd had to advocate a Catholic education, of course he did, and yet he hadn't liked what he'd seen of St Joseph's. There was a horrible feel about the place and though it had reminded him of his own prep school there was a subtle difference. The kids at the prep had parents, and, while a degree of covert humiliation occurred daily, the physical brutality was limited to the occasional pinch or rap across the knuckles with a ruler. He wasn't so sure that it was at St Joseph's.

Michael Leary had told him that he'd stayed in Señora Hipola's himself a few years back. It wasn't too bad a place either, basic but clean and the food was good. Señora Hipola did seem a bit of a tartar, mind, and you wouldn't want to cross her if you could help it. Michael Leary had certainly come up trumps. He had booked them into this place, the monastery of Santa Eulalia, the convent of Santa Anna, and also in to a lodging house in Santiago itself.

He wondered what would happen to Michael Leary if the village school closed. It wasn't likely to stay open much longer if the St Joseph's orphans were shipped off to Australia. There were only a handful of local Ballygurry kids and Siobhan was off to England soon to the convent school in London.

Still, Michael Leary was a bright and well-qualified man, he could get a position easily in one of the top schools in Ireland, or anywhere else come to that.

His thoughts turned then to Solly Benjamin. His more than generous help with the money side of things had been an absolute godsend. The man had been an angel. He hoped Miss Carmichael and Miss Drew never found out who had financed this trip or there'd be all hell up. He wondered if Solly had sorted out his hypothetical mystery yet.

Father Daley yawned. He was tired after the long boat journey and the ride in the donkey cart had almost finished him off. Mind you, the look on the two women's faces would remain with him for ever.

Padraig, though, had loved every minute of it. He was having a whale of a time. He'd nearly bust a gut trying not to laugh. He was a smashing little lad, genius or not, he was funny and bright and damn good company. Quite how Father Daley was going to put up with a couple of weeks of constant whingeing and moaning from the old biddies was another matter. Nothing seemed to please either of them. Born to moan the pair of them. Still, sod them, he was looking forward to a hearty meal and a glass or two of wine tonight; a good night's sleep and he'd be fit for anything the following morning. He closed his eyes and sighed and was just drifting off into a pleasant doze when someone started banging urgently at his door.

The train squealed to a sudden halt and Carlos Emanuel was roused from a deep sleep. He supposed the train must have pulled into a small station or countryside halt, any moment now and they would be on their way again.

Then he heard the sound of loud, vulgar cursing. Carlos went out into the corridor to see if he could find out what was going on.

A yellow-toothed old crone standing in the corridor grinned at him and he smiled unenthusiastically back. In one hand she held a live chicken, its feet bound together with twine, and in the other a leather wine sack. The red-eyed chicken stared mournfully at the floor; the bewildered creature had shit prolifically during the journey and the corridor was now spattered with the stinking stuff.

'Going to be a long wait,' said the old woman, giving Carlos a smile.

'What's the problem?'

'The guard's just told me that there's a body on the line.'

'A suicide do you mean?'

The woman gave a loud cackling laugh. Carlos winced; the chicken flinched and lost control of its bowels, spraying liquid shit all down the old crone's apron.

He turned his head away in disgust and held his breath; his stomach was weak at the best of times.

'Not a suicide. Saint's breath! Just a drunken old nubeiro passed out across the tracks.' The old woman laughed. 'Lying flat out and naked as the day he was born and not happy to have been woken.'

'This is all I need,' Carlos muttered.

'He's refusing to move until he's been paid for his trouble! And he's threatening to put a curse on the driver to boot.'

Carlos smiled wryly. A nubeiro! He remembered the word from his childhood. A nubeiro was supposed to be a magical maker of storms and cloudbursts. These ignorant peasants lived in the Dark Ages and believed in all kinds of superstitious nonsense: sprites and goblins and all kinds of ridiculous make believe.

'Still, these things happen. There's no rush though, is there? Everything keeps for another day,' the old woman said holding out the wine sack and indicating to Carlos that he take a drink.

Carlos declined hastily; he could catch something off the filthy old crone: tapeworms, threadworms, the list of contagious possibilities was endless.

He went quickly back into the carriage and slumped down on the seat.

Forty minutes later the train started up and chugged slowly on its journey. As the train built up steam Carlos stared incredulously at the sight of a small wizened old man standing at the side of the track. He was toothless and ancient and stark staring naked! Carlos's eyes were drawn to the incredible size of the man's appendages. Holy Saint James! The scrawny old thing was hung like a prize bull.

The old man saw Carlos looking, grinned at him and made a lewd gesture, and Carlos turned his red face away. These peasant people were a queer, savage lot, barely human.

The train was an hour late arriving and there was no sign of the car that was supposed to pick him up at the station.

He managed to get a bus and make the painful arse-juddering ride across country to the small fishing town of Camiga. For most of the journey he was squashed in between a loud-voiced young woman and a tearful matron who had sat with her head in her hands crying quietly all the way. He had to keep a handkerchief pressed to his face to keep out the stink. The reek of sweaty armpits, unwashed bodies, fresh fish, stale garlic, chicken and goat and God knew what else.

At last the bus pulled into a small deserted square in Camiga.

He wasn't going to make it to Los Olivares tonight; he'd missed his next connection. Connection! That was a joke! There was no proper road up to Santa Eulalia so he had been meant to make the trip on a donkey cart. A donkey cart! He hated donkeys and all four-legged creatures. He wished fervently that he were back in the city. He hated everything about the countryside with a fierce passion, the constant smell of shit in his nostrils and all that hearty country food that played havoc with his delicate digestion.

Tomorrow he'd get to Santa Eulalia somehow, whether he had to walk, crawl or ride bareback on a donkey. He had instructions to find a monk, a Brother Francisco, and ask him, beg or bribe him, kidnap him if necessary, to return with him to the Villa Henri. It was a matter of life and death, though why in God's name his dying employer had to have confession and the last rites from some piss poor monk when she could have had the bastard Bishop himself was a mystery to him. Still, the idiosyncrasies of the aristocracy were of no concern to him. The Señora was a very wealthy old widow who had promised to leave him a good legacy in return for his faithful service. She had also agreed to pay him very handsomely if he came up with the goods in the form of the monk.

Lost in his thoughts, he stepped unwittingly in a pile of dog shit, yelped and swore heartily.

He climbed a steep hill leading out of the town, turned into a narrow lane and paused for a second to regain his breath.

There was a bar further down the lane, a rough-looking place but as he approached he could smell food cooking. He desperately needed to eat, to have a strong drink to sustain him and an hour's respite for his aching feet. He stepped eagerly inside the dimly lit Bar Pedro.

Father Daley, Miss Drew, Miss Carmichael, Padraig and a bemused-looking Señora Hipola stood in the lobby of the lodging house staring down at Miss Carmichael's open trunk. The trunk was empty except for a few chicken bones and some rotting apple cores.

Miss Carmichael, shaking with rage, looked up and glared at Padraig.

'It must have been him!' she screeched, pointing at Padraig. 'Those orphans are all light fingered.'

'I never touched anything,' Padraig growled.

'What exactly is missing?' Father Daley asked, trying to sound patient.

'Two dozen tins of sardines, the same of corned beef and Spam, luncheon meat, pineapple chunks, peaches, pears, semolina, rice pudding, prunes . . .'

Miss Carmichael drew breath.

'Four tins of ham, two boxes of candles, a torch, a hurricane lamp, a spirit stove, disinfectant, soap, two cotton frocks and a pair of my best walking shoes, a new hat, oh and . . .'

Miss Carmichael tailed off and the colour drained from her face.

'And, oh God, some very important letters. I want my things back now, you little swine from hell,' she hissed and lunged ferociously at Padraig.

Padraig ducked as Father Daley intercepted Miss Carmichael's flailing fists and stood between the trembling boy and the irate woman.

Señora Hipola stared open mouthed. In the name of the Holy Father, what sort of pilgrims were these?

'Hang on a minute, Miss Carmichael. Violence won't solve anything. Besides, I really don't think Padraig has anything to do with this. What would he want with those things anyway?'

'I don't even like corned beef or semolina and I wouldn't be seen dead wearing a frock.'

'I bet you like tinned peaches though.'

'I do but I didn't steal any.'

'Miss Carmichael, when do you last remember checking the contents of the trunk?'

'In Ballygurry. The morning before we left. Miss Drew and I checked together just before Donahue came to take it to the station, didn't we?'

Miss Drew nodded her head vigorously and blushed.

'And you haven't looked inside it since?'

'No. I had no need to.'

'So it's possible that the things could have been removed in Ballygurry?'

'No, it isn't, because the trunk was heavy, you saw that for yourselves. It took two men to carry it on and off the boat and it wasn't out of my sight on the quayside.'

'Yes, you're right. So, your things must have been removed while the trunk was here at Señora Hipola's.'

'Yes, and we know who is responsible.'

Father Daley turned to Padraig.

'Padraig, do you know anything about Miss Carmichael's missing things?'

'On my life, Father, cross my heart and swear to die, I don't.'

'Thank you. Go up to our room, Padraig, and wait for me there.' Padraig went, giving Miss Carmichael a look of utter hatred.

'Miss Drew, if you don't mind, I would like to talk to Miss Carmichael alone.'

Miss Drew followed Padraig reluctantly up the stairs.

'Miss Carmichael, while it is abundantly clear that you have unfortunately been robbed, I find it very disquieting that you choose to blame Padraig without a shred of evidence. Padraig is sharing a room with me and I assure you that we do not have a stash of corned beef or anything else hidden there. Now, we are on a pilgrimage, Miss

Carmichael, a holy journey, and I will not have it marred by your spiteful accusations.'

Miss Carmichael looked up at the priest. He was very impressive and even more handsome when he was angry. She still thought that Padraig had something to do with the theft of her things, but she wasn't brave enough, in the face of Father Daley's anger, to defy him. She'd swallow humble pie for now but she'd be keeping a sharp eye out for Padraig O'Mally and she'd have plenty to tell Sister Veronica when they got back to Ballygurry. He'd get his comeuppance all right and feel the nun's strap around his blasted backside.

Father Daley turned to Señora Hipola and spoke to her in Spanish. She replied, waving her arms around and wagging her finger at the ceiling. Then she bowed to Father Daley. She gave Miss Carmichael a curious look, crossed herself and went back into her kitchen to attend to dinner.

'Señora Hipola says that there are many thieves about these days. There are all sorts of foreigners and lunatics on the loose all over Spain. She says that by now your things will have been spirited away, probably by gypsies or vagabonds, who knows? She says you can report the theft to the police but that will probably mean that you will need to be interviewed and could mean us staying here a few extra days. She says that you will not need any extra food while you are under her roof; why at this very minute she is preparing you a feast!'

Miss Carmichael smiled weakly and made her way wearily up the stairs.

Father Daley called out, 'Miss Carmichael, tell me one thing.'

'What's that, Father?'

'Why are there lots of tiny holes punched in the top of your trunk?'

Miss Carmichael said, 'My mother used to shut me in there when I was a child if I wasn't top of the class or misbehaved and, er, other reasons besides. Without the holes I would have suffocated.'

Violante Burzaco had enjoyed a very interesting and yet disturbing day. Pig Lane had been busier than it had been for many years. The place seemed to have thrown off its usual torpor and buzzed with a peculiar and unexplained energy. She was sure that something strange was about to happen in Pig Lane, she could feel it in her waters.

From the balcony of her house opposite Señora Hipola's lodging house she'd been able to watch all the comings and goings, and it had been better than going to the theatre in Los Olivares.

By early afternoon there was a full house at Señora Hipola's; usually there was just the occasional travelling salesman staying overnight or a priest on his way to Santiago.

The first person to arrive at Señora Hipola's was a woman who came hurrying down the lane, head bent, worn-down clogs clacking noisily on the cobbles. The woman had only looked up as she arrived at the lodging house. As she did, Violante noticed that she had a newly blackened eye and a nasty gash on the side of her head. She had no luggage with her and kept looking back over her shoulder as though she was afraid of being followed.

Moments later a man emerged from the Bar Pedro, blinking in the sunlight. He looked up and down Pig Lane and then followed the woman into Señora Hipola's. He was a peculiar, mincing little fellow and a little the worse for drink. He was definitely not from round these parts, judging from the flimsy city shoes and the tight loud suit.

Then, just as the church clock chimed one o'clock, all hell

broke loose. There was a clatter of hooves at the far end of the street as old Antonio turned into Pig Lane with his donkey cart. The cart rattled noisily over the cobbles and the four passengers in the back were bounced around like drunken rag dolls.

The two middle-aged women clung to each other and screeched like harridans. Their screeching was echoed by old Antonio's hysterical laughter.

Mother of God! Violante Burzaco had never seen such a commotion. These people must be the foreign pilgrims that Señora Hipola had told her about. What a motley band of pilgrims they were too! As well as the odd-looking women, who were dressed as if they were going on an expedition to the North Pole, there was a very handsome but flustered-looking priest and a small boy who was holding on to his belly and shaking with laughter.

When the donkey cart pulled up sharply outside Señora Hipola's, old Antonio leaped nimbly down and helped the women out. There was more squealing then as the lewd old fellow had a surreptitious feel of the pair of them.

The red-faced priest paid Antonio and the old man shook the priest's hand energetically. Then he got back up into the cart, flicked his whip, and the relieved donkey clattered off along the lane.

The giggling boy and the flustered priest heaved the trunk through the doorway of Señora Hipola's, puffing and panting as they did so. The two peculiar-looking women followed them quickly inside.

Moments later the boy came back out into the lane. Violante leaned over the balcony and watched him with interest. He walked excitedly up and down, peeping curiously into doorways, peering down into the gutters as if looking for something important.

He had such a smile of happiness on his face, such an

excited sparkle in his blue eyes that she couldn't take her eyes off him. Excitement was bursting through his skin. Some children had the marvellous ability to express their joy physically. This boy had such an unbridled appetite for life and a fascination with everything around him that it made her skin prickle . . . It was as if Pig Lane had been awaiting his arrival. There was something about him, something quite beguiling and intriguing.

Eventually the boy went back inside the lodging house and then moments later reappeared on an upstairs balcony busily snapping away with his camera and singing softly to himself. Then someone had called out to him and he had disappeared quickly inside. Violante was disappointed. She could have watched him contentedly for hours. There was something exceptionally uncomplicated and innocent about him and yet at the same time an intricate complexity.

Violante was about to go back inside when something caught her eye. There was a shadowy figure moving around behind the doorway of Señora Hipola's house. She thought it might be the boy hiding behind the curtain so she watched the doorway intently.

A large nose emerged cautiously through the metal beads. Two large, wary green eyes followed the nose. Then they withdrew hastily back behind the curtain.

Violante caught her breath.

Her heart beat rapidly with the shock of what she'd seen.

She tried without success to steady her breathing.

She stared earnestly at the doorway. There! The unforgettable nose and the hypnotic green eyes reappeared. Dear God, she'd know that face anywhere, even after all these years. It couldn't be! But it was. How could it be so? The owner of those fascinating eyes had been dead and buried for years.

She closed her eyes momentarily and wondered what on

earth this could mean. When she opened her eyes again the fly curtains on Señora Hipola's house were jingling noisily. There was no sign of the face but she could hear the sound of someone scurrying away down the lane, and though she leaned over her balcony she saw only a pair of hairy, skinny legs and well-worn heels disappearing round the corner.

While she was puzzling over this, Señora Hipola's niece Marta came slowly along Pig Lane, lugging a battered old trunk across the cobbles. She paused for a moment outside the Bar Pedro and looked up towards the balcony where Violante stood in the shadows.

Marta was a beautiful-looking girl but today she looked pale and tearful, her young face smudged with misery. Her heart went out to the girl; it really was quite shameful that she was to be married off to Ramón. Poor Ramón didn't need a wife, he needed a nursemaid. Violante smiled down at Marta and waved and Marta smiled wanly back, then dragged the trunk angrily through into the house.

Piadora sat on the edge of the bed, her head in her hands. Her skull was still throbbing and she could barely see through her swollen eye. She supposed by now that Aunt Augusta would have realized that she'd run away and they would be scouring the fields for her at this very moment, but she wasn't going back, not even if they sent the army for her.

This morning had been the last straw.

As usual she had got up at dawn, turned out the hens from the barn, fed them and collected the eggs. She had fetched the goats from the stable and led them down to the lower pasture, swept the veranda, watered the many pots of flowers and drawn three pails of cool water from the well in the yard.

By the time she had finished her outside chores, Aunt Augusta was already calling out to be washed and dressed. Piadora had boiled more pails of water and filled the bath, lain out clothes on the bed ready for her aunt to wear. She had made *café solo* into which she had to stir four level spoons of sugar, toasted bread to just the right shade of brown, then drizzled it with two and a half teaspoons of olive oil.

She had been sent to search the house and find a book on the lives of the great saints, to retrieve a shawl from the veranda and do a host of other jobs that Aunt Augusta was more than capable of doing for herself.

By noon she had a severe headache and thought that if she remained inside the house a moment longer her head would explode and her mangled brains would spread out across the recently whitewashed walls. Five minutes more of her querulous aunt whining and complaining and ordering her around and she would have committed murder or suicide.

She had slipped outside to the quiet coolness of the washhouse and defused her pent-up anger doing the washing until gradually the throbbing in her head subsided.

She hadn't heard Aunt Augusta creep up behind her, and when the old woman jabbed her in the back with her stick Piadora had jumped and cried out in alarm.

'My hot chocolate, girl! I've been waiting for almost half an hour. I've been calling and calling you until I was almost hoarse.'

'I told you earlier, Aunt, Juanita is late bringing the milk. As soon as she arrives, I will make your chocolate.'

'And soon, when she leaves the Villa Romano to marry, you will have to go down to the farm to fetch it yourself.'

'Well, I've thought of that and spoken to Benito; he's willing to bring the milk up each morning.'

'Benito! You imagine that I'll have him hanging round my house. That dirty, flea-ridden lout of a boy! You think you can moon about making eyes at Benito and neglect your work?'

'Aunt Augusta, for heaven's sake, Benito is a boy of barely eighteen. I am nearly forty.'

'Don't remind me! Nearly forty years of age and still unmarried; it's a disgrace to the family. If you'd had a vocation and become a nun, well that might have saved the family's face.'

Piadora had felt her face reddening with anger. If she'd had her way she'd have been married years ago. If her bloody family had allowed her to marry the man she'd loved. But no! Instead she had been sent here with her mother until the baby was born and then afterwards left here to care for Aunt Augusta. She wasn't supposed to have stayed long, just until everything had been sorted out about the baby. But years had passed and she had never been called home.

'And if I had gone to the nuns, who would have slaved for you, eh? Who would have skivvied and worn their fingers to the bone for a . . . for a wicked and manipulative old woman who has covered up an enormous lie for the past twenty-odd years!'

Aunt Augusta had stood transfixed, her petulant mouth wide with surprise, the cold, hooded eyes flashing with fury. Then she had struck out viciously with her walking stick and caught Piadora a sharp blow around the side of the head.

When Aunt Augusta spoke, her voice was thick with venom.

'Remember, my girl, that this house and the allowance that goes with it is mine, a gift from your mother, and I can turn you out at any time. Any time at all! And then where would you go, eh? You are not welcome even in your own home after what you did!'

Piadora had raised her hand to her head and felt a trickle of sticky blood run slowly down her cheek.

She had pushed past Aunt Augusta and run out of the wash-house. She did not stop until she reached the cross-roads at the end of the lane. She was shaking, her heart thumping painfully.

Then she'd heard the far-off rumble of wheels and the parp of a horn. The battered old bus had come into sight, drawn to a screeching halt. In a split second she'd made her decision and clambered unsteadily on to the bus.

She sighed. Tomorrow she supposed she'd have to swallow her pride and go back to Aunt Augusta.

Padraig stood out on the balcony for a long time, unaware that he was being watched. From a shadowy doorway in Pig Lane a wizened, ragged old man gazed at Padraig in wonder. There was no doubting who the boy was, that was certain. The old man stood there for some time and then slipped in through the doorway of Señora Hipola's house.

Looking out to the right of the balcony, Padraig had a grand view over the rooftops of the huddled old town. On a distant hill a church tower reached towards the vast blue sky. On top of the tower an enormous bird was perched on a scruffy nest. He stared in fascination. It was the stork, the big bird that delivered babies in the dark of night. He'd seen pictures of the stork in story-books. It brought babies for rich people and left them in wooden cribs with lacy pillows and satin bows and it hid the poor people's babies in cabbage patches and under gooseberry bushes.

He smiled to himself then as he remembered the story his mother had told him. He hadn't been left under a cabbage bush by the stork. He was a love-child, his mammy had said, and he'd to remember that always. Whatever people said about him, he'd to remember that he was a special child and a wanted child. Although some people might call him other things, illegitimate and worse, he had once had a very brave daddy. For a long time after his mammy died he'd hoped there'd been some mistake and that the wind would change and his daddy would come looking for him, come sailing up the river. He hadn't thought about his daddy in a long time. He didn't know that much about him even.

Sod it. He wasn't going to think about anything like that and let it spoil his happiness. For at that moment Padraig felt so light, so carefree and happy that, if he wished hard enough, he thought that he might grow wings and fly. It was as if, standing there on the creaking balcony amidst the pots of flowers, he weighed nothing at all. Maybe, if he flapped his skinny arms up and down as fast as he could, his feet would leave the balcony and he would rise up past the dusty attic windows.

He closed his eyes and imagined gliding away over the rooftops and into the glistening sky, flying with the screaming gulls above the town. He could look down on the queer baby-carrying bird in its lofty nest. He would soar with the mountain birds and swoop and climb and drift on currents of sweet, clean air and would never have to go back to St Joseph's.

Opening his eyes, he looked across at the other houses on the opposite side of the lane. On some of the balconies there were tiny coloured birds chirruping madly in wicker cages, cages hung high out of the reach of marauding cats. Spanish cats were very peculiar things: thin, arch backed, long legged with tails like quivering antennae.

There were lines of washing tied across some of the balconies, jumbles of dripping drawers, darned stockings, woollen socks and brassières big enough to bring home the shopping in.

Through the opened window shutters of the houses, he could see shady rooms where black crucifixes hung upon the walls and the statues of brooding saints lurked in every nook and creepy cranny. It was going to be hard work trying to find the lost Irish virgin for Mr Leary. There were even more virgins in Spain than in Ireland.

Tomorrow he was going to get up early and do some detective work. He'd have a good hunt round the town. Try and sniff out some clues. It would be great if he could find the lost statue. He'd love to give something back to Mr Leary.

Just then the sound of the dinner gong echoed through the house. Padraig took the stairs two at a time and arrived in the dining room breathless.

Miss Drew and Miss Carmichael were already sitting either side of Father Daley like two pug ugly gargoyles. Miss Carmichael glared at Padraig and bared her strong teeth.

Frosty-faced old bag.

Miss Drew sniffed.

Skinny-nosed freak.

Father Daley smiled.

'Take a seat, Padraig, you must be hungry.'

'Starved, Father,' said Padraig. 'I could eat a scabby donkey.'

'It wouldn't surprise me if there was one on the menu,' said Miss Drew.

'Now, now, Miss Drew, I'm sure Señora Hipola will have something special prepared for us.'

Miss Drew coughed and looked down into her lap.

Just then a man came into the room. He was a dapper little chap who bowed stiffly to the women, nodded at Padraig and Father Daley and took a seat next to Padraig. Padraig sniffed surreptitiously. The fellow didn't smell much like a proper man at all; he stank of strong perfume, scented hair oil and onions.

'*Buenas tardes,*' Father Daley said.

The man looked up and nodded.

'Buenas tardes.'

Then the man and Father Daley rattled away in Spanish at nineteen to the dozen while the Ballygurry pilgrims looked on in astonishment.

'This,' said Father Daley eventually, 'is Señor Carlos Emanuel, and he is going to the monastery of Santa Eulalia tomorrow.'

'Where did you learn to speak such good Spanish, Father?' said Miss Drew.

'Ah, when I was a little boy I had a Spanish nanny and I wasn't allowed any pudding until I'd practised my Spanish. And then, later, thanks to the enthusiasm she gave me, I studied Spanish and French at university.'

'Would you ask him, does he know where I could find an Irish virgin, Father?' Padraig asked eagerly.

Father Daley blushed. Miss Carmichael kicked out at Padraig under the table and caught him a crack on the shin.

'Ow! You've a kick like a mule. What did you do that for?'

'To stop your filthy mouth, that's why,' she hissed.

'What's filthy about that? It's true, somewhere here in Spain there's a statue of the Holy Virgin that's been lost for hundreds of years. It was made in Ireland and brought here by some monks, Mr Leary told me.'

'It seems to me that Mr Leary would say anything except the truth.'

Conversation stopped then as a woman came quietly into the room. She nodded briefly at everyone and sat down quietly on the other side of Padraig.

Padraig turned to her and smiled. She smiled back shyly. She had the whitest teeth that Padraig had ever seen. She also had a whopper of a black eye. He peered closer. A real shiner. Purple and viridian. Lilac and mauve. Someone had given her a right clout by the looks of it. He hoped she'd given them a good bugger back.

A few moments later a young girl came out of the kitchen carrying a pitcher of water and a large earthenware jug of wine that she set down on the table.

Padraig had never seen such a pretty face before but he noticed that she'd recently been crying, because her eyes were red and swollen.

'This is Marta, my niece,' said Señora Hipola peeping out through the kitchen doorway and handing the girl a basket of bread. 'The lucky girl is to be married in two days' time.'

Father Daley translated for the Ballygurry pilgrims.

There were oohs and ahs from Miss Drew and Miss Carmichael. Señora Hipola beamed around at them all and disappeared back into the kitchen.

Marta lowered her eyes and glowered. She took her place sullenly at the end of the table and avoided looking at anyone. Instead, she busied herself breaking off small pieces of bread, rolling them brutally into tiny pellets and then lining them up round her plate as if they were bullets ready for firing.

A few moments later, a great clattering and shouting emanated from the kitchen and Señora Hipola came into the room carrying a large earthenware bowl that she placed with a flourish in the middle of the table.

'*Sopa de Abados*,' Señora Hipola announced proudly.

'Abbot's soup,' said Father Daley. 'In Spain they don't say food fit for a king because they haven't a royal family, so instead they say food fit for an abbot.'

Señora Hipola ladled out the soup generously and handed around the bowls.

Padraig had a good poke about in the bowl that was placed in front of him.

It looked like slices of bread with bits of sausage, some sort of peas and meat. It smelled good.

He lifted a spoonful to his mouth and tasted it.

'Delicious,' he said and set to with a gusto.

Father Daley whispered to Padraig, 'Say *"Muy bien, Señora Hipola!"*'

'Muy bien,' said Padraig with a grin.

'Said like a native.'

Señora Hipola clapped her hands and smiled from ear to ear.

Miss Drew and Miss Carmichael sipped the soup dutifully but without enthusiasm.

While her guests ate, Señora Hipola chattered away and when she eventually paused for breath Father Daley said, 'Señora Hipola was just telling me that we are honoured guests in her house. She says that there have been very few pilgrims staying here for many years but that in the past Pig Lane was a busy thoroughfare, full of inns and boarding houses, and even a convent. This house dates back over five hundred years in some parts. It has played host to princes and potentates, abbots and monks, nuns and pilgrims from far away. The great and the good, the meek, the dispossessed and the hounded have all passed this way on their way to Santiago de Compostela.

'There is even a far-fetched story that long ago a Jewish family were hidden for many months in Pig Lane during the years when they were expelled by Ferdinand and Isabella. Legend has it that they were locked in a secret room and died of starvation.'

'Food poisoning more likely,' Miss Drew muttered.

When the soup dishes were cleared away Señora Hipola returned with another enormous serving dish.

'Pulpo a la Gallega,' she announced proudly.

Father Daley raised his eyebrows and swallowed hard. He wondered for a moment if he should lie. He thought better of it.

'Octopus,' he said. 'Fresh from the sea this very afternoon.'

Miss Drew let out a low groan.

'Holy Saint Patrick,' said Miss Carmichael, making the sign of the cross.

Padraig peered inquisitively into the dish, looked up and said, 'Mr Leary told us that the octopus has eight testicles and two enormous eyes.'

Father Daley snorted.

Miss Drew moaned as if in mortal pain, threw down her spoon and hurried from the table with her hand over her mouth. Miss Carmichael followed hot on her heels.

'What did I say this time?' Padraig asked quizzically.

Father Daley was restless and unable to sleep. He'd drunk a few glasses of red wine to wash down the octopus but instead of making him sleepy it had woken him up. He lay in bed looking out through the windows at the night sky.

Tomorrow he thought they might spend the day in Camiga, the day after that they were off to Santa Eulalia.

After dinner, when everyone else had gone, Señora Hipola had lingered to talk to Padraig and himself. She'd told him that the monastery of Santa Eulalia had once been a very important place in these parts. Her father had worked on the land for the monks and his father before him.

In the old days it had been one of the largest employers in the district. For hundreds of years it had been a gathering place for pilgrims from all over Europe. After the numbers of pilgrims had dwindled, it had become a gathering place for artists, musicians and writers. They, she'd said with a sniff, were a very queer bunch of oddballs, all long hair and glazed about the eyes. Why, she still had a painting that had been handed down from one generation of her family to the next, an ugly old thing that she kept hidden in the attic for the sake of decency.

Father Daley had asked her at Padraig's behest whether she had ever heard of the lost Irish virgin, and strangely enough, much to Padraig's excitement, she had.

There were, she said, many tales about a group of foreign monks who had come to Spain to deliver a golden and bejewelled statue to the cathedral at Santiago. Some said that they had travelled on foot through the mountains but that a nubeiro had brought down a storm upon their heads, a storm that had raged for so long that they had taken shelter in a cave and then the mists came down and they had lost their way on the mountains.

'What's a nubeiro?' Padraig asked.

Father Daley translated.

'He's never heard of a nubeiro; where's the boy been hiding?'

'Nowhere,' said Father Daley. 'We don't have nubeiros in Ireland.'

Señora Hipola shook her head in disbelief.

'Why, I chased one away from here this very evening. A most peculiar thing they call Muli. He was hanging round trying to peep in through the front door.'

'Well, what exactly is a nubeiro?' Father Daley asked, trying to cover his amusement.

'A nubeiro,' she said, 'is a sorcerer, a magician who has the powers to conjure up storms and cloudbursts.'

'Why do they make storms?'

'It's like this,' she replied, 'if a nubeiro has an argument with someone, he can order up a storm to fall on that person's house, or even on a whole town.'

'Wow!' said Padraig when Father Daley had explained.

'But,' Señora Hipola went on, 'there are things that can be done to stop their tricks.'

'Why would anyone want to stop their tricks? I love storms,' Padraig said.

'You do?' said Señora Hipola. 'Well, you are a strange one.'

'How do people stop the nubeiro's tricks?' Padraig asked curiously.

'Well, if you know that you've upset a nubeiro and they are going to pay you back with a storm, you can light special candles to ward off their magic. Or else,' she went on, 'if the storm has already started you can pray to Saint Barbara to stop the storm.

'And also you can make balls out of wax, ask the priest to bless them and then you throw them up into the air as high as you can. That will stop the nubeiro's wily magic! Anyway, there aren't many nubeiros left now, thank the Lord.'

'Where have they all gone?' Padraig asked.

'Some of them have been turned into skeletons,' said Señora Hipola with relish, 'and others have been turned into dwarves.'

'Who has done that to the poor things?' Padraig asked indignantly.

'Why, the priests of course!'

'Have you ever turned a nubeiro into a dwarf, Father?'

'No, Padraig, between you and me I wouldn't know a nubeiro if one dropped in my lap!'

'But it's the priest's job to get rid of them! If a priest catches a nubeiro, then the nubeiro is honour-bound to unload their rain clouds. The priest tells them where he wishes the cloud to be emptied and the nubeiro must obey,' Señora Hipola explained.

'Ah, if only I possessed such power!' sighed Father Daley, smiling.

'If the priest exorcizes them, then the nubeiro will fall to the earth and, like I said, will be changed into a skeleton or a dwarf.'

Padraig had seen some dwarves once; there were two of them riding piebald ponies in a circus procession through the town. He hadn't realized then that the sad-faced little people were really nubeiros who had had their powers taken away.

'Ask her where the nubeiros come from?'

'Ah, they are all lunatics who have been turned mad by studying abroad in the schools of Saint Patrick,' Señora Hipola replied.

'Where are the schools of Saint Patrick?' asked Padraig.

'In England and Ireland,' Father Daley translated with a broad grin, 'where Señora Hipola says there are more lunatics than anywhere else in the world.'

'Ask her what happened to the Irish monks?' Padraig asked.

'Well, eventually the monks sought refuge in an isolated monastery of French or maybe Spanish monks; anyway, an untrustworthy lot on the whole. Some say that the monks in the monastery overpowered them and stole the statue, drugged them and blindfolded them and then let them loose on the mountain. The monks escaped to France where they lived the rest of their days like kings.

'Others say that the monks were robbed by Jews fleeing from Spain and that the monks were too afraid to return to Ireland because of the shame of losing the statue. And there was even a story that one of the monks fell in love and ran away with a nun from a convent.'

Padraig hadn't looked too convinced, and, soon after, they had said goodnight to Señora Hipola and gone to bed. Now, Father Daley looked over at Padraig in the next bed. The boy was exhausted and slept the sleep of the truly content. Talk about out of the mouths of babes and sucklings! When he'd mentioned the Irish virgin you'd have thought he'd pissed on the Holy Father's boots. And the testicles!

Oh God, that was hilarious. Miss Carmichael had looked positively murderous.

They'd been a strange band of dinner guests. The peculiar chap with the fancy clothes had said something very odd about going off to kidnap a monk and take him down south. They'd hardly got a word out of the woman with the bruised eye other than to say she was visiting a sick aunt, although she did make some quiet conversation with the bride to be, Marta. Marta had a face like a slapped arse throughout the entire meal; she didn't look exactly ecstatic considering she was soon to be married.

Eventually, overcome with restlessness, he got out of bed, crept quietly across the room and stepped out on to the balcony.

A honey-coloured moon glowed above the church tower where the stork made an eerie silhouette against the sky. The night air was cool and musky with the scent of fermenting seaweed, of sweet pine and candle smoke.

He sat down on an ancient wicker chair and looked out across the rooftops of the sleeping town. Then he realized that someone was talking quietly on the balcony below.

He strained his ears to listen. He wondered if it was Miss Drew and Miss Carmichael but then he remembered that their room faced out on to the courtyard at the back of the house. Besides, by now those two old bats would be hanging by their feet from the rafters.

He realized with surprise that it was Marta and the other, older woman with the black eye who were talking quietly together.

He really ought to go back to bed, it was wrong to eavesdrop on a conversation, but even so . . .

'Where will you go tomorrow, Piadora?'

'Back to my aunt, I suppose. I've no choice. I have very little money and nowhere to go.'

'Have you no other family?'

'My father is dead. I have a mother and a younger half-sister who I've not seen since she was a baby. They've had nothing to do with me for years.'

'Why is that?'

'It's a long story. A story woven with so many lies that it's sometimes impossible to separate the truth.'

'Do you miss them?'

'I missed my father dreadfully but he's been dead a long time now and there's no going back.'

'And your mother?'

'I don't miss her at all. And as for my sister, I hardly knew her,' the woman said and her voice was tight with bitterness.

There was an awkward silence then between the two women.

Father Daley wondered what could have happened to make her feel that way towards her own mother? She was heartless if you asked him. He still missed his own mother even after four years, and not a day went past when he didn't feel that interminable ache of loss in his belly.

'Do you have any family, Marta?'

'Just my father still living here but he's drunk most of the time. My brothers both went to live in South America, married over there and never came back. My mother died two years ago. Life's never been the same for me since. If she were alive, none of this would have happened. God, I'd give anything to get out of here.'

'Won't your father listen to you?'

'No, he doesn't listen to anyone. He's deaf to everything except the pop of a wine cork. He thinks this marriage is a good proposition. It is, for everyone except me. Ramón is from a good family with plenty of money. My aunt has her eye on his father, as a future husband and a pension all rolled into one. Did you ever want to marry, Piadora?'

'There was a young man once, a long time ago, but it didn't work out. My family disapproved.'

Father Daley swallowed the lump in his throat. The way she'd said, there was a young man once . . . her words were so full of regret and loss that they moved him close to tears. Perhaps she did have a heart after all. He closed his eyes, brushed away a tear and tried to keep his mind off his own past, his own lost love.

'See, you and I, we are opposites,' Marta went on. 'Your family stopped you marrying the man you loved and mine are making me marry one I don't.'

Father Daley sat quite still. The night lay so beautifully around the old town and yet the conversation was so poignant, so helpless that he was filled with an overwhelming sadness and despair.

'What will happen, Marta, if you refuse to marry this Ramón?'

'Refuse! There's no question of my refusing. My feet wouldn't touch the ground. They'll have me shut up with the nuns somewhere. And yet, you know, I think I would prefer even that to marrying a man I don't love.'

'Does Ramón love you?'

'Poor Ramón, he doesn't know whether it's Easter or Christmas half the time.'

Father Daley sighed and crept sheepishly back into the bedroom. He closed the window shutters quietly, blotting out the moon and the stars and the sad conversation from the balcony below.

When Padraig awoke, the shutters on the window were closed but shafts of watery sunlight pierced the gaps in the slats and made patterns across the bare floorboards.

Padraig yawned and stretched and wriggled his toes with pleasure.

One of the best things about being away from St Joseph's was waking up in the morning and not having Sister Agatha ring a bell next to your earhole, not having to hop about on the cold lino and wash in freezing water or queue to use the lav.

Spain was grand. Tip-top. He loved everything about it, the noisy excitement of the people, the colours and the smells, even the horrible ones. He didn't know how he was going to do it but he was never going back to live in St Joseph's, that was for sure. On the way back from Santiago he'd have to give them the slip.

He wondered, though, how Sister Immaculata was and little Donny Keegan. Tomorrow he'd buy a postcard and tell them both about all that had happened to him so far. He'd send it to Mr Leary and ask him to pass it on to Donny; he didn't trust Sister Veronica as far as he could throw her, and that wouldn't be far, she was the size of a house. He'd left Donny in charge of sorting the wet sheets out if anyone peed the bed.

Sister Immaculata had always given Padraig a secret pile of clean sheets that he'd hidden beneath the floorboards under his bed. She'd taken away the wet ones and washed them without anyone knowing so that Sister Agatha couldn't give anyone a beating.

He looked across at Father Daley, who was still fast asleep. He liked the priest; he was a good, kind man, and up for a bit of fun. He looked different when he was sleeping, without his priest's collar, more like a boy than a man. There was a pink flush of sleep about his face, the faint flickering shadows of his eyelashes sweeping across his cheeks. The planes of his face were washed in a mixture of early light and shadow. God, he wished he had some paper and a pencil. He'd like to draw Father Daley while he slept.

Suddenly he remembered the money that Mr Leary had given him. He had quite a bit of money in the pocket of his shorts for the first time, foreign money. He'd buy a drawing pad and a pencil and he'd sketch. God almighty. There was no one to stop him. He could do anything he liked.

Padraig got out of bed. He stood up and stretched his arms towards the ceiling and enjoyed the sensation of every bone in his body unfurling, the click of sleepy tendons and ligaments, the quiver of waking muscles. He felt his blood stirring itself and he thought that it was wonderful to be alive. And he was alive, more than he'd been for ages.

It was so good to wake up slowly without having to throw himself down on to his knees, to feel the judder through his cold bones. It was good not to hear the whistle of dormitory prayers through chattering teeth.

There was no smell of piss or fear in this room. No smell of carbolic soap or damp toast.

I am alive and I'm not afraid. I am not angry, he whispered to himself.

And outside this lovely room the sun was warming the roofs of the town and filling up the world with colour and light.

I didn't say my prayers last night and yet I didn't die in my sleep. Thank you, God. I don't have to eat porridge and burned toast. I don't have to feel the icy eyes of Sister Agatha and Sister Veronica boring into the back of my head.

He touched his head. His hair was growing back fast; he could feel the kink of a curl fighting its way through his scalp. He remembered his mammy making corkscrews of his curls with her fingers, cutting one thick curl off and keeping it pressed between the pages of a book.

He felt sad for a moment. If he did run away, the few things that he'd been allowed to bring to St Joseph's he would never see again. The small shoebox would be thrown away. Inside the box was the photograph of his mammy in a silver frame, the book with the lock of his hair between the slippery pages, the letters tied up with blue ribbon. Hastily he pushed the thoughts from his mind, and crossed the room quietly. He squeezed his bare toes against the wooden floor; beneath his feet the floorboards were worn and warm. A thousand people could have crossed this room before him but none was as happy as he.

He picked up Father Daley's gold watch from the washstand and turned it over. It was smooth and cool to the touch. He turned the watch over. It was a lovely watch with faded Roman numbers on the face. It was six o'clock. There were two hours before breakfast.

He dressed quickly, looking down sadly at his grey clothes. He hated grey; it wasn't a colour, it was a feeling. It reminded him of gloomy rooms and miserable faces. If he had enough money, he'd buy some new clothes. Maybe he'd buy a blue or yellow shirt, purple or even pink? Not feckin' grey or brown. He was sick of shit colours in shades of bloody drab.

He picked up his camera, closed the bedroom door quietly and tiptoed downstairs. The lobby was deserted and quiet except for the tick of the lazy clock. The front door was already open and the metal fly curtain in place over the doorway.

Miss Carmichael's empty trunk was still in the lobby. He walked round it slowly and carefully, hands behind his back, the way he thought a detective might look at the evidence. The hinges at the back of the trunk had been broken, so all the thief had had to do was lift up the lid from the wrong side, no need for the key. It was funny though, who would have wanted to steal all those tins of food? And how would they have carried them away down Pig Lane without being seen?

Kneeling down he lifted off the lid and stared at it in alarm. There were scratch marks on the inside as if someone had been shut up in there and been trying to get out. He shivered. He'd read stories where people were buried alive in wooden coffins and had worn down their fingernails trying to get out. He replaced the lid hastily and stood up.

Señora Hipola was clattering about and singing tunelessly in the kitchen at the back of the house. Padraig winced. She had a voice like the screech of chalk on a blackboard, making his teeth squeal with pain.

The smells of fresh coffee and warm bread wafted out from the kitchen. Padraig's stomach rumbled noisily. He passed swiftly through the curtain, barely making a noise.

As he stood in the early morning light, the air in Pig Lane seemed to hum with a peculiar excitement, as though something unusual was about to happen at any moment.

Pig Lane was deserted. The shutters on most of the houses were still shut fast. Far above his head the fiesta bunting flapped gaily. The faded colours of the triangular flags seemed much brighter than yesterday. The cobbles of the lane were strewn with velvety petals that had blown down from the flowerpots on the balconies. He stepped carefully to avoid crushing them.

A fresh breeze was blowing up from the sea and the curtains on the doorways began to jingle as though unseen ghosts were passing through them. The sign above the Bar Pedro creaked knowingly.

Padraig sniffed. The breeze was sharp with the salty smell of the sea, the whiff of freshly landed fish mingling with the sweet perfume of the balcony flowers.

He looked up through the narrow gap above the clustered houses. The sky was the palest of pinks and the sunlight outlined the stark chimneys with a glimmer of buttercup light. The wings of the reeling gulls were tinged with gold.

Someone was playing the guitar softly up in one of the attic rooms.

The Bar Pedro was already busy and tobacco smoke drifted out through the barred windows and tickled his nose. He could smell hot oil, aniseed, beer and wine, onions and chocolate.

The bar window was curtained with smoke so he crept up to the door and peeped warily through the fly curtains. A group of men were standing at the bar. Tall knock-kneed men with sharp elbows and tongues. Short wobbly fat men with bellies of dough. The smoulder of sucked cigarettes pricked the air like floating glow-worms.

Padraig carried on down Pig Lane and stopped outside a shop. From inside, the smell of warm bread and cakes wafted out into the lane and his belly rumbled noisily. Feeling in his pocket for the money Mr Leary had given him, he took out a handful of Spanish coins, potatoes they were called.

He peeped in through the doorway of the shop. He felt nervous about going inside. What should he say? How much would things cost? He didn't know the words for bread or cakes.

Taking a deep breath, he pushed through the curtains. He loved the noise they made as he passed through them. One day when he was a grown-up he was going to have fly curtains over the doors of his house and shutters on the windows and flowerpots instead of curtains. And he was going to buy an easel and a paint box like Mr Leary's and he would paint pictures that made your head spin and your heart turn over.

It was as warm and dark as a cave inside the baker's

shop. Behind the counter an old woman who was as fat as a pudding stood with her back to him, humming happily as she stacked sticks of bread into a basket. From a shelf above the woman's head a virgin looked down sorrowfully on all the cakes she could never eat. She was dusty with flour and a cobweb hung round her shoulders like a lace shawl.

Padraig stood before the counter and waited. He licked his finger and ran it along the sugary counter and popped the tiny crystals into his mouth. They fizzed on his tongue, melting deliciously against the top of his mouth.

Eventually the old woman turned round. She stared at Padraig in surprise as though he were a friendly ghost. Then, as if someone had put a match to an oil lamp, her face lit up into a radiant smile. She leaned across the counter and patted Padraig's head, ran her fingers down his cheek and cupped his chin. Then she stood back and looked him up and down. If he'd been a horse, Padraig thought, she would have checked his teeth.

Padraig pointed shyly to a tray full of what looked like long twisty doughnuts sprinkled with sugar.

He held up one finger and beamed.

The woman lifted two cakes from the tray and wrapped them in a piece of paper and handed them to him. He offered her a handful of money but she shook her head and laughed gaily.

The cakes were still warm and fresh from cooking. He waved to the woman and she laughed again and waved back. The curtains jingled wildly as he stepped back out into the lane.

He was so hungry that he wanted to swallow the cakes whole, but instead he bit off small pieces, rolling them slowly round his mouth. He had to deliberately slow himself down. The cakes were delicious, warm and sugary, and they melted in his mouth and he didn't want the feeling to end. When he'd taken the last bite he licked the paper, chewed it into a ball and swallowed it. Then he turned out of Pig Lane and into a road that was called the Calle San Lorenzo.

The Calle San Lorenzo was a steep hill that led down towards the sea. Pig Lane was scruffy in a pretty kind of way, but here the houses were one-storeyed hovels. On the window-sills, cats with ripped ears slept with one eye open, their tails twitching like snakes ready to strike. Dead and dying cockroaches were scattered across the dusty road.

Padraig stepped carefully on the cobbles, avoiding the cockroaches and keeping an eye out for slivers of fish guts and the twisted volcanoes of wormy dog turds that littered the road.

A small boy wearing only a long soiled vest watched him slyly from a doorway, blinking his red-rimmed eyes, while a fly paddled in a weeping sore on his cheek.

Outside the houses, a line of ancient men sat in silence on a rickety bench. Their faces were as wrinkled as currants, their eyes milky with age. Thick hair grew from their noses instead of their heads. The few teeth they had were long and wobbled as they chewed on tobacco. They chewed like lazy cows and launched gobs of spit into the morning air, gobs as big and slimy as oysters. Some of them had clay pipes clamped tightly between their leathery lips, and they blew beautiful smoke rings high into the breeze.

A gust of wind came up the hill, bowling the cockroaches away across the cobbles, scattering the cats from the window-sills. The old men turned their eyes towards Padraig and watched him intently. A smile started up on the nearest old face and travelled eerily along the line.

Padraig felt a frisson of fear run up his backbone. He had a terrible urge to run, to escape from the old men's gaze.

He walked on quickly. Suddenly, the old men began to

stamp their wooden clogs like flamenco dancers warming up. Padraig shivered and began to walk faster. The old men stamped their feet faster and faster. Padraig broke into a trot and the old men's laughter followed him down the hill.

At the bottom of the hill he turned swiftly into a dark, narrow alley and walked slowly along it. It was similar to Pig Lane except that the houses were smaller, squashed even closer together.

Suddenly, he stopped halfway along the alley and stared in fascination. There, in a small grotto set into a wall of one of the houses and covered by thick glass, was another statue. There were small drops of moisture on the back of the glass as though the virgin's breath had misted the glass during the night.

She looked lonely behind the glass, shut away from the world. He would have liked to break the glass and take her out, give her an airing and blow the cobwebs off her. She was a small slender virgin with creamy-coloured skin and a faded blue robe. But she had a gormless look about her, as if she wasn't quite all there. There were red paper roses entwined round her tiny feet.

Padraig stood on tiptoe and took a good look at her. It looked as if the statue was made from china, like the one in the baker's shop, and not precious metal. He didn't think this was the lost Irish virgin and decided not to take a photograph. He didn't want to waste his film.

He walked on slowly, glancing surreptitiously over his shoulder; he felt sure that someone was following him. He stepped quickly into a doorway and waited, keeping his breathing quiet. He peeped out of the doorway. There was no one there, but he couldn't get rid of the feeling that someone was on his tail.

When he came to the end of the alley he found himself in a large square. The square was deserted and silent except for an old woman who was sweeping dust and pigeons from outside her house.

In the centre of the square there was a fountain. He ran across to it excitedly and jumped up on to the edge.

In the middle of the fountain a life-sized boy statue stood on a raised block of stone.

Padraig gawped in astonishment. The boy was as naked as the day he was born. And he had his mickey on show for the whole of Spain to see. And out of his mickey, in a wide arc, poured a stream of non-stop water.

The boy was smiling and pissing at the same time! God almighty, if he'd ever dared to do that in Ballygurry he'd have been locked up and the key thrown away. Wait until Miss Drew and Miss Carmichael had a look at this. They'd be fainting and swooning all over the place.

Taking his eyes reluctantly from the statue, he kneeled down, dipped his hands into the fountain and let the water trickle between his warm fingers. He would have liked to take off all his clothes like the statue boy and frolic about in the fountain. Instead, he splashed his face, enjoying the coolness on his warm cheeks. Then he cupped his hands and drank thirstily, the water was sweet and cool and lovely on his lips.

Standing up, he walked slowly round the edge of the fountain, one foot in front of the other like a tightrope walker in a circus.

He imagined the roll of drums in the big top. He pretended to lose his balance. Wobbled dangerously. He imagined the horrified gasp of the audience. He pictured their faces, bog eyed, mouths hanging open, holding their breath.

He steadied himself. Took a few more faltering steps. He stood on his hands. Let his feet drop over his head. He took a low bow and another. The crowd roared.

Then he stood quite still, looking at the statue. He copied the pose. Feet about six inches apart, hip bones tilted, bum clenched. He let his bones slip into the same shape as the boy. He practised the same lopsided smile, the cheeky tilt of the head, the one eyebrow raised. He held the pose.

All of a sudden he realized that the old woman had paused in her sweeping and was watching him carefully, leaning on her broom and squinting at him with a very odd look on her face.

Embarrassed, in case she thought he was going to pull out his mickey and piddle in the fountain, he jumped down and walked across the square towards the church, hands in his pockets, whistling nonchalantly.

The church didn't look like any of the churches he'd ever seen in Ireland. It was as big as a castle and made of scratchy pale stone with rough windows cut out from the walls. There was a door big enough for giants to pass through without stooping. High up near the roof a cloud of bees buzzed busily and then disappeared one by one into a large crack in the wall.

Padraig stood in the shade of the church wall, rubbing the palm of his hand against the stone surface. It felt warm and rough to the touch.

It was then that he noticed the man. He was sitting on the ground, soundly asleep, with his head and back resting against the wall.

Padraig stiffened with excitement. He crept closer. The man wore a faded black cloak, wrapped round his body even though it was warm. He had the biggest feet that Padraig had ever seen. He could be charged ground rent for them. On his head he wore a wide-brimmed hat that was tilted so far forward it covered most of his face. On the ground by his side stood a dusty knapsack and a silver flask.

Padraig smiled. This man was the Old Pilgrim. Peregrino

Viejo. The man he had seen in the photograph in Mr Leary's scrapbook back in Ballygurry.

Padraig held his breath. There was a yellow butterfly resting on the brim of the man's hat. It was the most beautiful butterfly that he had ever seen. Each time the man breathed, the butterfly's wings riffled gently.

What was it Mr Leary had said about him?

That he was as elusive as a rare moth?

That it was rumoured he was an axe murderer?

Padraig kneeled down and peeped cautiously up underneath the hat.

The man wasn't sleeping at all. Two amused eyes stared back at Padraig.

Then suddenly the church bells began to clank and clatter. Pigeons flew up from under the eaves and a dog barked from a doorway. Padraig leaped back in alarm. The noise echoed loudly round the square and he put his hands over his ears to keep out the sound.

He looked up at the church. These were the strangest sounding bells that he'd ever heard. It was as though a lunatic were up in the tower bashing them with a frying pan.

Moments later when he looked round, the man was gone. He'd vanished into thin air. Padraig looked anxiously across the square but there was no sign of him at all.

Shite! Double shite and hairy backsides. He'd had a chance to talk to the Old Pilgrim and he'd messed it up just because a few old bells had started up a racket.

There on the ground, though, was a blue silky scarf that the man had left behind. Padraig picked it up. It was old and worn, of the most glorious shade of blue he had ever seen. He wrapped it tightly round the fingers of his left hand. The material was so soft that it made him shiver at the touch. He lifted it up to his nose. It smelled gloriously of wood smoke and fresh tobacco, of horses and dandelions.

He walked slowly back across the square and kicked out disconsolately at a stone. He was real mad at himself; he wasn't much of a detective if he'd let the Old Pilgrim slip away from under his nose. Retracing his steps back past the misty virgin, he turned into the Calle San Lorenzo and once again he had the feeling of being watched.

He climbed the steep hill and walked warily past the old men. They ignored him as he passed, they were sleepy now, their faces turned to the sky like tired sunflowers. He turned into Pig Lane. The window shutters were open on the houses now and smoke coiled up lazily from some of the chimneys. The smell of coffee and fried bread filled the air. Water dripped down from the flowerpots on the balconies. A bedraggled cat stalked across the cobbles. The caged birds on the balconies sang their thin little songs as though they would burst.

As he was about to go into Señora Hipola's house, the curtain parted and two women came out. It was the pretty but miserable girl who was soon to be married and the one with the white teeth and the black eye. Last night the pair of them had looked so down in the dumps and yet now they looked as if they hadn't a care in the world. They walked quickly past Padraig, whispering furtively together, and hurried away down the lane without seeming to notice him. As they turned out of Pig Lane, he listened to the fading echo of their rising laughter; women, he thought, could be very odd.

Miss Drew woke with a start and sat up on the side of the bed. Nancy Carmichael was still asleep and muttering incoherently under her breath. She was a very restless sleeper and had cried out in her sleep several times in the night. Miss Drew looked across at her and smiled. She'd known Nancy Carmichael ever since they were fellow pupils who had sat side by side in the classroom at the Ballygurry school. Chalk and cheese they had been. Nancy had been the cleverest girl in the whole school; she'd been good at everything she'd turned her hand to. There wasn't a subject that gave her any trouble. Miss Drew had been a hopeless student who had struggled with her schoolwork. She'd copied most of her work from Nancy when she could. She'd longed to have the brains that Nancy had, the quick way she understood things, and yet for all Nancy Carmichael's cleverness there was something odd about her too.

There had always been a jittery nervousness about her. It was easy to rattle her and the slightest criticism reduced her to tears. Everyone in Ballygurry had known that she'd pass the scholarship to Saint Mary's convent school, and she did with flying colours, but at the last minute Mrs Carmichael wouldn't let her go. Instead Nancy Carmichael had left Ballygurry and, it was said, had gone to stay with an aunt in Cork, not that that fooled anyone. It was all the talk that she'd gone into a hospital for people with bad nerves, and when she came back she never did go to the convent school but stayed at home looking after the house and her mother until she'd died a few years back.

Miss Drew smiled to herself and carefully removed her hairnet and hairgrips. She knew now why Nancy Carmichael had never had the confidence she should have had. If she hadn't rifled through the trunk that day in Ballygurry and seen the pile of letters then she would never have known the truth. Now it was all quite simple. Oh yes, she'd been envious of Nancy Carmichael for all those years, but not any more. Oh no! Miss Nancy Carmichael would be at Miss Drew's beck and call for the rest of her days when she realized that her secret was out.

She sat listening to the sounds of the strange house. There was a faint scrabbling noise somewhere in the room.

Mice.

Rats.

She crossed herself, slipped her feet quickly into her shoes and tied up the laces.

Her stomach rumbled noisily.

It must have been that disgusting soup last night. There was all kinds of muck in it, funny-looking beans and lumps of bread. Ugh! She could have been poisoned. Food fit for abbots her foot. Fit for pigs more like.

Her stomach gurgled again and a sharp pain made her flinch. She dressed hurriedly, picked up her wash bag and towel and made her way downstairs.

There were no inside lavatories in the lodging house at all, just chamber pots beneath the beds. Even in France, which was barely civilized, there had been inside lavatories. Disgusting though they had been, at least they hadn't had to go outside. Here they had to cross a courtyard at the back of the house to get to the lavatory and the bathhouse. She vaguely remembered Father Daley telling them where it was last night.

She crossed the courtyard quickly. The pains in her stomach were gripping now and there was no time to hang around.

She stepped gingerly into the open-sided stable. An ancient donkey eyed her nervously then edged towards her, baring a mouthful of yellow teeth.

Hastily she opened the door to the lavatory and went inside. She shuddered. Lavatory! It was nothing more than a privy! There wasn't even any newspaper on a nail.

Ten minutes later she edged past the donkey and climbed the stairs to the bathhouse above the stable. There was a notice on the door. PELIGRO! SE PROHIBE LA ENTRADA. Ha! It must be Spanish for bathroom. Miss Drew went into the room, closed the door and drew the rusty bolt across.

She looked dubiously down at the bath. It didn't look as if it had been used in years. It just showed that the Spaniards weren't too particular where hygiene was concerned. She took out a cloth from her wash bag and a small bottle of disinfectant and spent a good five minutes wiping the thick layers of dust and grime from the bath.

With difficulty she turned on the taps. There was a noisy gurgling sound and then a rush of rust-coloured water spluttered into the ancient bath. The last time Miss Drew had seen a bath like this a horse had been drinking out of it in a field.

There was no hot water but it was tepid to the touch and she'd never minded a cold bath. A little privation was good for the soul. After a few minutes the water ran clear and Miss Drew fitted the plug into the hole.

She undressed, sprinkled some lavender bath salts into the water and waited for the bathtub to fill. When it was ready she stepped gingerly over the side of the high-sided bath into the water.

Miss Drew sighed, closed her eyes, and settled back for a good long soak. She didn't think much of Spanish plumbing; there were all kinds of groaning and creaking noises coming from the pipes. Downstairs in the stable the old donkey began to bray plaintively.

This pilgrimage really wasn't as she'd imagined it at all. The journey on the boat hadn't been too bad, she supposed; at least the food had been plain and plentiful. But as soon as they'd landed in Spain things had gone from bad to worse. She blushed at the thought of that terrible ride in the cart with the filthy old thing with the wandering hands. Then the food last night! It was disgusting. Octopus! And fancy Miss Carmichael having her things stolen from under their very noses! This town was probably full of cutthroats and robbers. They could be murdered in their beds or worse.

Miss Drew opened her eyes and stared hard at the bath taps. They were most definitely lopsided. Spanish builders obviously hadn't got the hang of a spirit level; they were as useless as the cooks. Five minutes more and then she'd get out, get dressed and go down to breakfast, though God only knew what horrors were in store for her there.

Carlos Emanuel ate a hurried breakfast of fresh bread and drank a bowl of particularly good coffee. Señora Hipola gave him elaborate directions on how to find the early bus that would take him to Los Olivares and the name of a man there who would take him in a cart to the monastery of Santa Eulalia. Señor Emanuel paid for his night's lodging and left thankfully.

He walked briskly along Pig Lane and made his way back down towards the port, where a dilapidated old bus was parked alongside the cannery. He weaved his way through the market stalls towards it. As he was passing a fish stall he noticed the girl from the lodging house. She was standing at the back of the stall as though she was hiding from someone.

She really was a very beautiful-looking girl. Then he saw the older woman; she was coming out of a shop carrying a bulging knapsack. He was startled by the expression on her face. Last night she had looked positively downtrodden and miserable and yet now she looked quite radiant. She could barely keep the smile off her face. The pretty girl stepped cautiously out from behind the stall and then the two women linked arms and hurried away, giggling together like two schoolgirls up to no good.

He hurried across to the bus. The folk in these parts were an odd, whimsical lot. The sooner he got to Santa Eulalia the better, then he would be on his way south again with the monk safely in tow, and not a moment too soon as far as he was concerned.

*

Father Daley was waiting in the lobby when Miss Carmichael came downstairs just as Padraig came hurrying in through the door, breathless and excited.

'Good morning, Miss Carmichael. A good night's sleep, I trust? Ah, Padraig, there you are, have you been out exploring?'

'Yes, Father. I found an old church and a statue of a naked boy and I saw the Old Pilgrim but he got away before I could speak to him.'

Miss Carmichael gave Padraig a withering glance. It made her feel tired and irritable just looking at him.

'Great stuff, Padraig,' Father Daley said with a smile. 'You must tell me all about it over breakfast. Now, I've just spoken to Señora Hipola, and she has very kindly laid out breakfast in the courtyard as it's such a beautiful morning.'

Miss Carmichael's heart sank. She thought of flies and bugs and the smell of donkey muck.

'Where is Miss Drew, by the way?' Father Daley enquired.

'I don't know. I heard the church bells ringing earlier so maybe she's gone to mass,' said Miss Carmichael, who was a little aggrieved that Miss Drew had gone out without telling her.

'Doubtless she'll join us in a while,' Father Daley replied cheerfully.

Señora Hipola had set up a table and chairs in the courtyard beneath a canopy of vines. In the far corner, a washing line was strung between two trees. On the line a wedding dress blew gently in the breeze. Padraig stared at the dress in amazement. It was huge. Gi-normous. Bloody massive. It was the biggest dress he'd ever clapped his eyes on in all his life.

'Blimey,' he said, pointing to the dress and giggling, 'you

could fit the bride and a half-dozen bridesmaids in there and still have room to dance a jig!'

'Don't be so rude, Padraig. It's beautiful material; it looks like Irish lace to me.'

The breakfast table was covered with a bright blue and yellow checked oilcloth and set upon it was a basket full of golden bread rolls and a large red coffee pot.

'Shall I play mother?' Father Daley said.

He poured coffee and milk into large white bowls and handed them to Padraig and Miss Carmichael.

Miss Carmichael sipped her drink and winced. The coffee was really quite good but there were no handles on the cups and it was like drinking out of a chamber pot; it was enough to turn a decent person's stomach.

It was a beautiful morning, though, and she had to admit that she'd had one of the best night's sleep she'd had in years. She had not been troubled by too many bad dreams and she felt an enormous uplifting of her spirits.

Padraig helped himself to bread and munched away happily. Miss Carmichael declined anything to eat.

Padraig thought the courtyard was a very pretty place to eat breakfast. Birds flew down and perched in the lemon tree and sang gaily. Way above their heads the sky turned a deeper shade of blue and the sun warmed their faces.

'Who is this Old Pilgrim fellow you were talking about, Padraig?'

'Ah, just an old feller who roams about all over Spain wearing funny clothes. Mr Leary said he was maybe an axe murderer or a defrocked priest. Mr Leary was dead keen to meet him because he knows all sorts about history and that.'

Father Daley raised his eyebrows.

'He doesn't sound the sort of man you should be speaking to, Padraig.'

'He looked harmless enough to me.'

'The devil himself would look harmless to you, no doubt,' muttered Nancy Carmichael.

'Anyhow, how about we make a plan for today? How about we do a bit of sightseeing, maybe have a meal out in the town? They say the sardines down at the port are wonderful. Miss Carmichael, I know, loves sardines.'

'Only Irish sardines, Father.'

Father Daley laughed.

Miss Carmichael bristled and blushed.

'Miss Carmichael, the sardines we eat in Ireland have probably been fished in the waters round here, canned here and then shipped to Ireland. Instead of eating them from a tin, we have a chance to eat ones caught fresh today.'

Miss Carmichael was not convinced, but she did allow herself a half smile. Padraig thought she looked quite nice when she smiled. He noticed that her nose, which was usually white and pinched, was peppered now with freckles, as if someone had got into her room at night and dappled her nose with a fine brush.

The donkey began to bray loudly over in the stable.

'It sounds as if something is spooking him,' Padraig said.

'How do you mean, Padraig?'

'They pick up things animals, like they have an extra sense.'

'Go on,' Father Daley encouraged him.

Miss Carmichael raised her eyebrows.

'We had a dog, a black and white collie called Sequana.'

'What sort of a name is that for a dog?' Miss Carmichael said, turning up her nose.

'I think it's a lovely name; it's the Latin word for the Seine.'

'What do they call the insane?'

'The Seine is the river that runs through Paris. Sequana was the goddess of the river.'

'Heathen nonsense,' said Miss Carmichael.

'Anyhow, Sequana took to her bed, wouldn't eat her breakfast even though she was a greedy beggar; she knew, you see, that something awful was going to happen.'

'Don't be so silly, Padraig,' Miss Carmichael said with irritation.

'It was true, though, because that was the day she died.'

'The dog?' asked Father Daley.

'No,' said Padraig. 'They took Sequana away while I was at the funeral and put a bullet through her head.'

Miss Carmichael didn't like dogs. They licked their own behinds and rooted up your skirt and tried to do unthinkable things to your leg.

Miss Carmichael sipped her coffee and wondered where on earth Miss Drew had got to.

Padraig went on.

'The clock had just chimed eleven when Sequana started howling . . . She'd only gone round the corner for a loaf of bread.'

'What is this nonsense about?' Miss Carmichael asked.

The birds held their song.

The wedding dress flapped like a schooner with the wind in its sails.

'She was knocked down by a lorry and killed.'

'Who was, Padraig?'

'My mammy,' he said quietly.

Miss Carmichael sucked in her breath.

Father Daley put a hand on top of Padraig's.

'It was in the newspapers and everything. It was two days before they realized who she was and came and found me and the dog.'

Father Daley looked hard at Padraig. Dear God. The poor little mite.

A smattering of dust drifted down into the stable from

the room above. The donkey sneezed.

Suddenly there was a noise. First a rustle and then an enormous cracking sound as though a huge tree had been felled and was falling close by.

The donkey stamped its hooves.

Señora Hipola appeared in the kitchen doorway looking agitated.

It all happened in a split second, but afterwards it seemed to Padraig like slow motion.

'Dios mío!' yelled Señora Hipola, and made the sign of the cross.

Suddenly claw legs slipped through the ceiling above the donkey's head.

The breakfasting pilgrims stared in frozen fascination.

There was a muffled scream.

The donkey bucked.

'What the fuck?' said Father Daley.

Miss Carmichael opened and shut her mouth like a frog after flies.

Then came the sound of rushing water and the smell of lavender.

The donkey disappeared beneath a deluge of water.

Then the bath and Miss Drew descended into the stable like an apparition in a Christmas pantomime.

But there was no laughter or clapping.

A cloud of dust blotted out the stable and the donkey. Señora Hipola was hissing and spitting.

Imbécil! Dios mío!

The donkey was roaring.

Miss Carmichael was trembling violently and slopping coffee all down her clothes. A brown stain widened across her white high-necked blouse.

Señora Hipola was pawing the ground with her foot like a mad bull.

The donkey was kicking his hard heels against the wood of the stable.

Padraig was hot on Father Daley's heels across the courtyard.

Dust settling like dirty snow.

Señora Hipola trying to quieten the donkey.

Padraig on tiptoe looking over into the stable.

Miss Drew with a face like a startled corpse.

The bath rocking like a fairground swingboat without the ropes.

'Cover your eyes, Padraig! Someone run for a doctor.'

Padraig kept his eyes wide open. He gawped at Miss Drew in wonder.

There was another loud cracking sound and more plaster falling, and then something else fell through the broken ceiling and landed with a clatter beside the bath.

It was an ancient chest, like a treasure chest.

Father Daley stared at the ancient chest that lay in the straw.

Padraig couldn't take his eyes off Miss Drew's chest. Miss Drew's titties were as pink and soft as a puppy's belly. There was a bird's nest in her lap, but sadly no eggs.

The Old Pilgrim took his breakfast in the Café Cristobal down on the quayside. The British boat was still berthed and would sail again in the early afternoon. He remembered vividly stepping down off the boat that first time years ago. He was a young man then, a reckless man whom he hardly recognized now. Then he had been an ill and broken man, his nerves shot to pieces, a desperate man on the run with a trail of misery left in his wake.

He'd boarded the boat in England without any concern as to where it would take him. All he'd wanted was to escape from the past.

Spain had been his salvation.

Now he spent several months of each year in different parts of Europe, occasionally he returned to England and Ireland, but only when he had to.

He sighed, dipped a sugary churro into a bowl of hot chocolate and ate it slowly. After breakfast he was going to go up into the mountains for a few days, explore a few places he had never been to before.

Last night he had stayed in old Antonio's house near the church. He had woken early and left, the old man's company he could stomach but not his breakfasts. Pigs' trotters and bread fried in lard was more than a man could cope with first thing in the morning.

He watched the early goings on in the port but his mind was mostly consumed with thinking about the little boy he'd seen earlier.

After he'd left Antonio's he had found a quiet place to sit near the church in the square to enjoy an early morning smoke. He'd been there quite some time before he'd looked up and seen the boy.

He'd watched the little lad with fascination as he had completed his imaginary tightrope walk round the wall of the fountain. He loved the way that children could become so engrossed in their own imaginary world, completely absorbed and unselfconscious in what they were doing. It was a childhood gift and didn't last long.

He had sat quite still in the shadow of the church hoping the boy wouldn't see him and stop what he was doing. He'd only just stopped himself from applauding when the boy had taken his final bows to his imaginary audience.

Then the boy had copied the pose of the statue. That was when he'd sat up in surprise and really taken note. The resemblance between the statue and this comical little boy was quite absurd. The likeness, albeit between tarnished metal and warm flesh, was quite remarkable. It had to be just coincidence, a trick of the light maybe. After all, the statue had been in Camiga for as long as he could remember and couldn't have been modelled on this funny little fellow. And, yet, something stirred in his mind . . . a half-thought, confusing and somehow important.

This child wasn't a local boy, that was for sure. His skin was pale; he wasn't a child who had spent long hours playing under a hot sun. With his dull grey clothes and skinny white legs he looked out of place in Spain, a scruffy sparrow in a cage full of exotic birds. The Old Pilgrim smiled; he was a chrysalis of a boy waiting for his transformation into a butterfly.

Now he drained the last of his hot chocolate just as the cannery siren blared out across the quay. He'd better get a move on if he was to make it up into the mountains by nightfall. He paid for his breakfast, left a generous tip and then strode across the cobbled quay, aware of but unconcerned by the curious eyes of the market traders who watched him go.

Part Three

Donny Keegan stood alone in the cave they called the Giant's Cakehole. It was cold and dank inside the cave, just the echoing plop of water dripping from the stalactites into the rock pools.

Plip

Plip

Plip.

He pushed his hands down into his pockets and whistled softly.

He wondered had Sister Immaculata stood right here where he was standing now when she'd decided to do herself in? Had she just sat in the cave and waited for the tide to come in and swallow her up?

He shivered violently. She must have wanted to die real bad to do a thing like that. He wondered did she maybe start to panic and change her mind but by then it was already too late?

It couldn't have been an accident because everyone in Ballygurry knew that the cave was dangerous when the tide was coming in. The fishermen had shaken their heads and said that her body might not be washed up for many months, or maybe not at all.

One of the fishermen, Archie Cullinane, had found some

of her clothes here in the cave the day after she'd disappeared. The grey habit and veil caught up in a tangle of seaweed and flotsam and jetsam amongst the rocks. Further down the beach one black sodden lace-up shoe lay half buried in the sand, and a woollen grey stocking was discovered hanging across the bows of one of the barnacled boats.

Donny struggled to hold back his tears. It was strange in St Joseph's without Sister Immaculata. After Padraig had gone she used to bring him clean sheets in case of accidents and he'd hidden them under the floorboards just like Padraig had shown him. There were hardly any sheets left now, no escape from night-time terrors and beltings for a wet bed.

The attic room where Sister Immaculata had slept had been cleared, scrubbed, disinfected and locked up. It was as though she had never been alive at all.

Sometimes at night he woke up and thought he heard her up there still, pacing the boards restlessly.

A gust of wind blew inside the cave and Donny felt the goose-pimples prick through his tight skin. He imagined the icy water reaching up over her feet, her ankles and knees. Then the awful bit where it came over your mickey . . . she wouldn't have had a mickey though. Women didn't. What they had down there was a mystery. Up and up the water would have risen, up to her neck. Oh God, he felt sick at the thought of it. Higher and higher until her mouth and nose were full of salty water and she couldn't breathe!

His nose began to run and he wiped away his snot and tears on the ragged sleeves of his pullover. The wet shrunken wool made the bits where he'd wiped sore and itchy. He wished that Padraig were here with him now because he felt afraid and Padraig had always made him feel so much braver. He stifled a sob. He couldn't believe that the old nun had taken her own life. He knew that it was a terrible sin to do that. Now, she'd never be allowed to be buried in a Catholic graveyard even if they did find her body, and she'd go straight to hell where the really bad people went, swearers and spitters, murderers and thieves.

He thought that was wrong because she had been a really good person while she was alive. She was the only one at St Joseph's who was kind to the kids. If she went to hell then he didn't want to believe in God any more. If Sister Veronica and Sister Agatha went to heaven what sort of a place would it be?

He kneeled down on the floor of the cave and wrote carefully in the wet sand with a trembling finger.

SISTER EMMAKULARTA. RIP. RISE IF POSSIBLE.

Then he leaped back in alarm as a wave broke with a resounding crack at the jagged mouth of the cave. Another followed swiftly and white foamy water surged up over his sandals and melted away the nun's name as if it had never been written at all.

A third wave swirled up round his knees. He waited for it to be drawn back, judged the timing and ran out of the cave. He raced headlong along the beach until he reached the boats. He rested against one to catch his breath. Then he took off his shoes and socks, tipped the water out of his shoes and wrung out his socks. As he dug his toes into the dry sand to warm them his big toe caught against something sharp. Pulling his toe back quickly in case it was a lurking crab, he bent down and dug in the sand with his hands. He lifted the necklace up, shook off the sand and looked at it closely. It wasn't a necklace at all but an old battered rosary. He swallowed hard. He'd seen Sister Immaculata holding it in her hands when they were in church. It wasn't like a normal rosary, it was a clumsily made thing and looked like it had been hand made, the beads were heavy and a milky blue colour, like blind people's eyes. He slipped it into the pocket of his shorts. He would keep it for ever and have something to remember her by. Like a good-luck charm.

He put on his socks and shoes and made his way across to the slipway and then along Clancy Street.

As he came level with Dr Hanlon's house a voice startled him and he jumped with fright.

'Jeez! You frightened me then,' Donny said, and breathed out with relief. He stared in fascination at Siobhan Hanlon, who had stepped out suddenly from the doorway of her house.

'Well, what do you think? Gorgeous or what?'

Siobhan was dressed in a baggy grey gymslip that reached almost to her ankles, a blue stiff-collared blouse, a blue blazer with a red badge, grey tie and a grey pudding-basin hat.

'N-nice,' he stammered.

'Nice! Give over. Who are you kidding! I look a right bleeding eejit! And guess what?'

'What?'

'I have to wear two pairs of drawers at the same time! Can you believe that? White cotton underneath and blue regulation baggies on the top! And three pairs when we have games lessons. Imagine, all that rushing about and the blood will rush to my arse and I'll probably drop dead of heatstroke.'

Donny blushed with embarrassment. Siobhan Hanlon didn't care what she said or who she said it to.

Siobhan looked Donny up and down inquisitively. His socks and shoes were soaked and his grubby face was smudged with dirt and tears; he was doing his best to stop his lip from wobbling. Donny Keegan was sweet. If she ever had a little boy she'd like one like him.

'What's up, Donny? You look like you've seen a ghost.'

'Nothin's up. I just had sand blow in my eye.'

'Where are you off to?'

'Nowhere much. Just up around the famine wall for a walk.'

'Can I come with you?'

Donny nodded half reluctantly; he was a bit afraid of Siobhan with her bold ways and her big gob.

'I'll catch you up in a minute. I'll just go and take this pile of shite off. I won't be half a tick.'

Donny squelched away up Clancy Street.

A breathless Siobhan caught up with him just as he was passing Mankey's Alley. They wandered away down past the silent station and climbed the rotten stile that led into the tinkers' field.

It was quiet in the tinkers' field as they walked side by side through the long prickly grass towards the famine wall. Poor, starving people in the great famine in the olden times had been made to build the wall. It didn't serve any purpose, they were just made to do it to earn some money.

All around them dandelion clocks bobbed in the breeze and red poppies bent under the weight of early bees.

Over the years people had scratched their names on the wall. Along with the names there were dates and faded love hearts with arrows through them; and filthy messages that made Siobhan laugh out loud. Donny thought that she had a real dirty laugh for a doctor's daughter.

SISTER VRONICKER IS A FLABBY ARSED OLD COW SO THERE.

SISTER AGATHA STINKS.

They wandered slowly round the wall together.

'Look,' said Siobhan. 'Theresa Patricia Drew. Ugh! Hey, Donny, did you know that the old witch is back?'

'Who, Miss Drew? From the pilgrimage? Are they all back?' he asked hopefully.

'No. Only her, worse luck. She got back yesterday morning and came straight to see Daddy, and guess what?'

'I don't know.'

'She has a bruise on her ARSE the size of the whole of Ireland!'

'Siobhan! How do you know?'

'Because I looked through the keyhole when she was showing Daddy!'

'You did not!' Donny giggled.

'I did too. She's shown him three times already. Do you want to know what it looked like?'

'No,' he said.

He did though. She was terrible rude was Siobhan but he couldn't help laughing. He was never ever going to get married but if he did he reckoned it would be fun to be married to someone like Siobhan who made you laugh all the time.

'It was this big!' she said, stretching out her arms as wide as she could. 'And her bum is covered all over in enormous pimples!'

'No way, you dirty devil!'

'And in between the pimples it was black and blue!'

'Give over! Why did she come back though?'

'Well, afterwards I heard her telling Mammy in the kitchen that she'd had the most terrible time out in Spain . . . She fell through a roof and was attacked by a mad donkey, and if that wasn't enough she was forced to eat octopus and there was a robber on every street corner. And she was disgusted because the other pilgrims were more interested in an old treasure chest that fell through the roof than her injuries.'

'What sort of treasure?'

'I never heard because Mammy opened the door then and gave me a right crack around the chops for listening at keyholes. Look. There. Martin Sean Donahue. That must be old Donahue from the bar. I can't imagine Donahue ever being a little boy. He's a miserable old bastard.'

'Siobhan, shh. Someone might hear you!'

'There's no one here to hear us. My name's there, look.'

SIOBHAN MARY JANE HANLON. AGED 10 AND THREE QUARTERS.

Donny blushed. She had written her name as close to Padraig's as was possible.

He had been going to scratch his own name next to Padraig's with a penknife but she'd beaten him to it.

'When do you go off to your new school?'

'In a couple of days' time. I'm going over on the boat and then a nun is going to pick me up on the other side. That's if I don't throw myself overboard on the way!'

'Don't say things like that!'

'Only joking, but I don't want to go. Donny, if I give you the address of the school will you give it to Padraig for me when you see him and tell him to write me?'

'Sure. If I see him. Why are you going so soon? I thought it was after the summer holidays.'

'Nope. Now the school is going to close I'm being sent early.'

'What do you mean the school will close? Course it won't.'

'It will. I heard Daddy say that once you lot are all sent off to Australia there'll be hardly any kids left.'

'I'm not going to Australia.'

'Sure, you'll have to.'

'My daddy will come for me before then,' Donny mumbled.

'Where is your daddy?'

'In England I think.'

'How long since you've seen him?'

'I've never seen him.'

Siobhan put her head on one side and drew a circle with the toe of her sandal in the dusty bare earth.

'You've never ever seen him?'

Donny shook his head.

'You don't even know what he looks like?'

'No.'

'How will you know it's him when he comes?'

'I don't know. Ah, sure he'll just say I've come for my son Donny Keegan, won't he?'

Siobhan supposed he would. It was funny to think someone had never seen their own daddy. She'd hate not to have seen her daddy, she loved him to bits.

Then it hit her like a thump in the belly from a wet sack of flour. Soon she'd be away from her daddy for whole weeks and months at a time. Her heart raced and her eyes felt scratchy with tears.

'What's up, Siobhan?'

'Nothin'.'

'Then why are you sad all of a sudden?'

'I'm not, all right? Look, what sort of a name is that anyhow?' Siobhan said, blinking rapidly and pointing at a name on the wall.

Fatgit Flaherty!

'There's another one, look. Bigbollocks O'Grady!' said Donny.

'Donny, did you know that Padraig sometimes used to

get out of St Joseph's at night and walk about the place on his own?'

Donny grinned widely.

'Yep, he told me. It's a secret, though, and you mustn't tell.'

'How did he get out?'

'There's a way of getting into Sister Veronica's room through a cupboard in the old laundry. Sister Immaculata showed him,' Donny said, lowering his voice to a whisper.

'Is that the poor old thing that drowned herself?'

Donny nodded and sniffed and felt for the rosary in his pocket.

'That was sad, wasn't it?'

'I know. She was real nice to everyone and they can't even bury her without a body.'

'Why do you think she did it?'

'She was always saying she wanted to escape or that someone was going to come and rescue her, but no one believed her.'

'Was she nuts?'

'A bit, but not in a scary way. She told Padraig that once she nearly got away.'

'How?'

'She said there was a peddler selling pencils who came to save her but that they locked her up and wouldn't let him in. She used to say all sorts of daft things like that. Just made it up as she went along, I reckon.'

'Well, she has escaped now, but what a way to go. God, fancy killing yourself like that. She'll have been eaten up by fish by now.'

'Shut up, Siobhan.'

'Or swallowed whole by a whale. Imagine being tea for a whale!'

'Don't!'

'That wouldn't be so bad, though, you can survive inside a whale's belly for ages and then hope that they sneeze or sick you up and then you can swim like billy-o for the shore.'

Donny brightened up a little at the thought. He imagined Sister Immaculata crawling exhausted up a faraway beach and someone kind finding her and looking after her.

'That would be good,' he said with a smile.

'Why did she show Padraig the secret way?'

'They were real good friends and they got in there once to listen to a meeting that was going on. Padraig was real upset after because that's when he found out they wouldn't let him go to that posh school.'

'Have you ever got in there?'

'You must be joking. But Padraig worked out that he could get out of the cupboard into the study and then climb out the study window and escape.'

'Fancy creeping around in the dark of night! I'd be terrified, but he is a brave bugger. Can you keep a secret, Donny?'

'Sure I can.'

'He told me that one night when he escaped he saw Miss Carmichael in the horse trough dancing naked.'

Donny giggled.

'He did not!'

'He did so! It was only her reflection, though!'

'Well, that's not what he told me.'

'What did he tell you, Donny?'

Donny lowered his voice.

'He said he saw the face of his mammy.'

'But his mammy's dead.'

'Exactly, Siobhan, so it was her ghost that he saw.'

Siobhan felt a shiver of fear skedaddle up her backbone.

'Padraig said that seeing her face was a sure sign that

somehow he was going to escape from St Joseph's.'

Siobhan bit her lip. She wondered why he'd told her that old nonsense about Miss Carmichael. She swallowed hard. He hadn't told her because he knew she couldn't keep a secret and he was right. She'd gone and told Sinead about the Black Jew's little girl, hadn't she? Still, fingers crossed, she didn't think Sinead would tell. If she did she'd paste the piss out of her.

'Would you like to get into the cupboard, Donny?'

'No way,' Donny said, and stared at her nervously.

'Are you scared to?'

'Nope.'

'Bet you are, too. Padraig O'Mally isn't afraid of anything.'

'I'm not afraid.'

'Let's get in there then and have a snoop around.'

'We couldn't.'

'I dare you, Donny Keegan. Double. Triple dare. Come on. Race you back to the stile. Last one there is a shitey stinkpot!'

Siobhan ran in front, Donny hot on her heels, the pair of them racing wildly through the long grass, leaving an explosion of dandelion clocks and buttercup pollen in their wake.

On her way back from Dr Hanlon's, Miss Drew called into Donahue's for a few odds and ends. As she opened the door the bell jingled above her head and Donahue looked up from the newspaper he was reading.

She was surprised to see Donahue looking quite bright eyed and bushy tailed, he usually looked a wreck whatever the time of day you came in.

'Morning, Mr Donahue.'

'Miss Drew.'

Donahue had known Miss Drew for most of his life and yet they still weren't on first-name terms. They'd sat in the same classroom together at the Ballygurry school; she'd been a spiteful little thing then, quick to tell tales, quick to drop anyone in it to get on the good side of the schoolmaster.

He still had the marks on his legs where she'd once jabbed him with a sharpened pencil.

'Well,' she said, 'it's grand to be back in Ballygurry amongst friends. No more foreign travel for me, that's for sure, as long as I live. Thanks be to God.'

'Ah, and how is that?'

Miss Drew leaned conspiratorially towards him and lowered her voice even though the bar was empty except for the ginger tom cat. And the cat, who had felt the toe of her boot up his backside many a time, slipped away hastily under the high-backed old settle.

'It was a nightmare out there. A terrible, hellhole of a place. It was full of savages and light-fingered lunatics. Oh, and the stink! It was enough to turn your stomach.'

'Your friend Miss Carmichael liked it enough to stay on then?'

Miss Drew twisted up her face into a hideous grimace.

'Miss Carmichael is no longer a friend of mine and I told it to her straight,' she said emphatically.

'Ah, get away with you. You've been friends for years, like a pair of them Pekinese twins.'

'Siamese, Donahue. Pekinese are a type of cat. Ah well, they say you never really know someone that well, someone secretive like Nancy Carmichael.'

Donahue scratched his head.

'Ah, she's not a bad old stick, a bit hoity toity at times but we've all got our faults, Miss Drew.'

'Well, Nancy Carmichael is not all that she's cracked up to be, you know.'

Donahue busied himself with wiping glasses that didn't need wiping, but Miss Drew pressed on relentlessly.

'Course we never really heard what happened to her father, did we?'

Donahue sighed. 'Died young as far as I can remember,' he said with a shrug.

Miss Drew cleared her throat and spat out the words as if they were slivers of glass.

'Illegitimate, more like. And I have the proof.'

Donahue jumped and almost let a glass slip from his hand.

How the hell did the spiteful old cat find that out?

'Ah, was she now? Well, Miss Drew, she won't be the first and she won't be the last.'

Miss Drew looked at Donahue through bright, narrowed eyes. She reminded him of a cat with a bird in its mouth.

'Well, I hardly think that she's the right sort of person to be on the church cleaning rota, or the orphanage committee, come to that. I don't think Sister Veronica will be over impressed when she finds out the truth.'

'Ah well,' said Donahue, 'there won't be any need for the committee for much longer with them orphans all being shipped off . . .'

'Well, anyhow, it's my Christian duty to see that people are aware of her, um, er, background.'

Poor Nancy Carmichael, Donahue thought; by the time this evil old shite-hound had traipsed around the village telling all and sundry what she'd found out, life wouldn't be worth living when Nancy got back from Spain.

'And before I forget, I'll take a tin of pilchards and a packet of fig rolls.'

Donahue lifted down a tin of pilchards and grinned. Miss Drew looked a bit like a pilchard herself! He hoped the bloody things had bones in and choked her.

'I'm off to see Mrs Cullinane, catching up on everything that's happened since I've been away.'

'You'll have heard about the poor old nun, I take it?'

'Dreadful business. It's a selfish thing and a sin to take one's own life. She wasn't really a proper nun, you know, she was a bit simple in the head and her family paid to have her looked after.'

'Well, she didn't seem simple what I saw of her. It's very sad all the same.'

Miss Drew did not reply but left the shop, and the bell above the door gave a mournful clang.

Donahue had a horrible taste in his mouth after the conversation with her. He was sorely tempted to pour himself a stiff drink; a man deserved a drink after talking to that sour-pussed old bitch. He changed his mind, poured a glass of dandelion and burdock, crossed to the window and watched Miss Drew scuttling across the road to spread the gossip about poor Miss Carmichael to Mrs Cullinane.

Old Mrs Carmichael, Nancy's mother, had been a friend of his own mammy. They'd been in service together when they were both young girls at Kilgerry House up near Rossmacconnarty.

He crossed the bar to look at an old photograph that had been hanging there in the bar for as long as he could remember. He took it down, fetched a cloth and began to wipe away layers of dust and grime. It was a group photograph that had been taken outside the front of Kilgerry House.

He hadn't looked at it properly in years and yet when he was a child he used to be able to point at each face and recall the names of all the people.

He tested his memory now.

There was his own lovely mammy at the end of the line wearing her housemaid's cap and apron, looking young, pretty and shy. God bless her, she'd been a good mother to him. At the other end of the row was his daddy, though at the time they were both single, just at the stage of making eyes at each other across the stable door or the coal scuttle. There was the cook, Miss Yeats. Lady Fitzallen. A slim, sad-faced woman with a faded prettiness about her.

'She'd the patience of a saint putting up with all his comings and goings, the dirty old goat, he's fathered more children than an alley cat, the dirty old dog,' his mammy used to say. She'd been very fond of Lady Fitzallen and had visited her up until her untimely death.

Lord Fitzallen was standing next to his wife. A smug-looking bugger if ever there was one. A right hard-faced old bastard. Donahue's daddy couldn't wait to get the hell out of Kilgerry. He said old Fitzallen treated his dogs better than people, including his own family.

Hell, what was the name of the old housekeeper, a big-boned piece with arms like a navvy and the snout of a boxer? Miss Innis or something like that. She had six fingers on one hand and four on the other, or maybe it was toes?

He scoured the photograph for Miss Carmichael's mother but couldn't find her. Nelly Jones she was called in those days. Ah, there she was at the back. A girl with a long horsey face, haughty looking like she had a bad smell under her nose. She'd been the nanny at Kilgerry. Damn! There was something else his mother had told him about her but he was beggared if he could remember it.

He looked more closely at the photograph. On the bottom, in a fine hand, someone had written, *Tenth birthday of Henry William Fitzallen.*

Of course! He'd forgotten all about poor Henry. He was the little boy who had hanged himself. There he was, standing in front of his mother, Lady Fitzallen, her hands resting protectively on his shoulders. He was a big-eared self-conscious-looking boy dressed in a sailor suit, his head tilted to one side, squinting into the sun.

Donahue shivered.

He'd hated hearing that story when he was little. Nelly Jones, Nancy's mother, had gone to call Henry William one morning as she always did, but had found his bed empty and discovered him hanging from a rope in the bathroom.

Apparently he'd had a beating off his father the night before for some wrongdoing or other. They never knew whether he meant to hang himself or if it was a prank that went wrong.

'He was a sensitive little fellow, a darling little boy. He thought the world of his mother. You can bet your life that there was more to that than met the eye,' Donahue's mammy had always said.

Nelly Jones had been so distraught that she'd left Kilgerry soon after.

Donahue smiled; he used to get really jealous when he was a little boy because every time his mammy had looked at the photograph she'd put up her hand to touch Henry's face. Many a time, on the sly, Donahue had glared up at the little boy and poked out his tongue when his mammy was out of the way.

Lady Fitzallen was never the same after the boy took his own life. She went to pieces completely and even though she had two more children she never recovered properly.

A year after Henry's death she'd given birth to another son, George, the same year Donahue had been born, and then a daughter many years later. They were a family cursed. There was some gossip about the boy George; Donahue seemed to remember that he had been sent off in disgrace. And then, years later, the only daughter had disappeared and never been found.

Dear God. Anyhow, his own parents had got well acquainted, a bit of how's your father and then Bob's your uncle and there was a quick wedding and a swift exit from Kilgerry and a long and happy marriage.

Nelly Jones, the nanny, had surfaced again a few years later, now called Mrs Carmichael, recently widowed, with a toddler, Nancy. She'd bought the little house in Clancy Street and lived out her respectable widowhood in Ballygurry. He'd never liked Mrs Carmichael much, she was a funny old stick with her airs and graces and swanky talk.

'She didn't get the money to buy that house by scrubbing floors, I'll be damned. There's more to Mrs Carmichael than meets the eye for all her swanky ways!' his mammy had muttered many a time, but she hadn't been a one for gossip and Mrs Carmichael's secret had been safe with her.

Donahue wondered how the hell beaky-nosed Drew had found out Nancy's secret. Nancy would never have told her. Come to think of it, he wasn't sure if Nancy even knew, herself. Poor old Nancy, when she got back she wouldn't be welcome in some quarters. She didn't deserve that, the poor bugger. She hadn't had an easy life with that mother of hers.

Donahue sighed. The world was a topsy-turvy old place for sure.

He was tempted again to pour himself a whiskey but he reminded himself that he hadn't taken a drop of drink since the day the old nun had taken her life. It had really shook him up badly that, even though he'd hardly known her. He'd thought of ending it all himself a few times, mind, after his wife had left but he'd never had the stomach for it.

Donahue replaced the photograph on the wall. He looked for a long time at his mammy. Tell the truth and shame the devil, she always used to say. And stand up for what is right. Listen to the little voice inside you, Marty. You have to face up to the facts.

He sighed heavily, walked to the door and pulled across the bolts. For the first time in many months he climbed the creaking stairs to the bedroom. He hadn't slept up there since Eileen had left him. For a long time after she'd gone he used to go up there and sit on the side of the bed for hours at a time just staring ahead of him.

The bedroom still had many reminders of Eileen. Most of her clothes she'd taken with her but her perfume was still there in the royal-blue bottle on the dressing-table along with a pink hairnet, a shocking-pink chiffon scarf and a handful of hair clips. There was also a pile of ironed, dusty hankies with a day of the week embroidered in each corner. They were all there except for the one with Wednesday on it. That was the day she'd upped and gone without a word of warning.

He picked up the pillow from her side of the bed and held it to his nose. He could no longer smell the sweet oily smell of her hair or the pungent whiff of setting lotion. Now the pillow smelled only of dust, cat hair and mildew.

He sat down on the bed and raised a cloud of damp dust that made him sneeze. He sat there for a long time until suddenly, in a moment of long-pent-up anger, he got unsteadily to his feet, swept the perfume bottle and other knick-knacks from the dressing-table to the floor. He screwed up the hankies, hurled them to the floor too, and dashed them all beneath his feet. Then shaking uncontrollably he lay down on the bed as big hot tears rolled down his large face. Eileen wasn't ever coming back, that was for sure. Like his mammy'd said, he had to face up to the facts, but God, it was awful hard.

*

Michael Leary walked slowly along the beach and sat on an upturned boat. He took out the letter from his pocket, put on his glasses and began to read it again as he felt the first tears prick his eyes.

> My darling Michael, why did you stop writing to me? All the letters I sent to your last address were returned to me. I waited so long for your letters I thought that you had forgotten me . . . I had no address for you until now . . . and my getting one is the strangest coincidence, but that's another story

Michael Leary was confused. He'd written to her every week since he'd left Spain. He read on.

> By the time you get this letter I will be a married woman.

Married! It hadn't taken her long to forget him then! He read on through a blur of angry tears.

> I cannot bear it but it must be so. I will always remember you, my sweet one . . .

What was the date today? He checked the date on the top of the letter . . . God almighty! She was already married.

She must have got his letters! That was bollocks! This was just her way of letting him down gently.

He stood up, ripped the letter into small pieces and threw it up into the air. The breeze caught greedily at the fragments and carried them off on the early evening air.

Michael Leary stalked across the beach, spat between his teeth and lit another cigarette.

He climbed up the slipway and walked up Clancy Street.

Outside Donahue's the strings of summer sandals were swaying in the breeze and the tin buckets and spades clanking restlessly. He passed the horse trough. The water rippled and stirred.

He stopped in his tracks and a shiver of fear riffled up his backbone. Christ! Seeing the face of that old nun staring up at him from the horse trough had knocked the bloody stuffing right out of him, especially with what had happened afterwards.

It was the night before the pilgrims had left for Spain. He'd been restless all that day and just before midnight he'd left the schoolhouse and walked along the beach, almost as far as the Giant's Cakehole. He'd lingered there a while, listening to the whistle of the wind as it got trapped in the cave. Then he'd walked back up the beach and along to the village. He didn't know what made him do it but just as he'd got level with the horse trough he'd heard the clock in Dr Hanlon's chime midnight. He'd never believed in all that rubbish about seeing faces in the water. Ballygurry was awash with old wives' tales.

He'd had a good look round in case anyone was watching out of their windows, kneeled down and peered into the water, laughing at his own stupidity. His breath had stirred the water. What a load of old codswallop. All he could see was his own wobbling reflection.

Suffering angels, he'd nearly had a bloody heart attack.

The wrinkled old face grinning at him like that over his shoulder, the wide toothless grin, and then the mouth moving as if she was trying to tell him something.

He'd begun to breathe too fast, felt a nauseous faintness creep up on him, and then he must have blacked out; he'd come to seconds later with a shock, face down in the cold water like a prize bloody eejit. Then he'd struggled to his feet, blowing and puffing, and looked all around Clancy

Street, but not a sign of the old nun. Yet for a few seconds afterwards he could still smell the mustiness of her clothes, camphor and candlewax.

It made him come over all queer now just thinking about it. It wasn't a bloody magic vision, though, it was her in the flesh all right. He should have tried to find her, at least have reported it to Sister Veronica, but he'd not wanted to get her into trouble. Instead, he'd hurried home, drawn all the bolts across the door and poured himself a very large, very stiff whiskey and then another three.

The next morning he'd woken with a head as thick as a simpleton's, and a mouth like the inside of a skunk's arsehole.

It was later that afternoon, after they'd seen the pilgrims off from the station, when she'd been discovered missing. The nuns had searched the grounds and the station and even scoured the Dark Wood but to no avail. She must have planned it all carefully, slipped away in the night and taken her own life. God help her, the poor old bugger must have lost her mind, gone daft in the head to do a terrible thing like that.

He couldn't rid himself of the vision of her face. At night when he closed his eyes he could still see her. A wobbling reflection, a maniacal smile. Sometimes the face would distort and grow younger. There was something, a fleeting expression in the eyes, that made him think of another face he'd seen somewhere. His head was full of jumbled thoughts and faces. Padraig's face. The painting Padraig had done of the wide-eyed girl in the wood holding a bunch of dandelions. A blur of eyes and noses and lips that kept him from sleep. He stepped quickly now into Donahue's; what he needed was a stiff drink.

Sister Veronica crossed to the window of her study and looked out across the scrubby lawns of the orphanage garden. Soon, when all the orphans were gone, she'd make a few changes to the place, put in some benches for the old folks to sit on, a nice little fish pond with goldfish, maybe an archway with yellow roses growing over it. Old people would appreciate that kind of thing.

Just then the telephone rang.

'Sister Veronica. St Joseph's orphanage.'

'Ah, sweet Jesus, the organ grinder herself, just the job.'

Sister Veronica winced. The voice on the other end of the phone was overloud and brimming with confidence.

'How may I help?'

'I wanted to have a word with you about a young man currently in your bounteous care.'

'To whom am I speaking?'

'Willy Flanagan of the Abbey school at your service, ma'am.'

A hiccup and a giggle travelled down the line.

'I have been sent, courtesy of the illustrious and winsome Michael Leary, who may I say set the ladies' hearts in Cork all a flutter when he posed naked for the life class . . . But I digress; I have been sent some paintings done by a young man in your charge. You know I daresay of the artist to whom I refer.'

'I do not.'

'Patsy, no, hang on, Padraig, that's it, Padraig O'Mally. And I'm telephoning to say that you may send the boy to me post haste. No need to take the examination. There will be a place kept warm at the Abbey for him, a place to hang his hat. Does he have a hat? Every budding artist should have an outrageous hat, don't you think? The boy, Padraig, oozes flair, he paints with the eye of an angel and the palette of the devil himself.'

'Padraig O'Mally is not here at present.'

'Well, when does he return?'

'That is of no consequence, but when he does return, Mr Flanagan, he will be boarding a boat, and when he gets off it he will be safely in Australia, where please God he will come across no more drunken Protestant schoolmasters.'

'Well, bugger me backwards, Leary said you were a difficult woman and he wasn't exaggerating. May I take this opportunity to wish you a long and incontinent life, madam.'

Sister Veronica slammed down the telephone and sat down heavily on her chair.

Michael Leary had a damned nerve. She'd been quite emphatic about Padraig not going to the Abbey school. And yet Leary had obviously been behind her back talking to this drunken lunatic of a man. Well, by God, Padraig would not go to the Abbey school come hell or high water. Padraig O'Mally was a brazen, troublesome little brat and she would put paid to Mr Leary's ridiculous plans. The first lot of children were sailing for Australia in a week. It was thought best to send them quickly, not give them too much time to brood. Padraig was due back from Spain after they'd gone but it was arranged that he would join up with a group from Dublin who were travelling later.

She stood up, and on a sudden whim she unlocked a cupboard, looked along a row of files and lifted one down.

Most of the orphans arrived at St Joseph's with a slim file and a small box of mementoes that were kept for them and given back on the day they left and not before. She'd only ever had a cursory look through the boxes. Usually, they contained a pile of cheap gaudy knick-knacks and a photograph or two of gormless-looking family groups.

Padraig George O'Mally. Mother's name: Maria Bridget O'Mally. There was an address on the South Circular Road in Dublin. Sister Veronica knew that that was the Jewish area of Dublin and yet the records showed that Padraig

O'Mally had been christened a Catholic. There was no name on the birth certificate where his father's name should have been. She reached up again and lifted down a battered old shoebox. Brushing the thick layer of dust off the top of the box, she carried it over to her desk.

There wasn't much inside Padraig's box at all, hardly a grand inheritance. There was a photograph of a young woman in an ornate silver frame, a battered and dog-eared leather-bound book and a pile of mildewed letters. The photograph was of a dark-haired woman, good looking in a brazen kind of way. She was sitting in what looked suspiciously like a bar. Her hand was supporting her chin; she held a glass in her other hand, while smoke from a cigarette drifted round her face. She was smiling and unafraid of the camera. Sister Veronica put the photograph down on the table, picked up the bundle of letters and undid the faded blue ribbon that held them together.

She opened the letter on the top of the pile. It was written on a piece of headed paper. The Granada Hotel, Santander.

> My darling girl, I was so sorry not to see you that last night before I left, but I had to move quickly, and besides your father had made his feelings quite clear . . . Here in Spain, despite all that's going on, the weather is splendid. I would give my right arm to have you here with me now if the circumstances were better. We could run into the waves together, fall beneath them and kiss until the tide turned. How I miss you. If I close my eyes I can imagine the taste of salt on your lips, the colour of your hair in the sun's light.

Sister Veronica coughed and tutted with disdain.

The letter went on in the same soppy lovesick vein as did the next three that she picked up, but the one she held in her hand now was written in a different tone and she read intently.

> My darling, sweet girl, please, for God's sake, don't do anything rash. I know how awful this is for you and how terrible to be alone at a time like this, but you must trust me. I will stand by you. For now, though, while we are apart, you must take note of what I'm saying. You must leave Kilgerry as soon as you can. I have an address in Dublin where you will be safe. Listen to me: there's an old lady called Gerty Wiseman, one of three old sisters who lives in the place they call Jewtown. I have written to her and she awaits your arrival; she will keep you safe and take care of you until the child is born and arrange any papers that you need to get away. If necessary she will get you safely to a house in London, she'll know exactly what to do. She's spent most of her life running away and is a dab hand at it. I am leaving for Vigo tomorrow and eventually across the north of Spain and then into France, but I will contact you at Gerty's as soon as I can. Do as I say, my darling, you will be in safe hands. I am beginning to doubt my reasons for fighting in this war; I did it really for Grandpapa because he loved this country so very much. Soon, when this damned war is over, we will be together, the three of us. How lovely it is to say those words, the three of us. I beg you not to be tempted to confide in your mother, she isn't strong or well enough to stand up for you. As for your father, there are still things that you don't know. You must leave as soon as you can. There is a funny little fellow, a foreign peddler called Muli, who calls at the village occasionally, he sells notepads and pencils; he will make contact with you

soon. He's an odd-looking little man but don't be alarmed by his appearance. Put your trust in him, he will not let you down. He will get you to Gerty's. She'll sort out how to register you and the child in a new name . . . it will be easier as they won't be able to trace you. When we are together again we shall be married as soon as we are able and then we will move away, anywhere . . . now my brave girl . . .

The nun read on avidly. It all sounded very odd and far-fetched to Sister Veronica. The writer of the letter must be Padraig's father, of course. It seemed O'Mally wasn't his mother's maiden name as Sister Veronica had supposed. So she wasn't originally Maria Bridget O'Mally by birth. Who the hell was she then? And why all this nonsensical subterfuge? The two of them must have been a pair of crooks or worse. She opened another letter and read on.

My sweet one, thank God that you are safe. I'm so glad that you are well and the sickness has now passed. Soon, soon I shall be back with you and holding you in my arms. I am heading up towards Santa Eulalia; remember, where Grandpapa lived for a while. I'll gather my strength there and then make for France as soon as I can. One good thing is that I think I may have some news about your brother for you. Don't get too excited just yet, but a chap I met used to be at school with George and he's sure that he saw George in Paris in a bar in the Rue Montagne . . . Do you know I still have the army greatcoat of his that you gave to me and it's still going strong. It has his name-tag sewn into the lining even after all this time.
I digress. This chap was damned sure it was him; he saw him a second time by the Seine but then lost him.

> I'll keep my ears pinned back for any more news. Give my love to Gerty, she's a funny old stick but as honest and true as the day is long. Stay safe . . .

Sister Veronica put down the letter on top of the others and stared in front of her for a long while.

Slowly and with an increasingly shaking hand she reread the letters, and as she read she felt the blood pounding inside her head, her eyes smouldering with fury.

Sister Veronica closed her eyes and imagined herself back in the gardens of Kilgerry House, walking alongside the walled kitchen garden, then on down the path that led towards the lake. God, how she had loved that house. If things had worked out she could have been mistress of Kilgerry . . . She could still remember the heady scent of the yellow roses, the sound of drowsy bees buzzing round the sweet peas. The lazy plop of a fish in the lake.

She remembered standing, hidden in the shade of the mulberry tree; round her feet mulberries were squashed into the grass and wasps burrowed deep into their red and sticky flesh. She feels nauseous, retches, has to steady herself against the tree.

On the jetty by the boathouse a man is poised, ready to dive into the glistening lake. A splash, then circles growing ever wider across the lake. Then the excited shout of a young child jumping into the lake and surfacing moments later in the man's arms, shrieking and laughing, droplets of water reflecting rainbows of light round both their heads.

A pretty, lively child who would have been about ten then. Another picture of the child sprang to mind. Laura wearing a cream dress, her dark hair braided with tiny yellow flowers, standing in the porch of the church, the smell of fresh flowers cloyingly sweet in the cool air, outside the porch the rain falling incessantly. She remembered the sound of hurrying footsteps and fervent whispers, the girl crying inconsolably into her bouquet. Someone close by screaming hysterically.

Sister Veronica opened her eyes and stared down at the photograph. Her heart beat quickly and her hands quivered with emotion. Dear God! She knew who Padraig O'Mally was now. A mystery never solved until now and now was too many years too late.

Now she was probably the only person alive who knew the truth. That stupid clot of a girl had got herself pregnant by some irresponsible eejit who had gone off to fight a war that was no concern of his. She threw the photograph down on to her desk and closed her eyes.

Padraig O'Mally, well I never. Dear God. No wonder Padraig was such a slippery little fellow with these two as parents. He was as devious a little swine as his good-for-nothing mother.

She picked up the photograph again and stared at it for a long time.

Oh, they'd been clever all right in covering up their tracks, too clever by half.

A slow triumphant smile spread across Sister Veronica's thin lips. How her brother must have grieved for his little sister! They'd been very close those two. He would have lavished care and affection on Padraig if he'd known of his existence. How she hated that man! He was the only man who could have saved her but instead he had ruined her life! Well, the contents of this scruffy old shoebox were the only proof that Padraig O'Mally was someone else entirely. And nobody would ever find out the secret about Padraig O'Mally as long as she had breath in her body.

She yanked the photograph out of the frame, then tore it from side to side, from top to bottom, ripped it into many small pieces, stood up and threw the pieces on to the fire and watched them curl and melt and finally disappear.

As the final pieces of the photograph disintegrated there was a knock on the door, and hastily Sister Veronica tore the letters in half and tossed them into the unused cupboard. Later she'd rip them to smithereens and then she'd burn the whole damn lot so that not a trace of the truth would be left.

Nora, the Hanlons' maid, was dusting the hallway half-heartedly and earwigging at the same time. There were raised voices coming from the drawing room and she hovered close to the door but far enough away to make her escape into the kitchen if it was suddenly opened.

'Well, James, do you have any idea where Siobhan is at this very moment?' Hetty Hanlon asked her husband.

'No, my dear, I am afraid I do not.'

'I thought not, because most of the time she's gadding about across the countryside like a perishing tinker child.'

'Don't exaggerate, Hetty, she's just a normal child, a very curious and imaginative child. There is nothing wrong with her, she gets on well with people from all walks of life, that's all.'

'And what is that supposed to mean?'

'That unlike you, Hetty, she has put no barriers up against the world. If she likes someone it doesn't matter to her which side of the tracks they are from.'

'Well, while you may be happy with her hobnobbing with all and sundry, I am not. All I want is for her to move in the right circles.'

'Well, soon she'll be in the convent learning how to be a bloody lady. Isn't that what you wanted all along?'

'Will you mind your tongue. At least she'll learn manners and deportment, how to conduct herself.'

'Yes, Sister, no, Sister, three bags full, Sister. She'll wear her knees out with praying. Walking with a book on her head and curtseying to the Sister Superior.'

'She'll have a good education.'

'No, Hetty, she'll have a mediocre bloody education. And, Hetty, I am sick of minding my tongue. I am sick of walking on damned eggshells in this house.'

'Are you now? Well, are you aware of what she's gone and done now?'

'I am not but I dare say you are about to tell me.'

'She's been telling that dopey child Sinead Cullinane that the Black Jew has a child locked up in his house against her will. James, Siobhan is a born liar and now Mrs Cullinane has told Miss Drew and they've both gone marching off up to St Joseph's parading Sinead as a paragon of virtue for confessing all she knew.'

'And your point is?'

'That she makes things up to make life more lively and sometimes I'm not sure that she's quite right in the head.'

'For God's sake, that's our child you're talking about.'

'Well, sometimes I feel that I hardly had a part in creating her.'

'I can assure you, my dear, that you did. I was there, you remember, when she came into the world.'

'Something I'd rather forget.'

'Well, as it happens Siobhan is not lying. He does have a child in the house.'

'What?'

'He does have a child in his house.'

'You mean it's true and you knew all along?'

'I did.'

'How, may I ask?'

'Because he swore me to secrecy when he called me up there to take a look at her.'

'And you never thought to mention it to the authorities?'

'He didn't want me to.'

'He didn't want you to! And I've sent Miss Drew and Mrs Cullinane away with a flea in their ears, telling them that they must be mistaken, that Sinead is a compulsive liar! And you, you're a doctor, for God's sake, and he probably has the child held there against her will.'

'Poppycock! The child was in very good health. He's taking good care of her.'

'Good care of her! A single man on his own with a child! It's not right, not right at all.'

'Well, God forbid! If you were to be taken off tomorrow I'd have to take care of Siobhan, wouldn't I?'

'And you'd manage?'

'Of course I'd manage. Men are not completely brainless when it comes to looking after children.'

Hetty Hanlon gave a high-pitched laugh.

'Now that I'd like to see! Without my discipline she'd be running amok!'

'Well, according to you she is already!'

'And where in God's holy name did this child come from?'

Dr Hanlon swallowed hard.

'That I don't know and neither does he. It's a mystery. Someone sent her to him with a label round her neck.'

'You'll be telling me next that the stork dropped her out of the sky, or maybe the leprechauns fetched her. God almighty, were you born yesterday?'

'Anyway, it's none of our business.'

'Ah well, I dare say Sister Veronica will think differently.'

'She, the old bitch, can think what she likes.'

'Don't speak of her like that. She's a good woman. Maybe she's a bit harsh but those children need discipline.'

'They need love! They need to be allowed to speak and make sense of what's happened to them. Knocking the fear of God into them does nothing to help, Hetty. It just makes them hard and bitter.'

'In my book Sister Veronica is a saint.'

'Sister Veronica is a sad and twisted individual. Her only vocation is to display cruelty and disdain to those who can't fight back!'

Hetty Hanlon stood speechless, staring at her husband and wondering whether he'd taken leave of his senses. He'd never dared to speak to her like that before. Or say such terrible things about the holy sisters. What the hell had got into him? Before she could find the words to reply, Dr Hanlon walked from the room and slammed the door, glaring at Nora, who had tripped over a broom and was lying helpless and flustered on the hallway floor. He slammed the front door with an unusual savagery and hurried down to Donahue's.

Siobhan was hiding in the thick bushes at the bottom of the drive that led up to St Joseph's. Donny had gone reluctantly ahead to check that the coast was clear. Now she was all alone she didn't feel quite so brave. Why hadn't she kept her big mouth shut?

She was wobbly with excitement and fear. Hell's bells, if the pair of them got caught there'd be bloody ructions.

'Hurry up, Donny. Donny, hurry up,' she muttered under her breath.

She listened out for any noise, the telltale squeak of a nun's shoes. She could hear the sound of cautious footsteps approaching along the gravel drive. Shit! What if it was one of the nuns? The leaves rustled.

'Donny, Donny, is that you?'

Donny's bloodless face peeped through the greenery.

'Are you sure you want to do this, Siobhan?'

'Yep,' she lied convincingly.

'We've to go in through the side door and hide in the laundry, check that no one is about, and then we'll get in proper.'

'What will they do if they catch us?'

Donny pulled his finger across his throat and grimaced.

Siobhan shivered.

'Wait there until I whistle. Like this.'

He whistled. It was a feeble little whistle.

'Can't you do it a bit louder? You sound like a sparrow with a sore throat.'

'Just keep your ears open and your eyes skinned. When you hear the whistle, run like hell to the next bush and then wait for the next whistle. Sister Agatha is out in the garden somewhere killing snails, so be careful, for God's sake.'

Donny scuttled off.

Siobhan waited. And waited. Damn and buggery buggery! She was dying to pee. Bursting. She clamped her knees close together. She tried not to think about it. That was worse. She jigged up and down on the spot. No good. Desperate now. She lifted her dress. Pulled her drawers down quick, slipped out one leg. Crouched down.

If she was in the convent in London she'd have pissed herself by now. She'd have at least two pairs of drawers to get off.

Sweet relief.

She liked peeing out of doors. The feel of the cool air on your bum. She peed a trickle and then a flood. Pissed like a mountain pony.

Donny's feeble little whistle barely made it over the sound of her peeing.

Bloody Nora. She shook herself off, stuck her leg back in her drawers and whipped them up quick.

Creeping out of the bush, she kept close to the edge of the drive, ten strides and then she threw herself behind a tree. She was breathing like a train and her heart was thumping wildly.

Another feeble whistle.

Same thing to the next bush.

The sound of someone singing tunelessly in the gardens, the sickening crunch of a snail shell beneath a cruel heel.

Then Donny grabbing her hand and pulling her out of the bush.

'Come on. Quick, get behind the shed over there. I'll go inside and make sure there's no one prowling around.'

'Okay. Say, Donny, are you scared?'

'Yep.'

'Me too.'

Siobhan, holding on to Donny's sticky little hand, stepped inside St Joseph's for the first time in her life. The smell hit her like a tidal wave. The place stank of cabbage and old custard skin, of strong soap, damp walls and rotting linoleum all mixed up with holy-smelling polish and incense.

Donny pulled her along a dingy corridor, through a door into the laundry, and there they stood with their backs against the door for several moments, struggling to catch their breath.

'Is this where Sister Immaculata used to work?'

'Yep. She always had to do all the dirty jobs.'

'God, it's spooky in here, Donny. What if her ghost is hanging around?'

'Pack it in, Siobhan, you're just imagining it. There's no one here, only us. And she wouldn't harm a hair of your head anyway.'

He didn't sound too convinced to Siobhan.

'Where do we go now?'

'Inside that cupboard over there. According to what Padraig said we crawl along a bit and there's a big hole at the back we can squeeze through to get into the cupboards inside Sister Veronica's study.'

'Are you sure, Donny?'

'I'm positive. Remember, Padraig told me he used to get out through the study window in the middle of the night.'

'Come on then, Donny, before I change my mind. It's now or never, I'm shaking that much.'

'You are scared then?'

'No, I'm feckin' terrified!'

Donny put his finger to his lips.

'I can hear someone. Quick.'

The blood drained from Siobhan's cheeks until she was the colour of chalk. Donny took hold of her hand and pulled her into the cupboard just as the laundry door opened.

They peeped through the crack in the door. Sister Agatha had come into the room and was looking round suspiciously, sniffing as though there was cat shite about.

Donny held his breath, squeezing Siobhan's hand tightly. They watched as the nun turned to go, turned back and sniffed the air again. Then with relief they watched the door close with a soft click.

'God!' said Siobhan. 'She looked a right old bag. Like old Nick himself dressed up in a nun's habit.'

Donahue was talking to Michael Leary when Dr Hanlon stepped inside the bar.

'Dr Hanlon,' said Donahue with surprise.

'Hello, Marty. A Guinness please, one for yourself and whatever Michael's having.'

'Thanks, Doctor, a Guinness if I may.'

'And yourself, Marty?'

'No, thanks all the same.'

Dr Hanlon raised his eyebrows.

'On the wagon,' Michael Leary said.

'Dear God, that's a miracle in itself.'

'It's not like you to be drinking in the day, Doctor.'

'Needs must when the devil drives . . .'

'Michael was just showing me a postcard he had from Spain,' said Donahue. 'Have a look at this.'

> Dear Mr Leary, having the time of my life. Stayed in some funny places. No sign of the Irish virgin but still looking. Miss Carmichael has learned to smile and Father D. drinks wine like it's going out of fashion. Taken loads of photos, bought a sketchpad. Off to the monastery today. Best wishes, Padraig O. Give my love to Sister Immaculata and Donny. Say hello to Siobhan but no kisses!

'God, he doesn't know about the nun's death yet. They were close those two by all accounts. Still, at least it sounds like he's enjoying it out there; let's hope he makes the most of it, it'll be the last holiday he'll have in a long time,' said Donahue.

'Poor little bugger.'

'What's up with you, Leary? Look like you've swallowed a bloody wasp,' Dr Hanlon said.

'Bit of bad news, that's all, on the female front, nothing I want to talk about. I was just thinking about Padraig. He's been offered a free place at the Abbey, you know, and that old bitch up at St Joseph's won't let him go. Willy Flanagan just rang me to tell me.'

'You're not surprised, though, are you? She'd never let him go there. Michael, that's not the Willy Flanagan who does all those mucky paintings?'

'One and the same, Donahue, but they are not mucky paintings. The human body is not a mucky thing.'

'Ah, well, a grown man drawing pictures of people's mickeys and women's thingummyjigs is not quite right in the head in my book.'

'Dear God, Donahue, your book would make a fascinating read!'

'Well I've heard that that Flanagan is one of them momosapiens.'

Dr Hanlon and Michael Leary spluttered into their Guinness.

'Donahue, you are bloody priceless.'

Donahue scratched his head and muttered, 'Well, it's not natural in my book . . .'

'Well, I pray to God you write this book one day, Donahue, it'll be a bestseller!'

'Ah, bollocks to the pair of you!' said Donahue. 'Anyhow, what will you do now the school is to close? Have you applied for another job yet, Michael?'

'I've applied for a couple of jobs, but I don't really fancy them myself. I don't know, something'll turn up I dare say.'

'It's going to be a dead place round here when St Joseph's closes,' Donahue said.

'Sure it'll be full of old codgers waiting to pop their clogs.'

'It won't be the same as having kids about the place.'

'Siobhan'll be lost in the holidays.'

'When does she go away to school?'

'The day after tomorrow.'

'You'll miss her.'

'I will that.'

'Can't she just go to school in Cork and come home weekends?'

'She could but her mother has other ideas. Hetty was at this posh school in London and says she met all sorts. The higher echelons of society, would you believe? Hetty also went off to a finishing school in Paris. That's where she got all her fancy ideas from and it's what she has in mind for Siobhan.'

'No offence but I can't imagine Siobhan in a finishing school,' Donahue said with a grin.

'She'd finish the buggers off all right, single-handedly,' replied Dr Hanlon smiling.

'She's bright that daughter of yours, she needs to be challenged.'

'I know that, Michael. But you can't argue with Hetty. She says she'll meet a grand set of girls from good families at the convent in London. When Hetty was there she was hobnobbing with all sorts. Spanish nobility, Italian princesses . . . One of the Spanish girls used to have all her clothes sent over from Paris.'

'They must have been millionaires.'

'Hetty and the Spanish girl were good friends, but when they were in the finishing school in Paris she had a fling with an unsuitable chap and the mother whisked her away. Hetty wrote to her loads of times but never got an answer.'

'Probably married with a castle full of kids by now,' Donahue said.

'I dare say. Anyway, Siobhan is in the shite at the moment.'

'How's that?'

'I'm afraid somehow she found out about the kid up at Solly Benjamin's house.'

'A kid?' said Donahue. 'I thought he had a bit of stuff up there.'

'No, that was all just gossip.'

Leary and Donahue listened mesmerized as Dr Hanlon told them the little he knew about the child.

'So where does Siobhan come into all this?'

'You know what she's like, she's a nosy little sod putting

her beak into other people's business. She saw the child, and apparently Padraig had seen her too in the Dark Wood. Anyhow, she told Sinead about her and blabber-mouth told her mammy and now they're off up to St Joseph's to see Sister Veronica.'

'Why, what can Sister Veronica do?' Leary asked suddenly.

'Anything she likes. She'll get the kid taken off him without a doubt.'

'P'r'aps that's for the best.'

'No. She's transformed him, that child, I've never seen the fellow looking so happy. It must have been a lonely old life living there all by himself. Ah, well, there'll be all hell up now.'

Suddenly the door opened and the three men turned to look at the newcomer. A small swarthy man, no bigger than a jockey, stood framed in the doorway.

'Come in,' said Donahue. 'We don't bite until the moon is full.'

The man grinned and walked jauntily across to the bar.

'Would you be wanting a drink?'

'I could murder a Guinness.'

A stranger in Ballygurry was an interesting occasion.

'Have you come on the train?' Dr Hanlon asked, knowing full well there was no train on this particular day.

'No. I came off the boat yesterday and hitched a couple of lifts, one from a halfwit of a farmer and then a couple of flatulent nuns.'

'I've never heard of the Flatulent order, are they French?'

Leary snorted into his beer.

The newcomer looked at Donahue as if he had a screw missing.

'Will you be staying long?'

'Until I finish me pint.'

Donahue giggled.

'Would that be an English accent?' he asked.

'London, mate, north of the river.'

'Have you friends here in Ballygurry?'

'Nope. I'm not staying. I've come to pick up a kid.'

The three men stared at him in amazement.

'What sort of a kid?'

'The usual type.'

'With horns?' asked Donahue.

The man looked askance at Donahue.

'A kid. My kid,' he spluttered into his pint, 'not a bleeding goat.'

He downed the rest of his pint swiftly.

'Cheers,' he said, 'I needed that.'

The bell jingled above the door as the man left.

'Ah well, he seemed a nice enough chap for an Englishman. Let's hope he gets to the kid before Sister Veronica and her band of washerwomen.'

'Will we go up and have a look?' said Donahue.

'Can't. I've a surgery to start,' said Dr Hanlon. 'And if Miss Drew comes in one more time to show me her bruises I may be tempted to end it all myself.'

Sister Agatha showed an excited Miss Drew and a flustered Mrs Cullinane into Sister Veronica's study. Miss Drew looked with interest at Sister Veronica. The nun was usually so composed in a chilly kind of way but now she looked positively rattled. Her hands were shaking and there were two spots of high colour on her cheeks.

Mrs Cullinane, hiding behind Miss Drew, was wishing fervently that she hadn't come at all and began to bob up and down on the spot anxiously.

Miss Drew was the first to speak.

'Sister Veronica, I know how very busy you must be and

I'm sorry to bother you but with Father Daley being away we didn't quite know where to turn.'

'Spit it out, Miss Drew, I haven't all day.'

Miss Drew flinched and continued.

'The first thing is that while I was away I learned something. Such a shock to me it was, but I feel I have to tell someone. Mrs Cullinane here agrees with me.'

Mrs Cullinane nodded her head anxiously and blushed.

'What is it, Miss Drew?'

'It's to do with Miss Nancy Carmichael. The thing is, Sister, by pure chance I came across a letter belonging to her by accident while we were away. Shocking, it was, quite shocking . . .'

'Get on with it, Miss Drew.'

'Well,' said Miss Drew with barely concealed glee, 'have you ever heard of a place called Kilgerry up Ross-macconnarty way?'

Sister Veronica stared unblinkingly at Miss Drew.

Miss Drew noticed that the pulse in Sister Veronica's neck raced feverishly.

'No, I'm afraid I have not.'

'Well, Miss Carmichael's mother used to work there as the nanny to the posh family.'

Sister Veronica swallowed hard.

'What has that to do with anything?' she asked impatiently.

'Well, you'd hardly believe it but Nancy Carmichael is illegitimate and you'll never guess who her father was . . .'

Miss Drew tailed off.

'Oh, I think I can,' said Sister Veronica quietly. She leaned heavily on the table, breathing hard. Her face was puce and beads of sweat bubbled on her top lip.

Miss Drew was delighted with the nun's reaction. Sister Veronica was absolutely livid, with a face on her like she'd explode. Serve Nancy Carmichael right for letting her come all the way home on her own.

Sister Veronica's head was in a spin. God Almighty! What else was she going to hear today? She'd had just about as much as she could stand.

To Miss Drew's dismay, she said no more but eventually straightened up and looked across at her. Sister Veronica steeled herself, drew herself up to her full height. She'd had quite enough shocks for one day. She could barely think straight.

'There was something else I believe that you wanted to tell me, Miss Drew?' she said distractedly.

It was dusty inside the cupboard where Donny and Siobhan were huddled together in fright. It was dark and smelled of mice and mildew.

Donny whispered to Siobhan, 'Siobhan, what's illegitimate mean?'

'Sure I don't know. It's some sort of incurable disease I expect.'

'Mrs Cullinane has heard some very shocking news, very shocking indeed,' said Miss Drew in a breathy croak. 'She wanted, well, we thought, that you should be the first to hear all about it.'

'What is it, Miss Drew?' Sister Veronica said, giving her a withering glance.

'It seems Siobhan Hanlon, who as you know is a meddlesome little devil, has told Mrs Cullinane's Sinead a secret that she made her promise not to tell on pain of having her teeth pulled out with pliers.'

In the cupboard Siobhan grabbed Donny's arm. 'Bloody cheek! When I get out of here I'll piss in her bran tub! And I'll kill Sinead,' she said through clenched teeth.

'Siobhan Hanlon is a proverbial pain in the neck. I fervently hope that the nuns in London will instil some discipline into the child. I think Dr Hanlon spoils her, myself.'

Siobhan nudged Donny in the ribs. 'Cheeky old bitch,' she hissed.

'Well, the thing is, Sinead, being a sensible girl, has told her mother the secret.'

'Sensible!' sniffed Siobhan. 'She's as thick as a donkey's dick.'

'And pray what is this enormous secret?'

'The Black Jew has a young girl locked up in his house against her will.'

'It's hardly news, Miss Drew.'

Miss Drew blushed.

'Ah, well, the thing is we all thought it was a young woman but according to Siobhan it's not at all, it's a little girl that he has trapped in there.'

'And how does Siobhan know all this?'

'Well, apparently she says that she saw them together up in that glass thing in the roof. And that Padraig had seen her too and he said she had a rosary, so she must be a Catholic.'

'Padraig O'Mally!' Sister Veronica spat out his name.

'Yes, Sister.'

'I might have known he'd be involved.'

'She hates Padraig,' Donny whispered.

'She hates everyone,' Siobhan replied.

'Where in God's name did this child come from? He's been living up there on his own for years.'

'I don't know, Sister, but it's all very odd, if you ask me.'

'We must go up there,' declared Sister Veronica, 'and ascertain if it's the truth. And if it is we shall take steps to remove the child and bring her to the safety of St Joseph's.'

'The three of us?' said Mrs Cullinane, and there was a quiver of fear in her voice.

'I'll phone the bishop first and tell him what we're going to do. But I for one, Mrs Cullinane, am not afraid of Solly Benjamin. There is great evil afoot in this village at the moment and we, the soldiers of Christ, must be brave! We have a child to rescue, a Catholic child by the sound of it.'

In the cupboard Siobhan clutched Donny's hand tightly.

'This is all because of me and my big mouth!' she whispered. 'We have to get there first and warn him.'

Donny nodded reluctantly. Siobhan thought that he looked as if he was about to be sick.

Solly Benjamin was sitting in a wicker chair under the horse chestnut tree in the garden. Beside him on a plaid rug Dancey Amati was playing happily with an old saucepan and a few old spoons.

Occasionally, Solly glanced down at her. She was a contented child and played happily for hours on her own. This was her favourite game, making pretend soup.

Dancey whispered quietly to herself, 'Take a fistful of garbanzos.'

She wandered over to the drive, picked up a pile of gravel and laid it on the rug.

'A clutch of white beans.'

For beans she had selected a mixture of odd-shaped white pebbles.

'Two wide-brimmed hatfuls of spring water.' Water from the garden tap had to do. For olive oil she squeezed the sap from buttercup petals.

Slivers of monastery beef were wrinkled leaves that she picked from the flowerbeds.

Honesty leaves for silvery garlic.

The tomato was a red rubber ball she had found close to the high wall.

She picked dandelion leaves with care, and though she didn't know which way was west she had a guess.

She put all her ingredients into the saucepan and stirred them thoroughly with a stout stick she found lying in the grass.

Dancey looked up at Solly and smiled. She had a wonderful smile that transformed her whole face. Solly wondered had she played this game in her previous life. She stood up now and wandered round the garden carefully examining clumps of dandelions. She had a thing about dandelions. She came back to the rug and placed the dandelion leaves she had selected carefully in the saucepan along with the other ingredients.

Now came the cooking. She had made a pretend fireplace from large stones she had gathered from round the garden. She put the saucepan on top of the fire and sat cross-legged, occasionally lifting the lid and peering inside.

After a while she picked up the saucepan, spooned the liquid and pebbles into two cups and held one up for Solly. At this point he always joined in the game and smelled the soup, smiled with appreciation and pretended to drink it.

He was just about to take a pretend mouthful when he was startled by a shout.

'Hey, mister! Over here!'

Solly looked up from his soup and was flabbergasted to see two small children standing on top of the high wall that bordered the Dark Wood. They were jumping up and down and waving at him madly.

He squinted in the bright sunlight. One of them was Siobhan Hanlon. The other one a little boy who looked terrified out of his wits.

'Hey, mister!' Siobhan yelled. 'Come quick!'

Solly stood up and hurried over towards the wall.

'What is it? Are you safe or is there a grizzly bear after the pair of you?'

'I'm real sorry and it's all my fault,' said the girl.

'What is?'

'I told them you'd a child up here and they're coming to get her. I'm real sorry, mister.'

Just at that moment the gates to the garden opened with a clank and rattle and Solly stared towards them in dismay.

The big beefy nun from St Joseph's was striding purposefully up the path, followed by the ferrety woman from the sweet shop and a petrified-looking Mrs Cullinane. Bringing up the rear was a thin-faced nun with a smug smile.

Dancey stood up in alarm and knocked the saucepan of soup all over the plaid rug.

She ran across to Solly and took hold of his hand.

'Feckin' hell!' shrieked Siobhan. 'We're too late, Donny, the old bitches are here. Scarper!'

Siobhan, in panic, grabbed hold of Donny by the arm. There was a screech and the sound of rustling leaves as she pulled him off the wall and they plunged headlong into the Dark Wood.

Solly thought that they looked like two angels falling from grace. Listening for the sound of breaking bones, he was relieved to hear the crashing of undergrowth as they fled through the wood.

Then he turned to face the delegation of hard-faced women who were marching up the gravel drive towards him and Dancey.

Sister Agatha waylaid Siobhan and Donny as they crept out of the Dark Wood. She took hold of an ear of each of them and yanked them across the road and up the drive towards the orphanage. Siobhan squealed and struggled to escape but Donny went quietly, speechless with fear.

Sister Agatha dragged them in through the front door and down the dingy, reeking corridor. Beneath her habit her keys clanked as though she were a jailer taking prisoners to the dungeons. She opened the door to Sister Veronica's study and pushed the pair of them roughly into the room.

A clock on the wall flinched and yelped a dissonant chime, pulled itself up short and ground to a halt.

Siobhan and Donny stood side by side on the rug. Siobhan shivered and glanced sideways at Donny. The state on him! Shite! His knees were banging together and his teeth were chattering so loudly they sounded like castanets being played by a drunk. Oh, hell's bells, it was all her stupid fault. She should never have dared him to get into the cupboard.

Siobhan stood stiff backed, biting her lip, her sweaty hands clasped in front of her as she looked up and up at the enormous nun.

'What do you think you were doing, Donny Keegan?'

'T-t-trying t-to warn him,' he stammered.

'And why may I ask?'

Donny tried to speak but couldn't get the words up over his quivering tonsils.

'We were trying to warn the Black— S-Solly Benjamin that you were coming for the little girl,' said Siobhan.

'You speak when you're spoken to, my girl!'

'There's no point asking a boy to speak when he's too afraid to open his mouth.'

With that Sister Veronica slammed her fist down on to the table and Siobhan jumped in fright. An old cat who had been happily perched on the window-sill woke with a start, arched his back and spat in alarm.

Donny Keegan gulped. Siobhan sucked in her breath with a whistling sound.

'Well, your silly prank will backfire, Miss Clever Clogs, because very soon the guards will arrive and the child will be brought here to me.'

'Won't that be just grand for her?' muttered Siobhan.

Why doesn't she keep her big mouth shut? Donny thought, but there was no point hoping, Siobhan always did what she thought was right.

'I would dearly like to slap that silly face of yours, Siobhan Hanlon, for God only knows you're in need of a good hiding, but when I've finished with Donny Keegan I'll have your mother up here and let's hope she'll knock some sense into you.'

Then she lifted a leather strap from a nail on the wall and slashed it down across the table. A china statue of a saint on the bookshelf leaped up in the air and landed with a clatter.

Siobhan was frightened almost witless but dying to laugh at the same time. Sister Veronica was off her rocker, nutty as a feckin' fruit cake.

'Hold out your hand, Donny Keegan.'

Donny flinched.

His tiny dirty outstretched hand shook. Siobhan glanced across at his face. His eyes were wide and his eyelashes glittered with tears, his chin was wobbling with fear.

Siobhan bit the insides of her mouth. She closed her eyes each time the strap was raised and winced as the leather made contact with the soft flesh of Donny's little hand.

Siobhan felt misery and fury ballooning up inside her at the unfairness of it all. She swallowed hard. Donny's hand erupted in lines of angry red weals. He was desperately trying to hold back his tears but he couldn't. His nostrils bubbled with snot and tears began to run unchecked, making tributaries of grime on his grubby face.

As Sister Veronica raised the strap again, there was a great banging on the study door.

'Wait!' screeched the nun. But the door opened and then seconds later all hell broke loose.

When the women had marched back down the drive Solly Benjamin had taken the child inside the house and bolted all the doors. He was paralysed with indecision and panic. Dancey was white with shock and would not leave his side. Solly tried his utmost to keep calm; he didn't want to alarm the child but he wasn't sure what to do next. He'd no doubt that Sister Veronica meant what she'd said about calling out the guards and having Dancey removed to St Joseph's. He didn't have a leg to stand on, either. He had no proof of who the girl was or what she was doing there.

He hadn't liked the look of Sister Veronica at all. She was a big domineering bully of a woman. No wonder that little Padraig had wanted to get out of there.

Solly knew that he had to make plans, but for the moment he was unable to make a rational decision. He thought of ringing Uncle Sammy in London but he wouldn't be able to help from that far away. Maybe, though, if he could get to Uncle Sammy's he'd know what to do for the best. One thing was for sure, he wasn't putting her in the care of those vile beings at St Joseph's.

Oh God! Someone surely would have made contact if they wanted the child back. Why the hell hadn't they?

Hurriedly he packed a travelling bag with essentials. He had plenty of cash on him and access to money was no problem. He began to pack the child's clothes in another bag but when he turned round she was standing there silently looking at him, holding her battered brown suitcase out towards him. He kneeled down and spoke to her even though he knew she couldn't understand a word of what he said. He tried desperately to sound confident and in control.

'I don't know if you can understand any of this, Dancey,

but I promise you that I am going to keep you safe. I know you are afraid but please don't be. We'll go away for a while just the two of us. Trust me, Dancey.'

And he held the child close, feeling the beat of both their hearts.

In her bedroom Siobhan lay on her belly and smiled grimly through her tears. Mammy had paddled her arse with the hairbrush when she'd got her home from St Joseph's. But that was nothing to the way those bloody cows had thrashed little Donny Keegan. Still, hadn't he had the last laugh!

Sister Veronica's door had burst open just as the strap made contact with Donny's hand. Jeez, it was like something out of a film except it wasn't in black and white.

'What in God's name do you think you're doing bursting in here uninvited?' Sister Veronica had screeched.

'I've come for my son, Donny Keegan,' the tiny glowering man in the doorway had said.

Honest to God. Just like that.

That's when Donny had fainted.

Out like a bloody light. Face down on the mat and arse towards heaven.

Siobhan giggled just thinking about it, and winced. God, her own arse was hurting but it had been worth it. Padraig would have loved it. Oh, you should have seen Sister Veronica's face. Bloody lovely it was! And the air in the room was blue. Donny's dad could swear like . . . like a bloody good swearer.

'Get your hands off that child! What's a bloody big lump of a woman doing battering a small child like that? You're nothing but a bleeding savage. He's been through enough already. Touch him once more and woman or not I'll put you flat on your bleeding arse!'

For a minute Siobhan had been worried because Sister Veronica was enormous and could probably have pasted the daylights out of the fellow, but she was so shocked at the interruption that she just stood with her trap open, feet splayed and the pulse in her neck doing overtime.

Holy hell, it had been marvellous!

Lying there on her bed as daylight faded Siobhan suddenly remembered the papers in her pocket. While she and Donny had been in the cupboard at St Joseph's she'd stretched out her hand and found a pile of papers. Unable to see what they were in the dark, she'd slipped them into the pocket of her skirt.

She got up from the bed now and pulled out the papers from her pocket. They looked like letters that had been ripped up.

Outside her room a floorboard creaked. Shite! Mammy on the prowl. If she got caught with a pile of stolen letters she'd have another pasting. She hurried across to her school trunk, bent down and slipped the letters carefully into a rip in the lining of the trunk, covering it with a pile of regulation pants and itchy-looking vests.

Solly wondered how long it would take for the Guarda to get to Nirvana House? They'd have to come from Rossmacconnarty, which was a good hour away. An hour! He'd never do it. How he wished now that he'd learned to drive and bought himself a car.

Outside the sun was sinking fast and golden-winged gulls screamed and soared in the last red light before night fell on Ballygurry. At least soon they'd have darkness on their side. If they made their escape through the Dark Wood, they could come out further down the road closer to the station. Maybe someone, a stranger, would pass through in a car, a tractor, anything.

They made it past the station and down to the crossroads, turned right towards Rossmacconnarty. They had travelled about a half-mile or so down the road when they heard the sound of an engine. Seconds later a black car overtook them.

Further down the road the car turned round and Solly and Dancey were blinded by the glare of headlamps. There was a shout and the sound of car doors slamming. Two men in dark clothes leaped out of the car and ran towards them.

Solly Benjamin bowed his head in despair and held tightly on to Dancey's hand.

Part Four

Santa Eulalia

The Ballygurry pilgrims were over three hours late arriving at the monastery of Santa Eulalia. The storm that had raged fiercely for most of the day had passed and the night air was fresh and cool.

The mule cart wound its way slowly up the steep mountain track. Padraig, who had slept for most of the journey, with his head resting in Father Daley's lap, was jolted from sleep as the cart hit a bump in the road.

'We're nearly there, Padraig,' Father Daley said and yawned tiredly. 'Just around the next bend.'

Padraig sat up and rubbed his eyes. Pale moonlight drizzled the track and he was aware that they were passing through a small cluster of dilapidated houses. A donkey brayed fretfully somewhere close by and a dog ran out of the darkness, barked lackadaisically at them as they passed by and then disappeared back into the shadows.

As they passed the last of the tumbledown houses a figure loomed out of the darkness on their left.

'What's that?' asked Miss Carmichael fearfully.

Father Daley spoke to the driver in Spanish.

'It's all right, the driver said don't worry. It's only the

statue of the Blue Madonna. He says in olden times it was famous and people came from miles around to put prayer requests at her feet but they don't much now.'

'Would you ask him how long it's been there?' Padraig asked sleepily.

'Hundreds of years apparently.'

Padraig looked eagerly at the shadowy statue. Its eyes gleamed eerily in the silvery moonlight. In the morning he would find his way back down here but after all the excitement at Camiga this morning all he wanted to do now was eat and sleep.

'Santa Eulalia!' the driver announced, turning his head to address them.

High above them on a rocky perch above the deep river valley, the monastery of Santa Eulalia was cocooned in moonlight, a swathe of mist drifting around the crumbling turrets.

'Wow!' said Padraig sleepily. 'Would you look at that!'

'A bit spooky don't you think? Like Dracula's castle,' said Miss Carmichael with a nervous giggle.

'Oooooo,' said Padraig making ghostly movements with his arms.

Miss Carmichael giggled and ruffled his hair fondly. She was getting used to Padraig O'Mally, he wasn't such a bad little fellow when you got to know him.

Padraig looked up at the monastery and shivered. It was beautiful enough to knock the breath out of you, but awesome too.

The mule cart climbed more slowly now and after several minutes turned into a deserted cobbled courtyard. A dog howled mournfully from a broken-down barn and bats sliced silently through the air above their heads.

Pulling up outside a large wooden door, the three pilgrims clambered stiffly down from the cart.

Padraig was the first to notice the bell-pull in the wall next to the enormous door. He tugged it heartily, then leaped back in alarm as a large grille set into the door opened instantly and an impish face popped out at him, like a cuckoo in a clock.

'*Hola! Bienvenue!* Come in, come in.'

A small wiry monk opened the door and greeted the weary pilgrims excitedly.

'I am Brother Bernardo. I have welcome to give for you and food also, if you follow me, you must be starved!'

He led them across a high-ceilinged, stone-flagged hallway lit only by spluttering candles set into niches in the uneven walls.

Padraig stopped and sniffed the air curiously. The monastery smells reminded him of Sister Immaculata; camphor and candle wax and old age. He'd really missed Sister Immaculata; she was one of the few things he did miss about St Joseph's.

'Come on, Padraig, pick your feet up,' Father Daley called out, and Padraig hurried to catch up.

Brother Bernardo showed them into the refectory and soon they were seated at one of several large scrubbed wooden tables. Brother Bernardo brought them earthenware jugs of wine and water, fresh bread and black-rinded cheese; large oddly shaped tomatoes and slivers of red onions. He set before them a bowl of sweet grapes and furry-skinned peaches.

As Padraig ate hungrily he looked round the room with interest. There were large paintings hung on the walls and not the sort you'd expect in a monastery. There were big colourful canvases similar to the ones Mr Leary had in the schoolhouse back in Ballygurry, only these looked like they'd been done by a child. There were also sketches of faces done in charcoal, and half-naked bodies of men and women. It was difficult to get a really good look in the candlelight but in the morning he'd look at them properly.

The pilgrims ate their feast hungrily and even Miss Carmichael drank two glasses of red wine. Padraig noticed that within minutes it had brought the blood to her cheeks and a sparkle to her eyes. She was getting more like a human being by the day.

Brother Bernardo spoke good English and he seemed happy to practise it on them.

'You,' said the smiling brother, 'are first pilgrim in many year. We welcome very well and hopes you tells everyone this is good place to stay. Then maybe we make lots of money and don't have to close, eh?'

The pilgrims nodded in agreement.

'Why would you have to close, Brother?' asked Father Daley.

'Not many monks left now, most very old and Santa Eulalia is not owned by us, belongs to an old lady, Isabella Martinez. The monastery now it needs many repairs and is not self-sufficient any more. When the old lady dies, who knows what will happen to us?'

'That's awful sad,' said Padraig. 'I think it's just real lovely here.'

'I understand that you know Michael Leary?' Brother Bernardo enquired.

'Indeed,' Father Daley replied. 'He's Padraig's teacher.'

'He was very good friend with Brother Francisco but today Francisco has gone with a man to hear confession of our benefactor, a very sick woman. She's a distant relation of Brother Francisco. When she dies that could be it for us here.'

'Carlos Emanuel came here yesterday to collect Brother Francisco, didn't he?'

'Yes, funny little man. Very impatients. Can't wait minutes but wants to be gone.'

'Mr Leary got shot when he was staying here, didn't he?' Padraig asked eagerly.

Brother Bernardo looked nonplussed.

'An old monk thought he was a pig and shot him . . .'

'Oh, *sí*, Brother Anselm. Big hunter in his day. He very eccentric. Bad shot with gun but he don't use one no more. Too old now, thank the good Lord.'

Then he rattled on in excited Spanish and Padraig and Nancy had to wait patiently for Father Daley to translate.

'He says that Michael Leary was here for quite a while at the end of the war. He was a great help to the monks. A comical chap, always on the look-out for some lost statue. Brother Anselm thinks he was a bit strange in the head. He used to drive Brother Anselm mad with all his questions about the statue.'

'That's because one of the monks who lost the statue was his ancestor and he wants to find out all about it,' said Padraig.

Brother Bernardo went on to tell them that Michael Leary had just left when the other Englishman came.

'Rosendo, a man who lives down in the hamlet, found him and brought him here. He was a young man who had been wounded in the fighting down south; he was trying to cross back into France and make his way home. He's buried here, the poor man, down in the graveyard. The monks wrote to his family but no one ever wrote back or came to see the grave. He was from same country as you.'

'What was he called?' Father Daley asked even though it was hardly likely that they would know the man.

'George. Let me think, that's it, George Fitzallen.'

Nancy Carmichael drew in her breath and turned quite white.

'Are you all right?' said Padraig with concern.

'Yes, yes, I just swallowed my wine too fast, that's all.'

It seemed to Nancy that she could never be free from the damned Fitzallen family; why even here in the middle of nowhere she couldn't escape them.

Although Nancy seemed to lose her appetite at that point, Padraig and Father Daley ate their fill.

Brother Bernardo led them back through the flickering hallway, up a steep winding staircase and along a narrow corridor.

The monk carried a candelabrum and the shadows of the pilgrims writhed eerily along the whitewashed walls.

Padraig had the horrible feeling that someone was behind him; a frisson of fear caught him between his shoulder blades. Turning his head slowly he saw the lurking shadow, a bent-backed thing close to the top of the stairway. There one minute and gone the next. Padraig shook his head, rubbed his tired eyes and yawned.

Then as they passed an open doorway he caught sight of an old monk lying prostrate on a bed. Padraig stopped and peered nervously into the room.

The monk lay as still as a stone bishop on a cathedral tomb. His bony hands were clasped across his sunken chest, his head raised up on a pillow. His eyes were closed, his bloodless lips collapsed in a pallid grimace. His skin was the colour of translucent ochre and violet thread veins lay beneath the surface like contour lines on a map. The skeletal bones of his skull looked as if they were about to break through the taut skin at any moment.

Padraig stared at him in horrified fascination. This must be Brother Anselm, the man he'd seen in the photograph in Mr Leary's scrapbook. The big beaky nose was a dead giveaway.

At that moment the old monk opened his eyes and looked across at Padraig.

Padraig flinched under his gaze. The monk blinked lizard-like and his mouth twisted into a ravaged, almost toothless smile. For a second he struggled to sit up but then collapsed back on to the pillows.

Padraig shivered violently; fear seeped up from his feet, rattled on up his backbone.

'Come on, Padraig, keep up,' Nancy Carmichael called out to him.

Padraig turned his face away from the old man and hurried towards the others, who stood waiting for him in an oasis of candlelight further down the corridor.

Father Daley climbed thankfully into his own bed and blew out the candle on the bedside table. He pulled the freshly starched sheets up over him and lay for a while looking up at the huge moon through the opened shutters. Padraig, in his bed on the opposite side of the room, was already curled up in a ball, dead to the world and snoring softly.

Father Daley yawned; he was absolutely exhausted what with the journey and all the commotion at Señora Hipola's that morning.

The weather had changed quite suddenly during the previous night and the storm had blown into Camiga without any warning.

He had been woken at just before six by the shutters banging against the bedroom window. He had looked out into a very different Pig Lane. The lines of bunting that were stretched across the lane were whirling madly. Flowerpots had crashed to the ground from the balconies and broken geraniums were strewn across the cobbles. A dog was chasing its tail like a thing possessed. The sign that hung above the Bar Pedro clanked loudly, and on the balconies songbirds clung shrieking to their perches inside their swinging cages.

Then the screaming had begun downstairs and Father Daley had dressed hurriedly and gone to see what was going on.

Down in the lobby Señora Hipola was standing with her apron pulled up over her head, hollering and stamping her feet like an overwrought tap dancer.

'Calm yourself, Señora Hipola. Whatever has happened?'

Nancy Carmichael and Padraig came hurrying downstairs moments later, their eyes still heavy with sleep.

It was a good five minutes before Father Daley could get any sense from Señora Hipola. When he finally coaxed her out from under her apron she said that Marta, her ungrateful niece, had done a bunk in the middle of the night. Señora Hipola had discovered her bed empty this morning and her few belongings gone. What was Señora Hipola to do? The wedding was to take place tomorrow. The dress was bought, the guests invited. Holy saints, the shame of it all would kill her. What would people say? What would she tell Ramón and his father?

'Are you absolutely sure that she's gone? There's no mistake?'

'Yes, yes, I am sure. Violante Burzaco said she saw them hurrying off together at the crack of dawn.'

'You said "them". Who else do you mean?'

'The other woman, the one with the blackened eye. I never liked the look of that one. Piadora she was called. The moment I set eyes on her I knew she was trouble! She's gone too, though at least she had the grace to leave payment for her stay.'

Señora Hipola continued to wail and bawl and stamp her feet.

Then to add to the commotion all the church bells of

Camiga began to ring out and that had set Señora Hipola off even more.

As the pilgrims stood looking on at the distraught Señora the whole house shook under the buffeting of the winds and echoed with the clattering of bells. Dust blew in under the door and swirled round their feet and a pile of ash fell with a dull thud into the grate.

Then they all jumped as a large head appeared in the doorway that led out into the courtyard.

The old donkey, escaped from his stable, stood in the entrance blinking nervously at them.

'Poor old devil, he's afraid of the storm,' said Padraig. 'Shall I go out and calm him down and put him back in the stable?'

'I'll come with you,' Father Daley said with alacrity, leaving a disconcerted Miss Carmichael to cope with Señora Hipola's histrionics.

Padraig and Father Daley had led the sad-faced old donkey across the courtyard, which had taken a pounding from the storm and was in a sorry state. The ground was strewn with fallen lemons and straw and the oilcloth from the table had blown away into a corner. On the washing line the enormous wedding dress ballooned in the ferocious wind.

'Get him in the stable, Padraig, and then we'd best get that dress off the line, though God knows it'll not be needed now.'

As they bolted the stable door an enormous gust of wind blew into the courtyard. Chaff and straw flew up into the air and lemons hurtled to the ground like small bombs. On the washing line the enormous wedding dress billowed and somersaulted, neck over hem, arms flailing wildly. Then suddenly it broke from its moorings, and before Father Daley and Padraig had a chance to rescue it it was carried up, up and away on the back of the rampaging wind.

They had stood together staring in horrified wonder as the dress, more like a barrage balloon now, soared and dipped and then disappeared from sight over the rooftops.

They'd had to wait hours for the storm to subside until eventually they had left a tearful Señora Hipola waving at them from the doorway.

What a day!

Across the room Padraig was muttering restlessly in his sleep. Father Daley closed his eyes, listened to the call of a barn owl somewhere outside, heard the dog bark down in the courtyard and then fell into a deep and blissful sleep.

Nancy Carmichael opened the shutters on the windows of her bedroom. The cool night air, fragrant with herbs, wafted into the room and felt like a balm on her tired skin. She breathed in greedily and looked out longingly into the night.

Beyond the narrow window the sky was a deep indigo bowl, peppered with stars, the moon a waxy orb spinning high over the mountains. In the far distance the hazy lights of Los Olivares and Camiga blinked lazily. A keen sea breeze blew up the deep valley, whimpering through the pine trees, murmuring through the long grass down by the river.

Nancy Carmichael shivered with pleasure.

The sheer drop down into the valley was both terrifying and yet exhilarating. She felt like a princess in a tower looking down on her fairy-tale kingdom. Like Rapunzel waiting for her prince! She giggled at the thought and told herself not to be so silly. A princess at her age indeed. Besides, she didn't have long enough hair to let down!

She was just a slightly tipsy woman in her forties letting her imagination run away with her.

Turning to the right she could see the rough cart track that led up from the tiny ruined hamlet to Santa Eulalia. The track was dappled with moonlight and Nancy could just make out the statue of the Blue Madonna. Tomorrow, she thought she'd take a walk down there and leave a prayer at her feet.

As she stood there she felt unaccustomedly at peace with herself; indeed, undoubtedly the happiest she had ever been in all her life. She felt like shouting out to the sleeping world below. Quite what she would shout out she wasn't sure. It was as though, especially since Miss Drew had gone, this pilgrimage had opened her eyes to enjoyment, and she was freeing herself little by little from her troubled past.

She was about to close the window shutters in case something unpleasant flew into the room while she slept; there could be bats, bugs, huge moths on the loose. Then she changed her mind; she was sick and tired of being afraid of things, always living on the edge of real or imagined fears. Bugger it and sod it! For once she'd let the sweet cool air roll over her while she slept.

She undressed slowly and then looked down at the pile of her clothes. They really were most unsuitable for this climate. They were drab, old-fashioned garments that made her look years older than she really was.

As soon as she could she would buy something more summery. A cool cotton dress or skirt maybe, in a nice bright colour, maybe a pair of those rope-soled espadrilles. She'd throw away her stockings and go bare-legged, let the sun brown up her legs a little. She picked up her flannel nightdress and was about to pull it on over her head, then changed her mind.

Usually, last thing at night she got down on her knees and went through the long list of people to pray for. Her mother, Aunt Maisie and Uncle William, Grandmother Jones . . . All of them long dead and buried. And lastly but not least, for poor dead Henry William Fitzallen.

But tonight, damn it, she wasn't going to pray for any of them. They could do without her prayers for once. Henry William had dogged her daylight hours and her dreams for too many years. Henry, the little child from Kilgerry who had killed himself. The poor sweet boy whom her mother had found hanging by his slender neck, eyes bulging, a puddle of still-warm urine on the floor beneath his dangling sandals . . .

She was filled then with such a rush of emotions: fury, sadness, frustration, loss. She had carried that little boy on her conscience, been made to pray for his soul, pray for forgiveness for as long as she could remember.

Sometimes when the madness was upon her her mother had shut Nancy in the trunk and slammed down the lid. *I will let my own child suffer to assuage his sin,* she had said.

Nancy began to tremble now at the memory. Her breathing grew tense and erratic. Her ribs felt like an iron cage, her heart a trapped moth, fluttering frantically. She had always hated the dark.

'No, Mammy, please, Mammy, no!'

But her frantic pleas always went unheeded and the lid would slam down and she would be trapped alone in the terrifying darkness. Beyond the lid she would hear the sound of her mother's rosary beads clacking, the deranged muttering of fervent prayer. The sound of her own fingernails scratching the lid of the trunk, her own muffled screams.

Dear God, she had been a little child, much younger even than Padraig, a child shut up in the suffocating darkness because another poor child had killed himself in fear and despair.

For a long time she had thought it was because her mother felt guilty for not preventing his suicide. It was only years afterwards that Nancy had found out the awful truth.

She had listened to her mother's ramblings during the last days before she died and eventually pieced it all together. Henry had seen something, something awful, something no child should ever see. He had come upon them together in the attic bedroom. His father and his nanny. He had caught them in the act.

Nancy's mother had begged Lord Fitzallen not to beat the boy, but he'd said that he would shut the boy's mouth for him. She'd said that in loyalty to his mother and fear of his father the boy had killed himself. He couldn't live with what he'd seen and keep a secret of it.

And after her mother's death Nancy had found the hidden letters, the ones that had disappeared from her trunk. Dear God, if they got into the wrong hands her secret would be out. She should have left them in Ballygurry, they'd have been safer there.

Nancy had always been led to believe that her father had died when she was a year old. According to her mother he was a good, kind man who had worked on the railways. He'd had a heart attack at the age of forty and died. It had all been a pile of evil lies. The good, kind man who had supposedly stood over her crib and sung softly to her was the figment of her mother's warped imagination. A made-up man. She was illegitimate. Her mother had already been pregnant at the time Henry had taken his life. After the boy's death, when she found out she was expecting a child, she'd had to leave. She'd gone to Dublin until Nancy was born, stayed there a few years, concocted the story about dear Mr Carmichael and then set up home in Ballygurry. Nancy held back her tears. Well, tonight, sweet child Henry, you and I must be parted. We never even met, did we? We were both innocent children and didn't deserve to suffer so at the hands of adults. She, for one, was sick of sin and suffering . . .

She eventually fell asleep to the echoes of owls calling across the mountains. As she slept the moon cast a soft shadow across her smiling countenance, a naked woman coming slowly towards peace.

The clock down in the refectory chimed the midnight hour and Brother Anselm awoke from a troubled sleep. He lay still for a while thinking that perhaps he'd dreamed seeing the frightened boy looking in at him from the doorway. Then he remembered how Brother Bernardo had been wittering on for days about the Irish pilgrims who were due to arrive.

He'd thought that it was queer, that after all these years pilgrims should decide to come to Santa Eulalia again. Apparently, though, it was something to do with that meddlesome Leary fellow.

He looked across the room at Brother Bernardo, who was supposed to be keeping a vigil at his bedside. There always seemed to be someone watching him these days. It was as if they were afraid he was going to do something outrageous.

Brother Bernardo was soundly asleep, his chin resting on his chest, candlelight sending shadows skittering across his nodding bald head. In another hour Brother Tomás would arrive to take over from Brother Bernardo and Brother Tomás would remain awake until the dawn.

Brother Anselm struggled to a sitting position and swivelled his legs round to the edge of the bed. His head felt too heavy for his body. His tongue was swollen, like dough proving. Rancid saliva filled his mouth, his few remaining teeth ached and his breath was hot and fetid. His swollen belly was full of turbulent gas and even his piss was peculiar, the colour of cabbage water, the stink of it as rank as compost.

He got slowly to his feet, steadied himself and crossed the room shakily. Beneath his cotton nightshirt his testicles swung like pendulums.

Despite the darkness of the corridor he made his way without stumbling, feeling his way along the walls. He knew every inch of the monastery, every hidey-hole, every nook and cranny.

Turning the handle on the guest bedroom door, he opened it without a noise. He stood quite still, gathering his strength, then he stepped cautiously inside the room and listened. Someone was breathing heavily, someone sleeping very deeply. The softer sound of a child's breath . . .

Moonlight flooded the room through the opened shutters. He shuffled over to the side of the bed and looked down at the sleeping occupant. His heart jumped painfully. The sight of a child sleeping had always moved him; there was something so innocent in their complete abandonment to sleep. He brushed a sudden angry tear from his sunken cheek.

He stooped closer to the boy, holding his breath. Holy St James! He began to tremble and had to put out an arm and lean against the wall for support.

The boy called out suddenly in his sleep and Brother Anselm stiffened with fright.

Dear God, he'd only got a fleeting glimpse of the boy in the doorway. Now he caught his breath. This was a ghost of a boy come back from the past to haunt him. Come back to sniff out his inheritance, no doubt. He put out his hand towards the child's face, felt the warm skin, the whisper of hot breath on his hand. He withdrew his hand quickly. No, this was no ghost, no figment of his imagination.

Who the hell was this boy? His arrival could mean nothing but trouble. He had to think of a way of getting rid of this boy before he ruined everything. But how?

He glanced round the sparsely furnished room. On a rush-backed chair beside the sleeping boy's bed lay a sketch-pad. He picked it up and turned the pages. His heart juddered painfully as he looked at the beautifully executed sketches.

There was no mistaking the girl! Although he hadn't seen her for many years he would have known her anywhere. The marks of her ancestry were there, stamped on her face, especially those eyes. She had the look of her grandmother, and someone else besides . . .

What was this boy doing with a sketch of the girl? Where had he seen her? Pepita had told him that they were off to America to begin a new life together, that she would never trouble him again. Dear God. Like mother like daughter. He felt his heart contract painfully. Reminders of the past were there on these pages bringing the dead to life, a past from which he knew only death would afford him escape.

He replaced the book on the chair with a quivering hand.

The boy whimpered from the depths of his dreams.

Brother Anselm returned to his bed but he could not sleep. He listened to all the usual night-time sounds of Santa Eulalia, the screech of the owl scouring the meadow for mice, the cluck of a rattled hen in the tumbledown barn, Quixote the monastery dog tottering on his three arthritic legs sniffing feverishly for rats. The careful footfall of ghosts stepping back through the centuries to tell their tale.

Padraig dreamed that he was back in Pig Lane, standing on the balcony at Señora Hipola's house. There were people standing on all the balconies in Pig Lane, as if they were waiting for a grand parade to start. Suddenly a shout went up and the people pointed excitedly towards the sky.

Padraig looked up. There in the turbulent sky the huge wedding dress that had hung on the line in the courtyard was floating high above the church tower. On its lofty nest on the tower the startled stork was screeching, flapping its wings in fury . . .

As Padraig stared in fascination he realized that someone was trapped inside the dress. As he watched he saw that a string hung down from its hem, trailing towards the earth. It was like a giant dress and a kite at the same time. The dress whirled and twirled, swooped and plunged towards Pig Lane. The onlookers on the balconies shrieked with glee and ducked as the dress hurtled towards the lane.

Padraig recoiled as a face appeared amidst the billowing lace. Sister Veronica! Her eerie grey-brown eyes were wide with fear, her large teeth bared in terror, the mole on her cheek sprouting a clutch of fierce black hairs.

Up went the dress and Sister Veronica. The onlookers clapped and cheered. The stork screeched.

Then Padraig had looked down over the balcony and seen her. Sister Immaculata! She was holding on to the kite string and dancing up and down Pig Lane, a look of utter glee on her wrinkled face. She was reeling in the kite, letting it soar . . .

Then suddenly a boy came running down the lane behind her. It was the boy statue come to life, the naked boy stepped down from his place in the fountain and chasing behind Sister Immaculata.

Fearless, eager to join the fun, without a thought for his safety Padraig leaped over the balcony and floated down into the lane. The onlookers cheered and Padraig joined in the chase. The statue boy looked back over his shoulder and winked at Padraig. He followed the boy and Sister Immaculata, skipping and laughing along statue-filled alleyways, until he realized that they were in the grounds of the monastery. The sky grew suddenly darker and it began to rain.

High above them the wedding dress kite lost height and then came crashing to the ground. Padraig looked down at the crumpled dress lying amidst the dandelions and daisies, but there was no sign of Sister Veronica among the muddied bundle of torn lace.

Sister Immaculata let go of the kite string like a disgruntled child with a broken toy. She was standing beside a grave and she rapped on the headstone with her knuckles as though it was a door. To Padraig's horror and amazement the headstone creaked open slowly. The statue boy and the nun stooped down and stepped inside and beckoned for Padraig to follow, but he shook his head sadly. Then the door closed with a click.

When he turned round Sister Veronica was standing behind him beckoning him to come to her. He backed away from her, turned to run, but his way was blocked by the hook-nosed Brother Anselm, who was brandishing a smoking shotgun. There was no escape. He turned again and Sister Veronica was upon him, slapping her enormous hand across his mouth, stopping him from breathing . . . the sound of gunshot echoing inside his head.

He awoke screaming and thrashing round in the bed. Suddenly someone was wiping his forehead, cradling his head, talking to him softly . . . He could smell her perfume, the softness of her breasts, the tickle of her hair on his face . . .

'It's all right, you'll be fine, you've had a bad dream. Hush now, sweetheart,' Nancy Carmichael said as she stroked his hair. 'I'm surprised Father Daley has slept through the racket you were making. You were shouting loud enough to wake the dead!'

*

Rosendo Angeles was woken by the wind moaning in the chimney and a sudden fall of ash into the fireplace that scattered the mice foraging for crumbs in his kitchen.

Rosendo groaned as he surfaced slowly from his dreams. The ill-fitting shutters rattled and a cold draught stirred up the dust and cobwebs. Rosendo rose from his bed, shivering in the cold morning air.

He threw some dried fir-cones and pine needles on to the dying embers of the previous night's fire. The flames crackled lazily as he ladled water from a large stone jar into a battered metal jug and set it to boil.

It was his habit every morning before taking his breakfast of barley coffee and stale bread smeared with olive oil, to walk up the mountain track to the shrine of the Blue Madonna.

As he lifted the latch on the outside door, without warning a fierce gust of wind blew it inwards with such a force that it threw him back against the kitchen wall, knocking the breath out of him.

'Holy Moses!' He hung on to the latch with all his strength for fear of the door being ripped from its rusty hinges. He tried without success to force the door shut as the wind circled the kitchen, moaning testily, jiggling the tin pots and pans that hung on hooks embedded in the walls. Once inside the room, the wind seemed to gain in strength, a mini-hurricane setting the wooden crucifix that hung above the fireplace into slow revolutions on its rusty nail. Rosendo stared in fascination as the twisted body of Christ spun faster and faster until it blurred into a multi-armed creature, spinning like a Catherine wheel pinned to the wall.

Mother of God! This must be something to do with that nubeiro who'd been hanging round the place recently. He always brought trouble with him. The last time he'd been around, there'd been a terrible storm and in the middle of it a painting was stolen from the monastery.

Suddenly the wind dropped; spent of its fearsome force, it blew into the fire, sparking up the kindling, breathing life into the glowing embers, then heading away up the chimney, drawing the eager flames behind it.

Rosendo made the sign of the cross, steadied his breathing, then crossed the kitchen and straightened the crucifix with a trembling hand.

Tonight he'd light a blessed candle and put it in the window; that would put paid to that wily nubeiro's tricks.

The sun was rising: a small watery ellipse dusting the mountain peaks with a soft, grey-pink flush of glimmering light. He walked towards the stable, unhooked the rope that secured the door and stepped inside. He loved the earthy primeval smell of the beasts, the sweet-smelling litter of chaff and straw, wood ash and peelings that lay in a deep carpet on the floor.

Alfredo the donkey was calmer this morning. In the night Rosendo had woken to the sound of him braying plaintively and had hurried out to check on him. It was most odd because he was such a placid creature normally, yet he'd certainly been spooked by something last night.

Now, he stamped his hooves and lifted his big head, his deep dark eyes gleaming with joy at the sight of Rosendo.

Rosendo smiled and clicked his tongue. Alfredo was as constant as the tides in his affections. He and the donkey went back a long, long way. It was more than ten years since he'd taken Alfredo in. He remembered the day quite vividly. The donkey trudging carefully up the track, the man slumped on his back, blood seeping through his shirt. A handsome man, even though his face had been contorted with pain. He'd been shot and had lost a great deal of blood. The monks had taken him in, but the poor soul had lost consciousness soon afterwards and died two days later.

Alfredo, shut up in the barn, had roared and kicked and had escaped on a regular basis always to be found down at the man's grave.

Rosendo had offered to keep the stricken beast and he had stayed with him ever since. Now, Rosendo stooped to fill the manger with chaff and barleycorn. He giggled as the donkey nuzzled his ear playfully. Rosendo stood up, scratched the space between the donkey's ears as the beast nodded his great head, baring his old yellow teeth in pleasure. Rosendo peered over into the next stall and smiled. Dolores the pig slept soundly on as she did every morning, refusing to wake until the world was bright and the sun warm on her bristly back. If his parents had still been alive she would long ago have been turned into pig broth and black puddings, her trotters would be hanging from the hooks in the kitchen. But he hadn't the heart to kill her even though the widow Alvarez constantly hinted that it had been a long time since they'd had a pig killing.

He left Alfredo enjoying his breakfast, and Dolores her sleep, closed the door to the stable and made his way on up the rough track.

The wind was cool and Rosendo shivered in his thin clothes. It was a strange, unsettling wind, which made goose-pimples erupt on his skin, the hairs quiver on the back of his neck; a wind that made him feel nervous and excited at the same time.

Here and there he stooped to pick a handful of the brightly coloured spring flowers that grew in abundance alongside the track and then carried on his way.

The Blue Madonna was a stone statue that had been inexpertly but lovingly sculpted by an unknown hand many centuries before. She stood on a worm-chewed wooden plinth in a grotto that had been roughly hewn from an enormous boulder. The blue paint of the madonna's robes was faded now and the pink of her face was cracked and flaking but Rosendo still thought she was beautiful. She had a tranquil, soft, tired smile and one eyebrow was raised as if she were about to ask a question but wasn't sure if she should. A mark beneath her eyes reminded him of a smudged tear, the lips slightly parted as if trembling.

He had made this small pilgrimage nearly every day since he had been a little boy. It had always been the custom of the local people to nail scraps of paper to the wooden plinth, paper prayers for the sick and dying, for the departed, requests for miracles and cures, entreaties for everyday things.

When he was a boy the hamlet had been a thriving place with its own blacksmith and a small bar-cum-shop. Then, the madonna's plinth had always been covered with paper requests. Now, only three of the houses in the hamlet were still lived in. The rest were derelict, the tiles on the roofs long gone and the broken walls gradually subsiding into the rich green grass of the mountain. The families who had lived there for generations had been lured away to the larger towns to work in the new factories and canneries. Others had moved further away, down to the coast to work in the hotels and cafés that served the tourists who now came in increasing numbers each summer. There were only two other inhabitants left, the widow Paquita Alvarez, her simple-minded son Felipe and their three tortoiseshell cats. Rosendo sighed sadly. Perhaps the time had come for him to hitch Alfredo to the cart, gather his few possessions together and move away too. He was only forty-five after all; he was still strong and he had his health and most of his own teeth. There was time enough left to make a new life for himself in one of the big towns, get one of those new fancy apartments with electric lights and running water.

Pah, he spat angrily into the wind. Where would he keep a flatulent old donkey, eh? And a troublesome pig with wanderlust? Besides, who would put an eye to the others if he were to go? Someone had to gather the firewood in for the winter and take the cart down the five-mile track to the nearest village to bring back provisions. Someone had to dig them out when the heavy snows came. It was too late to think about change now; he should have been more adventurous and gone years ago.

He reached the shrine of the madonna and stooped to pick up a glass jar. He tipped out the wilting flowers and dirty water, filled the jar from the spring that gushed out from behind the rocks and put in the fresh flowers that he had picked. He placed the jar carefully at the madonna's feet. Such dainty feet she had, delicate little toes painted the same pink as her face. She really could do with a lick of paint, though. He'd take Alfredo down to Los Olivares one day soon and try and get a good match of paint, give the old girl a good spring clean.

He kneeled down on the springy mountain grass to pray. Maybe one day soon the Holy Madonna would answer his prayers. Then things would be okay.

Rosendo clasped his calloused hands together and bowed his head. He took out his own paper prayer from his trouser pocket. The same request was written on it as always. He must have written hundreds, no thousands of them over the years. He could have written it with his eyes shut. Sticking the paper down on one of the many small rusty nails that were embedded in the wood, he made the sign of the cross and slowly rose to his feet.

Suddenly a ferocious blast of wind roared through the trees overhanging the grotto. Leaves and twigs blew down round his head, whirling in an eddy round the feet of the madonna. As the wind tore at his paper prayer, it fluttered wildly for a second, then was ripped away from the rusty nail. It rose into the air, twirling and coiling on the lip of the wind. Rosendo reached out frantically to try and retrieve it but the wind whipped it beyond his grasp. Higher and higher it climbed on the currents of strangely perfumed air. He watched in fascination and frustration as it was carried up, up and away until it was just a small speck drifting away over the roof of the monastery high above him.

Rosendo sighed, turned on his heel and made his way back down the track, dipping his head against the rough gale. From the stable he could hear Dolores the pig, awake now, grunting and squealing impatiently for her breakfast. Rosendo shivered, shrugged, pulled his thin jacket more tightly round his body, the wind whipping his silvery hair across his face, bringing tears to his eyes.

Then he heard the noise. He stopped in his tracks, hardly able to believe his ears, and looked upwards in alarm at the monastery of Santa Eulalia. The monastery bell was ringing. The last time it had rung had to be twenty-odd years ago. Back in those days it had rung at all hours of the day and night. Now, the unfamiliar sound echoed across the mountains, a hoarse, arthritic, rasping knell.

The wind died down and the bell groaned to a stop. Rosendo shook his head in disbelief and hurried on his way. Something peculiar was afoot round these parts, that was for sure.

When Padraig awoke, Father Daley had already dressed and gone downstairs. Still slightly shaky and bewildered from his nightmare, Padraig got out of bed and hurried over to the window, eager to see daylight.

Outside, the sun was rising and a soft, pinkish glow was

spreading up the valley. The air was alive with birdsong and he could smell wood smoke and strong coffee brewing.

He dressed rapidly and hurried along the corridor, thankful that the door behind which old Brother Anselm lay was now shut. He climbed down the stairs and made his way across the hall. The shutters on the windows were open and the hallway was bright with sunshine, although a fresh breeze added a chill to the air.

In the dining room Father Daley and Nancy were taking breakfast and Brother Bernardo was running to and fro bringing fruit and baskets of bread, chattering excitedly as he went.

'Morning, Padraig. Miss Carmichael, er, Nancy was just telling me that you'd had a nightmare. And a lot of help I was, sleeping right through!'

Padraig blushed. He'd thought that he'd dreamed that Miss Carmichael had stroked his head until he'd fallen back into a dream-free sleep.

'I just had a bad dream, that's all, Father, I'm fine now.'

Nancy thought that Padraig looked a little pale this morning. Each day, though, since they'd been away from Ballygurry his features had grown a little softer; he was putting a little flesh on his bones, too. His hair was growing back very quickly, the soft dark springy curls framing his face like a cherub's.

'Who did all these paintings?' Padraig asked with interest as Brother Bernardo came out from the kitchen.

'Ah, the big, er, bright ones,' he said pointing, 'are by our own Brother Anselm. The small ones done by many different peoples who stayed here over the years. That one my favourite there. It's by a man called Luciano. He was very good artist, came to stay here many summers, before my time of course. Luciano also made the famous statue of the little boy in Camiga.'

'The boy without his clothes?' Padraig said.

'*Sí*, that's the one. The one making a big piss.'

Nancy Carmichael spluttered into her coffee and blushed. Padraig tried unsuccessfully to stifle a giggle.

Padraig would have liked to meet this fellow Luciano and take some lessons from him. He could paint brilliantly, that was for sure. He remembered the awesome painting in Mr Leary's house, the painting of the lopsided house beneath a sky where the stars were exploding fireworks. That was by Luciano too!

He looked up at the painting with total admiration. It was a picture of the monastery of Santa Eulalia by moonlight. The monastery looked almost as it had when they had arrived last night. There were even swathes of mist painted round the turrets. All the windows of the monastery were in darkness except for one. The one where Padraig and Father Daley were sleeping!

Padraig left his seat and got right up close to the painting. There was a small figure in the lighted window, someone leaning out into the night. A child staring up towards the sky that blazed with stars. It looked like someone had added the little boy as an afterthought.

In the bottom left-hand corner of the painting a shaft of moonlight illuminated the statue of the Blue Madonna. He could even see a few paper prayer requests at her feet. Moonlight caught the whites of the virgin's eyes. Padraig scratched his head; although the perspective of the painting was perfect, the colours great, there was something that didn't ring true, but as hard as he stared he couldn't work out quite what was wrong.

He looked next at Brother Anselm's paintings. Bloody hell, they were awful. All thick swirls and splodges the way a bored child might paint, trying to cover the paper as quickly as possible and then get on with something they found more interesting. Padraig didn't think much of Brother Anselm's artistic talent.

'Brother Bernardo,' he asked, 'there's a mark on the wall there as if a painting had once hung there.'

'Ah, yes, very, very sad. About ten years ago it was stolen away in the night by a thief.'

'Was it one of that Luciano's paintings?'

'No, it was one of Brother Anselm's.'

Padraig's eyebrows rose involuntarily and he wondered who in their right mind would have taken Brother Anselm's painting when they could have taken Luciano's.

'Did they ever catch the thief?'

'No. The police they talked to old Muli, an odd little fellow, who was hanging around at the time but they had to let him go.'

'Was it ever found?'

'No.'

After a breakfast of fresh eggs cooked in oil, chunks of crusty bread and steaming bowls of coffee, the three pilgrims and Brother Bernardo stepped outside into the courtyard.

A few monks came ambling out of a barn carrying an assortment of ancient gardening tools. They looked so decrepit and frail that a puff of wind could have lifted them off the ground and blown them to kingdom come.

As if to prove the point, a hearty gust of wind swept round the courtyard sending the hens into a frenzied scuttle towards the cover of the barn. The old monks wobbled dangerously on drumstick legs and Nancy held on tightly to her skirts.

Suddenly a bell began to clang up in the tower. Brother Bernardo sucked in his breath with a bronchial whistling sound. The old monks stopped in their tracks and a hoe clattered noisily to the ground. The monks crossed themselves, then began to chatter and hug each other while the Ballygurry pilgrims looked on bemused.

'Mother of God! You see!' said Brother Bernardo grinning from ear to ear. 'You pilgrims are a good omen for Santa Eulalia. The bells! They were all rusted up; they have not rung in twenty years! It is an omen. I feel it in my old bones!'

In the Villa Castelo, Brother Francisco looked down at the old woman who lay in the four-poster bed and shuddered. He felt cold to his very core despite the warmth of the afternoon.

Even close to death, Isabella Martinez still had that hard cruel smile impressed on her pale tight lips, and her eyes retained that wary watchfulness he remembered from his childhood. She held her blue-veined hand out towards him but he could not, would not, take it. He made the sign of the cross and turned his face away from her.

As he opened the door and stepped into the coolness of the corridor an old peasant woman shuffled past him into the room, looking up at him with lively inquisitive eyes. She was old but she had a peculiar air of great energy about her. She wore a faded brown dress and down-at-heel shoes, and on her head a green beret was pulled down tightly over her ears giving her a comical look.

He stepped back fearfully when he saw the look of peculiar triumph on her wrinkled face as she looked down at Isabella in the bed. She had a look of undisguised glee that was quite out of place in a deathbed scene.

The old woman looked back at him, scrutinized his face carefully. She spoke eagerly.

'She has made a confession to you, yes?'

Brother Francisco nodded.

'It's my time now to speak with her. I've waited long

enough and death will not deprive me of this pleasure.'

Brother Francisco looked down for the last time at Isabella Martinez. She lay quite still, eyes closed as the old peasant woman approached the bed. Then she rallied for a moment, her eyelids flickering, then opening wide as if startled.

The old woman bent her head closer until she was almost face to face with Isabella, who stiffened visibly, her eyes bright with terror. Her mouth moved and she whispered something hoarsely that Brother Francisco could not make out.

'Yes, Isabella, it is me. The past cannot be held at bay for ever.'

Brother Francisco turned away and closed the door softly. He thought sadly that a lot of people might have a score to settle with Isabella Martinez.

He had already made up his mind not to stay a moment longer at the Villa Castelo. He had listened to her confession and he knew that Isabella couldn't possibly last more than a day or two. He wanted to get out of there as soon as possible and back to the peace of Santa Eulalia.

People were already arriving at the villa to visit Isabella in her last hours. There were villagers and workers from the estate, all come no doubt out of frightened respect. None of her closest family had arrived. Isabella, it seemed, was to be a very lonely woman in death.

'Is Piadora coming to the funeral?' he'd asked Carlos Emanuel.

'No, Brother. I have spoken with Isabella's only sister, Augusta. Piadora, it appears, has gone, left, abandoned her poor old aunt without a word. Augusta is on her way here now. By the terms of the will, as the next eldest she will inherit everything. She will be a very rich woman that one, a good catch for any man.'

'What about the other, er, younger daughter?'

'Pah! She wasn't her daughter, you know. She was the illegitimate child of the daughter Piadora, but the good señora brought her up as her own. She has been gone from here for years. I never knew her. Upped and off with some rough-necked fellow apparently. Cut off without a penny that one. Neither of the daughters was any good, if you ask me. It's scandalous, though, that neither of them will be here for their own mother's funeral, don't you think?'

Brother Francisco had bitten his lip to keep silent, to stem the tide of his enormous anger. He had heard many a deathbed confession in his time but none as chilling as the one made by Isabella Martinez.

When the bell finally stopped ringing and the commotion in the courtyard had died down, the old monks had shuffled off to their work on the land and Padraig settled down on an old stone bench in a small alcove out of the breeze.

Chickens strutted across the courtyard, dipping and pecking at the cobbles, and a three-legged dog ran across to him and sniffed excitedly round his legs. Padraig stroked the dog and wondered why there were so many three-legged dogs in Spain. How had they all come to lose a leg?

Padraig looked round about him with interest. The monastery was a real higgledy-piggledy place; it would be a great place to play hide and seek. He imagined the orphans of St Joseph's running round the courtyard and racing across the meadows that surrounded Santa Eulalia. It would be a lovely place for kids to live.

The ancient walls of the monastery had been cracked by the harsh winter frosts and the roof bowed by the deep falls of snow. There were bullet holes in a few of the windows and he wondered if the loony Brother Anselm had made them when he was taking pot-shots at flying pigs or short-sighted schoolmasters. Swifts and martins had built their nests beneath the eaves and the summer sun had faded the stone of the walls and bleached the statues of the stone saints in their mossy niches to a deathly hue.

Padraig took a well-chewed pencil from his pocket and began to draw in the sketchbook he'd bought in Camiga with the money Mr Leary had given him.

He worked quickly, feverishly, trying to draw from memory. When at last he was satisfied he closed the book and sat for a long time, staring ahead of him, lost in his thoughts.

A few minutes later Brother Bernardo came out of the barn, scattering corn for the chickens that scuttled behind him clucking and pecking at each other. Seeing Padraig, he waved cheerily and came and sat down beside him, throwing the last of the corn to the frantic chickens.

'You an artist?' he said, nodding at the sketchbook.

Padraig blushed to the tips of his ears.

'I'd like to be one day but I don't expect I will.'

'I can look, yes?'

Padraig handed him the book shyly.

Brother Bernardo opened it at the first page, looked at the sketch and then looked with surprise at Padraig.

'This very good, very much, very good.'

'Thanks,' Padraig replied, blushing again with pleasure and pride.

It was a sketch of Sister Immaculata that Padraig had drawn from memory. He was very pleased with this drawing because he'd got her large nose just right, and the twinkling crinkled eyes and the lopsided smile. Padraig smiled and said fondly, 'That's Sister Immaculata, she's an old nun who is real kind to me. I'm going to buy her a nice present while I'm here and take it back for her.'

The monk turned the page and studied the next sketch.

Padraig looked down at the drawing he'd done of the little girl in the Dark Wood.

'This one here, look, like a little nun in her cloak and hood. Ah, see look, she is holding the *diente de león*.'

'What's *diente de león?*' Padraig asked.

'In English I think teeth of the lion.'

'Ah,' said Padraig, 'dandelions.'

'From the *diente de león* you can make very good soup.'

'Can you?' said Padraig with a hint of disbelief in his voice. He'd never heard of anyone eating dandelions.

'*Sí*, one day soon I make the dandelion soup for you, eh?'

'That'd be grand,' Padraig replied.

Brother Bernardo began to laugh uproariously as he looked at the sketch that Padraig had just completed.

'Who in the name of the Holy Father is this?'

Padraig grinned.

'Just someone from a dream I had last night.'

'Very bad dream, eh? Funniest bride I ever seen. Don't look happy woman this one. I wouldn't like waking up in bed next to that one, eh?'

Padraig looked up at the chuckling monk and giggled.

'No way. She's another one of the nuns who looks after me. Not a very nice one either,' he said with a shudder.

The monk scratched his head.

'She's a nun. A bride of Christ, eh?'

Brother Bernardo thought it was a funny thing for a little kid to draw.

'You should show these to Brother Anselm. He knows lot about art.'

'Brother Anselm is the old scary man in the bedroom near me, isn't he?'

'*Sí*. He studied art in Paris before become a monk. In the dining room you see many of his paintings. One time there lots of artists come to Santa Eulalia. Very good some. Some not good but think they am. Come with me if you like and I show you paintings in the Great Hall. Very old. Very good, I think.'

Padraig put away his pencil, picked up his sketchpad and followed Brother Bernardo inside the monastery and down a dim, cool corridor to the left of the refectory.

They stood together in the Great Hall studying a huge fresco on the wall. It was faded and flaking in parts but most of the colours were still bright.

'Wow,' said Padraig. 'Would you look at that!'

'This was found when we were cleaning the walls, Padraig. Just think, it was hidden away for hundreds of years!'

Padraig looked eagerly up at the fresco. It seemed to tell a story, as if each of the three sections was a chapter in a book.

In the first section there was a group of big-bellied monks gathered round a pompous-looking monk who seemed to be telling them a story. All the monks wore cream-coloured robes except for one, who wore brown. The monks in white wore lots of jewellery, large rings and bejewelled crucifixes. Next to the monks stood a group of ragged men with long hair and beards, one of whom was fishing a bone from a cauldron.

Padraig looked again at the group of monks. They were all standing together under a lemon tree, and in their midst stood a three-legged dog who was piddling over the feet of the storyteller. The dog was almost identical to Quixote. Padraig thought that this artist must have had a good sense of humour.

'How come there are so many three-legged dogs in Spain?' he asked.

Brother Bernardo shrugged and said, 'I don't know about

Spain but there's always been dogs like that at Santa Eulalia.'

'How old do you reckon this painting is?'

'Hundreds of years, I think. No one really knows.'

Padraig looked with interest at the second section, where another group of big-bellied and red-faced monks in cream robes were filling the goblets of two other monks from wine sacks. Next to them a monk sat at a table, counting a huge pile of money. There was the dog again, piddling against the leg of the table.

The third section was completely mystifying. There was a peculiar little man in the background, a shrivelled-up little fellow dancing naked above what looked like a pile of earth. Above his head were several clusters of dark clouds and in between them was a fork of angry lightning. He looked like some kind of little devil prancing up and down and causing mischief. Beneath him a group of monks were prostrate on the floor, others trampling on them as if trying to escape. A group of laughing children were running away, with the dog at their heels. Behind them the ragged men stood round an overturned cauldron, one of them looking down in wonder at a ring that lay in the palm of his hand.

Padraig stood looking up at the fresco for a long time. The artist had really caught the individual expressions of the different people.

'Brother Anselm thinks this many hundreds year old, but he thinks we should paint over them again.'

'Why does he want to cover them up? They're wonderful,' Padraig said.

'Who knows? Just an old man being contrary.'

Padraig was absolutely enchanted by the fresco and the closer he looked the more detail he observed. He marvelled at the bright blue of one of the monk's mischievous eyes, the detail on a red ring that the pompous-looking one wore on his little finger, a rosary one of the ragged children was clutching in her hand. He thought that he could look at the fresco for hours and still find something new to admire.

'Is it okay if I come again to have another look?'

'*Sí*. Yes, come soon any time you like in case Brother Anselm escapes and takes a paint brush and covers it all over!'

'Escapes?' said Padraig fearfully. 'Is he meant to be locked up?'

'No, he's not dangerous but he sometimes gets forgetful and wanders off. Why only last week we found him wandering down near the Blue Madonna with a hammer.'

Padraig made a mental note to keep the bedroom door shut and stay well out of Brother Anselm's way.

Miss Carmichael took a slow walk down the mountain track towards the hamlet. She was truly enjoying herself, she felt so alive, so happy; she had removed her stockings and garters and the cool breeze felt wonderful on her bare legs. She hadn't gone about with bare legs since she was a very small child.

The breeze dropped as she neared the Blue Madonna and the sun felt hot on her face. She kneeled down at the feet of the statue and made the sign of the cross. It was a very old statue by the look of it; the body was quite crudely carved and yet the face was a masterpiece of emotions. She put out her hand and felt the madonna's cheek; it was smooth and cool to the touch. As she touched the shadowy tear on the face, she felt a tremor of emotion run through her.

Taking the piece of paper that she had already written on, she placed it on a nail at the feet of the madonna, where it fluttered in the breeze. Then she got to her feet slowly and carried on down the track. The few crumbling houses of the hamlet were run down and looked deserted except for the thin wreaths of smoke that drifted up from the chimneys of two of them. She supposed that years ago it must have been a pleasant little place in which to live, very isolated but exceptionally beautiful. The views down the valley were absolutely magnificent. She walked quickly and quietly past the houses, not wanting to disturb anyone inside. From an opened window a boy of about eighteen watched her curiously, a half-witted boy by the look of him. His mouth hung open and dribble ran down his chin. He waved his hand slowly, laboriously. Nancy waved nervously back and hurried on her way.

Just past the last house she turned down a narrow track that led towards the river. Taking off her shoes, Nancy felt the grass soft and cool beneath her feet. She walked for a long way down the track that was bordered on the right by a dense pine forest.

Occasionally she stopped and listened. All she could hear was the sound of birdsong and the occasional clank of what she guessed must be a cow-bell. There was something else, though; she was sure that she could hear the sound of footsteps on the grass some distance behind her.

What if it was a brown bear? She'd heard that there were bears up here in the mountains. Dear God, she could be eaten alive. For God's sake, Nancy! Chiding herself for her stupidity, she carried on her way. After a while she arrived at the riverbank and followed the fast-flowing river further down the valley.

The day was glorious, the sound of the water soothing to her ears. The sun rose higher into the wide blue sky and the last wisps of cloud evaporated above the mountain peaks.

Further downstream she sat down thankfully for a rest near a sheltered pool. A bee buzzed nearby and a hawk screamed overhead and plummeted to the earth. A dragonfly skimmed the water and a butterfly rested on a quivering blade of grass at her side. She felt as though she was completely alone in the world.

Nancy lay back on the grass, her head pillowed by a mound of soft moss. She closed her eyes, felt the sun's rays dappling her eyelids and she began to doze, completely unaware that two pairs of eyes watched her intently from the cover of the wood.

When she awoke some time later she felt drunk with the heat. It was unbelievably hot. Already her pale shins were turning pink in the sun. Slowly, she slipped off her tweed skirt and jumper and sat in her cotton petticoat and drawers. She wondered if she dared step into the cool water and paddle to cool herself down.

She kneeled down at the water's edge and peered into the sparkling water. It didn't look too deep close to the bank but it was hard to gauge how deep it was further out towards the middle. She was wary of water because she had never learned to swim so she wanted to be sure that it would be safe. She leaned forward, backside in the air, quite unaware of the sudden movement behind her. She had already hit the water face first by the time she realized that she had been pushed.

She opened her mouth to scream but she disappeared beneath the cold water, the scream never making it past her lips. Water rushed into her nose and throat as she sank deeper into the sparkling, whirling, weedy depths.

Padraig stayed in the Great Hall for a long time, looking intently at the fresco and trying to work out the story that was being told. Then he left Brother Bernardo to continue with his chores and took a walk down the track to see the statue of the Blue Madonna, hoping that he'd catch up with Nancy, but there was no sign of her anywhere.

He shrugged, whistling softly to himself; she must have got bored and gone back up to the monastery for a lie down. Grown-ups did a lot of lying down.

Padraig kneeled down and examined the Blue Madonna and as he did he felt a tingle of excitement run up his backbone. It was a very old statue, that was for sure. He couldn't tell what it was made from but it was very cool to the touch. He rapped it with his knuckles. Ouch! It was made of something bloody hard. Picking up a small sharp stone, he scratched the paint near the base of the statue. A flake of dark-blue paint fell away, revealing another. Layer upon layer of slightly different shades of blue paint. He scratched the paint again and sighed. There must be twenty layers at least. Underneath the very last layer of blue paint he came to white stone and, sadly, definitely not gold. This one wasn't the lost Irish virgin either! He'd got quite excited about this statue, wondered if it had been Santa Eulalia where the Irish monks had stayed. He examined the statue inch by inch but there were no clues to be found. He was about to try and squeeze in behind the grotto and get a proper look when he heard a noise nearby. He looked down towards the houses. A man had come out of one of them, crossed into a barn and come back out carrying a large stick. The look on his face startled Padraig; the man looked absolutely furious. Padraig ducked down and watched curiously as the man stalked off down the track and then turned to his left down a smaller track. Padraig didn't like the look of him one bit! Abandoning his examination of the statue, he decided he'd come back another time and get a better look.

As he climbed the track he looked up towards Santa Eulalia. The steep walls seemed to have been built into the rock face itself. He could see the arched window of the room where he and Father Daley had slept, the very window that the artist Luciano had drawn in his painting. A few windows along to the left he saw a light shining. For a moment he thought it was the reflection of the sun on a mirror. Screwing up his eyes, he peered up at the window and he knew instantly that he was being watched. Someone was standing at the window with binoculars watching him as he made his way back up the track to Santa Eulalia. He knew instinctively that it was old Brother Anselm, the monk who gave him the willies.

Despite the ferocity of the midday sun, Brother Francisco walked all the way from the station in Los Olivares to Santa Eulalia. The track was steep and the going hard but he needed time alone to think before he got back to the monastery. His mind was in absolute turmoil, racing feverishly to try to make sense of all that he had learned at the Villa Castelo.

He cursed himself now for his own crass stupidity; his shallow acceptance of what he had been told and foolishly believed without questioning for all those years. What an imbecile he'd been! For God's sake! He'd just believed everything he'd been told and never thought logically about anything at all.

He had grown up on the estate of the Villa Castelo; Piadora had been his second cousin. She had been more than that, though! She had been a friend, a soul-mate, indeed for a while as a teenager he'd been quite besotted with her.

He'd been away studying at the seminary in Barcelona when she'd written to say that she was at a finishing school in Paris and was having the time of her life.

Then she'd stopped writing and he'd heard that she had been whisked away from Paris to her aunt's house in the country, and he like everyone else had assumed the worst.

The gossip was that she'd had an unsuitable relationship while she was staying in France, got herself pregnant and been sent off until the baby was born. That she had never returned to the Villa Castelo was natural, the shame would have been too great amongst the aristocratic circles in which she'd moved.

Her mother Isabella had taken on the illegitimate child as her own. He remembered the child vaguely; he'd seen her on his few trips back while his parents were still alive. She was a very pretty girl but spoiled and petted like a lap dog. Everyone had pitied Isabella when the child turned out badly and had run off at sixteen with one of the labourers. Like mother like daughter they'd said and shaken their heads. Bad blood would out in the end they'd said. The saintly Isabella had done her Christian duty and look how she had been repaid!

Isabella Martinez! She was no saint, that was for sure. She'd always had a way, though, of fooling people into thinking she was good. He had never liked her when he was a child; he'd been afraid of her withering looks, her caustic tongue. The instincts of children were pretty sure indicators he'd always thought. She was a shrewd, cunning woman who wouldn't let anyone stand in her way. He remembered his mother telling him that when they were children she'd drowned her own twin sister's pet rabbit and then put the blame on her. She was a powerful woman and not to be trusted.

Now he knew the truth, but it was too late to make amends. He trembled with the enormity of the knowledge imparted to him.

Piadora hadn't had a baby at all! She'd never been pregnant. It was all a pack of lies! The fact that she'd had a liaison with some chap was just used as an excuse. It was Isabella who had given birth to the child! She had hurried

Piadora away to her younger sister Augusta, who must have been in on the deception. At the time Isabella's husband had been out in South America so it had been easy to cover up.

Months later she had returned to the Villa Castelo with the baby but Piadora had not returned with her. Piadora had been left, banished, blamed and ignored. Bad blood would out! Isabella's blood!

May she rot in hell! He grew red in the face as he climbed the track to Santa Eulalia. Isabella hadn't told him who the father of the child was. She had told him, however, that she had not left the monastery to the brothers as she had promised Brother Anselm. Brother Francisco sighed; Santa Eulalia was breathing its last. Now he had to impart the news to the monks. They would have a few months at the most before they were asked to leave.

Brother Anselm watched Padraig avidly as the boy bent down to inspect the statue thoroughly. His hands shook and he had to grasp the binoculars tightly to keep the boy in his sights. He was a clever little devil this one, that was for sure; poking his nose into things that didn't concern him.

Brother Bernardo had told him earlier how lovely it was that the boy had been so interested in those damned frescoes. But he wouldn't get his hands on Anselm's treasures, not if he had anything to do with it. He'd made damned sure that that other meddlesome Irishman Leary had stopped snooping about. A couple of pot-shots had laid him low and dampened his curiosity.

The boy looked up at where Brother Anselm stood at the window and as he did the monk drew back inside the room. As the boy climbed the path and got closer he trained the binoculars on his face, watching him until he turned the bend and was lost to sight.

He remained at the window for some time until eventually he saw Brother Francisco toiling doggedly up the track. As he got closer, Brother Anselm saw the expression on his face and he knew without being told that as Isabella Martinez had approached death she had needed to confess. He wondered with a shudder just how much she had told Brother Francisco.

He swivelled now and looked to his left out across the meadows. As he steadied the binoculars he noticed the small man standing motionless in the long grass. Brother Anselm knew that the man was looking back at him and a tight knot of fear twisted in his guts.

When Nancy Carmichael failed to appear for lunch and by late afternoon still hadn't arrived back at the monastery, Father Daley began to get worried. He sent Padraig off into the grounds to look for her while he looked round inside the monastery. Although Padraig searched among the barns and in the kitchen garden there was no sign of Nancy anywhere.

Padraig and Father Daley walked down the track towards the hamlet calling out her name as they went.

'Where on earth do you think she's gone to? I mean there's no shops or anything around,' Father Daley said.

'The thing is, Father, she's been acting a bit odd lately.'

'How do you mean, Padraig?'

'Well, she drinks wine for a start, and Miss Drew and her were always preaching about the evils of the demon drink back in Ballygurry.'

'I suppose.'

'And,' said Padraig, 'she has taken to going without her stockings; now, that is very odd, don't you think?'

'Is it?'

'Of course! Have you ever seen Miss Carmichael's bare legs before?'

'Er, no, not that I've noticed.'

'And she laughs more.'

'That's true.'

On the side of the riverbank they found her lace-up shoes and a folded handkerchief but there was no sign of Nancy Carmichael.

It was cool and dark in the monastery chapel. Brother Francisco entered quietly and found Brother Anselm and Brother Thomas near the front of the chapel on their knees, heads bent in prayer.

Brother Francisco kneeled beside them breathing heavily, his heart beating rapidly. Brother Thomas smiled across at Francisco, got to his feet and left the chapel.

When Francisco was sure that they were alone he said, 'Don't beat about the bush, Anselm. You knew Isabella Martinez well for many years. Tell me the truth. Did you know about the baby?'

Brother Anselm turned round slowly to face Brother Francisco.

'I did, God forgive me,' he said and lowered his eyes.

'And you did nothing?'

'What exactly did Isabella tell you?'

'That she was pregnant by a man who wasn't her husband and the only way she could save face was by pretending the baby was Piadora's, to save her marriage. It was a despicable, disgraceful thing to do to her own child.'

'That's true, Francisco, but her husband by all accounts was a very jealous man. He would have gone berserk if he'd known the truth, probably killed her. She was a desperate woman, you understand.'

'Well she pulled the wool over your eyes all right. A jealous man! He was a wonderful man, a gentle, sensitive soul.'

'I didn't know,' Brother Anselm stammered. 'She told me that he was a monster of a man.'

'A monster! The only monster in this sad story was Isabella. And she sacrificed her own daughter, let her husband believe that Piadora had given birth to the illegitimate child. Her husband was away in South America for almost a year while this was all going on. The poor man died not long afterwards, believing all those lies. God knows what sort of life Piadora's had living with her Aunt Augusta, never being allowed home . . . and now to cap it all she's run off somewhere, so there isn't any way of contacting her.'

Brother Anselm was trembling and his chest creaked with the effort of breathing.

'Do you know who the father of this child was?' Brother Francisco asked.

Anselm shook his head.

'Did Isabella mention the will, Brother Francisco? Did she say what might happen to us here at Santa Eulalia?'

'She did indeed.'

Brother Anselm held his breath.

'All the money, the estates, including Santa Eulalia, have been left to her younger sister Augusta. Of course they would have been left to her twin, Thérèse, but she's been dead for years.'

Brother Anselm stiffened, let out a low moan of pain and buried his head in his hands.

'It was a payback to Augusta, I suppose, for keeping her grim secret for all these years. It looks, Brother Anselm, as though we are finished.'

Brother Anselm held back a sob. She had promised him,

promised him faithfully that she would leave the monastery to the brothers! He should have known not to trust her.

'Maybe we could buy Santa Eulalia back from the sister?' he said hopefully.

Brother Francisco snorted.

'What with? God knows we have barely enough money to keep going from day to day.'

Brother Anselm smiled wanly. There might just be a way of saving the monastery if only that nosey little bastard of a boy didn't go and spoil everything.

By late evening Father Daley and Padraig were beside themselves with worry over Nancy's disappearance and contemplating getting up a search party.

Then, just before dinner time, a dishevelled and shoeless Nancy Carmichael waltzed into the refectory and took her place at the table. She seemed more than a little tipsy and kept giggling and hiccupping, but was completely tight-lipped about where she'd been. Father Daley and Padraig had to make do with the unlikely explanation that she'd kicked off her shoes, walked too far downstream, fallen asleep and not woken until it was dark and had to run all the way back barefoot.

As they ate, Padraig took sly glances at her across the table. Her hair looked as if it had been washed and dried in the sun. The face paint and powder were gone and the bloody awful pink lipstick too. The sun had turned her face a pale-golden colour and emphasized the blue of her eyes. There was a looseness about her neck and shoulders that hadn't been there before and a twinkle in the once down-turned eyes. It was as if Nancy Carmichael had walked out this morning as one woman and come back as another.

After supper Padraig took Nancy to the Great Hall to show her the fresco.

'It's great, isn't it? Imagine, it's been hidden for maybe hundreds of years and then suddenly it's found again. It looks as if it's telling a story, doesn't it?'

Nancy Carmichael looked up at the fresco, humming cheerfully to herself.

'What's that tune, Nancy?'

'Padraig, shame on you! "When Irish Eyes are Smiling", of course . . .'

Padraig gasped.

'Padraig, what's up?'

'Nothing. Just an idea. Miss Carmichael, you know Mr Leary has a problem with his eyes?'

'I do indeed, which is why he wears those thick pebbly glasses. Come to think of it, he looks a bit like that fellow there who's squinting,' she said, giggling and pointing at one of the monks.

'Well, why does he have a problem like that with his eyes?' Padraig persisted.

'I couldn't tell you, Padraig, I suppose it's one of those things, hereditary.'

'Like three-legged dogs?'

'Padraig, what in God's name are you going on about?'

'Doesn't matter. I'm thinking, that's all.'

'Me too, but not about frescoes, I can tell you. You want to give that brain of yours a rest. Too much brain work can be bad for you. Anyhow, I'm off for an early night before that Brother Anselm comes looking for me again.'

'Brother Anselm? Why is he looking for you?'

'He's a most peculiar old thing. This morning he kept pestering me to death, asking all sorts of questions. Where do we come from? How long are we staying? And all about you; he seems quite taken with you, Padraig. Do you know he even asked if I was your mother. Fancy that!'

'He was the one that shot Mr Leary, you know. You want to be careful; I don't like the look of him myself.'

'Padraig, your imagination is running away with you. I'll see you in the morning. And for goodness sake, Padraig, get those fingernails scrubbed, look at the state of them!'

Padraig looked down at his blue-paint-stained nails.

'Nancy, did you put a prayer down at the statue's feet?'

'I did.'

'And did it get answered?'

'Oh, yes, Padraig.'

And with that she winked, hiccupped and was gone.

Padraig took a last look at the fresco and sighed, then he went upstairs to his room where he stood at the window looking down into the valley far below. The river was a silvery ribbon coiling and twisting its way down towards the distant sea. The moon was high and full and a million pinpricks of stars were scattered across the sky.

He listened carefully; he was sure that he could hear the sound of someone giggling down below on the track. He leaned out of the window just in time to see two shadowy figures slip down past the Blue Madonna.

Padraig went across to the washstand, poured water from the wash jug into the bowl and picked up a bar of soap. Reluctantly he washed his face and the back of his neck and watched the water in the bowl grow scummy. Then he scrubbed his filthy nails with a nailbrush and soon the water was streaked with blue.

Father Daley was still down in the refectory talking with Brother Francisco and Brother Bernardo and probably wouldn't be up for a while, so Padraig put a chair against the back of the bedroom door while he was on his own. It wouldn't keep anyone out, but the noise of it moving would warn him; he didn't like the thought of Brother

Anselm being only a few doors away down the dimly lit corridor.

Padraig undressed and got into bed and lay for a long time thinking about everything that had happened since they'd left Ballygurry. He remembered how angry he'd been when Nancy had accused him of stealing the things from her trunk. Blimey, back then he would never have called her Nancy. He giggled as he thought about Miss Drew hurtling naked through the roof of the stable. He hadn't been sorry to see the back of her!

He remembered too his disappointment when Father Daley prised open the lid of the chest that had fallen down beside Miss Drew. He'd been really excited, hopping up and down, urging Father Daley to hurry. He'd conjured up thoughts of long-hidden treasure, gold coins and jewels and silver goblets, but all that the chest contained was an old moth-eaten suit and a filthy mackintosh with a faded tartan lining. At the bottom of the trunk was a leather-bound notebook, and Padraig's spirits had soared; it was bound to contain a map and coded instructions that would lead them to buried treasure or maybe even the Irish virgin.

Señora Hipola had lifted the clothes out gingerly and put them aside for burning, but only after she had slyly gone through all the pockets on the look-out for loose change. Seeing Padraig running his finger down the leather cover of the book she had told him to take it if he wanted it, and he still had it in his suitcase.

Señora Hipola couldn't remember whom the trunk had belonged to, some careless traveller, no doubt, who had stayed there over the years and forgotten it.

It didn't seem like he was going to find the statue of the Irish virgin. It must have been stolen; the jewels had probably been picked out of it and the gold melted down, after all it would be easier to get rid of small amounts of gold rather than humping a great big statue around.

Then he set to thinking about Brother Anselm's painting and who would be daft enough to pinch it. He remembered Brother Bernardo telling him that Brother Anselm knew a lot about art. Padraig thought that he might know a lot about it but he couldn't create it for the life of him.

And whatever had got into Nancy Carmichael, running about barefoot and without her stockings and staying out for hours like that on her own and coming back half cut? She wouldn't get away with throwing wine down her throat in Ballygurry, she'd be the talk of the place.

He wondered what it was that she had asked the Blue Madonna for when she laid her request at her feet. He thought that maybe he would write out a wish himself and ask if he could stay in Spain for ever and never go back to St Joseph's.

He slipped his suitcase out from under the bed and undid the clasps. Sifting through his clothes, he found the leather-bound book and opened it. It smelled strongly of mildew and the blank pages were stained as though at some time they had been soaked through. He turned the pages but there was nothing written on any of them. Towards the back of the book two of the pages were stuck together. Maybe someone had hidden a map between them?

Excitedly he tried to prise them apart with his fingernails but they were stuck fast. Reaching for his small penknife, he tried to insert it carefully between the pages. He worked patiently away for a while and finally made a tiny opening, slipped the point of the blade between the pages and wrenched them apart . . .

A piece of paper slipped out. Bugger! It was just a piece of boring old card. He turned it over and read the faded writing.

> Mr and Mrs Egbert Brennan cordially invite you to the marriage of their daughter Vera Mary Brennan to . . .

He sighed, tossed the stupid card back into his suitcase and climbed into bed, where he fell asleep thinking about the pictures of the monks on the fresco. He didn't hear the door scrape against the chair as Father Daley stumbled into the room, nor did he hear him giggle and fall into bed as the door clicked shut.

He woke in the darkness several hours later to the sound of shouting and someone hammering on the door.

Before Padraig could rouse himself, Father Daley was out of bed and hopping across the room. When he opened the door Padraig saw Brother Bernardo standing there, his ashen face illuminated by the glow of a candle that he held in a shaking hand.

'Father, I need your help. Someone has broken in and stolen another painting, but the worst thing is Brother Anslem has gone missing and so has one of the guns.'

'Stay there, Padraig, and don't move out of the room. Wedge the door with the chair.'

Padraig was trembling as Father Daley dressed hurriedly and followed Brother Bernardo down the corridor.

He was too afraid to stay in the bed so he got up, wedged the chair back in place as Father Daley had told him, and sat upon it. For a while he could hear raised voices downstairs, then a door slamming shut and a dog barking excitedly. And then a terrible quivering silence settled over the monastery.

Every creak made Padraig flinch. His ears ached with listening too hard for the slightest sound. His nerves were raw, his teeth ached and the hairs on his neck tingled with fearful expectancy.

He wondered whether Nancy was asleep in her room or

was she, like him, sitting on a chair pushed up against the door? He was half tempted to tiptoe along the corridor to her room, but as he put his ear to the door he was sure that he could hear the sound of someone breathing heavily. Was Brother Anselm lurking outside in the darkness of the corridor waiting for him to make a move? Padraig hugged himself tight with his arms, felt his heart squeeze up with fear. His knees were knocking and his ears pounded with the rushing of his blood. His mickey had shrivelled like a slug under salt.

Eventually, unable to bear the tension any longer, he got up off the chair and tiptoed across to the window. Down near the hamlet he could see lanterns bobbing in the darkness. He watched them moving along past the dilapidated houses until they were sucked up by the night. Padraig left the window and made his way silently back to the chair. A floorboard creaked outside the door and he chewed his fist with fear.

Suddenly the sound of a single gunshot fractured the silence. The noise loosened the bones of his skull, lurched his belly up painfully between his ribs, as it echoed on the chilly air. Padraig stood up and made his way unsteadily back across the room to the window and peeped warily out. He could see the frantic bobbing of lanterns down near the Blue Madonna and hear someone calling out in pain.

He could not bear being alone in the room a moment longer. He moved the chair, opened the door and came face to face with a grinning Brother Anselm.

The Old Pilgrim, sleeping soundly on the floor of a shepherd's hut, was woken by the sound of a gunshot. He sat bolt upright, the noise reverberating inside the hut, struggled to his feet, opened the door and peered outside.

The night was dark, heavy clouds were drifting across the

moon. Ahead of him the monastery of Santa Eulalia was a black silhouette against a star-blown sky, wisps of mist drifting up above the turrets.

He put on his hat, pulled his cloak tightly about his body and set off across the mountainside.

The monastery was in darkness except for one window where a light burned brightly. The Old Pilgrim stood still and contemplated the sight before him in wonder. A figure came into view in the lighted window. He drew in his breath, watched as a larger figure approached the smaller one . . .

Then there was just blackness where the arc of light had been.

A second gunshot reverberated round the mountainside.

Hunters, no doubt, out on the prowl under cover of darkness. The Old Pilgrim made his way back to the shepherd's hut, found his wine sack, took a long draught and sat for some time deep in thought.

This was the first time that he'd been up to these parts and seen the monastery of Santa Eulalia and yet he'd seen almost the same view of the monastery somewhere before. It was an uncanny feeling which sent his mind scurrying back over the past to more than twenty years ago.

He smiled now as he remembered the early light reflecting off the River Seine, the sound of the Parisian boatmen calling out to each other, the smell of oil paint and turpentine and French cigarette smoke strong on the morning air. On an ancient stove milk bubbled in a saucepan and the aroma of freshly made coffee escaped from the spout of a red enamel pot. The crumbs of croissants and bread were scattered on the table, a smear of jam on a white plate. A child singing enthusiastically as he pretended to wash up on the deck.

After he had landed in Spain all those years ago he had

holed himself up in Camiga as he had contemplated the enormity of what had happened to him. Then he had been overcome with the urge to move, to keep on moving and never stop. Thus he had made his way slowly up through the Pyrenees and on through France.

He'd spent a while in Paris that first winter, working in the anonymity of noisy kitchens in large hotels or waiting tables in back street inns. Then a stroke of luck had come his way. He'd heard that an artist who lived on a barge moored on the Seine was looking for a general dogsbody to do some cooking and child-minding.

For six months he'd enjoyed a blissful existence living on the barge called the *Sequana*. Everything had been a new experience for him. He'd shopped for the first time in his life, going each morning to the busy markets to buy meat and vegetables. He'd bought second-hand recipe books and a French dictionary, struck up conversations with housewives in street cafés, learned their language and culinary secrets. Then in the evening he'd cooked in the galley kitchen and the three of them had eaten together.

At other times he'd explored Paris with the irrepressible grandson of his employer, the ten-year-old Raffy. And, somehow, being with Raffy had softened the grief he had felt at the loss of that other child. Raffy was a sweet-natured but impulsive little chap, swift to get into mischief but quick to say sorry.

His employer, Federico, had risen early each day and painted in the mornings when the light was right and the weather clement. He was secretive with his work, never allowing anyone even a glimpse until he was finished.

Each afternoon he moved his canvas and easel back into a small cabin at the back of the boat where the Old Pilgrim and Raffy were forbidden to look.

Then one afternoon as he and Raffy had sat up on deck,

a string of expletives in several languages rent the air. Raffy had jumped up with fright, guilt stamped indelibly across his small face.

Federico came roaring on to the deck, his face suffused with anger. He'd lunged at Raffy, scooped him up and dangled him headfirst over the side of the barge . . .

Later he had taken the Old Pilgrim down below and shown him his grandson's handiwork.

That was the first glimpse before tonight that he had had of the monastery of Santa Eulalia. Just like tonight he'd seen the monastery silhouetted against the sky, one window illuminated.

Pointing to the window, Federico began to see the funny side of things. He began to laugh. And, oh, such a laugh he had. A swell of laughter in the belly, a wave bursting through his chest, breaking out through his mouth, stopping passers-by in their tracks, sending the cat scuttling for cover . . .

'Look what he has done!' Federico guffawed.

The Old Pilgrim had looked nervously at the painting. Raffy had taken a brush and painted in a small boy in the lighted window, a small boy looking up at the stars.

'I say to him, Raffy, you have ruined my work, and he looks at me so perplexed. But, Grandpapa, he says, this is such a beautiful place, wouldn't you want me to go there too? And he's right, he shall go there.'

'Where is this place?' he'd asked Federico.

'Ah, this is my secret place, the place of my dreams. You must go there one day, savour its peace.'

And then, before Federico could reveal the name of the place, all peace had been shattered as two gendarmes boarded the boat to break the news that Raffy's parents had been killed in an avalanche.

Soon afterwards Federico had shut up the barge and he

and Raffy had moved on together, wrapped up in their grief. The Old Pilgrim had lost contact with them after a few years. He had always remembered them fondly, though, they were a part of his good times, a part of his healing.

He knew that Federico had died about fifteen years ago, because he'd read a report about it in a French newspaper. He was quite a celebrity by then and was making enormous amounts of money. Good luck to him too, he'd richly deserved his success. He'd never heard any news of little Raffy, though. He'd be about thirty by now; he hoped that life had treated him well.

The Old Pilgrim dragged himself reluctantly back to the present and knowing now that sleep would not come easily he packed away his few belongings in his knapsack and left the hut.

He made his way laboriously across the mountain, the dew seeping swiftly up through his broken boots. Eventually he came to a track that led up the mountain towards the monastery. When he reached the top he turned and looked back down the valley. It was a fantastically beautiful place, almost surreal in its lofty splendour.

He walked quietly into a cobbled courtyard where an unseen dog announced his arrival enthusiastically. He was sorely tempted to ring the bell because for once the thought of a comfortable bed and a monastery breakfast were very appealing, but he didn't yet feel ready for company, so he stepped up his pace, left the courtyard and set off on a track that led over the mountain.

He walked for some time but clouds were banking and soon the moon was hidden and it became unsafe to continue. He sat down on a mound to wait for the moon's reappearance before he went on his way.

When the moon eventually reappeared, he looked about him and smiled. He had wandered off the track and now found himself in a small graveyard. All round him were wooden crosses, stark and strangely beautiful in the moonlight. He cast his eyes over the ones nearest to him.

BROTHER ALOYSIUS 1889–1943

BROTHER PEDRO 1910–1939

There in the midst of the wooden crosses was a stone headstone that looked most incongruous and foreign among the simple hand-carved crosses. He approached it with trepidation, stooping as he got closer so that he could read the short inscription.

He read the words slowly, disbelief growing by the second.

Good God! It was most extraordinary. He must be hallucinating, have wandered maybe into a madman's dream. Slowly he traced the indented letters of the name before him with his finger. Then he threw back his head and his wild laughter rang out across the mountains.

Father Daley, Brother Bernardo and Brother Francisco had reached the spot on the mule track just below the hamlet when the first shot rang out. The three men stood together in petrified silence trying to work out where the noise had come from when they had heard a muffled shout further up the track.

'This way!' Brother Bernardo yelled and set off with Father Daley and Brother Francisco on his heels.

As they reached the Blue Madonna they saw Nancy Carmichael lying on the ground at the feet of the statue. Her eyes were closed, her face an unearthly shade of white in the darkness. They looked in horror at a dark-red stain growing wider by the second across the bodice of her starched white blouse. A man was stooped over her and as they approached he looked up at them in alarm.

'Hell's teeth! Jesus and all the saints! What the fuck have you done to her?' shouted Father Daley, and he lunged at the man.

In the confusion that followed, Father Daley threw several fierce but badly timed punches. The man punched Father Daley only the once but rendered him unconscious and changed the shape of his nose for ever.

As Father Daley lay prostrate, a benign smile spreading across his face, the man turned to Brother Bernardo and spoke.

'Brother Bernardo, we must get help quickly. We must carry her to my house, fetch Brother Tomás to look at her. Maybe even send for the doctor from Los Olivares.'

'What happened, Rosendo?'

'I don't know, one minute we were walking together and the next, BANG!'

Brother Anselm stood in the doorway looking across the room at Padraig. Padraig looked steadfastly back, trying not to seem afraid; but he knew from the way his eyes were stretching and his chin was wobbling that he wasn't doing a very good job of it.

There was a quivering dewdrop on the end of Brother Anselm's hooked nose. He was dribbling profusely like a baby cutting new teeth. His rotten teeth were bared in a terrifying grimace. In his gnarled hands a shotgun wobbled dangerously.

Brother Anselm took a step closer to Padraig and the boy backed away. He knew that there was no escape except out through the arched window behind him. If he leaped out of the window he would fall to his death, tumbling over and over and smashing himself to bits on the rocky track below.

The old monk began to mutter, and frothy spit filled up the corners of his mouth like a rabid dog. His red-rimmed eyes bored into Padraig.

Brother Anselm took another step forward.

'I am very clever man. See, I make them think I have run off with gun. I shoot at the woman. Really, though, it's you that I want to shoot.'

'What woman?' Padraig said in a voice that was little more than the croak of a dying frog.

'Don't play the games with me. I know why you come. You and that mother of yours.'

Jesus, he'd gone and shot Nancy. He was a lunatic. Nancy hadn't done anything to hurt him.

'I haven't come to play games, honest to God, and I don't have a mother.'

'You come to take back my treasures. Looking everywhere, sniffing about . . .'

'I don't want the statue, if that's what you mean. I was just interested to know where it is, that's all; you can keep it.'

Brother Anselm shuffled closer.

Padraig stepped backwards knowing that soon nothing would separate the two of them except the gun.

A moth fluttered gaily in through the window and flew straight towards the wavering candle flame. Padraig bit his lip. There was a hiss, hot wax dripped down the candle and on to the holder. The moth flapped away into a corner, wings flailing helplessly.

Brother Anselm's eyes narrowed dangerously as he pointed the gun directly at Padraig.

Padraig knew that he was at the mercy of a lunatic and he didn't know what the feck to say to calm him.

Suddenly his gaze was drawn to a movement out in the corridor. He swallowed hard. Please God, he thought, I must be dreaming. Let me wake up . . .

Standing out there in the corridor was the shrivelled-up old man from the fresco, except that he wasn't naked but dressed, or rather wrapped, in a multitude of threadbare rags and there was no fork of lightning above his head. He was standing very still just beyond the doorway, his finger pressed tightly to his lips.

Padraig looked back at Brother Anselm. He was so close now that Padraig could feel his hot fetid breath on his own face, could hear the rattle of his groaning chest. He smelled stale piss and papery old skin.

Padraig pressed his back up against the window and felt the night air cool on the back of his neck riffling his newly grown hair.

Someone had told him once that hair kept on growing after a body was dead. And sometimes dead people farted and the force of the fart made them sit up on the mortuary slab with a satisfied grin on their chalky white faces. And that sent mortuary attendants skittering away jibbering with fright.

Oh, Jesus, he was afraid; he wanted his mammy, he wanted Sister Immaculata to hold him tight, Nancy Carmichael to stroke his head . . .

Brother Anselm pushed the barrel of the gun into the space between Padraig's nipples. Nipple was a rude word. Like fanny and tits. Oh God, even in his last moments he was thinking filthy thoughts. He'd go straight to hell . . .

Then suddenly the rag man stamped his foot and let out a terrible shriek and Brother Anselm turned round in alarm.

There was a sharp exchange of agitated Spanish. Padraig closed his eyes, felt a stream of hot itchy piss shoot down his left leg. The gunshot exploded, plaster flew from the walls and the candle went out.

*

Rosendo Angeles whistled as he made his way up the track towards the Blue Madonna. He kneeled down at her feet and bowed his head in prayer.

'Most holy, gracious mother, I give thanks to you for answering my prayers. Please God, grant now that the woman you have sent me makes a full recovery.'

He stood up, made the sign of the cross and carried on up the steep path, stooping to gather flowers as he went.

In the infirmary Brother Tomás looked down on the woman sleeping peacefully in the bed. Thank God the bullet had only grazed her shoulder. It was the shock that had affected her most. He had cleaned the wound and dressed it, given her a sleeping draught. Now a good long sleep and she should awake refreshed, if a bit sore.

Brother Tomás made his way across to the window and looked sadly down the valley. Soon they would have to leave the monastery and five hundred years of history would come to an end. Then he saw Rosendo making his way eagerly up the track carrying a bunch of freshly picked flowers. He smiled. So the Blue Madonna had finally rewarded his patient supplications to her over the years. Why, Brother Tomás had rarely seen such a lovesick chap.

How odd that Rosendo should wait all these years and then suddenly a pilgrim turns up out of the blue and steals his heart. Ah, the world was a strange old place all right.

Alone in the chapel Brother Francisco bowed his head in prayer and gave thanks that the two pilgrims had been spared. It was a miracle that the woman and boy had not been killed. Why the hell had Brother Anselm done it? What had two strangers done to make him so violent?

They hadn't got much sense out of the boy last night. He'd been a jibbering wreck when they'd found him, almost delirious with terror. Father Daley had translated what the boy had said about Brother Anselm trying to shoot him and how a rag man from the olden times had saved him. There was no doubt that someone had saved him, though, because he was alone when they found him cowering on the floor, but they'd also found a raving Brother Anselm tied securely to the bed in his own room.

Maybe the news that Isabella had not left the monastery to the monks had finally unhinged him. After all, Santa Eulalia had been a large part of his life. And now he was going to end his days locked up in an asylum.

Rosendo Angeles sat at the side of the bed and watched Nancy Carmichael as she slept. He took her hand in his own, stroked it gently and watched the sleepy smile transform her features. God, she was beautiful. He smiled to himself then as he remembered that first meeting.

He'd gone up to the stable that morning only to find that Dolores the pig had escaped again. She was like bloody Houdini. The trouble was every time she got out Alfredo set off behind her like a faithful minder.

It was a good job he'd had an inkling Dolores had taken a fancy to a boar that lived further down the valley on an isolated farm. He'd only just got to the river in time, to find Alfredo and Dolores standing on the bank watching the woman thrashing hopelessly in the water.

He'd jumped straight in and pulled her to the bank, a trembling half-drowned woman wearing only her underwear . . .

As Rosendo watched Nancy Carmichael he was unaware that she was only pretending to sleep. She was enjoying the feel of Rosendo's warm hand on hers, his comforting presence obliterating the pain in her shoulder, the soft touch of his lips on her cheek.

She let her mind drift back over the past few days. The

terror of tumbling into the glistening water. Frantically she had thrashed to the surface, sunk again, surfaced, sunk, surfaced again. Then suddenly she was lifted up, up out of the sparkling, beautiful, terrifying water and laid down on the soft riverbank. An anxious handsome face loomed close to hers. He had given her the kiss of life, little knowing that she didn't need it. Oh, and what a kiss it had been.

Having swallowed Brother Tomás's sleeping draught, Padraig had been pulled down deep into a dreamless sleep and woken in the morning heavy headed and calm until he remembered with a rush the events of the night before. He sat up and began to panic but was calmed by a nearby voice. He looked up to see Father Daley looking down at him anxiously.

'Padraig, it's all right. Calm down, little fellow.'

'Where is he, Father? Put the chair back up against the door quick. Don't let him in!'

'It's all right, son, he's not here, he can't harm you now.'

'Where is he, Father?'

'They've taken him away to somewhere secure. You've no need to worry.'

Padraig relaxed. Father Daley had called him son. No one had ever called him that since his mammy had died.

Suddenly the tears came in a torrent, splashing down his feverish cheeks, trickling down his neck. His chest began to heave. Oh Jesus, he wanted to talk, to spill everything out, but his throat was a burned-out cave, everything about him felt broken.

Father Daley looked down at him, a skinny little shrimp of a thing, a boy racked with enormous pain. He leaned tentatively towards Padraig, took him in his arms and cradled him. As he felt the little rib cage heave against him with emotion, he experienced a sudden rush of tenderness, a tenderness he hadn't felt since his own mother had held him close. He held the boy tightly and soon his own silent tears fell on to the boy's head.

Later, Brother Bernardo brought Padraig breakfast in bed. He came in to the room smiling cheerfully, carrying a wooden tray that bore an earthenware bowl containing two coddled eggs in oil, a hunk of freshly baked bread and a bowl of steaming hot chocolate.

After he'd eaten, Padraig made his way along the corridor to see Nancy Carmichael, but when he approached the door the sight before him took him aback. A man, the bad-tempered-looking man he'd seen down in the hamlet, was bending over her as she lay in the bed. He was stroking her cheek and cooing like a pigeon. A right lovesick gimp. Ugh! It was disgusting! He wasn't going to stop and watch that kind of thing; he'd come back later when the eejit was gone. He tiptoed silently away down the corridor and as he passed Brother Anselm's room he saw with relief that the bed was stripped and the room was empty.

He walked quickly on down the stairs and into the refectory, where Father Daley was talking quietly to Brother Francisco. When they saw Padraig they fell silent and Father Daley smiled.

'Father, do you mind if I go out for a walk by myself? I'd like a bit of fresh air.'

'No. No, Padraig. You're okay on your own, though?'

'Sure, I'm fine. Is Nancy going to be all right?'

'According to Brother Tomás she'll be up and about tomorrow. I'm afraid, though, that we'll have to go down to Santa Anna without her, but God willing she'll be able to come with us to Santiago de Compostela.'

Padraig took a walk along the mule track that led away from

Santa Eulalia and across a large expanse of meadow land. Brother Bernardo had told him a few days earlier that they would take that road when they went on down to Santa Anna. Padraig walked along it for some time, then stepped off the uneven track and ambled through a trail of trampled daisies and dandelions.

Eventually he came to an outcrop of rocks beyond which there was a sheer drop hundreds of feet down into the river valley below.

He lay down in the grass on his belly and turned things over in his mind. He trembled as he remembered the terrible look of hatred in Brother Anselm's eyes last night. But why? What had he ever done to Brother Anselm? And why had he shot Nancy? Nancy wouldn't harm a fly. Thinking about Nancy he remembered how happy she'd been the other night when she'd been humming that song, 'When Irish Eyes are Smiling'.

After she'd gone he'd looked closely at the painting. The monk in the brown robes had deep-blue eyes, whereas the white-robed monks round him had dark eyes and swarthy skin. His skin was paler, pinker. He looked more like an Irish fellow than a Spaniard. In his hand he held a rosary and it was the rosary that had caught Padraig's eye. He'd seen one something like it before but he couldn't work out where. There was a group of similar pale-skinned monks in the background, some of them swigging from goblets, others holding out goblets to be filled from wine sacks. These ones had wide grins and rude-looking eyes.

Maybe, just maybe the fresco showed the group of Irish monks who had brought the statue to Spain. There was no sign of a statue in the fresco, though.

Then when he had scrubbed the blue paint from under his fingernails last night the colour was almost identical to the blue on the fresco, a peculiar shade of blue with a hint of lilac.

Padraig sniffed. He kneeled up and shuffled forward on his knees and peeped over the edge. A thin curl of smoke was drifting up from somewhere further down the rock face.

The view from here was brilliant but it churned his stomach and made him feel giddy. It was like being in an airplane, he guessed, because cows and sheep down in the valley looked as tiny as insects. He was about to scramble back up to his feet when he heard the sound of singing coming from below.

He got as close to the edge as he could without falling but it was impossible to see past an overhang of rocks a yard or so below him.

The singing stopped abruptly. He sniffed again. No more singing, just the tantalizing smell of woodsmoke and sizzling fish.

Then suddenly he was flipped gently on to his back like a big fish himself, being turned with a spatula. The sunlight blinded him momentarily. Shading his eyes against the glare, it was some moments before he realized that he was looking up into the eyes of the strange little rag man who had saved him from Brother Anselm last night.

He was a man with a face as shrivelled and dark as dried seaweed, eyes as black and damp as limpets.

The cave was surprisingly large, cut into the rock face high above the valley and only accessible through the dark tunnel down which the odd little man had led Padraig.

A thick rope was strung across the front of the cave and on it were hung an assortment of animal skulls in various sizes that rattled in the breeze. In a brazier, on an overhang of rock, a fire crackled beneath a blackened pan.

Padraig was impressed; it was a fabulous if dangerous hideaway.

He looked again in fascination at the oddly dressed little man.

'Thanks for what you did last night.'

'That's quite all right. Pleased to meet you again, Padraig O'Mally.'

Padraig blinked in surprise. The weird-looking fellow spoke English but with a peculiar twang to it, almost Irish sounding.

He swallowed hard; half of him was terrified and the other half intrigued. The fellow looked deliciously mad.

'How do you know my name?'

'We met before, briefly, a long time ago,' the man answered with a smile and held out his hand.

'My name is Muli,' he said.

'Where did we meet, Muli?'

'Ah, you won't remember. You were tucked up warm beneath your mammy's coat.'

'You knew my mammy?'

'I did indeed, and she was a wonderful woman. I'm only sorry that I wasn't around when she passed away to give you a helping hand.'

'Why did you save me, Muli? He could have killed you.'

'Ah, it was nothing.'

'You saved my life.'

The man waved his hand dismissively.

'How did you know that he was going to come after me?'

'I was just hanging around the monastery, that's all, keeping an eye out. I heard the first shot, thought I'd just take a peek.'

'Muli, would you tell me something? Were you there in the monastery the night we arrived?'

Muli grinned.

'I was, why do you ask?'

'I saw someone hiding at the top of the stairs and thought I was imagining it.'

'I was just checking, that was all.'

'Do you live in this cave all the time, Muli?'

'On and off when I'm not travelling.'

'How do you live, though, for like food and that?'

'I live by the lip of the wind.'

'Come again?' Padraig said, puzzled.

'The winds bring me everything I need. A few apples and plums blown down here and there on the mountain, sometimes in a storm a bird will get blown in here and then I pluck it and bung it in the pot. This fish, for example, was dropped by a startled eagle.'

'Honest?'

'No, I caught this one myself just before dawn.'

'How come you speak such good English?'

'Ah, for many years I travel, selling pencils and pads, all over the place I go . . . wherever the wind calls. Wherever the nubeiro is needed.'

'Bloody hell, are you a nubeiro? I've heard all about them! You can make storms and that at the drop of a hat, isn't that right?'

'A little more than the drop of a hat, maybe, but yes, I can conjure up storms. Are you afraid of storms, Padraig O'Mally?'

'No, I love them.'

'Why do you love them?'

'I don't know, it's the excitement, the electricity and like that lovely fresh smell afterwards as if the world has been shook up a bit . . .'

'Like things might change?'

'Yes, like there's a bit of hope. Why do you make the storms?'

'It was my destiny to be a nubeiro. Like my mother before me, her father before her . . . we just help things along a bit sometimes.'

Padraig caught sight of something at the back of the cave and gasped. He pointed with a shaking finger at the bundled wedding dress at the back of the cave.

'You did that?'

'I helped,' Muli said with a slow grin. 'The poor girl couldn't get married without a dress, after all, could she?'

'I saw that happen, saw it take off. The girl, the pretty one at Señora Hipola's, was supposed to wear it for her wedding but she ran away.'

'Did she indeed? Maybe when the wind changed it made her restless, gave her a shove. Take a look at the back of the dress, Padraig O'Mally.'

Padraig flinched.

'Ah, you are afraid because it is the dress from your dream?' Muli asked.

Padraig gawped at Muli.

'How do you know about my dream?'

'Sometimes we share our dreams, Padraig. Sometimes dreams serve to point us in the way we should be going or where we have come from.'

Muli shuffled to the back of the cave and picked up the dress, fiddled round with the neck and revealed a label.

'A clue!' he said, holding the dress towards Padraig.

Padraig looked at the label.

'Does it mean anything to you?'

Padraig read the label.

FLORENCE GALLIVAN. CORK

'She must have been a big woman this Florence Gallivan. Is that who it belongs to?' he asked.

'No. No. Florence Gallivan was the name of a dressmaker in Cork.'

'Then how is it a clue?'

Muli smiled, a secretive smile.

'It's a piece of a small puzzle. One of many small puzzles that make up one enormous puzzle.'

'I still don't understand.'

'You will, Padraig O'Mally, you will. Already you are trying to solve many puzzles, is that so?'

Padraig nodded.

'I am, but at the moment I'm kind of confused.'

'Things going round and round in your head but nothing makes sense?'

'That's right. Have you ever seen one of those glass snowflake domes that rich kids have? You know, there's a scene inside and you shake them and the snow makes a blizzard. Siobhan Hanlon has one back in Ballygurry.'

Muli nodded enthusiastically.

'What's inside your dome, Padraig?'

'A lost statue and . . .'

'And what else, Padraig?'

Padraig was silent.

'A face in a horse trough?' Muli proffered.

'My mammy's,' Padraig said in a faltering voice.

'It's a hard thing to lose someone you love, isn't it, Padraig?'

'Do you know how it feels, Muli?'

'I do, Padraig. Even a queer-looking thing like me feels loss.'

'Was it your mammy that you lost?'

'No, not my mammy, my mammy is still alive.'

Padraig wondered if Muli was a bit short-changed up top. No way could his mammy still be alive, he was as old as the hills.

'No, it was a woman called Thérèse that I lost a long time ago, but enough of that. Small boys aren't interested in romance. Tell me what else you see in the dome.'

'I'm not sure, every time I think I can see it it goes all blurred.'

'It feels as though you have shaken up the dome but all the snow is refusing to settle?'

'Yep.'

'It will settle, Padraig, it will, and then all will be revealed.'

Padraig felt suddenly faint, the smoke from the fire was making his eyes water, the smell of the fish made him nauseous. Muli's face swam in front of him, a blur of lively eyes and a wobbling grin. He stumbled and Muli took hold of him.

'Here, take a drink of this,' Muli said, and his voice sounded to Padraig as if it came from a faraway place.

Padraig took the leather bag that Muli held out to him and drank deeply.

'Muli,' he said, 'when I saw you last night I thought you were the man from the fresco.'

Muli grinned widely.

'And so I am, Padraig, so I am.'

'That's not possible, though. It was painted hundreds of years ago. You look old, but not that old.'

'Maybe it's not me exactly but an ancestor of mine.'

Padraig's head swam as he tried to keep all his thoughts on the go.

Muli went on.

'That's enough thinking for now. Come with me, Padraig O'Mally, for I have some secrets to show you.'

Muli led him back up the slanting tunnel that led away from the rear of the cave and eventually brought them out in the middle of a large clump of long grass on the mountainside.

'Sit down over there,' said Muli.

Padraig sat cross-legged on the grass.

'Now,' said Muli, 'to take your mind off solving mysteries I will show you a few tricks of the nubeiro. Not to be attempted by the faint hearted. Though you could try these out and come to no harm, only those who have the wind in their soul can practise this kind of magic.

'Right. The first thing that I show you is the *fumeira*. It is one way to conjure up a storm but not one to carry out in front of any ladies.'

'Why?'

'No more questions. Watch and see. First I find a molehill. Like this one here.'

Padraig stared at the molehill, a mound of fine earth a few feet away from where Muli stood.

'Then I take off my fine clothes.'

Padraig laughed.

'Now, being a shy fellow I won't actually strip naked, but I take off the clothes, wrap them in a bundle, place them on the molehill and set light to them. Then, I stand upon them and then . . .'

Muli's eyes were glinting with such humour and wickedness that Padraig shivered in anticipation.

'What then?'

'Like magic, I disappear into the sky with the smoke and then da da da, like magic, within moments you have the storm!'

'You mean you can make a storm just like that wherever you want?'

Muli nodded, his face grown very serious now.

'What is the second way?'

'Ah, the second way, and no less successful is the *polyvorina*.'

Padraig rolled the word round on his tongue and enjoyed the feel of it.

'Now I will show you the *polyvorina*.'

'And will we have a storm?'

'But certainly.'

Muli made a low bow to Padraig.

'Señors, señoras, señoritas, the great and marvellous Muli will perform today for you the *polyvorina*!'

Padraig bit his nails in excitement, never taking his eyes off Muli. The old man beckoned to Padraig and he followed him across the grass to a bare patch of ground that looked as though someone had been busy preparing it for planting. Padraig sat down and watched as Muli scooped up handfuls of dusty earth and began to pile them into a mound.

'The *polyvorina* is perhaps the best one to show you. It wouldn't do after all to take off my clothes in front of such a grand gentleman as yourself.'

Padraig grinned up at him, laughed aloud.

Muli worked furiously for ten minutes or so and was soon sweating from his efforts.

'Remember these things I show you today, for I am a very old man and my powers grow weaker.'

'I will remember them,' said Padraig honestly, for he had a fine memory.

When the pile of dust was almost as high as Padraig's head, Muli stepped back and closed his eyes as though he were praying. Padraig wondered what he was going to do next.

After a few moments Muli opened his eyes and smiled, a ragged, comical smile. Then quick as a wink he turned his back and pissed on to the pile of earth.

Padraig leaped to his feet and stared in admiration. Muli pissed as fast and furious as a frightened donkey. He pissed an ocean. As the hot stream hit the pile of earth, dust rose into the air and Muli was soon hidden from his sight.

The dust found its way into Padraig's throat and made

him cough. His eyes watered and he batted at the air with his hands to clear it away.

Slowly, the cloud settled. A thin layer of reddish-brown dust now covered Padraig's arms and legs. Muli was gone. It was as if he had been spirited away by magic. Padraig turned round and looked across the mountainside. A soft wind stirred the grass, but there was no sign of Muli, not even the mark of his bare feet on the dusty ground.

Padraig called out his name. He turned round and round but there was no sign of the queer little fellow, just the sound of the breeze in the long grass and the shriek of an agitated bird passing overhead.

The sky grew dark, angry purple clouds blanked out the sun and a cool breeze riffled through the grass. Below in the valley cow-bells clanked.

Away in the distance the monastery of Santa Eulalia glowed with an incandescent light. Far away the clouds banked above Camiga, thunder growled and the first fat drops of rain began to fall.

Padraig stretched out his arms wide and ran towards Santa Eulalia, nose-diving, curling and weaving through the clouds of poppies and dandelions that dipped their heads at his passing.

Part Five

Donahue had driven on the left-hand side of the road since leaving the ferry, while his passengers huddled down in their seats, eyes covered by trembling hands. In his wake lay a lorry loaded with hay that had swerved too late into a ditch, a cyclist with a limp, and the echo of a stream of French obscenities from pedestrians and motorists from Calais to Paris.

The passengers' backsides were bruised from the miles of bouncing up and down on the hard leather seats while the French countryside flashed by outside the car windows.

As they had entered a small village, an old man crossing the road waved his stick cheerily at the car. Donahue waved back and put his foot down to the floor.

The side wind took off the old man's beret.

Chickens scattered, geese flapped their wings and an ancient woman bending down at the side of the road had her skirt blown over her head by the back wind.

Donahue in his mirror looked in amazement at the huge bare French behind.

'Vive la France!' screeched Donahue.

Leary, a man to avoid religion whenever he could, muttered a string of Hail Marys and crossed himself at regular intervals.

The car bumped and bounced over a level crossing.

Through the back windscreen they could see a train hurtle past. Startled French railway passengers gawped and raised their Gallic eyebrows. A gendarme at a cross-roads blew his whistle and put out a hand to stop the car.

Donahue stopped for no one.

The gendarme crossed himself and then launched himself into a flurry of geranium pots . . .

As the car pulled up outside the Hotel du Pont stars were bursting into a huge Parisian sky and a full orange moon glowed above the city's rooftops. Donahue's passengers uncovered their eyes and staggered exhausted and traumatized on to the pavement.

After a night's rest Donahue and Leary sat opposite each other at a table outside the hotel. Donahue picked up a peculiarly shaped bread roll and stared at it curiously.

'What the hell is this?' he asked.

'It's a croissant, Marty, and it won't bite. For God's sake eat the bloody thing and stop examining it,' Michael Leary said, grinning, his eyes twinkling behind his thick spectacles.

Donahue took a bite of the croissant and chewed on it thoughtfully.

'Quite nice for foreign muck. Very tasty actually. Flaky and buttery and very satisfying to the taste buds.'

He took a hearty swig from his bowl of coffee and sighed with pleasure. Sitting there contentedly with Leary at an outside table in Paris not a stone's throw from the famous River Seine, Donahue decided that he was having the time of his life and wondered why he'd never taken to the road and travelled before.

'I never imagined I'd enjoy being on foreign soil this much. Mind you, the way they drive over here is enough to send you on the bloody drink. Behind the wheel they're all lunatics!'

Michael Leary rolled his eyes skywards. Being in the passenger seat next to Donahue had been the only time in his life that he had ever rejoiced in his appalling eyesight. Donahue just aimed the car in the direction he wanted to go and God help anyone who got in his way.

The two men were taking breakfast while they waited for Solly Benjamin and Dancey to return from their quest to discover if Madame Mireille still kept the dress shop on the Rue Bernard.

'Do you think they'll discover anything about this red cardigan that Dancey has in her suitcase?' Donahue asked.

'God only knows. It looked like a bloody dishrag to me, but it had the label in it saying Madame Mireille, so I suppose every avenue, or *rue*, as they say over here, has to be explored. Still, are you glad you came, Donahue?'

'Indeed I am. Spur of the moment decision and all that. I'd love to have seen their faces in Ballygurry the day after we'd gone.'

'Ah, their tongues will be hanging out waiting for a drink in Donahue's, eh?'

'Ah, not that long. I posted the keys to Dermot Flynn, asking him to look after it in my absence; he always had designs on running the place anyway.'

'You can't beat a bit of travel, Marty. There was no future for me in Ballygurry; I'd already received notice to quit with all the kids going off.'

'Ah, I should have shifted my lazy arse out of Ballygurry years ago. Michael, will you order me a couple more of these crotchet thingies, I'm bloody ravenous.'

Leary signalled for the waiter, lit a cigarette and smiled across at Donahue. He'd never seen him looking so happy, he was positively glowing, like an overgrown and over-excited kid.

Solly and Dancey took a taxi to the Rue Bernard and stood looking up and down the street. Solly didn't hold out much hope of finding the shop after all this time. Madame Mireille had seemed ancient when he was a boy; it was a shot in the dark all right.

He held Dancey's hand as they walked together along the street looking at all the shop fronts. There was no sign of the dress shop, and Solly thought that it had probably closed years ago.

They crossed the road and looked on the other side, but with no success. Solly was about to call it a day and return to the hotel when an old man came shuffling along the street towards them. Solly called out to him and marvelled at how, despite all the years away, his own command of French had come back to him since his arrival in the country.

The old man looked up with rheumy eyes, squinted at Solly and cocked his head on one side. He was very hard of hearing and Solly had to repeat his question several times. The old man pondered for some time and then walked away. Solly looked down at Dancey and shrugged, and then the old man glanced over his shoulder and beckoned Solly and Dancey impatiently to follow him.

They followed him back along the Rue Bernard and turned left down a dark alleyway where the old man stopped in front of a small shop. Looking up, Solly was delighted to see the familiar name, faded now, above the window. Madame Mireille.

Of course! He'd thought that the shop was on the Rue Bernard; he remembered now that it was the pâtisserie that was on the Rue Bernard, where they used to stop after his mother had finished her interminable clothes shopping.

He thanked the old man profusely, then opened the door, and he and Dancey stepped inside the shop. Solly felt about ten years old again as the familiar smells of face powder and strong lavender perfume assailed his nostrils, and though he couldn't see anyone out in the shop, he could sense that Madame Mireille was somewhere close at hand.

He coughed loudly and shuffled his feet. A faded green chenille curtain which hung down over a door at the back of the shop suddenly stirred and a withered, bent-backed old woman appeared. Madame Mireille felt her way towards them painfully, slowly, and Solly realized with a shock that she was blind.

He spoke first and watched with delight as her face broke into a fond smile and she held out her cheek for him to kiss.

'Ah, Solomon,' she said, 'it's many years since you've been here. Such a bored little boy always when you came here with Maman. And she was a very beautiful woman, was she not?'

'She was, Madame Mireille.'

'But you haven't come all this way to talk about your mother, eh?'

'No. I've come to see if I could find out something, to try and solve a mystery.'

Madame Mireille listened intently, and when he'd finished speaking she nodded slowly. Solly put the red cashmere cardigan into her wrinkled old hands. She felt the material carefully between her twisted fingers, searching out the small buttons on the front of the cardigan. Finding one, she traced a finger carefully round its shape.

'Ballet slippers,' she said, and smiled knowingly.

Solly looked closely at the buttons. He hadn't taken much notice of them before, buttons were merely buttons, after all.

'Mademoiselle Martinez,' she said brightly.

Then she began to jabber away at incredible speed and Solly had to ask her to speak more slowly.

It transpired that Señora Isabella Martinez used to buy many clothes from Madame Mireille when she came to stay in Paris.

'She brought a man with her sometimes, her brother, she said he was. Brother, my arse! I am not as green as I'm cabbage looking. He was supposed to be some sort of an artist. The way they looked at each other there was no way he was her brother. Her lover more like!'

The girl, her daughter, then a teenager, had had a penchant for ballet. Madame Mireille told how she had bought the buttons from a traveller from Chartres, then sewed them on herself by hand. She'd sewn them on to seven or eight cardigans and blouses for the young lady. They were very good customers.

'The girl was a bit of a devil. She gave them the run-around, that's for sure. A precocious madam, and an eye for the men even at that young age! Not a bit like her elder sister; chalk and cheese they were. She was a lovely girl the elder one. She'd been at school in England; I used to send over clothes several times a year. There was no shortage of money with Señora Martinez, that was for sure.'

Madame Mireille insisted that she make coffee, and the three of them sat for a long time as the elderly dressmaker relived some of her past.

Finally, Solly bid her an affectionate farewell, and when he and Dancey left the shop there was a spring in his step. He was a little closer anyway, at least he had a name, and perhaps if he could trace this Señora Martinez it might just shed some light on where Dancey had come from and who had sent her to him.

Solly and Dancey headed back towards the hotel and

found Michael Leary and Donahue still sitting outside in the early morning sunshine.

'Any luck?' Michael Leary asked, and was astonished when Solly nodded and sat down to recount all that Madame Mireille had told him.

'That's strange,' Donahue said, wiping croissant crumbs from his chest. 'Do you remember, Michael, when Dr Hanlon was talking about a girl who was at school with his wife?'

'Sure I do. A Spanish girl who had her clothes sent over from Paris. She and Hetty wrote to each other for years, then suddenly she lost contact.'

'Is that a coincidence or what? I wonder if it's the same person.'

'Well, there's a way of finding out,' Donahue said, grinning from ear to ear.

'How?' Solly asked.

'Two ways in fact. Telephone Mrs Hanlon and ask her the name or else contact Siobhan and get her to ask at the school. She'd love that, ferreting about for information.'

Solly was excited by the headway they were making, but he was troubled, too. He'd grown very fond of this silent little child, and he had to face facts, no one had come looking for her, had they? Whoever had sent her to him didn't seem to want her back.

Siobhan Hanlon was sitting alone in the schoolyard when Sister Mary Michael called her inside to take a telephone call.

She followed the nun along the darkened corridor, past the gimlet-eyed statues, and stepped nervously inside the small wooden telephone cubicle outside Sister Helen's study.

Siobhan was surprised to be summoned to take a

telephone call, because parents were requested not to telephone unless there was an absolute emergency. Sister Mary Michael had told her that this was an exception because it was her old schoolteacher on the telephone asking how she was doing with her schoolwork.

'Hello,' Siobhan said nervously.

'Siobhan, is that you?'

'Yes it is. Is that you, Mr Leary?'

It was great to hear a familiar voice. She'd been so homesick since she'd been at the school.

'Siobhan, listen, I want to see if you can find out something for me. Would you mind helping out?'

'Not at all!' she said with enthusiasm.

'Are there any old school photographs up on the walls at St Martha's?'

'Yes, sure. They go back about as far as the Black Death I think.'

At the other end of the line Leary smiled.

'Can you find the one your mother was in?'

'Course, but why?'

'Well, your mother had a friend when she was at school, a Spanish girl, and we want to find out anything we can about her. We think that her second name was Martinez.'

'There's three girls with that name in my year alone. Couldn't you just ask Mammy?'

'No, I rang your parents at home but the maid said they've gone off to Dublin for a few days. Anyway, I thought you'd like to do a bit of detective work.'

'Great. I'll have a scout round tonight. There's one nun here who comes from up near Rossmacconnarty way who's been here for yonks, I might try asking her. She seems as lonely as I am and the only friendly one here,' Siobhan whispered. 'Are you in Ballygurry, Mr Leary?'

'No, I'm in Paris. Me, Donahue, Solly Benjamin and the little girl.'

'Wow! What are you doing there?'

'Siobhan, we've run away.'

'You never have! Why?'

'Remember the little girl that you saw in Solly's?'

'Yep.'

'We've come to look for her family. Tomorrow we're driving down towards Spain.'

'Wow and double wow! Mr Leary, will you see Padraig in Spain?'

'I hadn't thought of that. I doubt it.'

'If you do will you tell him something from me?'

'Sure.'

'Tell him to write me else I'll flatten him.'

'Siobhan, you'll have to speak up, I can hardly hear you . . .'

Siobhan's voice came faintly down the line. Leary couldn't make head nor tail of what she said.

'Siobhan, you're a grand girl, do you know that?' he yelled down the phone.

Siobhan had a lump in her throat the size of a plum, and a tear made its way down her hot cheek.

'Siobhan, what did you say? Speak up!'

And then the line went dead.

Señora Hipola, coming into the house from the courtyard, stopped in her tracks and stared in disbelief at the four people standing in her lobby.

There were two men that she had never set eyes on before. One was a slim dark-haired fellow, the other a barrel-chested, florid-faced man with a grin like a slash in a paper bag. The third was Señor Leary, who had stayed here in her house a few years back. And most surprisingly of all, there amongst them, looking absolutely petrified, was the little Amati girl.

The girl looked up at Señora Hipola uneasily, keeping a tight hold on the dark-haired fellow's hand.

Señora Hipola looked from the girl to Señor Leary questioningly.

'Señora Hipola, I wonder if it would be possible for you to give us rooms for a few nights.'

Señora Hipola pursed her lips.

'Do you have that one's mother with you?' she said, narrowing her eyes and pointing at a cowering Dancey.

'No. Why, do you know this girl?' Leary asked excitedly.

'Of course I do! Dancey Amati, she's called. And you can tell her mother from me that she'll feel the rough side of my tongue if she turns up here again. She upped and left here in the middle of the night, still owing a month's rent.'

Leary spoke rapidly to Solly and Donahue, relaying all that he'd just heard.

Solly was astonished.

'Tell her I'll pay the money that she owed, but ask her does she know the mother's name?'

Leary duly transalated.

'Sure I do. Pepita Amati.'

'Does she know where she is now?'

But Señora Hipola was as much in the dark as the rest of them.

'One minute Pepita Amati is here, swanning about the place in her high heels and dancing for hours alone up in her room, clomping about enough to bring the ceiling down. Pah! The next thing she is gone. Mind, if you ask me the child is better off without her.'

'Pepita Amati,' mused Leary. 'Well, at least we know her name now.'

'This gets curiouser and curiouser,' said Solly.

Señora Hipola showed them up to their rooms and Solly settled an exhausted Dancey down for a nap, kissing her gently on the forehead as he did so. He sat and looked down at the child as she closed her eyes and drifted off to sleep.

The closer they were getting to solving this mystery the more uneasy he was beginning to feel. It was clear that the mother wasn't up to much, and if they did find her, and she took Dancey back, what would happen to the girl then?

He waited until Dancey was asleep, then he got up, closed the door to the room quietly and went downstairs to find Leary and Donahue, who were sitting out in the courtyard drinking wine and talking.

'Have a glass of wine, Solly, damp down your worries for a while.'

Solly sat down with a sigh, accepted a glass of wine, drank deeply and soon felt his spirits a little restored.

'Let's have a recap on what we know so far,' Leary said, lighting a foul-smelling cigarette.

'Well, I only know that the child was sent to me by someone who knew my name and address but obviously I don't know them.'

'You're sure that you don't know any floozies like her mother?' Donahue said with a giggle. 'No skeletons in your closet?'

'None whatsoever. I am positive about that, Donahue.'

'We have one lead. If we can trace the Martinez family we may get somewhere, except that there are millions of people called Martinez in Spain. And if we do find them they may know nothing about her,' Leary added, blowing smoke rings into the air.

'All we know is that the mother was called Pepita and that she trotted about in high heels, danced alone in her room while the kid worked, and left suddenly owing money.'

'Now why would she do that?' Solly mused.

'Trot about in high heels?' asked Donahue.

'No! Leave suddenly like that?'

'To escape from someone? To meet someone?'

'But why send the child to me?'

'God only knows.'

'So where do we go from here?'

'Well, we can wait to see what Siobhan comes up with. But we also know that this girl is called Amati, so links with this Isabella Martinez could be tenuous. This Pepita Amati might have found the cardigan, stolen it even . . .'

'Does Señora Hipola know anything else about them?'

'No. She said they arrived one day looking for rooms. The mother was very secretive, kept to herself except for where the men were concerned. She didn't work, apart from the occasional shift in the brothel, but she put the child to work down in the cannery, poor little mite.'

'Where's the cannery, Leary?'

'Down in town. I worked there for a while. A bloody awful place to work, all stinking fish guts and blood. It was terrible working there in the heat!'

'That solves something,' Solly said.

'What's that?' Donahue asked.

'Her dislike of fish.'

'Whose?'

'Dancey's. She always ate whatever I put down for her except fish, the look on her face when I opened a tin of sardines once was a picture.'

'Ah well, if you'd spent hours every day down in the cannery it would be enough to put anyone off.'

'Do you think we've much chance of finding the mother?'

'I don't know, Donahue, and the trouble is will she want the child returned to her? And if we do return her, will she dump her again at the first opportunity?'

'Well, what's our next move then?' Leary asked.

'I'm damned if I know,' Solly said, shaking his head sadly.

'Was there anything else in the suitcase that could give us any clues?'

'No, there was just an old rosary and a scallop shell with a painting on it.'

'A painting of the Madonna?'

'That's right, how did you know that?'

'A lot of the monasteries on the route to Santiago used to make them, they were a sort of souvenir with a trademark painting. Have you got it with you?'

'Sure, I'll just go and get it.'

While he was gone Donahue said, 'Do you know, although we've come all this way I think Solly's actually terrified that we might find the mother. After all, it doesn't sound as if she was very good to the child, now, does it?'

Just then Solly returned with the scallop shell. Leary studied it for a moment, sat up and declared triumphantly, 'Bingo! It's from Santa Eulalia. Look, there's a mark on the back there. This one has been done by a chap called Brother Anselm.'

'Where is this place, Santa Eulalia?'

'Not that far from here. A day's ride up into the mountains. It's an old monastery where I stayed a few times. It's right off the beaten track. Father Daley and the others have been staying there but they'll have moved on by now to Santiago de Compostela. Look, there's a slim chance that the monks might know who she is. Do you reckon that it's worth a try?'

Solly nodded slowly.

'Shall we drive up tomorrow?'

'Thank God, Donahue, that it's impossible to get a car up

there. The thought of you driving on narrow roads in the mountains gives me the heeby jeebies.'

'Well, that's bloody gratitude for you.'

'Donahue, how much driving had you done before you shut the car away when your, er . . .'

'When Eileen buggered off and left me for another man, do you mean?'

Leary and Solly nodded in embarrassed silence.

'I hadn't driven in my life before this trip,' said Donahue.

'What do you mean you hadn't driven?'

'This trip is the first time in my life that I've ever sat behind a wheel. I've been damned good, too, haven't I just?'

Solly and Leary made no reply but raised their glasses and downed the contents in one. Then Leary said, 'Well, anyway, you'll only get the car as far as Los Olivares, then I'm afraid it's a mule track all the way.'

'May I suggest dinner down on the quay tonight. Then a good night's sleep and then off to Santa Eulalia in the morning,' Solly proposed.

'Grand,' said Donahue. 'As long as we don't have to eat muck.'

Dancey had only pretended to fall asleep. As soon as Solly had gone she got off the bed and walked nervously across to the window and looked down into Pig Lane. It was just as it had been when she'd lived here with Mama. She shivered and looked back towards the door, imagining that at any moment Mama might walk in. She felt the old familiar feeling of sickness rise up inside her. At least the Old Pilgrim and Solly had looked after her well. She'd had plenty of food in her belly and hadn't been left on her own in the dark at night at all. She didn't like being back in Señora Hipola's. What if they found Mama and gave her back and then she did the same thing again . . .

She remembered that last day quite clearly . . .

She was standing in a field. The sun was hot, the breeze laced with the smell of herbs and flowers. Cow-bells clanked.

She began to count aloud, slowly and carefully.

Uno.

Dos.

Tres.

Cuatro.

She closed her eyes as she counted and silver spots began to dance on the back of her eyelids. Then came the deep dark redness and finally blackness.

Cinco.

Seis . . .

'No peeping,' Mama called out from somewhere close by, her voice a breathy excited rustle on the warm afternoon air.

Dancey listened intently. She heard the sound of Mama's feet on the grass somewhere behind her, the swish of her cloak in the soft breeze.

Usually, in their games of hide and seek, Dancey only had to count up to twenty. This time, though, because she was such a big girl now, Mama had said she must count to a hundred.

She counted again.

Siete.

Ocho.

Nueve.

Diez.

Somewhere close by she heard the busy fizzing of a bee. She kept quite still.

Once, a year or so ago, she had found an orange lying in the deep grass of an orchard. She had picked it up eagerly, turned it over in her hands only to discover that half of it had been eaten away, and she had stared fascinated at the maggoty sphere.

Then suddenly a wasp had flown out from the centre of the broken fruit. She had been too startled to drop the orange. The wasp had flown straight at her. She had seen its tiny fierce eyes. Closer and closer it came until there was a burning pain between her eyes. Hot shocked tears and then a lesson learned. Stinging insects got impatient and madder as the summer waned. It was best to keep very still, hardly breathing.

Veinte.

Veintiuno.

The noise of the bee grew fainter.

She yawned sleepily. They had been walking since the first light of morning and now her legs were aching, her toes, pinched by her boots, were burning. She dropped down on to the springy grass and lay on her back, her arms behind her head. The grass tickled the back of her knees, she could smell wild garlic growing nearby.

She imagined the blue of the sky above her, a sky as wide and tall as for ever.

She opened her eyes just a little. The sun pierced the gap and made them water.

Cuarenta.

Cuarenta y uno.

Not too far away she heard the sounds of a mountain stream rattling over smooth pebbles. A shepherd whistling tunelessly.

Noventa.

High above, a hawk cried out and she pictured the shadow of its huge wings gliding across the grass. Beneath her tired body the earth hummed with warmth.

The sun was hot on her bare legs and the heat drew out the greasy animal smell of her hair and skin. Her clothes smelled of the smoke from last night's fire and the oily fish that they'd eaten.

She listened for any tell-tale sound of Mama. She knew that she would be hiding somewhere close by, behind a thick bush or a big tree. Maybe she was already crouched down in the deep waving grass waiting to be found.

Sweat drizzled down between Dancey's shoulder blades, the string of her drawers cut into her hot skin.

She yawned again.

Away over on the rough track the wheels of a cart turned noisily on the rough road and the hollow clop of hooves echoed mournfully.

The wheels of the cart stopped turning.

A donkey brayed, then whinnied fretfully.

Then the wagon trundled on faster; she heard the crack of a whip and a gruff voice urging the donkey to speed up.

Giddy up!

Ciento.

Dancey opened her eyes, blinking against the harsh hot light of the noonday sun. She stood up lazily and stretched out her arms above her head.

'Mama! Coming, ready or not!'

But she hadn't seen Mama again. Tears streamed down her face now as she remembered the terrible fear she had felt when she couldn't find her mother . . .

Now, her heart felt as though it were swelling and filling up her chest so that she could barely breathe. Slowly, for the first time, the truth dawned on her. It hadn't been an accident. Mama had played the game of hide and seek to make sure that she got away. Mama had known exactly what she was doing.

Mama who was the insect with a sting in her tail. Mama who was as treacherous as those stinging insects that got more impatient and madder as the summer waned.

*

On a rainy Saturday afternoon Siobhan Hanlon was reading in her cubicle in St Elizabeth's dormitory. She had grown restless and lost concentration, she was sick of being cooped up inside St Martha's and she started turning things over in her mind.

She hoped Mr Leary rang again soon because she had done her detective work for him and found out what he wanted to know.

Siobhan had innocently struck up a conversation with Sister Bonaventure about her mother's time at the convent.

Sister Bonaventure had taken Siobhan up to the top corridor where the classrooms of the older pupils were and they had studied several photographs taken of the whole school together.

'Here,' she said. 'Take a look at this one. See if you can find your mother there.'

Siobhan had looked along the rows of girls until at last she pointed at a much younger-looking version of her mother.

'There, you see, she would have been about fifteen in that photograph.'

'She had a friend, a Spanish girl, when she was here, is she in the photograph too?'

Sister Bonaventure looked at the photograph again.

'Yes, there she is, next to your mother on her right.'

Siobhan looked at a dark-skinned girl, a girl with a broad grin and two thick plaits tied with ribbons.

'What was her name?'

'Oh, let me think, it's on the tip of my tongue. Something Martinez. The first name escapes me. You could look it up, though. There are yearbooks in the library which all the girls sign before they leave.'

'Thanks, Sister Bonaventure.'

In the library Siobhan had lifted down the heavy red leather-backed books from the shelves. The year was written in gold lettering on the spines. There it was: 1922! She had taken the book over to a table close to the window, where she turned the pages carefully, running her finger down the listed names.

Each page was drawn up into three columns. One for the name of the pupil, their home address in the second and in the third the place they had gone on to study.

There was her mammy. Henrietta Mary Connolly. Address: Killigrew House, McNulty Lane, near Cork. Written in the next column was the Convent de la Croix, Rue Martin, Paris. That was the finishing school her mammy was always going on about.

Further down the page she saw another name. Piadora T. Martinez. The address was Villa Castelo, Benita and next to that the Convent de la Croix, Rue Martin, Paris.

Lying back on her bed in the gloomy cubicle she wondered when Mr Leary would telephone again and also how he was getting on in Spain. It was then that she remembered the ripped-up letters she'd found in the cupboard in St Joseph's and stuffed into her pocket.

She fished out the pile of letters from inside the lining of her trunk and sat cross-legged on her bed piecing the bits of paper together. It took her some time before she was able to read them.

At first she blushed at all the talk of kissing on the lips in the sea, but as she read on she realized that whoever these people were they weren't even married but they were going to have a baby. How could you have a baby if you weren't married? Siobhan didn't think it was possible. And what the frig was a pile of smutty letters doing in Sister Veronica's cupboard?

As she read the last letter she frowned with concentration.

> My darling, darling girl. Thank God that you are well and the child has been delivered safely. I can't believe that I have a son. I am the happiest man alive. I cannot wait to hold you both in my arms and never let you go. I think that Padraig George is the perfect name. God bless you both, my angels.

Siobhan felt the tears running down over her cheeks. She thought of Padraig now and her heart ached for him. She knew that he'd never seen these letters, because he'd told her that every orphan had a box of belongings that they weren't allowed to see until the day they left St Joseph's. Why had someone tried to destroy Padraig's belongings?

The convent of Santa Anna lay in the very heart of the labyrinthine town of Murteda. The roads that led to the convent were so narrow that it was only possible to take a mule in one direction; there was no way of turning round unless the mule was backed inside a house and then pointed in the opposite direction.

Hidden away though it was at the end of a particularly narrow alley, the traveller approaching the small door set into the ancient walls was immediately aware of the multitude of glorious smells that emanated from the convent.

Soap bubbles drifted out from the windows of the laundry and blew away across the rooftops, leaving a hint of lilac lingering on their wake. The scent of strong soap and starch mingled with the whiff of freshly ironed linen.

From the kitchen came the aroma of beef cooking in hot oil and the mouth-watering smells of freshly made marzipan and newly baked bread.

Standing at the window in her study, Sister Perpetua watched the priest and the small boy make their way up the alley towards the convent. These must be the pilgrims from Santa Eulalia, and a right handsome pair they were too.

She heard the bell ring out and the sound of heavy footsteps crossing the flagged stone floors as one of the postulants went to open the door.

Sister Maria pulled across the grille in the door and took a sly peek at the new arrivals. Then she lowered her eyes and opened the door.

She led the way quickly across the hallway to the visiting parlour where Sister Perpetua had told her earlier to seat the visitors.

Sister Maria indicated that they take a seat and then turned to leave, tripping over her trailing shoelaces as she did so. She cursed under her breath, Padraig giggled and Father Daley nudged him. Red faced with embarrassment, Sister Maria scuttled out of the door just as Sister Perpetua appeared in the hallway.

'Decorum, Sister, remember decorum at all times. Perhaps if you tie your laces more securely you will prevent another fall from grace,' she said kindly, smiling at the flustered postulant.

'And, Sister Maria, ask Sister Matilde to make up another bed on the second floor. We have an unexpected pilgrim arriving presently.'

'Yes, Sister Perpetua,' Sister Maria stammered.

'She won't be eating with everyone else, but will have all her meals in her room as she prefers to be alone.'

'Yes, Sister,' said Sister Maria and made a dash for the safety of the kitchen.

Sister Perpetua shook her head and sighed. Sister Maria was such a clumsy article; there was a lot of work to be done with that one before she made a half-decent nun.

She shivered then as a chilly draught caught at her shoulders. Glancing out of the window, she saw that the sky above the rooftops of the town was black with foreboding clouds. They were in for one hell of a storm by the look of it.

The rain was torrential and Donahue could barely see through the windscreen of the car; the wipers had packed up some time ago. The previous night they had contemplated going up to Santa Eulalia but Leary had made contact with Siobhan again and she'd told them the last known address for Piadora Martinez. They'd made the decision to go to the Villa Castelo in Benita and see what the Martinez family could tell them about Dancey Amati.

They had reached the crossroads where Señora Hipola had told them to take a right turn but the road was blocked by a fallen tree. Donahue stopped the car and had to shout to be heard above the noise of the rain pounding incessantly on to the roof.

'What do we do now?' he asked.

'I'm going to get out and take a look,' Leary said.

He was gone only seconds before he returned to the car soaked to the skin, his glasses streaming with rainwater, his hair plastered to his head.

'We'll not be going down towards Benita, there's other trees been brought down further along the road.'

'Is there anywhere else we could stay?' Solly enquired.

'We're not too far from Santa Eulalia,' Leary said.

'Is there any chance of us maybe spending the night there?'

'Not unless we could find a donkey with water wings,' Leary said. 'I think our best bet is to keep to this road, head on to the first town and put up for the night wherever we can. We'll have to try and get to the Villa Castelo tomorrow.

Surely to God the rain's bound to let up by the morning. It can't keep on at this rate.'

'Is it usually this bad at this time of the year?' Donahue asked.

'No. If you ask me there's a nubeiro and his tricks behind this storm.'

'A what?' said Donahue.

'A nubeiro, a maker of storms, there's a few of them round these parts.'

Donahue raised his eyebrows.

'For an educated man, Leary, you don't half talk some shite!'

The Old Pilgrim took shelter in a broken-down barn on the outskirts of a small village, and from the doorway he marvelled at the sheer force of the storm. Lightning flared above the mountain peaks, springs erupted from the ground and hurtled away in search of a river. Thunder rolled and clattered and the rotten eaves above his head groaned under the onslaught of the storm.

He made his way across the barn to a pile of hay and settled himself down. He felt quite feverish and his head was aching badly. He'd try and get a bit of sleep and then, as soon as the storm let up a bit, he'd set off again and try and find some lodgings for the night. He'd spent too many nights on the road of late and now he yearned for a hot dinner, a soft bed with clean sheets and a long uninterrupted sleep.

Padraig stood at the narrow window of the bedroom in the Convent of Santa Anna and looked out across the dripping rooftops of the town.

It was almost dusk now and the shutters were drawn on most of the windows of the houses. There would be few people venturing out on a night like this.

A sudden flash of lightning lit up the lane and illuminated the figure of someone hurrying along towards the convent. Padraig could hear the squelch of water through their shoes as they splashed along, a muttered curse as they stepped on a loose cobble and black mud squelched up over their feet.

Padraig got up close to the glass and looked down on the shadowy figure below. It looked like someone old and withered wrapped round in a dripping black cloak. He wondered for a moment if it was Muli.

The bell rang twice and echoed inside the convent. Padraig heard someone hurrying to open the door. He stepped out into the corridor to see if he could catch a glimpse of the new arrival. An unshaded light bulb swayed in the draught as the front door was opened, casting a wavering, eerie light across the uneven walls.

Padraig heard footsteps climbing up the stairs and moments later a nun's face appeared. The nun caught sight of Padraig and turned her face away quickly, but not before he had recognized her as the clumsy one who had tripped over her own feet. She was followed by the mysterious cloaked figure, who was wheezing and panting with exertion with each step. The nun led the way up the second flight of stairs and then Padraig heard a door being unlocked, before being quickly closed again. Moments later the nun reappeared, ignored Padraig's cheery smile and clattered hurriedly back down the stairs. Padraig poked out his tongue at her back and went back into his room.

In the convent kitchen Sister Maria whispered to Sister Matilde as they prepared vegetables for the evening meal.

'This storm seems to have washed up all sorts of people. The pilgrim I've just taken upstairs is a most peculiar-looking thing. Never said a word to me at all, just stared at me like I was a ghost.'

'How long is this one staying?' Sister Matilde asked.

'Sister Perpetua didn't say, just that we had to take all meals to the room until further notice.'

'Do you know anything about the fellow in the infirmary?'

'Not much, just that he's some tramp that Sister Perpetua has taken pity on. He was found collapsed on the road leading into the town. Two men helped him along and Sister Perpetua has called for the doctor to check him over. He's exhausted, apparently, and has a high fever.'

Just then Sister Perpetua appeared in the doorway and coughed loudly. The two postulants fell into red-faced silence; it was forbidden to speak while they were working.

'Sister Maria, I need a hand with our poor patient if you could spare the time from your gossiping.'

Sister Maria put down the knife and the potato she had been peeling, smiled at Sister Matilde and followed Sister Perpetua out of the kitchen, across the hallway and down the corridor that led to the infirmary.

There were three empty beds in the room but in the fourth a man lay sleeping. His troubled face was dark against the whiteness of the sheets, he had one hand cupped beneath his cheek and the other was hidden beneath the bed covers.

'Pull up a chair to the bed, Sister Maria, and keep a close eye on him. The doctor has been called but may have some difficulty getting here in this weather. There is a bowl of water and a cloth here, I want you to bathe his head, try and bring his temperature down. He's been delirious this last half hour.'

Sister Perpetua left the room and Sister Maria moved a

chair across to the bed and sat nervously down. The man lay quite still, the only noise in the room the sound of his laboured breathing.

Anxiously Sister Maria picked up the cloth, dipped it into the bowl of water, wrung it out and began to bathe the man's feverish forehead.

He moaned softly and stirred in his sleep, his eyelids flickered and he opened his eyes and looked up at a wide-eyed Sister Maria.

He began to speak to her urgently, rambling in a foreign tongue. Sister Maria was at a loss what to do to help him. Suddenly he reached out and grasped her hand and as he did so she noticed the ring on his little finger.

It was a large oval ring inlaid with rubies and diamonds and must have been worth an absolute fortune. It was very peculiar because he was supposed to be a tramp; his clothes, which had been laid out on a chair, were grubby and threadbare.

Just then the door creaked open and Sister Maria saw that it was Sister Perpetua returned with the doctor.

With relief Sister Maria fled along the darkened passage and as she turned the corner she almost fell over the small nosey boy who was hanging round in the shadows.

'Shoo!' she said, flapping her hands at him, 'Shoo!'

Grinning widely, the boy disappeared upstairs taking the steps two at a time. There was something odd about the nuns in Santa Anna's, they all seemed frightened of their own shadows.

Later, Sister Perpetua showed Padraig and Father Daley into a wood-panelled dining room at the rear of the convent. From the dining room a door led off into the kitchen and from there came the sound of clattering and the occasional burst of stifled giggling.

'Well, Padraig, are you feeling quite recovered now?' Father Daley asked.

'I am, Father, but I still can't understand why Brother Anselm did what he did to me and Nancy.'

'Ah, Padraig, I just think the fellow is senile. Brother Francisco said he's been going downhill for a long time, doing all kinds of peculiar things before we even arrived.'

'What sort of things, Father?'

'Well, Brother Francisco told me that he'd taken a hammer to one of the statues in the grounds and knocked the head clean off it.'

'Why would he do that?'

'Because, Padraig, his old brain is addled, he doesn't know what he's doing half the time. Put him out of your thoughts now. He's banged up out of harm's way.'

Padraig wasn't so sure that Brother Anselm was senile, plain wicked was more like it.

'Just think, Padraig, that in a few days' time we will be in Santiago de Compostela at the shrine of Saint James and then in the wink of an eye we will be on the boat on our way back to Ireland and Ballygurry.'

'Well I'd rather be in Spain getting shot at than back in St Joseph's.'

'Don't be silly, surely it's not that bad, Padraig.'

'It is, I hate it. And probably they'll send me to Australia anyhow and I'll be stuck shearing sheep or rounding up kangaroos for the rest of my bleeding days.'

'Padraig, mind your tongue.'

There was an enormous crash of thunder overhead. The crockery on the table rattled and the light bulb swung dangerously on its quivering flex, and then suddenly the room was plunged into darkness.

Someone started screaming hysterically in the kitchen at

the same moment as the bell on the door was pulled impatiently.

'What the bloody hell is going on?' Father Daley spluttered.

'Mind your tongue, Father Daley,' sniggered Padraig.

There was a commotion out in the hallway and suddenly Sister Perpetua's startled face hovered in the doorway in a pool of flickering candlelight.

Behind her a group of shadowy figures huddled close together.

'Someone put a peseta in the electric meter or one of us will go arse over tit in a minute.'

'Father Daley, that sounds like Mr Donahue's voice!'

'Don't be soft, Padraig, what would Donahue be doing over here? He'd have trouble finding his way to the end of Clancy Street never mind to Spain, he's always drunk.'

'Which one of you cheeky buggers said that?' Donahue asked.

'Mind your mouth, Donahue,' Leary muttered, 'there are nuns around.'

The light flickered back on.

Father Daley and Padraig blinked in the sudden burst of brightness and stared flabbergasted at the group of people huddled behind Sister Perpetua.

Father Daley was the first to gather his wits and speak.

'What in God's name are you lot doing here? And who's the little kid?'

'She's called Dancey Amati,' said Padraig.

Dancey Amati looked at Padraig in astonishment. He was the kind little boy who had found her in the wood. Suddenly, she let go of Solly's hand, went over to Padraig and planted a big kiss on his cheek.

Padraig blushed.

'Ah, he has a way with the ladies has Padraig. It's a good job Siobhan isn't here to see this,' laughed Donahue.

'Ah, hush up,' Padraig said.

'Who is she?' Father Daley exclaimed.

'It's a long old story, Father,' said Solly Benjamin, 'and we're all absolutely exhausted. But now we're here why don't we sit down and catch up on all that's gone on.'

There was uproar then as everyone started to talk at the same time.

Bedlam persisted until Sister Perpetua, who had been hurrying to and fro bringing candles, began to ring a handbell and the deafening noise shut everyone up within seconds.

Five minutes later they were all seated round the dining-room table. Outside the convent the wind roared and the rain battered unceasingly against the window-panes.

Michael Leary had filled everyone's glasses with wine and the two dim-witted postulants had begun to ladle soup into dishes under the watchful eye of Sister Perpetua.

Padraig, sitting next to Dancey, looked down at his soup with interest. On the top of it was floating what looked like dandelion petals. He stirred it with his spoon and the petals swirled round the dish and made patterns on the surface of the soup. Dancey began to stir hers too, pointed down at the soup and then smiled at Padraig.

'What's this?' Donahue said, looking down into his brimming dish.

'Dandelion soup. It's popular around these parts,' said Leary. 'I've only had it the once but it's delicious.'

'Dandelion soup! Jumping Jehosaphat. We'll all be pissing the beds tonight.'

'For pity's sake just eat it and shut up.'

'My mother used to make dandelion soup. She said her family had made it for generations, she used to call it

Spanish-Jewish dandelion soup, but I don't have a clue why,' said Solly.

As they ate, Solly recounted for Father Daley and Padraig how Dancey had turned up on his doorstep and how Sister Veronica, Sister Agatha, Miss Drew and Mrs Cullinane had marched up to Nirvana House threatening to take her away with them.

Then Donahue told how he was in the bar talking to Leary when Archie Cullinane came in to tell them what had gone on up at Solly's place. That was it. Leary and Donahue had made an on-the-spot decision.

'The car had been sitting in the garage for all that time unused. It was time to do something. We started her up and drove straight to Nirvana House only to find that the birds had flown. We finally caught up with Solly and Dancey at the crossroads and Bob's your uncle and Fanny's your aunt, here we are! Mind you, we frightened the life out of the pair of them, they thought we were the Guarda. In two shakes of a lamb's tail we were out of there and off on an adventure.'

'I've just realized, Solly,' Father Daley interjected, 'that the mystery present you were telling me about that night when I came for a drink, it was the little girl, wasn't it?'

Solly nodded.

'And all the talk was that you had a loose piece from Cork shacked up with you,' said Donahue with a wide grin.

'So what exactly are you doing in Spain?' Father Daley continued.

'On a wild-duck trail and not getting very far,' said Donahue.

'We're trying to solve the mystery of who Dancey is and where she comes from,' Solly explained.

'And have you found out anything?'

'Well, the biggest stroke of luck came in Paris,' Solly continued. 'You see, Dancey had an old cashmere cardigan in her suitcase with a label in the back. It was bought from a shop belonging to a certain Madame Mireille. As it happens, I knew the shop from years before, my mother was a customer there. To cut a long story short, Madame Mireille was able to tell us who had originally bought the cardigan but unfortunately didn't have an address.'

'But then,' interjected Donahue, who was on his second bowl of dandelion soup, 'Siobhan Hanlon, the little belter, came up trumps.'

Padraig gulped.

'She did? Is she with you over here?'

'No. The poor little thing is shut up with the nuns in London and not very happy,' said Leary.

'We knew from Dr Hanlon that Siobhan's mammy had been at school with a Spanish girl. Siobhan did a bit of detective work and hey presto the name of the girl was Martinez and Siobhan was able to give us her last known address at a place called the Villa Castelo.'

'So what brings you here then?' Padraig asked.

'We got caught up in this storm and the road we were meant to take was blocked. A chap directed us here and said we'd be able to get a good meal and a bed for the night.'

The younger of the two postulants who had been standing silently in the background began to clear away the soup dishes.

'We knew we wouldn't make it to the Villa Castelo tonight, so I'm afraid the meeting with Señora Martinez will have to wait until tomorrow,' Solly explained.

The other postulant, who was carrying a pair of delicious-looking golden-skinned chickens in from the kitchen suddenly lost her footing, and if it hadn't been for Leary's fleetness of foot the chickens would have been launched into the middle of the table.

As Leary leaped to her aid and relieved her of the heavy serving dish, she looked up at him and he was taken aback by the look of absolute panic in her eyes. Quickly, though, she turned away, blushed profusely and hurried back into the kitchen.

'So you won't make any more headway until you get to the Villa Castelo and talk to this family, assuming that they do know something about the child?' said Father Daley.

'That's right, and it might all be a waste of time. I mean Dancey's mother could have pinched the cardigan and this Martinez family may know nothing about her.' Solly sighed.

'According to Señora Hipola, Dancey's mother was a flighty piece of goods,' Donahue added with relish.

'One piece of good news from Ballygurry, though, Padraig, is that Donny Keegan's daddy came for him,' Leary announced.

'Honest to God? That's great, the lucky devil.' Padraig was delighted and made Mr Leary tell him at least three times the story of how Donny's father had burst into Sister Veronica's study and whisked him away.

Leary realized with a shock that Padraig and Father Daley hadn't heard the awful news about Sister Immaculata. He didn't feel that this was quite the right time to tell them and decided he would have a quiet word with Father Daley when the boy had gone off to bed.

'How's your pilgrimage been so far?' he asked.

'Exciting and scary as hell,' Padraig said. 'Nancy Carmichael got shot by a mad monk.'

'I was just wondering where she was. Is she all right, Father?' Leary asked with concern.

'Sure, just a surface wound, that's all. She'll be fine and will be arriving here tomorrow in time to come to Santiago with us.'

'It was Brother Anselm who shot Nancy and he tried to

kill me too and I was saved by a man dressed all in rags who can conjure up storms . . .' Padraig rattled on without taking breath.

'See, Donahue, he means the nubeiros, the makers of storms I was telling you about.'

'Nubeiros my arse!' laughed Donahue.

'Anyhow, Nancy has a man who's after kissing her all the time, it's disgusting,' Padraig said, curling his lip.

Donahue, Leary and Solly gazed at Padraig in disbelief.

'Is that right, Father Daley?' Donahue asked with wide-eyed incredulity.

Father Daley nodded and turned crimson.

'Dear God, I thought she was on a holy pilgrimage not a quest to find a man. I can't imagine Nancy Carmichael with a man.'

'Well, she has one,' said Padraig. 'And she has thrown away her stockings and drinks wine by the bucketful.'

'Don't add yards on, Padraig,' Father Daley said, giving him a warning look.

'And do you want to know what else she does?' Padraig asked, enjoying Donahue's astonishment.

'Does the Pope shit in the woods? Of course we do.'

'She sleeps naked.'

Donahue spat wine into his lap and began to cough.

Leary banged him hard on the back.

'Were you serious, Padraig, about someone trying to kill you?' said Leary, changing the subject.

Padraig, his tongue loosened by the wine he had been surreptitiously drinking, replied, 'Honest to God, Mr Leary, it was the same fellow who put the bullets through your knackers.'

'You never mentioned that, Leary, is that why that woman finished it with you?' Donahue said. 'Because you'd no tackle?'

'I was not shot through the knackers, Padraig, but I was shot. Brother Anselm claimed he was out shooting boar but I never quite believed that,' Michael Leary said, blushing profusely.

'Where were you when he shot you, Mr Leary?'

'Down by the Blue Madonna.'

Padraig sucked in his breath, then hiccupped.

'That was where Nancy was with her fellow when she was hit. The thing is, though, Brother Anselm told me that he only shot her to cause a distraction so that he could get at me.'

'Padraig, you never said any of this before,' Father Daley said.

'I'm only just remembering it, Father. It was all muddled up in my head before.'

'Why do you think he wanted to harm you, Padraig?'

'I don't know, Mr Leary, Father Daley reckons that he's just nuts. But he kept on going on about my mother, he thought Nancy was my mother and that we'd come to take back his treasures.'

Mr Leary took a long swig of his wine and was silent for some minutes thinking of what Siobhan had told him on the telephone.

She'd read out to him parts of the rambling letters that she said she'd found in the cupboard in St Joseph's, and it had been obvious from the letters that there was a mystery regarding Padraig's birth. For a start, why would his mother have changed her name and why was she running away? What did the pair of them have to hide?

Then Father Daley said, 'It's a small world, isn't it? Brother Bernardo up at Santa Eulalia was telling us that there was an Irish fellow, wounded in the war, who's buried in the graveyard there.'

'Is there, by God? Father Daley, can you remember his

name by any chance?' Leary said, trying to keep the urgency out of his voice.

'I can. The funny thing is I seem to remember that the mention of his name worried Nancy, she went very quiet at the time.'

'What was the name?' Michael Leary could hardly contain his excitement.

'George Fitzallen.' Father Daley enunciated the words clearly.

The name meant nothing to Leary but he was aware that Donahue had dropped his fork with a clatter and his mouth was hanging open with shock.

'Do you know the name, Marty?'

Donahue pulled himself up. He didn't want to say too much, didn't want to compromise Nancy Carmichael.

'Sure, well I didn't know him, just heard of him, like.'

'What do you know about him?'

'Just that he and his family lived in a grand house called Kilgerry over Rossmacconnarty way. And that he was sent away in disgrace over a woman or something.'

'Well, the poor bugger didn't make it back, anyhow,' Leary said.

Donahue had gone very quiet and Leary gave him a sideways glance. Donahue knew more than he was letting on, that was for sure. He could be a deep bugger when he had a mind to it.

Donahue was thinking that life really was most odd at times. Whoever would have thought that one of the Fitzallens would end up buried in the middle of Spain? No wonder Nancy had gone quiet at the mention of his name, but obviously she hadn't said anything. Well, sure as eggs he wasn't going to give anything away to anyone.

Leary pondered on the fact that in the letters Siobhan

had read to him there'd also been a mention of Padraig's father making his way to Santa Eulalia. Was it possible that this George Fitzallen was Padraig's father? Leary made a rapid calculation. Padraig was ten going on eleven now. The dates fitted near enough. The poor bugger could have been on his way home to see his lover and his child but never got there. Why had Nancy Carmichael gone quiet at the mention of his name? Why had Brother Anselm thought that Nancy was Padraig's mother?

Anyhow, if the fellow buried up at the monastery could be proved to be Padraig's father then surely the boy was entitled to know who his father was and where he was buried. He'd have to talk to Father Daley on the quiet later and see what he thought about it all.

He smiled across at Padraig. The boy was looking a damn sight better than when he'd last seen him. He was glowing with health and his once pale skin was peppered with freckles. It was a bloody shame they'd have to break the news about Sister Immaculata and ruin his happiness, but if they didn't one of them was bound to let it slip and that would be worse.

'Don't look now,' Donahue whispered, 'but I don't think those two nuns who've been serving us are quite right in the head. The one nearly threw the chickens down our throats and the other one is staring through the crack in the kitchen door and looking at us as if we're from another planet.'

Leary looked up quickly but as he did the nun bobbed down out of sight.

'She's probably never seen such a handsome fellow as yourself, Donahue. She's no doubt thinking of renouncing the veil at this very moment.'

'Do you reckon?' asked Donahue.

No one answered him for at that moment Padraig's glass

clattered on to the table and he fell into a delicious and inebriated sleep.

Father Daley carried Padraig up to their room, tucked him up in bed and returned downstairs where Michael Leary told him about Sister Immaculata's suicide.

Later, as he lay in bed listening to the winds buffeting the convent, he thought about that day at St Joseph's when he'd opened the cupboard door in Sister Veronica's study and seen Sister Immaculata and Padraig crouched down together. He could picture her face as she had grinned at him wickedly, winked and put her finger up to her lips.

Looking back she seemed a feisty old thing, not the type to give up on life and do away with herself. He remembered, too, the look of terror on Padraig's face.

God, he hadn't liked the nuns at St Joseph's one little bit. He didn't relish the thought of returning Padraig to the sisters, but he knew that he'd have to. That poor little sod would be bundled off to Australia. Hell, life was hopelessly cruel sometimes.

Donahue stayed down in the dining room for a long time after the others had gone up to bed. Sitting there alone he felt quite depressed thinking about his eventual return to Ballygurry. He'd have to go back, though, there was no doubt about that. He had no other way of supporting himself and he didn't even speak the language over here. Everything that he owned was tied up back in Ballygurry; it was where he belonged, he supposed.

His thoughts turned then to Nancy Carmichael. Fancy, all these years she'd been a devout spinster and now she was having a fling with some Spanish fellow. Well, she might as well enjoy herself while she could, she'd soon be back in St Bridget's polishing pews and dusting the statues.

By now, Miss Drew would have done the rounds of Ballygurry and Nancy Carmichael's long-guarded secret would be common knowledge.

Ah well, he thought, he'd better get to bed, they'd a long journey ahead of them tomorrow. He climbed the stairs and began to make his way along the corridor. Halfway along he stopped in his tracks. A shadowy figure was bent double outside the room he was sharing with Michael Leary. And if he wasn't much mistaken they were looking through the keyhole!

A floorboard creaked beneath his feet. The figure outside the door stiffened, looked round towards where Donahue stood.

Donahue stood stock-still. Jesus! It was one of those queer bloody nuns. Peeking through keyholes wasn't a very holy thing to be doing, surely to God.

Suddenly the nun stood up and hurried along the corridor in his direction. Donahue shrank back into the shadows as the grinning nun passed him, oblivious to his presence. Crossing himself, he scurried along the corridor, let himself into the room and locked the door.

Michael Leary stood at the window for a long time looking out over the rooftops of the town. He had been both fascinated and horrified at the news that Nancy Carmichael had been shot. And it was bloody odd that she'd been down near the Blue Madonna, the same place he'd been when he'd been shot at.

And what the hell did Brother Anselm have against the child Padraig? He didn't go along with the view that Brother Anselm was merely senile. He was a wily old bugger.

Why had Brother Anselm thought that Nancy was Padraig's mother? And what treasures could they possibly be after? The monks at Santa Eulalia were on the bones of their arse.

He yawned then and undressed. He spent five minutes doing his nightly exercises. Then he slipped naked beneath the freshly starched sheets of his bed moments before Donahue came stumbling into the room.

Solly sat for a long time on the edge of Dancey's bed stroking her head until her eyes closed and she drifted into a deep sleep.

He wondered if tomorrow they'd finally be able to discover where she had come from, where she belonged. If they didn't, then he supposed he'd have to contact the authorities here in Spain. It would probably be better that she went into a Spanish orphanage where at least she would be among children of her own nationality. Maybe, though, if they went back to Ballygurry and she did go to St Joseph's she'd at least be with Padraig. She had a soft spot for that little fellow all right.

He leaned over and kissed Dancey softly on the forehead and she smiled from the depths of her sleep.

Sister Perpetua turned off the lights downstairs, lit a candle and climbed the stairs wearily. She made her way quietly along the corridor where the postulants' rooms were, paused outside the last door and listened.

From inside the room came the sound of excited whispering and stifled laughter. She put her ear closer to the door. She drew in her breath suddenly, felt the blood rush into her cheeks as she heard a snippet of the conversation. Then she rapped on the door and there was immediate silence within the room. Sister Perpetua shook her head and made her way slowly and thoughtfully to her own sparse room at the opposite end of the corridor.

*

During the night the storm had blown itself out. In the morning a watery sun rose above the steaming rooftops of Murteda and a fresh warm breeze blew along the cobbled streets of the town.

In the dining room Donahue looked at Nancy Carmichael across the table and couldn't believe the transformation in the woman.

It was a miracle and she hadn't even got to Santiago de Compostela yet! Her face had softened round the edges and a smile came quite naturally to her lips now, animating her whole expression and making her eyes crinkle up and sparkle. She'd done away with that bloody awful pink lipstick, too, and the orange face powder. Dear God, she had legs with knees attached.

He was dying to ask her about this fellow of hers but he supposed he ought to be tactful and wait for her to mention it first.

Neither of them spoke for a few moments. Donahue cleared his throat.

'I hear you've found yourself a man, Nancy Carmichael.'

'Well, you don't beat about the bush. I have indeed, Martin Donahue.'

'Will you be taking him back to Ballygurry? I'd love to see their faces back there if you did.'

'What do you mean "if", Donahue?'

'You're not serious about taking him back?'

'No, Donahue, I am not.'

Donahue heaved a sigh of relief. Things were going to be bad enough for her with all the spiteful stirring Miss Drew had been up to, never mind the scandal if she turned up with a foreigner on her arm.

Their conversation was interrupted then as the door opened and a bleary-eyed Padraig came into the room.

'Morning, Padraig. Did you sleep well?' Donahue asked.

'Yes, but I have a bit of a headache and Father Daley has just told me about poor old Sister Immaculata.'

'That was tragic news, Padraig. Look at it this way, though, the poor old girl won't be suffering any more now,' Donahue said kindly.

'I suppose so, but she was so good to me and all the other kids. She didn't have a bad bone in her body. St Joseph's will be awful without her.'

He turned away from Donahue then to hide his welling tears and suddenly noticed Nancy.

'Nancy, I didn't see you there,' Padraig cried.

Donahue stared incredulously as Padraig went straight across to Nancy Carmichael, put his arms round her neck and kissed her on the cheek.

Another bloody miracle! Back in Ballygurry Nancy and Padraig hadn't been able to bear the sight of each other.

'What happened to Sister Immaculata, Padraig?'

'She killed herself, Nancy. Drowned herself in the Giant's Cakehole.'

'Dear God!' uttered Nancy. 'Are they sure it wasn't an accident?'

'It couldn't have been,' Padraig said. 'She was always warning us to stay out of there when the tide was on the turn.'

'That's tragic. Do you think she'd lost her mind?'

'I don't know, Nancy, I mean she was always a bit different, a bit mad in a nice way, but I don't think she was simple at all. She just didn't want to be at St Joseph's, but they wouldn't let her out.'

'How do you mean, Padraig?'

'She wasn't allowed out in the daytime and they used to lock her up at night in the attic.'

'Dear God, why?'

'So she wouldn't be able to escape. If she escaped they wouldn't get the money,' Padraig said.

Nancy and Donahue stared at Padraig in disbelief.

'What money, Padraig?' Nancy asked.

'Are you pulling our legs?' Donahue said.

'No, she told me once that when she died, St Joseph's would get a lot of money from her family.'

'Well, God rest her poor soul,' said Nancy.

'Ah, God, she must have been put in the convent by her family, against her will. I'd heard they used to do that sometimes, and St Joseph's would have got a pay-off when she passed away,' Donahue said, remembering the two old women from years back.

'Anyhow, how did you get here, Nancy?' Padraig asked, sniffing.

'Rosendo brought Brother Francisco and me down in the donkey cart. The two of them have gone back to Santa Eulalia but Rosendo is coming back here tomorrow.'

'Rosendo is her fancy man, Donahue,' Padraig said, brightening up.

'Don't be so blunt, Padraig.'

'Pot calling the kettle black!' laughed Nancy.

Donahue whispered, 'Look, here come the gruesome twosome,' as the two postulants came shuffling in from the kitchen bringing baskets of bread and jugs of coffee.

'They give me the willies, those two, peeking at you from under those wimples. Especially that younger one; I wouldn't trust her as far as I could throw her, snooping about the place!'

The door opened then and Solly and Father Daley came into the room.

'Where's Dancey and Mr Leary?' Padraig asked.

'Dancey is still asleep and Michael is trying to telephone the Villa Castelo,' replied Solly.

'It'll be the parting of the ways after breakfast,' Father Daley said as he sat down. 'You lot off to Benita and us on our way to Santiago de Compostela.'

'When do you actually leave for home?' Solly enquired.

'We sail from Camiga in three days' time.'

Padraig looked down into his lap and surreptitiously wiped a tear away.

Michael Leary came into the dining room looking down in the mouth.

'What's up?' Donahue asked.

'Bad news, I'm afraid. I've just spoken to a chap on the telephone called Carlos Emanuel.'

'Who the hell is he?' Donahue interrupted.

'He's a servant at the Villa Castelo. Anyhow, the news is that Isabella Martinez died two days ago.'

'Damn!' Solly ejaculated. 'Is there no other member of the family there that we could speak to?'

'He passed me on to her sister, a woman called Augusta, a right frosty old bat. She said quite emphatically that she knew nothing of anyone called Dancey Amati and neither did she wish to.'

'Well, that's us scuppered then,' Donahue said sadly.

'Father Daley, Isabella Martinez was the woman Brother Bernardo was talking about,' Padraig said.

'I don't remember that, Padraig.'

'I do. He said that Santa Eulalia was owned by an old woman, and that was her name, Isabella Martinez.'

'Ah, you're right, I fancy. That was who Brother Francisco was off visiting, giving her the last rites.'

'Where do we go from here then, Solly?' Leary asked.

'God only knows. Back to Ballygurry?'

Donahue slumped in his chair and sighed heavily.

'Bloody hell, I was just beginning to enjoy myself,' he muttered.

All conversation was halted then by an ear-piercing scream that came from the kitchen.

'I told you those two are never bloody right,' Donahue said. 'Like a pair of frigging banshees about the place. Will we go and see what's going on in there before they wake the bloody dead?'

Before anyone had time to move, the two postulants burst through the door followed by the most peculiar and ancient-looking man that any of them had ever seen.

The bright-eyed little man made a low bow to the open-mouthed audience.

'I am Muli,' he said. 'The Nubeiro.'

'Pleased to meet you. And I'm the Queen of bloody Sheba,' Donahue snorted.

Padraig, who had been watching the two hysterical nuns, turned round, saw Muli, jumped up and ran across and hugged him.

'Do you know this peculiar article, Padraig?' asked Donahue.

'Muli is the one who saved my life when Brother Anselm was after me!'

'He doesn't look as if he could punch his way out of a paper bag. He's all skin and bone.'

'I believe that I am in the midst of pilgrims?' Muli said, looking round with interest at the assembled group.

'Not exactly,' Leary replied.

'If not holy pilgrims then those who are seeking for the answers to something, am I right?'

There was a great deal of nodding and nudging while the postulants cowered together in a far corner of the room.

'I believe,' said Muli, 'that you all hold a piece of a puzzle in your hands but without the help of each other you cannot solve the puzzle. Now, Padraig here, I know, has been trying to solve the puzzle of the lost Irish virgin.'

Donahue sniggered.

Leary kicked him under the table.

'Well, if you find her, Padraig, save her for me.'

'Ever since Mr Leary told me about the statue I've been searching all over the place for it, but I haven't nearly solved the puzzle yet, Muli,' Padraig said with disappointment.

'But you have unearthed some clues, yes?'

'I suppose so.'

'Tell us what you do know, then.'

'Well, I wondered at first if the Blue Madonna down in the hamlet below Santa Eulalia was the lost statue. It was very old for a start, but when I checked it out it was made of stone and the lost statue was made of gold.'

'So it wasn't the statue that you were looking for?'

'Nope. But I noticed one night when I scrubbed my nails that some of the blue paint I'd scraped off the statue was the same colour as the blue paint on the fresco in the Great Hall.'

'There wasn't a fresco in the Great Hall as far as I remember,' Leary said.

'That's the funny thing, the monks found it by accident when they were scrubbing the walls. It's really beautiful and yet Brother Anselm wanted them to paint over it again. Isn't that an odd thing for someone who loves art to do?'

'He's not right in the head, though, is he?' Father Daley said.

'Anyhow,' Padraig continued, 'I wondered did whoever paint the fresco also paint the statue all those years ago, on account of the colour being the same?'

'What would that prove?' Leary asked.

'Well, that they could be about the same age.'

'Anything else?' Muli asked.

'Yes. Nancy gave me a clue.'

'Did I?'

'You were humming "When Irish Eyes are Smiling".'

'Oh yes, and I was surprised that you didn't recognize the tune.'

'Well, I did recognize the tune,' Padraig replied. 'It was just that it made me think of something else.'

'I'm lost already,' Donahue sighed.

'Well, you see, some of the monks painted in the fresco had blue eyes and some of them had brown. Most of the people over here in Spain have brown eyes. I wondered, like, were these blue-eyed monks in the fresco the ones from Ireland who brought the statue here to Spain?'

'And were they?' Solly asked.

'Well, I don't suppose we'll ever know for sure, but Nancy pointed out that one of them did look a little bit like Mr Leary. And, you see, I knew that it was one of Mr Leary's ancestors who had been accused of stealing the statue.'

'Is that right, Leary?'

Leary nodded and smiled.

'Anything else, Padraig?' Muli prompted.

'The three-legged dog. There's one at Santa Eulalia called Quixote and there was one in the fresco. I asked Brother Bernardo why there were so many three-legged dogs in Spain.'

'And what did he say?' asked Donahue.

'Well, he said that there had always been three-legged dogs at Santa Eulalia, and that got me to wondering if the dog in the fresco was an ancestor of Quixote. The same way that I wondered if the squinting monk was an ancestor of Mr Leary's.'

'Go on, Padraig,' said Michael Leary, who was fascinated.

'Well, the strangest thing of all was that Muli was in the picture too.'

'Don't be ridiculous,' Donahue laughed with derision. 'I

mean he looks bloody ancient but he can't have been hanging around for hundreds of years.'

Muli smiled at Donahue and his eyes twinkled gaily as he said, 'There have, like three-legged dogs, always been Nubeiros hanging around at Santa Eulalia.'

Donahue shook his head and grinned.

'That's about all I found out about the Irish virgin, but there were a lot of things that didn't seem quite right at Santa Eulalia.'

'What sort of things?' Michael Leary asked.

'Well, there was a mark on the wall in the refectory where a painting had once hung. Brother Bernardo said that it was where one of Brother Anselm's paintings had hung, but it had been stolen about ten years ago.'

'What's odd about that?' Donahue said.

'Well, if you've ever seen any of Anselm's paintings you'll know that only a halfwit would steal them, because they're awful. That was strange, because Anselm was supposed to have been an artist himself, wasn't he?'

'That's right, I remember you saying that he'd studied in Paris,' Father Daley said.

'So why were they so bad? And even stranger, there's a painting on the wall by someone called Luciano and it's brilliant. Surely a thief would have pinched that if he wanted to make some money? Mr Leary has a painting by him back in Ballygurry that he calls his pension, but he told me that he'd never sell it.'

'He might have to now his job's gone, though,' said Donahue.

'Never,' said Leary emphatically.

No one spoke for a while until Michael Leary said, 'Talking of Luciano, one of his paintings turned up in America last year out of the blue.'

'How do you mean out of the blue?'

'Well, he was quite a prolific painter in his time and yet very few of his paintings have been found since his death.'

'Did it sell for a lot of money?'

'Thousands,' Leary said.

Muli turned his attention next to Solly Benjamin.

'And you, sir, I believe that you have travelled many miles with your companions to try and solve another mystery.'

'That's correct. As most of you here know, I was sent a child, a little girl called Dancey, who arrived at my house in the dead of night.'

'That would be the night that you had the peculiar dream about the dwarves and nuns?' Muli enquired with a grin.

Solly looked at Muli in disbelief.

'Yes, it was,' he stammered, but he didn't elaborate. 'Anyhow, she was sent to me by someone whose identity I don't know. I have been trying to find out where she came from and who sent her, and today we were going to Benita to follow up a clue.'

Muli looked steadfastly at Solly.

'But the news has reached you that Señora Isabella Martinez is dead?'

'How did you know that?'

'Ah, I hear things on the wind, my friend.'

Solly shook his head and then said, 'Padraig, what was it you said earlier about the monk studying in Paris?'

'Just that Brother Bernardo said that Brother Anselm was an artist before he became a monk and that he studied in Paris.'

'Madame Mireille!' Solly cried.

'What about her?' Donahue asked.

'I remember she said that Isabella Martinez used to bring a man with her to the shop sometimes. She said that he was her brother and he was an artist too. Madame Mireille said that the way he and Isabella looked at each other made her think that he was her lover not her brother!'

'Good God! You don't think it could be Brother Anselm, do you?' Leary asked.

'Why don't we ask him outright?'

'Because,' said Father Daley, 'he's locked up and half out of his mind.'

'Padraig, do you remember the photograph?' Leary said excitedly.

'What photograph, Mr Leary?'

'The one in my scrapbook, which was taken outside the café. Remember, the one of the pregnant girl and Brother Anselm!'

'I do. Blimey, do you think that she might be Dancey's mammy then?'

'Maybe,' said Leary quietly.

'That doesn't help us know where the mother has gone, though,' Solly said.

'But Anselm must know who the girl is,' Leary added.

'Maybe the dirty old sod is Pepita's father,' posed Donahue.

'Who's Pepita?' Father Daley asked.

'Pepita Amati is Dancey's mother. Señora Hipola told us her name,' Leary said.

Suddenly a voice spoke out.

'I think I may be able to help you with some of your questions.'

'Who the hell are you?' demanded Donahue.

'My name is Peregrino Viejo, the Old Pilgrim.'

There was a sudden silence as everyone turned to look at the tall, striking man who must have come quietly into the room some moments before he had spoken.

Padraig said, 'I've seen you before outside the church in the square with the fountain. I still have a lovely blue scarf that you left behind.'

The man smiled at Padraig and said, 'It's funny, you know, because I was sure that you and I would meet again one day.'

'What did you mean you could help us? I don't see how you can, sir, unless you can tell us where we can find the girl's mother?' Solly said impatiently.

'I'm afraid I can't tell you that, although I would hazard a guess that she's long gone from these parts.'

'Come on then, man, spit out what you do know,' Donahue urged.

'I found the child Dancey abandoned up near Santa Eulalia. She was in a terrible state, terrified and barely able to speak. But she managed to tell me how she had become separated from her mother. They were playing a game of hide and seek. Dancey was told to close her eyes and count to a hundred. When the poor child opened her eyes there was no sign of her mother. She had been abandoned.'

Nancy Carmichael gasped.

'What sort of woman could do that to her own child?'

Michael Leary glanced at Nancy. She would have made someone a great mother. He looked then at Padraig and was transfixed. He looked from Padraig to Nancy hardly believing his eyes! There was most definitely a resemblance between the two of them. He'd never have noticed it before but now that Padraig's hair was growing longer and the sun had sprinkled his skin with freckles he could definitely see it. It was small wonder that Brother Anselm had thought them related.

'Anyhow, Dancey and I went in search of her mother but I didn't really expect to find her. Dancey could tell me very little about her past except that they'd lived in many different places, never staying anywhere long. We were together for many months but in the end I had to let her go.'

'Why?' asked Padraig simply.

The Old Pilgrim smiled sadly.

'There are times when the blackness comes upon me, a deep despair that lasts sometimes for many months. It wouldn't have been right to subject the child to that.'

'But why on earth send her halfway across Europe to me, a man you don't even know?' Solly asked angrily.

'Because many years ago, Solly Benjamin, you did me a very great favour.'

'I did? Well, it's news to me!'

'You did indeed and I never forgot your generosity.'

'I'm in the dark still,' said Solly.

'It was at Rossmacconnarty station, a filthy rainswept day not unlike yesterday. I was a broken man and you gave me something that was precious, and I knew at that moment that you were a man of honour, a good and trustworthy man.'

'My God,' Solly said, staring hard at the Old Pilgrim. 'The man in the waiting room! I remember it as clear as if it were yesterday. You wore a mackintosh and I thought it was odd because your clothes were good quality but they were filthy. I gave you some money and . . . and the ring. But how did you know where I lived?'

'Your name and address were written on your suitcase and I never forgot them, always hoped I'd be able to repay you one day.'

'But how did you know I was still living there; after all, it was years ago.'

'I had someone check that you were still registered at that address. And now I have something to return to you.'

He removed the ring from his finger and handed it to Solly Benjamin, who closed his palm tightly round it as his eyes welled with tears.

'Thank you.'

Padraig jumped to his feet with alacrity.

'Would you let me see that ring, Solly?'

Solly held out the ring for the boy to see and Padraig drew in his breath with astonishment.

'Where did you get it?' he asked.

'It's been in my family for generations. There was some story that it was given to one of my distant ancestors by a holy man to help them flee from persecution.'

'But your ancestors didn't ever sell it?'

'No, but if you look closely there are one or two stones missing that must have been sold at some point,' Solly explained.

'Solly, in Santa Eulalia there's a monk in the fresco wearing a ring just like this one. And in the last part of the fresco there's another bearded man holding the ring in his hand. Maybe, Solly, this is the ring from the fresco!'

'That's a bit far-fetched, Padraig,' Father Daley said.

'Well, if you go to Santa Eulalia and take a look you'll see for yourselves.'

'He's right, you know,' Muli said. 'Think about it, Solly. You've told us that someone gave one of your ancestors that ring to help them on their way. There were many Jews expelled from Spain, many of them may have fled along the pilgrim trail.'

'It could be that your ancestors once passed through Santa Eulalia, like Mr Leary's did,' Padraig said, 'and you, Solly, like the monk in the fresco, passed the ring on to someone else in need!'

'Everything seems to lead back to Santa Eulalia,' Leary said thoughtfully.

Dancey Amati came slowly down the stairs and paused in the hallway. She sniffed the air excitedly and breathed in the welcome smells of tobacco and horses, wood smoke and hay and, above all else, dandelions.

Take a fistful of garbanzos
A clutch of white beans
A handful of dandelions
Two wide-brimmed hatfuls of spring water
A slosh of olive oil
Some slivers of monastery beef
Two cloves of silvery garlic
One enormous wrinkled tomato . . .

The words had stayed with her all this time. She had repeated them so many times, over and over in her head, like a charm to keep herself safe.

She stepped nervously towards the dining-room door, her heart beating wildly. Then she saw him.

'Peregrino Viejo!' she yelled.

At the sound of her voice everyone turned to look at her.

Solly swallowed hard. She'd been silent for so long, he'd thought she might never speak.

The Old Pilgrim turned round and held out his arms; she ran to him and was caught up in his embrace. He was lifting her up and up, kissing her cheek, stroking her hair, the feel of his warm tears like silk on her own skin.

'There is no more beautiful sight than a child being reunited with a loved one,' Muli said softly.

'And now I have a story to tell you about another child.

'Some years ago, here in Spain, a desperate young man who had come out here to fight in the war asked me to help him.'

'Who was he?' asked Padraig.

'Patience, Padraig, patience.'

Muli continued quietly.

'I was asked to visit a village in Ireland and wait for a

young woman to contact me, a very beautiful young woman as it turns out. I met her there and arranged to take her to a safe house in Dublin and leave her in the care of an old woman called Gerty Wiseman.'

Michael Leary listened intently.

'The young woman was unmarried and pregnant and she was fearful of what her father might do to her if he found out about the baby she was expecting. She was terrified that she would be made to give up the child for adoption. She went to stay in Dublin with Gerty and there she waited for the return of her young man, who had promised faithfully to come for her and the child.

'The child was duly born but the father never came. She would, I expect, have assumed that he had been killed out here in Spain in the civil war and that, like many others, his body lay in an unmarked grave.'

'So do you think the man buried at Santa Eulalia could be . . .' Father Daley interrupted but then fell into silence.

'I don't think that she ever really gave up hope of seeing him again, did she, Padraig?'

Everyone in the room looked at Padraig.

Padraig stared at Muli as if he were in a trance.

'No. She used to say that one day, when the wind was blowing in the right direction, he'd sail up the River Liffey and find us and we'd all be together again.'

Padraig fell silent and swallowed hard.

'Then,' Muli took up the story again, 'tragically, Padraig's mammy was run down and killed. Gerty Wiseman, I'm sure, would have looked after him, but she, by this time, was dead. Of course, there was no father's name on his birth certificate, and Padraig's mother had already changed her name to avoid being found by her family. It was assumed that Padraig was an orphan and he was whisked off to St Joseph's orphanage in Ballygurry.'

Leary interrupted, 'It sounds like this fellow who was buried up at Santa Eulalia could very well be Padraig's father. What was his name again?'

'George Fitzallen,' said Father Daley.

The Old Pilgrim spoke then.

'George Fitzallen is not this boy's father.'

'How the hell do you know that?'

'Because,' the Old Pilgrim said quietly, 'I am George Fitzallen.'

Donahue looked across the room at Nancy, who had paled to the colour of chalk.

'But George Fitzallen is buried at Santa Eulalia,' Father Daley exclaimed.

'You've a fine complexion for a dead man,' Donahue said.

'Who the hell is buried in that grave, then, if it isn't you?' Leary asked.

'I have no idea. I saw the grave for the first time myself only the other night.'

'How bloody odd. That must have given you a right turn,' Donahue said, 'seeing your own tombstone like that.'

'Remember Brother Bernardo said that he wrote to the family of the man but he never had a reply,' Padraig said.

'My father wouldn't have cared less about my death,' the Old Pilgrim said. 'I was not welcome in my father's house.'

'George Fitzallen! Bloody hell!' Padraig said excitedly. 'I've just thought of something else.'

'What is it?' Michael Leary asked.

'The trunk that that we found in Señora Hipola's house in Pig Lane when Miss Drew fell through the stable roof! I thought there was going to be treasure in it, but there wasn't, was there, Nancy?'

'No, there wasn't, just a pile of dirty old clothes.'

'Can you remember what sort of clothes, though, Nancy?' Padraig asked.

'Sure, just a filthy old suit and a mackintosh.'

'Yes,' Padraig continued, 'a dirty stinking mackintosh with faded tartan on the inside and leather buttons.'

'What in the name of Saint Patrick has a pile of old clothes got to do with anything?' Donahue said.

Padraig looked directly at the Old Pilgrim and said, 'They were your clothes, weren't they?'

'Yes, they were,' the Old Pilgrim said quietly. 'I stayed in Pig Lane when I first arrived in Spain. I wanted to get rid of everything from my past life and I left the trunk behind.'

'Well, all this talking is fine and dandy but we don't seem any closer to solving any mysteries,' Donahue said.

'Your name was on the wedding invitation I found!' Padraig cried. 'Wait while I remember the words . . .'

The Old Pilgrim twisted his hands anxiously.

'Padraig, what wedding invitation are you on about?' Leary asked impatiently.

'I found it between the pages of a book that was in the trunk. Let me think now what it said. "Mr and Mrs Egbert Brennan . . . something or other . . . invite you to the marriage of their daughter Vera Mary Brennan to George Fitzallen . . ."'

'So did you get married?' asked Donahue.

The Old Pilgrim shook his head.

'That day at the station,' said Solly, 'there were wedding bells in the background. I remember thinking what an awful day it was to get married . . .'

Padraig's mind was racing. He felt again as though he were inside a glass dome that someone had shaken madly and the snow, like his thoughts, was blizzarding, refusing to settle.

He shook his head, waited for his thoughts to arrange themselves.

'Florence Gallivan,' he murmured. 'That was the name on the label in the back of Señora Hipola's wedding dress . . .'

Muli nodded at Padraig in encouragement.

'I left her at the altar,' the Old Pilgrim mumbled.

'Florence Gallivan?' said Donahue. 'No wonder! No one will blame you for that. I went to her shop in Cork once with my mother. Florence Gallivan must have been ninety if she was a day and that was years ago.'

'He wasn't marrying Florence Gallivan, he was meant to be marrying Vera Mary Brennan,' Padraig continued.

The Old Pilgrim shuddered and closed his eyes.

'Why didn't you want to marry her?' Nancy spoke quietly.

'There was a very delicate situation I'd rather not speak about in front of, er, youngsters.'

Donahue nudged Leary in the ribs and grinned.

'Was this Vera Mary Brennan in the pudding club?' Donahue ventured.

'She was pregnant, yes.'

'That's disgraceful, man, leaving a girl in the lurch like that with a child on the way.'

'But she wasn't pregnant by me.'

'Oh right,' said Donahue, wrinkling his brow in confusion.

'My father demanded that I marry her to save her reputation or he would let the world know of the, er, delicate situation . . .'

Donahue jumped in.

'I remember now, it wasn't a woman you were caught with but a—'

Father Daley gave Donahue a kick under the table and smiled encouragingly at the Old Pilgrim.

'He's one of them momosapiens!' Donahue whispered.

'Will you shut up, Donahue,' Leary muttered.

Father Daley stared open-mouthed at the Old Pilgrim.

'Well, er, who did put her in the family way?' Father Daley asked.

Nancy Carmichael cleared her throat, and spoke.

'I expect it was this man's own father, Lord Fitzallen, who was the father of the child.'

The Old Pilgrim stared at Nancy in incredulity.

'She wouldn't be the first young girl he'd got pregnant, I for one know that only too well,' Nancy said.

Michael Leary could hardly believe his ears.

The Old Pilgrim looked steadfastly at Nancy as though he had just come face to face with a ghost.

A ripple of shock went round the room.

Dr Garcia drew back the grille on the cell door and looked in at old Brother Anselm, who was sitting motionless in a high-backed chair facing the iron-barred window.

He selected a key, unlocked the door and entered the cell. Brother Anselm did not stir even as the doctor placed his hand on the old man's cold papery one.

When Brother Anselm had first been brought in he had fought like a madman, but now he was calm, he just sat for hours and hours staring at the window.

Dr Garcia drew up a chair and sat down next to Brother Anselm, who stirred suddenly and turned to face him, his rheumy old eyes like lonely planets in an undiscovered universe.

It was quiet in the cell except for the rattle of Brother Anselm's chest. From somewhere outside came the sound of a caged bird singing.

'Isabella, is that you?' Brother Anselm whispered in a faltering voice.

The doctor did not reply, he was used to the inane chatter of the insane.

'You came after all, I told them you would . . .'

Outside, the bells of Santa Anna began to ring loudly.

'When I am well again we must escape . . . you and I, I have treasures, we can be together, the two of us, we can find the child . . .'

Dr Garcia sighed as he listened to the old monk's ramblings.

'It's the child I worry for, Isabella, our granddaughter . . .'

The warder wondered did the childless, at the end of their lives, always grieve for the family they never had? When his time came to die would he too curse the fact that he had never married? Would he wish that he had children to leave behind as a legacy? Maybe, like this poor old man, he would fantasize about imaginary lovers and phantom children.

Brother Anselm stirred.

'Is that someone at the door?'

'There's no one there, Brother Anselm.'

'Is that her?' he asked eagerly.

Dr Garcia took hold of the old monk's wrist. The pulse was weak, irregular, he wasn't long for this world.

'Is it my granddaughter come to see me?' Brother Anselm asked querulously.

'It's me, Dr Garcia, do you remember me?'

Brother Anselm stared at the doctor vacantly.

'Are you expecting your granddaughter, then?'

'Is she here? I must see her before, before I die,' he said more urgently. He grew more agitated, drumming his heels against the chair, clenching and unclenching his fists, grinding his few remaining teeth.

'How about if we go to the window, eh? See if we can see her coming?'

Brother Anselm smiled.

'She is coming then?'

'Maybe, maybe, soon she'll be here,' the doctor lied.

It would soon be time for him to give Brother Anselm his medication, probably for the last time. What harm would a few minutes looking out of the window do?

There was no stopping Nancy Carmichael once she'd started.

'This man's father, Lord Fitzallen of Kilgerry, was an out-and-out shite-hound who paid scant regard to anyone's feelings other than his own.'

'Steady on, Nancy, old girl, that's this fellow's father you're talking about,' Donahue said, putting his hand on her arm.

'I, too, hold a piece of this puzzle and for years I've kept it a secret. But this pilgrimage has taught me something very valuable: that at last I can be true to myself.'

Leary looked from Padraig to Nancy and back again. God almighty, the resemblance was there for anyone to see.

'I repeat, Lord Fitzallen was a philandering pig of a man. I make no apologies for what I say or for slandering this man's father, for I'm sure that the whole of Ballygurry knows by now that Lord Fitzallen was also my father.'

'My God,' the Old Pilgrim said, cupping his face with his hands. 'That means, doesn't it, that you are . . .'

'A bastard,' said Nancy Carmichael.

Padraig gasped and giggled with nerves.

'No, no I didn't mean that,' the Old Pilgrim stammered. 'I mean, that you and I are related.'

'I am your half-sister, I suppose,' said Nancy, and smiled shyly at George Fitzallen.

'Bloody hell,' said Donahue, wiping the sweat from his brow, 'I never thought that secret would see the light of day!'

'You knew?' said Nancy, rounding on Donahue.

'My mother worked up at Kilgerry, remember, with your mother. I've known for years.'

'And you never let on?'

'It wasn't my place and I thought you had enough on your plate with that bloody awful mother of yours.'

'Martin Donahue, you are a true gentleman and I thank you for that.'

Donahue beamed.

The Old Pilgrim said, 'My father had got Vera Mary Brennan pregnant. She was the daughter of one of his friends. He had a penchant for young snooty girls. She was a queer, dangerous sort of girl was Vera. She had her mind set on becoming the mistress of Kilgerry but my father would never have left my mother, because she held the purse strings.'

'The dirty old dog!' said Donahue.

'Anyhow, I'd had a fling with a, well, with someone rather unsuitable, and my father found out. He blackmailed me then and said I must marry Vera Brennan or else my secret was out. Vera would then eventually get her wish and become the mistress of Kilgerry when I inherited, and my father would be saved from scandal. But I just couldn't go through with it!'

'What a bastard!'

'I know, I'm not proud of what I did.'

'Not you, man, that father of yours.'

Padraig, who had been quiet for some time, got up and left the room, then came hurrying back some minutes later.

'What was she like to look at, this Vera Brennan?' Padraig ventured.

'What's that got to do with anything?' Michael Leary asked him.

'Is this her?' Padraig asked, opening his sketchbook and holding up the page to the Old Pilgrim.

The Old Pilgrim stared down at the page in horror.

'Who is it, Padraig?' everyone asked almost at once, clambering to their feet to get a look.

Donahue looked down at the page.

'Suffering angels!' he cried. 'Would you look at that!'

'You'd a lucky escape, man,' Father Daley said with sympathy.

'Vera Mary Brennan is Sister Veronica,' whispered Padraig, and shivered.

While everyone was staring incredulously at the sketch of Sister Veronica, the Old Pilgrim was oblivious to the conversation going on round him.

He was remembering a day long ago when he was standing in his new suit, shivering with fear at the front of a cold, flower-filled church.

He'd turned and looked behind him at the congregation, a blurry sea of expectant faces. His mother's head was bowed, her gloved hands fidgeting nervously in her lap. His poor mother, a tired, sad woman worn down by pain, deceit and misery.

His father's smug, arrogant face stared defiantly back at him. He'd heard the noise at the back of the church, the sound of the organist turning the pages of music.

He remembered the startled faces looking at him in dismay as he'd hurtled down the aisle towards the open doorway. The angry shouting of his father, the strangled gasp of a choirboy, the noise of an altar candle spluttering.

Averting his eyes from his intended bride, he'd looked down at his little sister, standing there in her bridesmaid dress, holding a posy of freesias. He'd bent and kissed her and that was the last time he had seen her . . .

He was woken from this reverie by the sound of the boy's voice.

'The dress,' said Padraig. 'That dress on the line at Señora Hipola's, that was the same dress that this Vera Brennan wore on her wedding day, wasn't it, Muli?'

Muli nodded.

'That enormous great thing that flew away in Camiga?' Father Daley asked.

'Yes. The one that Marta was meant to be wearing for her wedding . . .'

'Marta!' exclaimed Michael Leary.

'That's right,' said Padraig. 'She was staying at Señora Hipola's. She was a very pretty lady but dead miserable looking! She was meant to be marrying some chap but she ran away.'

'She did?' said Leary.

'That's right,' said Padraig.

'Thank you, God,' said Leary, punching the air.

'What's bothering me is, who is the fellow buried up at Santa Eulalia?' Solly asked.

'I think I might know the answer to that,' Michael Leary said.

All heads swivelled towards Leary.

'Siobhan Hanlon told me that she'd found a pile of ripped-up letters in a cupboard in St Joseph's. The letters were written by Padraig's father.'

Padraig looked at Michael Leary with wide eyes.

'The letters from the box! I was meant to be able to read them when I left St Joseph's.'

'Well, someone, and it doesn't take much working out who, had tried to destroy them, but luckily Siobhan and Donny had got into the cupboard to hide and Siobhan, being the nosey little article that she is, had picked them up.'

Padraig smiled; she was a grand girl was Siobhan, apart from all the kissing and soppy stuff.

'In one of the letters that Siobhan read out to me, Padraig's father mentioned something about still having the army greatcoat that Padraig's mother had given to him, the coat belonging to someone called George. And that he'd heard that someone had seen George in Paris.'

'Oh my God, Laura . . .' the Old Pilgrim whispered.

'Who's Laura?' Padraig asked.

'Laura is, was, my little sister.'

'And Padraig's mother?' Father Daley whispered. The Old Pilgrim looked at Padraig, resting his hands on the table for support.

'Which makes Padraig your, oh hell I'm lost. Is there anyone in this room who isn't related?'

'My nephew, my sister's child,' the Old Pilgrim said almost inaudibly, and he gave Padraig such a look of tender bewilderment that it made Nancy's eyes fill with tears.

Padraig was speechless, lost in a world of his own. He looked at the Old Pilgrim and then at Nancy. For a moment he remembered the wobbling reflection of his mammy's face in the horse trough at Ballygurry.

Nancy and this George Fitzallen were his family. He had a family like other people.

His heart pounded painfully as the memories came rushing back. He spoke then without knowing what he said, words coming from a long time ago.

'My mammy used to say that one day my daddy would come sailing up the river Liffey on the *Sequana* . . . She used to say that when he came he would take us back with him to Paris and we would look for her brother and find him and then the four of us would go wherever in the world we wanted to go . . .'

The Old Pilgrim groaned and sat down heavily in a chair.

'The first time I ever saw you in the square in Camiga I knew that you reminded me of someone.'

'Of your sister, Laura, of course,' said Nancy softly.

'No. He has the look of Laura round his eyes but he takes more after someone else.'

'Who?' asked Nancy.

'Raffy.'

'Who in the name of St Peter is Raffy?' said Donahue.

'Rafael Federico Luciano, the grandson of Federico Luciano, the painter.'

'Blimey O'Riley,' said Padraig.

'How in God's name did he ever meet Laura?'

'In Paris, I expect,' said Muli. 'As soon as she was old enough she went looking for you, her long-lost brother, but instead she met Raffy. He lived in Paris for a while on the *Sequana* after his grandfather died.'

'Federico and Raffy never knew my real name, they, like everyone else, called me the Old Pilgrim.'

'After the death of his parents, Raffy had spent many summers at Santa Eulalia with his grandfather. That's probably why he was making for there just before he died. He probably felt that he would be in safe hands,' Muli said.

'Brother Anselm would surely have recognized him, though. He'd been at Santa Eulalia for years and would have been around in the time when Luciano had stayed there,' Leary said thoughtfully.

'It served Anselm's purposes, maybe, to let everyone assume that this man was George Fitzallen.'

'But why?' asked Solly.

'Think about it,' Leary said. 'Padraig said why would anyone want to pinch one of Anselm's paintings when they could have a Luciano?'

'Maybe Raffy knew that a lot of his grandfather's paintings had been left at Santa Eulalia. He'd have become a very rich young man if he'd sold even a few of them,' Muli said.

'What are Anselm's paintings like, Padraig?' Solly asked.

'Like those of a kid who can't paint, like he was just trying to cover the canvas up as quick as he could.'

'My guess is that beneath these paintings of Anselm's you will find genuine Lucianos hidden. And each one will be worth a bloody fortune,' declared Leary.

'The girl in the café!' said Padraig. 'The one who was pregnant, the one that we think was Dancey's mammy. In the photograph, I remember, by the side of the table, there was something large wrapped up in paper. I reckon Anselm gave her the painting! I bet they got rid of Anselm's rubbish and underneath they had the real thing hidden; the Luciano.'

'But why would he do that?'

'Perhaps she was blackmailing him?' Nancy said. 'If he was her father? Maybe he had to keep her quiet? Maybe she needed money to get away?'

'And the jewels, Mr Leary. Do you remember what you said about the pawnbroker in Paris? That some of the jewels believed to be from the statue had turned up there! And that a Luciano painting was recently sold!'

'My God, Padraig, so I do!'

'I think we may safely say that this mother of Dancey's is long gone and is probably a very wealthy woman by now.'

Sister Perpetua came into the dining room and sent the two postulants scuttling back to the kitchen. Then she insisted that the Old Pilgrim return to the infirmary for a rest.

Muli took Padraig out for a walk to get some air. They walked slowly together away from the convent of Santa Anna hand in hand.

'Are you all right, Padraig?' Muli asked.

'I am, Muli, just a bit shocked that's all. There's loads I want to say to Nancy and the Old— George Fitzallen, but I haven't quite got the words in the right order yet.'

'It'll take time for it to sink in for all of you. Best to take things slowly for now.'

'Muli, there's a painting in Santa Eulalia of the

monastery at night. There's a boy in the window looking up at the stars, I always wished that it was me . . .'

Muli smiled.

'Well, in a way, Padraig, it is.'

'Muli, I think I know now what was wrong with the painting! There was something not quite right about it.'

'How do you mean?'

'The Blue Madonna!'

'What about her?'

'She was facing the wrong way!'

'Explain yourself, Padraig.'

'The way he, my great-grandfather, had painted it, you could see her eyes, but from the angle he'd painted the monastery you wouldn't have been able to see them. It's as if the statue had been turned around! Now why would he deliberately paint it all wrong like that when everything else about the painting is perfect?'

Muli smiled an enigmatic smile.

'Slowly but surely, Padraig, you are getting there.'

'Do you know why he did that, Muli?'

'I do.'

'How?'

'Because he told me.'

'Will you tell me?'

'Presently,' said Muli, 'I will.'

'The statue of the Irish virgin wasn't stolen exactly, was it? It was more like borrowed? Someone, Mr Leary's ancestor maybe, removed the stones and gave them out to people in need. I don't suppose we'll ever know exactly. Just like the ring that Solly had. Do you think that is what happened, Muli?'

Muli nodded.

'I wonder, though, whatever happened to the statue.'

'The statue is very safely hidden, Padraig.'

Padraig's eyes sparkled with excitement.

'Ever since its arrival at Santa Eulalia the secret of its location has been handed down through the generations. Only one monk and one nubeiro knew the secret at any one time. But when old Brother Tomás handed the secret down to Anselm just before he died, I began to get worried. I never really trusted Anselm.'

'He was a bad man, wasn't he, Muli?'

'In some ways, Padraig, he wasn't cut out to be a monk. If he'd been brave enough he should have done something about it.'

'Once you're a monk or a priest, don't you always have to be one?'

'Oh no, Padraig. Mr Leary's ancestor the monk didn't remain a monk.'

'How do you know that?'

'Just from stories handed down; remember there have always been nubeiros at Santa Eulalia.'

'So what happened to him?'

'He met a girl, they married, had children . . .'

'Bloody hell!'

'Santa Eulalia was a busy place in the old days; people came from all over, princes and paupers, Jews and Irish monks. Some passed through on their way to Santiago de Compostela, some fell in love and stayed . . .'

'Maybe Father Daley won't be a priest for ever,' Padraig said.

'Maybe,' said Muli.

'Tell me then, Muli, did Brother Anselm know where the statue was hidden?'

'At one time he did, but I confided in one other person about my worries and we decided that something had to be done!'

'Who was the other person, Muli?'

'Your great-grandfather, Federico Luciano.'

'Bloody Nora!'

'Federico and I decided that we had to move the statue.'

'Where was it hidden?'

'It used to be hidden inside the statue of the Blue Madonna, in a hollowed-out space. We removed it and transferred it to a very safe place.'

'So it *was* hidden there!'

'And you were right, Padraig, the statue did used to face up towards the monastery, but working in the dark we cemented her back in facing the wrong way. When Luciano painted that painting of the monastery he must have been remembering the way the statue once was.'

'Wow! Who gets to know about the secret next?'

Muli took both Padraig's hands in his own and whispered, 'It is hidden safely inside the statue of the pissing boy in Camiga!'

Padraig drew in his breath with wonder.

Paddington, London

Worming their way in through the dirty net curtain, shafts of weak sunlight brought a smidgeon of warmth into the dreary room.

Donny Keegan crossed to the window and looked out over the cluttered backyards. A train rattled along the railway tracks and an impatient driver honked his horn over on the High Road.

He turned his head and looked across at his daddy, who was sitting at an oilcloth-covered table scouring the newspaper for jobs. He had the stub of a pencil clamped between his teeth and his last Woodbine perched behind his ear.

'Have you found anything, Daddy?' Donny asked.

'No, son, there's nothing much in here for the likes of me.'

'Will we be all right, though, Daddy?'

'Well, we won't end up in the workhouse, whatever happens. We'll pray for a stroke of luck, Donny. Who knows? One day we may be rich like that fellow.'

'What fellow, Daddy?'

'The one here in the paper, look.'

Donny glanced down at the newspaper. There was a photograph of a handsome man with too many teeth smiling down at his pretty, dark-haired bride.

Yesterday in Manhattan, Mr Melville Smith, a self-made millionaire, married an unknown chorus dancer, Felice Olivares. Miss Olivares, an immigrant, met Mr Smith at a Spanish restaurant, where she says it was love at first sight . . .

'And the size of his cheque book, I dare say,' Jimmy Keegan said. 'Listen, Donny, I've five bob left to me name, but money isn't the be all and end all, son. Something will turn up out of the blue.'

'Like you did when you came for me at St Joseph's?'

Jimmy Keegan looked at his son and smiled.

'Something like that. Here, do us a favour, Donny, and sharpen this pencil.'

Donny took the pencil from his daddy and searched in his pocket for his penknife. Tongue between his teeth in concentration, he sharpened the pencil to a fine point and handed it back.

Then he felt in his other pocket and took out Sister Immaculata's rosary. He pulled the grimy net curtain to one side and held the rosary up to the light.

The beads were an unusual milky blue colour but as he looked more closely he could see that there were dark shadows at the centre of each bead.

'It looks as if there is something in the middle of these

beads, Daddy,' he said.

His father looked up absentmindedly.

'Do you see?'

'You're right, give us a look.'

'Shall I try and get one out?' Donny asked.

Inserting the tip of the penknife into the setting that held the beads in place, he worked carefully to remove one of them. He tipped it into the palm of his hand, then passed it to his daddy.

Carefully, Jimmy Keegan scraped away the layers of grime around the centre of the bead and then pulled it into two pieces. Inside the bead was a hollowed-out space where a dark-red stone nestled.

'Crikey,' said Donny. 'What is it?'

Donny's daddy worked the stone out with the tip of the penknife and set it down on the table.

'That, my son, and the other little beauties hidden in there, are, if I'm not mistaken, our passport out of this bloody place!'

Spain

Solly and Dancey strolled through the ancient streets of Murteda. Solly, preoccupied with his own thoughts, was silent, but Dancey skipped along beside him, humming happily to herself.

After a while they came to the outskirts of the town and continued walking through the deserted cloisters of a crumbling abbey until eventually they turned into a deserted square.

Dancey ran ahead of Solly, turning occasionally to smile back at him.

Then she stopped suddenly in the middle of the square and turned her head slowly, looking up at an ugly grey building where all the windows were heavily barred.

Solly caught up with her. She stood quite silently looking up at one of the windows.

Solly followed her gaze. A frail old man stood in the window looking sadly down at her through the bars. Beside him a man in a white coat was checking his watch.

Dancey raised her hand and waved at the old man.

Tentatively, the old man raised his hand and waved back.

Dancey smiled up at him, blew him a kiss and then she was off skipping across the square, scattering pigeons.

Solly looked up. The old man stood quite still, more like a statue than a man. Then he smiled, a radiant smile. Marvelling that the smile and hand wave of a young child could give such joy to a perfect stranger, Solly walked quickly on to catch up with Dancey.

At dinner time everyone gathered together in the dining room except for Michael Leary and Nancy Carmichael, who were nowhere to be found.

Sister Perpetua seemed quite agitated as she supervised the postulants in their serving duties and occasionally gave Father Daley a despairing look.

Donahue noticed with relief that another older woman had replaced the peculiar postulant, the one he'd caught looking through the keyhole.

Nancy eventually arrived in the dining room, looking radiant and holding the hand of a sheepish Rosendo, who bowed at everyone and then took his seat next to Nancy.

'Where on earth is Leary?' Solly asked.

'Probably he's found a bar somewhere and is drowning his sorrows at the thought of going back to Ballygurry,' Donahue said sadly.

Father Daley said nothing; he'd wait a while to see if Leary turned up and if he didn't then he'd speak to the adults when they were on their own.

Sister Perpetua had spoken to him earlier and was very concerned because Sister Maria had disappeared and old Sister Marguerite swore that she had seen Sister Maria going into Michael Leary's room.

Then, suddenly, all thoughts of Leary and Sister Maria evaporated as Padraig gasped loudly and pointed with a trembling finger.

An old woman had appeared in the doorway and stood there looking round inquisitively at everyone in the room.

'Padraig, it's rude to point!' admonished Father Daley, thinking that she must be the pilgrim who had been taking her meals alone in her room.

She was a most odd little woman, dressed in a threadbare brown paisley dress, thick tights and clumpy shoes that had seen better days. On her head she wore a green beret pulled down tightly over her ears. Her small wrinkled face peeped out from beneath it, as shrewd and inquisitive as a monkey's.

'Dear God in heaven,' declared Nancy Carmichael, 'she's wearing my dress that was stolen off the washing line in Ballygurry and my old gardening shoes!'

'Thérèse Martinez,' whispered Muli, getting unsteadily to his feet.

The old woman nodded in acquiescence.

'Martinez?' said Solly in astonishment. 'Not belonging to the family from the Villa Castelo?'

The old woman nodded.

Sister Matilde put her hand to her face and stumbled, and only Solly's quick thinking saved her from falling.

Padraig was watching Muli with interest.

A tear slid from Muli's left eye and made its way slowly down his wrinkled brown cheek.

For a moment Padraig saw the whole room reflected in that one fat teardrop. He remembered the words that Muli had spoken to him: 'Even a queer-looking thing like me feels loss.'

Padraig sat quite still, afraid to move in case the dream was broken.

Donahue, overcome with all the recent emotion, looked into the twinkling eyes of Sister Immaculata, freshly risen from the dead. He let out a low moan and promptly fainted.

Spain 1977

The bell rang out from the monastery of Santa Eulalia and the echo mingled with the clanking of cow-bells down in the valley and the shouts of children at play.

Uno.

Dos.

Tres.

A small, dark-haired girl stood in the centre of the courtyard and counted slowly at first, then faster.

Cuatro, Cinco, Seis.

All around her chickens clucked and pecked among the cobblestones and a three-legged puppy pissed over a pot of geraniums, then scuttled off into the barn in search of rats.

Henri, a wiry, tousled-haired boy, followed the dog into the barn. He looked round, searching out a place to hide, and saw the dust-covered trunk in a far corner. He lifted the lid and peered inside, there was plenty of room to hide. Then he climbed hesitantly into the trunk, pulling the lid back in place.

Siete.

Ocho.

Nuevo . . .

Veintiuno . . . Treinta . . .

The scurrying children squeezed in behind the bleached

statues that stood around the courtyard in their mossy niches. A hushed silence, punctuated by the occasional giggle, descended.

'*Ciento*! Coming, ready or not!' the girl cried.

In the barn, inside the trunk, the boy waited.

Slowly, his eyes grew accustomed to the gloom and he realized that there were tiny holes in the top of the trunk through which pinpricks of light filtered.

Then he remembered the story that Señor Padraig had told them about the trunk.

Once, many years ago, in a foreign country a brave old nun who had been locked away in a terrible convent decided to escape. She had emptied the trunk of its contents and climbed inside.

Hidden inside the trunk she had travelled across the sea on a boat undiscovered and then when she had arrived in Spain, when no one was looking, she had climbed out and set off on an adventure.

Henri sniffed; the trunk smelled faintly of candle wax and camphor. He shivered and hoped that he'd soon be found, he didn't fancy spending hours trapped in the darkness.

Señor Padraig had told them that she had been sent away to the convent because her twin sister was a very wicked woman who had done some awful things for which the nun had been blamed. But when the old nun appeared back in Spain she went to her sister's house where she lay dying. Being the oldest in her family she inherited a fortune. And being kind she had given away all her money to start an orphanage up here in Santa Eulalia.

Outside, beyond the barn, he could hear the shouts and excited yells of the other children as they were discovered in their hiding places.

Inside the trunk he whispered a prayer in memory of the old nun. If it wasn't for Santa Eulalia he would still be begging in the streets of Naples and wouldn't have had any chance in life at all.

The smell of beef sizzling in hot oil drifted out from the kitchen windows, and inside the trunk Henri sniffed. Dandelion soup! That must mean visitors were coming. He closed his eyes and waited to be discovered . . .

In the kitchen the cook helped a small boy to roll up his sleeves, lifted him on to a chair and pulled it up to a scrubbed kitchen table.

'Let's see what you can remember, Enrico, my little one,' she said as she looked down at the small orphaned boy who had arrived at Santa Eulalia less than a week before.

'I'm not little any more! I'm nearly six. And I can remember! It's easy, Señora Dancey. Listen!

'Take a fistful of garbanzos . . .'

'A clutch of white beans . . .'

Señora Dancey Martinez clapped her hands together in delight, then pinched the boy's nose fondly.

'We must hurry, though, eh? We have people arriving this evening and we still have much to do!'

'Who is coming?' the boy asked, looking up at her.

'Señor Daley and Señor Fitzallen will arrive very late. They are flying here from England and staying for two whole weeks.'

'Are they nice?' Enrico asked.

'Oh yes, you will like them very much,' she said, looking across at the photograph of the two men that had been taken in their garden in the cottage in Devon where they had lived together for many years.

'Is anyone else coming?' Enrico asked.

'Who knows?' she said mysteriously. 'Whoever the wind blows in.'

*

In one of the guest bedrooms Marta turned back the freshly ironed sheets, plumped up the pillows then walked across to the window.

Far below, the track led down past the Blue Madonna towards the hamlet. The freshly whitewashed houses gleamed in the sunshine and the splash of colours from the flowerpots on the window-sills gladdened her eye.

The yellow table umbrellas outside Rosendo's café riffled in the warm breeze. If she listened carefully she could hear the metal curtains jingling above the doorways of the houses where the older orphans lived under the watchful eyes of Nancy and Rosendo. From the barn, the pig, Dolores the third, was calling out plaintively to the boar further down the valley.

She sniffed the air. Nancy Angeles was already busy in her kitchen and soon the bar in the café would be laden with dishes of mouth-watering tapas.

Nancy and Rosendo's sons, Gregorio and Martino, would soon arrive along with other hungry men, all of them exhausted from a morning's work on the monastery land that stretched far down the valley.

Marta picked up the battered binoculars from the window-sill and lifted them to her eyes.

Further down the valley she could see a small figure toiling up the track towards Santa Eulalia. A traveller or a pilgrim who had lost their way, maybe.

Training the binoculars in the other direction she could see two old men walking slowly across the meadows, talking animatedly together. They could talk for Spain those two!

Soon, when all the talking had tired them out, they would stroll down the track, pause before the statue of the Blue Madonna for a few moments and then make their way to Rosendo's bar. There they would douse their hot tongues with beer and fill their bellies with Nancy's delicious food.

She smiled to herself as she watched them. Solly had his arm under Michael's to give him support and was leading him carefully, making sure that he didn't stumble. She choked back a tear. She found it hard sometimes to see him so helpless. Still, it wouldn't do to be maudlin, and Michael, God love him, coped with his blindness so well.

Putting down the binoculars, she picked up a feather duster and waved it briskly across furniture and walls, and thought that one day they really must fill in those bullet holes in the plaster.

Down in the monks' graveyard, Piadora Benjamin walked slowly among the wooden crosses, stopping here and there to read a name.

BROTHER TOMAS 1840–1927

BROTHER ALOYSIUS 1889–1943

BROTHER FRANCISCO 1903–1947

She smoothed the top of the cross and thought fondly of Brother Francisco. He'd died far too young but at least he'd known that Santa Eulalia had been saved.

She walked on through the maze of wooden crosses that marked the lives of generations of monks who had lived and died at Santa Eulalia.

She kneeled now before a stone headstone and closed her eyes.

She offered up a prayer for her aunt, Thérèse Martinez, whom she had met for the first time that incredible night long ago in Santa Anna. She smiled as she remembered poor Sister Perpetua's face when she and Marta had been discovered masquerading as postulants. Dear God, they'd been a sorry pair of would-be nuns in the making.

She turned her thoughts again to Thérèse, sweet, eccentric Thérèse who had, thank God, been able to spend the last happy years of her life here at Santa Eulalia reunited with her childhood sweetheart Muli.

Piadora opened her eyes and stood up. She looked out across the meadow and saw him standing there in the long grass, a small wizened figure dressed in rags, smiling wistfully in her direction.

A thickset, handsome American stepped off the boat in Camiga and made his way across the cobbled stones towards the cannery. He checked his map, found Pig Lane marked on it and set off with a spring in his step.

He glanced occasionally at his map, turning it round to get his bearings. He went down a few blind alleys before finally finding himself in a beautiful square. He wandered across to a fountain in the centre of the square and sat down on the side of it, marvelling at the beautiful statue of a small boy taking an eternal leak into the fountain.

He looked up to see a tall thin bespectacled man approaching him from the direction of the church. The man smiled and pointed excitedly at the statue as he got closer.

'That's damned odd,' he said, squinting through his spectacles.

'How do you mean? It looks good to me.'

'Well, I was here many years ago and I swear to God that boy was pissing in the other direction.'

He looked down at a book he was carrying.

'Another funny thing, it's lost weight. See, here in this guide book it says that the statue of the boy weighs so many kilos, but I remember it used to be heavier than that.'

He shrugged, scratched his head and walked away.

The American watched him go, got up and strolled on. He turned into a narrow alleyway and walked on past a bar above which a sign creaked ominously, and then he saw the door to the gallery.

He had come to Spain with the intention of buying a Luciano and he wasn't planning on returning to the States until he had one.

A few years ago he had managed to buy one in New York at considerable expense from the widow of Melville Smith. And now it held pride of place in his home in Manhattan.

As he stepped inside the gallery a bell tinkled lack-adaisically above his head. The assistant, who was engrossed in a book at her desk, looked up and got to her feet but he gesticulated that she should remain seated.

She smiled up at him; he was a handsome man and everything about him from his sleek haircut to his beautifully pressed clothes indicated wealth.

He walked across the room and stood before an enormous canvas. It was a painting of what looked like a gigantic teardrop that magnified a section of an ancient wrinkled cheek.

As he looked closer he realized that the tear drop reflected a group of people.

A blue-eyed boy with a look of absolute wonder and joy on his face.

Two nuns clinging together in terror.

A man whose eyes were hidden by thick-lensed spectacles, and a tall sad-faced man with a wide-eyed little girl cradled in his arms . . .

The gallery assistant watched the man furtively as he put his hand to his head and stepped back from the painting as if alarmed by it.

Then he seemed to pull himself together and walked further down the gallery, his soft-soled shoes whispering across the boards.

He stood solemnly before another picture and the girl could see the rise and fall of his chest, the rapid pulse movement in his neck.

The painting before him looked like part of a horse trough. There were two small hands holding on to the sides, knuckles white and sinewy with shock. The vague reflection of a boy's face in the water. A big-eared boy with huge astonished eyes . . .

He moved on slowly down the gallery. At the next painting he threw back his head and laughed so loudly that the assistant dropped her book.

The picture showed a bewildered nun climbing out of a trunk, one hairy leg hooked over the side. The nun had a look of absolute triumph on her face and in her hand she was clutching a tin of corned beef! By God, he'd give anything to meet this Luciano fellow!

He turned away from the painting and saw the assistant looking at him with undisguised interest.

'I'll take that one,' he said, indicating the teardrop painting and pulling out his wallet.

'Not for sale, I'm sorry.'

'That one then.'

'Not for sale.'

He smiled at her, ran his fingers through his beautifully cut hair and hurried out of the door, leaving behind the scent of his aftershave and the echo of the bell . . .

The woman climbed steadily up the rough track, the sun hot on her pale face, burning the backs of her calves. It was early evening by the time she reached the small hamlet and she was completely exhausted. She slumped down gratefully into a chair beneath the shade of an umbrella, lit a cigarette and closed her eyes.

When she opened them she was embarrassed to find that an old man was standing next to her, looking down at her expectantly.

She ordered a lemonade and a tortilla and was delighted that he understood her Spanish, because for the last two years she had struggled at a night class to learn the basics.

When she felt revived she stood up, struggled to wriggle back into her rucksack, paid her bill and went on her way.

Further along the track she paused before a statue that was set into a grotto which had at some time been carved out from the rock. She kneeled down and looked curiously at the small pieces of paper that were stuck on to rusty nails at the feet of the madonna. She smiled. The pieces of paper were prayer requests, no doubt. Perhaps she'd write her own.

Dear Madonna, I have had a bloody gutsful of men, so please, please send me an affectionate eunuch with plenty of money!

Ha! As far as she was concerned she was done with men. She stood up stiffly and continued to climb the track, every muscle in her body complaining now, and an irritating trickle of sweat making its way down her spine.

Then, as she turned a bend in the road she looked up and saw the monastery of Santa Eulalia in all its craggy splendour.

The sound of children's voices travelled down to her on the wind and far above her head a hawk screamed and plummeted towards the earth.

Okay, she thought, so it was beautiful, but what was she doing here? Why the frig had she listened to that funny little man she'd seen in the alleyway in Soho? A queer little tramp done up in multi-coloured rags! Why had she taken some arsehole's advice and set out on a pilgrimage through Spain; she wasn't even religious, for God's sake! She was a middle-aged woman getting over a nasty divorce and still coming to terms with the death of her beloved father. What she needed was a fortnight by a hotel swimming pool, not a solitary trek through the arse-end of nowhere in search of a saint's bones.

More than anything at the moment she needed a bloody stiff whiskey or seven. Right, she decided, tomorrow she'd put an end to this crap, throw in the towel and head for the beach. She'd sleep the night up in this bleeding eyrie of a place and then tomorrow she was out of there.

The taxi driver was on his way home to his wife Carmen when he saw the man hurrying across the cobbled quayside down near the cannery. He pulled over and called out through the window.

'You looking for a ride?'

'Sure.'

'Where to?'

'The monastery of Santa Eulalia.'

The driver raised his eyebrows. He wasn't often asked to drive up there.

'Sure, jump in.'

For the next hour the American cowered in the back of the taxi. Jeez, this fellow was mad as hell. He didn't drive the car, more like aimed it in the direction he wanted to go.

On the few occasions when he dared open his eyes he got a glimpse of chickens scattering and bent-backed old women in black waving their fists. For the first time in many years he prayed and crossed himself.

By the time they arrived at the monastery it was dark and the man staggered from the car. He paid the grinning driver and looked at him more closely; for a moment he thought that he looked kind of familiar.

Then he looked up at the sky above him and was mesmerized by its beauty. A honey-coloured moon glowed above the brightly lit monastery and stars blistered the skies. It was breathtaking.

He was interrupted then by a torrent of foul language, and looked round to see a middle-aged woman staggering across the courtyard under the weight of a heavy rucksack.

The woman struggled the last few steps across to where he stood, threw down her rucksack and moaned, 'God, if someone doesn't pour a whiskey down my throat in the next few minutes I swear the blood will rush to my arse and I'll die of heat exhaustion!'

The taxi driver spluttered, came hurrying over and helped yank the woman roughly to her feet.

He turned then to the American and said, 'Donny Keegan, will you stop standing there like a gormless eejit and ring the bell, this woman is in need of resuscitation.'

Donny Keegan, his head spinning, did as he was bid and rang the bell-pull. Then he leaped back in alarm as the grille in the door was pulled back and a pair of amazingly blue eyes stared out at him from beneath a head of grey curls.

Then the door was pulled back and a man stood framed against the light.

The woman stared dumbfounded at him, her eyes wide, mouth hanging open unattractively.

'Siobhan Hanlon, would you stop pulling that face, because the wind might change and God forbid, you'll be stuck like it for ever!' Padraig said throwing his arms round her.

'Dear God,' she said, 'couldn't I just eat you up.'

And she sniffed the glorious smell of his skin: tree bark and pencil shavings, oil paint and freshly picked dandelions.